June 15, 2022

To a couple of
great Canadians—
Nice to see you,
Hope you like
this book and
enjoy the Montana
memories (even if
they are from
the 1860s)

All the best,
Gregory [illegible]

Man from Montana

Man from Montana

Gregory J. Lalire

FIVE STAR
A part of Gale, a Cengage Company

Five Star Publishing, a part of Gale, a Cengage Company

LIBRARY OF CONGRESS CATALOGING-IN-PUBLICATION DATA

Names: Lalire, Gregory, author.
Title: Man from Montana / Gregory J. Lalire.
Description: First edition. | Waterville, Maine : Five Star, [2021]
Identifiers: LCCN 2019057356 | ISBN 9781432871178 (hardcover)
Subjects: GSAFD: Western stories.
Classification: LCC PS3612.A54323 M36 2020 | DDC 813/.6—dc23
LC record available at https://lccn.loc.gov/2019057356

First Edition. First Printing: April 2021
Find us on Facebook—https://www.facebook.com/FiveStarCengage
Visit our website—http://www.gale.cengage.com/fivestar
Contact Five Star Publishing at FiveStar@cengage.com

Printed in Mexico
Print Number: 01 Print Year: 2021

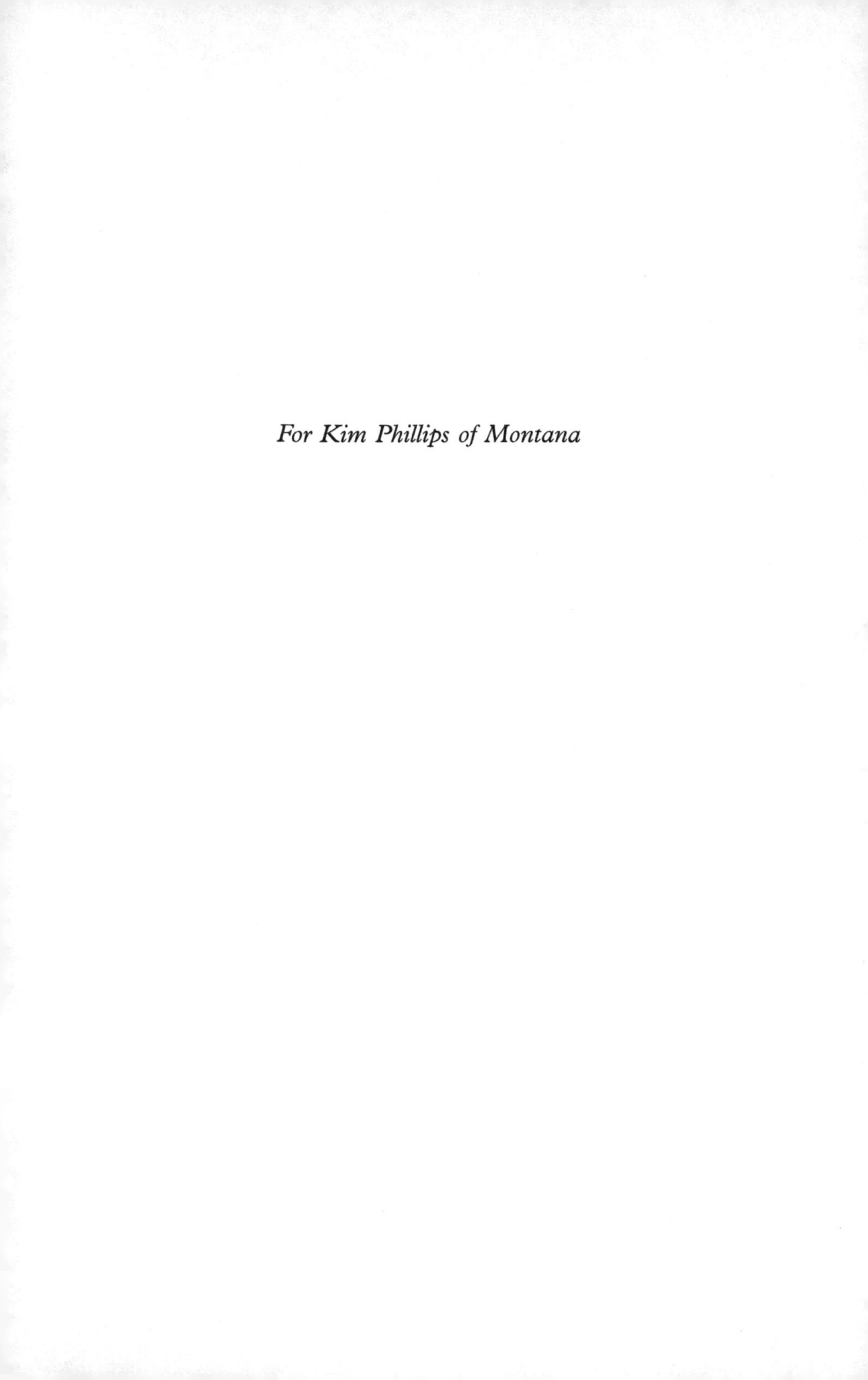

For Kim Phillips of Montana

PREFACE

Man from Montana. That's what they call me nowadays in Red's Saloon in downtown Missoula, Montana—well, either that or Red Ranger. I'm not too proud to answer to either name. It pays off with free drinks seven nights a week. Too much drink should have killed me years ago, but here I am. I'm a survivor. That fact mystifies me when sober. You see, I haven't tried all that hard to stick around. "How is it you've stayed above ground this long?" ask other Red's customers emboldened by strong drink. "Just unlucky I guess," I reply, and they buy me another round for sounding clever. Last century nobody ever attributed cleverness to me. I suppose an old dog, especially one with nothing much left to lose, can on occasion teach himself a new trick.

My real name, Woodrow Russell Hart, doesn't carry any weight on either side of the Clark Fork, let alone the Rockies. It's been eighteen years since onetime friend and onetime savior W.A. Phillips came out with that damned dime novel *Man from Montana: How He Escaped the Noose,* in which I was that man—aka "Red Ranger," the fearless, gallant, long-haired hero. Truth is, Red Ranger was nothing like the real me, though my red hair often became shaggy in the olden days. It isn't red anymore. It faded with age through a spectrum of colors and is now silvery white. I'm fine with that. It's enough being Red Ranger in Red's Saloon. I don't need to be *Red,* too.

Phillips's overblown tale, featuring bloodcurdling episodes

and climaxing in Red Ranger's hairbreadth escape from the Missoula County Jail, is taller than a ponderosa pine. For a while—never underestimate the American public's obsession for unbelievable, colorfully costumed pale-faced heroes—it sold like hotcakes in the Land of the Shining Mountains and on the East Coast. When the book was published in 1895, literary (using that term loosely) critics called W.A. Phillips the next E.Z.C. Judson, better known as Ned Buntline, the "King of the Dime Novels" who had died of heart failure nine years earlier in the state of New York. Phillips thought about calling his champion "The Red Revenger," but Buntline had already used that name in the title of one of his far-fetched adventure tales. Phillips went with Red Ranger in the story but not the title and chose *not* to precede the name with a "the" because it sounded too stilted and affected for a man of action, not of words. "What an auspicious debut," wrote one fervent reviewer in 1896. "Phillips can do for Red Ranger, the Montana man, what Buntline did for Buffalo Bill, now the Wyoming man."

Not even close, as it turned out. One big difference is that Buntline's Buffalo Bill Cody was based on a genuine frontier scout turned showman, while Phillips's Red Ranger was based (more loosely than a gay lady's bodice) on me, frontier nobody turned drunk. What's more, Buntline wrote more than four hundred novels. *Man from Montana: How He Escaped the Noose* was, as far as I know, Phillips's only book. He did make enough money from initial sales to go prospecting for gold up in the Klondike. Last I heard of him was in 1901 when he was at Wyatt Earp's Dexter Saloon in Nome, Alaska, where he still was prospecting some but mostly rubbing elbows with the former "Town Tamer of Tombstone." Yes, I've lost touch with Wilberforce Anaconda Phillips (always W.A. to friends and enemies alike) as well as with my dear sister Lucy, my greatest supporter for half a century. By century's end, though, she was fed up with male-dominated politics in Washington, frustrated in her effort to ensure women throughout the nation the right to vote, and weary of greedy, egocentric American men. She left D.C. to attend the Exposition Universelle of 1900 in Paris, France, and, as far as I know, has never returned to the States.

I don't know how many copies of *Man from Montana: How He Escaped the Noose* have sold in the 20th century. I don't expect that W.A. Phillips, wherever he may be, is still living off the royalties. I do know that to some degree the name Red Ranger lives on, and not just in Red's Saloon. In the fall of 1909, while I was crossing the Clark Fork on the Higgins Avenue Bridge, a lady of some years ran up to me from behind and said somebody told her I was the actual Red Ranger. I think she was of sound mind, but she did try to pull off my red mask when I wasn't wearing a mask, let alone a red cape, and of course my hair, what was left of it, was anything but red. I told her if she wanted to know the absolute truth about the one and only Red Ranger, she should come to Red's Saloon that evening with plenty of dough in her purse. Much to my surprise, she did show up at Red's and bought me several drinks. I told her the truth about Red Ranger and me, making it abundantly clear that we were separate people—one a fictional hero, the other a true-to-life do-nothing. She must have seen the difference for herself; Red Ranger never would have aged so poorly. Regardless, before departing at closing hour, she squeezed me tight, rubbed what was left of my silvery white hair, and declared, "You, my modest friend, are a treasure, more so than all the gold, silver, and copper in this treasured state." I nodded, since I was as drunk as her.

Come to think of it, nobody in the four years since then has approached me outside the confines of Red's to suggest any connection between me and Phillips's larger-than-life protagonist. Regardless, before I kick the already holey bucket, I aim to set the record straight and tell the world who I really am. What follows is my true story, straight from the horse's mouth. My working—or nonworking, if you will—title is *Man from Montana: The Man Who Wasn't.* I don't expect it to sell a lick should it get published. And if it doesn't, so what. I'm too old to care—as old as windswept and seemingly barren Water Works Hill, which I can barely make out through my north-facing window. The first horseless carriage showed up on Higgins Avenue a dozen years ago. Time moves that swiftly. The Old Days are gone and forgotten. Just the other morning I saw an aeroplane fly into Missoula from Milltown. Hell, I've been situated in this state since before it was even its own bloody territory, but let me make one thing perfectly clear: I *ain't* from Montana.

—Woodrow Russell Hart
Somewhere on West Front Street
Missoula, Montana
Fall 1913

Chapter One

I was born poor and poorly in Washington, D.C., on July 4, 1848. My mother must have been present, but I was her ninth boy, so she dwelled on me for about a minute and a half. My father was even less impressed. He had grandiose visions of becoming a master stonemason, building great government works in our nation's capital, so on the day of my birth he was off watching—along with 20,000 other people—the 24,500-pound marble cornerstone of the Washington Monument being laid. Any one of the other observers likely would have made a better mason than Lyman Hart. When a year later he accidentally (or otherwise, according to my mother, Olive Hart) severed his left hand with a stone-cutting tool, it ended his dreams of a solid vocation, which would have been shattered soon enough anyway due to his clumsiness and lack of skill. Afterward, my father devoted himself to hard drink and debauchery. He died too young, looking twice his age. As for my brothers, some of them took odd jobs to sustain our family; others ran amok in the city; and the oldest two rushed to California in search of gold (Adam drowned in a river crossing on the way; Hiram made it to the Far Coast but was never heard from again). I would have gone with them but I was barely one.

In *Man from Montana: How He Escaped the Noose,* hack writer W.A. Phillips makes up many things and exaggerates even more but—I suppose to his credit—never says I was born and/or raised in Montana. "As a boy he was from the namby-pamby, effeminate East—Washington, D.C., to be specific," W.A. writes, "but he became a man in the Wild West—Montana Territory to be specific. Everybody, whether for him or against him, whether living on the Potomac River in the shadow of the White House or on Grasshopper Creek in the shadow of the gallows, knows Red Ranger as the Man from Montana!" In his first chapter W.A. Phillips passes quickly over my (that is Red Ranger's) background, and what he says is ludicrous. According to him, I swam three miles in the Potomac, upstream, at age nine (about that time, being unable to swim, I nearly drowned in a swamp); helped our four family slaves (we had none) escape the city on our family schooner (we didn't have as much as a leaky rowboat or a homemade raft) when I was eleven; became a Union drummer boy at thirteen in 1862 (had no interest in joining up to fight anybody and never played any musical instrument); within months thwarted a Rebel plan to kidnap President Lincoln's youngest son, Tad (never laid eyes on the lad); and at fourteen was sent by the grateful president to Montana Territory on special assignment to keep an eye on Virginia City reprobates intent on accumulating gold by any means to support the Confederacy. (I did skedaddle west then with older brother Rufus but only to escape poverty, our parents, and the War of the Rebellion, and to perhaps find gold for ourselves; what's more, Montana Territory had yet to be carved out of the northeast corner of Idaho Territory.)

W.A. left Rufus completely out of his wild narrative, which isn't right, but the author believed a strong, self-reliant, self-made young man like Red Ranger would never tail after an older brother of questionable character. Truth was, I wouldn't have dared venture westward without Rufus. On March 3, 1863, when the president signed into law an act "enrolling and calling out the National Forces," Rufus was eighteen and eligible for the draft. He had Rebel leanings that he mostly kept to himself and declared he was absolutely against the killing of his fellow man, including his brothers (though no Hart had yet signed up to fight for either the North or the South). "It's a rich man's war, but they want the poor man to fight it," he complained, after failing to steal the $300 fee necessary to gain an exemption. He wanted me to lie about my age and be his substitute, but I told him I had already taken enough abuse as the youngest of nine brothers and besides that the sight of bright red blood and severed human limbs made me faint. Rufus was good about it, not punching me, yanking my hair, or gouging my green eyes the way he used to do whenever I was too stubborn to be bossed by him. "No worries, bub," he told me. "We can't beat the bastards, but we won't join them. You come along with me, bub, and we'll go far. It'll be just you and me—two daring young men from Washington headed for the goldfields."

So that's what I am—a *man from Washington,* though, of course the "young" part hasn't applied for many years and the "daring" part was never apropos for yours truly. Rufus was as prone to exaggeration in speech as W.A. Phillips would be in his scribblings. No matter what W.A. later wrote, I didn't have any "real" boyhood adventures or accomplishments. It certainly wasn't carefree, what with my own worries and fears, our dogged poverty, and those disinterested parents. By the way, my not-so-old man would die of alcohol poisoning before the war was done, and my mother would marry a one-armed Union officer and leave town with him to help reconstruct the South (I reckon they didn't finish the job, dying as they did hand-in-hand during the cholera epidemic in Atlanta). Still, I had one sister, Lucy, who tried to make up for the meanness and neglect of my brothers; a grandfather who handed out books to read and rock candy to savor; and a hard but caring Aunt Clementina who nursed me through any number of childhood illnesses. I also had the run of some fairly safe streets and alleys, and just two blocks away I could get a clear view of the Executive Mansion, or White House (though W.A. was of course off base when he wrote I was the one who first applied white lead paint to the presidential stones). Furthermore, a man will always have a connection with the place of his birth, especially when he almost grew of age there.

Rufus had the notion of robbing an Army payroll to finance our westbound journey, but there was no need. One of Lucy's more adamant suitors was a Pennsylvania Railroad big bug named William Penn Norton. Now Lucy didn't want me to go west (though she thought it might be best for draft-evader Rufus), because she was very protective of me. I had a full head of deep, hard-to-overlook red hair in those days, and she was convinced the red savages would take my scalp. Mr. Norton, who resented Lucy's unwavering love for her miserable family, assured her that no redskins rode the rails. "But the tracks only run as far west as St. Jo," asserted Lucy, who was not only beautiful and kind but also better book read than all us brothers combined. "That's far enough," replied her suitor, who mapped out the entire rail route from Washington, D.C., to St. Joseph, Missouri, and booked passage for Rufus and me. Saying goodbye to Lucy, my parents (though they hardly said goodbye back), my other living brothers (though some were still beating me up), the White House (though I never actually stepped onto its lawn), and the Potomac (though I never tried to swim in it) made me all-powerful sad. But once the train started rolling and I saw there was life outside of Washington, my tears dried fast.

No wild Indians attacked the trains I was on—not even hack W.A. Phillips went that far. But he did say how a brave brakeman and I (the future Red Ranger) repulsed a Rebel attempt at rail sabotage near Harrisburg, Pennsylvania. For the *two* Hart brothers in real life it was smooth railing all the way, the last stretch on the Hannibal & St. Joseph Railroad. St. Joseph, being a jumping-off point for the Oregon Trail, was a bustling place and too expensive for our tastes. We couldn't jump off soon enough. The remainder of Norton's travel money allowed us to buy a converted farm wagon with one yoke of already tired oxen, and with our last 40 cents, we paid the fee to ferry across the Missouri River (after cutting in the line of waiting wagons, which almost got Rufus in his first gunfight, without a gun). We couldn't afford to put supplies in our wagon bed, so as we rolled slowly west, we had to do odd jobs (and, no, I never scouted for the wagon master, as Phillips had it in that unfortunate book), beg, and even steal—all things that Rufus had been doing back in Washington.

One of our oxen lasted maybe seventy-five miles, and when we reached the adjacent landmarks Courthouse Rock and Jail Rock an hour after the rest of the wagon train, we lost a wheel and abandoned our dilapidated vehicle. Fortunately, a wealthy lady with four children and a hired driver instead of a husband took a shine to both Rufus (for his broad shoulders, above-average height, and self-assurance) and me (for my thick red hair and exceptional innocence) and allowed us to accompany the Wadsworth family's covered wagon. I got along famously with three of the four children (the fourth one, who turned fifteen two weeks before I did, was jealous of his mother's affection for me). Parting at Fort Laramie was such sweet sorrow (thank you Shakespeare and Grandpa Hart). Rufus and I would never forget the last kisses planted by Amanda Wadsworth (on Rufus's lips, on my forehead) or the Army mount she bought for us. The Wadsworths stayed with the train, which pressed on to Oregon's Willamette Valley, while the Hart brothers took turns riding our gift horse as we accompanied John Bozeman and a train of forty-nine wagons on his newly established shortcut road to the goldfields.

After just 150 miles, a formidable party of Northern Cheyennes and Sioux, whose faces and horses were painted, stopped us at the Rock Creek crossing, and Mr. Bozeman lent Rufus a Colt Army Model 1860. These were the first Indians I had seen in my life. Not long before Rufus and I hopped on the train in April 1863, fourteen chiefs and two squaws from the West visited the East Room of the White House to talk peace with the president. I never saw one of them out on the city streets, but William Penn Norton, the railroad man and Lucy's suitor, was in the room when Mr. Lincoln shook hands with each of them, including the squaws, and told them that pale-faced people were *not* as disposed to fight and kill one another as "our red brethren." The Indians must have thought the Great Chief of the White People was out of his mind, what with palefaces butchering each other right and left, north and south, in a great war. But, as Mr. Norton reported to Lucy, the Indians said nothing offensive, and the president gave a medal to one of them, Cheyenne Chief Lean Bear, to honor his commitment for peace. None of this eased Lucy's mind, and she was surprised that not one of the lesser chiefs present attempted to scalp Abraham Lincoln or at least trim his beard. "The red devils don't mind their manners out West, Woodie," Lucy insisted. "They'll all want your beautiful hair to hang from a tepee pole, and at night they will all gather 'round this pole to dance and sing."

I told myself that Lucy read a little too much of the wrong kind of material for her own good, but I must say when I saw those painted Indians at Rock Creek, I immediately remembered her warning and needed to bite my knuckles to keep from screaming. Rufus stared straight ahead stone-faced, but I heard him tapping the six-shooter against his pant leg. The warriors meant business and demanded that we emigrants turn back or be killed. Almost all the wagons did so, but bold John Bozeman forged ahead with nine men, including self-assured Rufus, and one frightened boy—me. We rode (me on the same saddle as Rufus) through the nights and slept during the days to avoid the "hostiles," as Mr. Bozeman called them. It took us three weeks, but we all made it safely to Virginia City on a route named for him. Because Rufus stood guard so well en route, Mr. Bozeman gave him a gift of the .44-caliber Colt.

Naturally W.A. Phillips told it differently. He wrote that the Indians found us near the Powder River and killed three of Bozeman's friends in the surprise attack but lost thirteen of their own, including one killed by me (the first of many killings of hostiles attributed to me in *Man from Montana*). W.A. borrowed some of his "facts" from an actual clash a year later involving northern Plains warriors and members of the 450-wagon Townsend train. Thing is, he needn't have bothered borrowing facts and making up even more "truths" to create a blood-and-guts story that would keep his readers riveted to the pages. Enough actual fighting and killing, massacring and abusing, saving and revenging was going on in the West to entertain the masses who didn't read Shakespeare. W.A.'s bigger mistake was centering all that deadly and gruesome action around me in my Red Ranger guise. Sure, I really did hear some things and see some things—lamentable things. It couldn't be avoided. But I was in the middle of nothing.

I asked W.A., who once loved Lucy Hart almost as much as himself: "Why me? Why not write your wild tales about a real-life hero who actually experienced wild things, someone like John Bozeman?" The author, as quickly as it took him to give his mustache a tug, simply replied that he liked me, as if he were doing me a favor. But then he mentioned how Mr. Bozeman was killed "too soon" under mysterious circumstances in 1867 either by Blackfeet Indians; his partner, Tom Cover; or someone else, and he couldn't change that unfortunate fact. "My hero *must* be a living hero like Ned Buntline's Buffalo Bill Cody," W.A. insisted. "And Red Ranger still lives!" I'm sure anyone could find holes in his logic the way I did. The only thing Mr. Cody, who was born two years before me, and I have in common is that we both have managed to stay alive this long. Buffalo Bill has always had more dare, flair, and even hair (though his was golden, not red) than me and is in fact a showman extraordinaire who promotes both self and a *wilder* Wild West. I have never promoted either. I am who I am, *not* who I am *not.* Same goes for the so-called Wild West, both the real thing and Mr. Cody's show of that name. They are what they are. I suppose I could also say *Man from Montana: How He Escaped the Noose* is what it is. But I can't. Some things just *ain't* right.

Chapter Two

Hanging is a nasty business, anyway you cut it—legal, illegal, or somewhere betwixt. Rufus and I rode into Virginia City in the fall of '63 having never previously seen noose, road agent, vigilante, or gold nugget. We sure enough got an eyeful of all four in the next few months. The first three of those objectionable things caused me to gasp, choke, and involuntarily clutch my frail neck. Rufus, as always, reacted differently. As for gold, seeing it (usually from afar and always out of reach) caused me to feel as if my fingers had just been held over hot coals, though that only happened in *Man from Montana: How He Escaped the Noose*. Rufus, on the other hand, would give his right hand—heck, his whole life—to possess gold for a little while. At the same time, he wasn't one to back down in the face of unpleasantry or adversity on account of he had a certain amount of gumption. Who can explain the difference between brothers? We came from the same place—same parents, same poverty, same longings for something more. I have no explanation. I'm not that smart. I do know one thing—Rufus, though no hero, was far more like the hardy and adventurous character W.A. Phillips later invented than I ever was.

Virginia City was just one of the settlements along Alder Gulch, the other principal ones being Summit, Highland, Junction, Adobetown, and Nevada City. They all owed their existence to gold claims, which were duly recorded, but prospectors had been pouring into the gulch for some five months, and there were hardly any claims left worth claiming. What's more there was no system of law enforcement in place. A man with his face mostly hidden behind a black scarf held me up on Virginia City's Wallace Street, but I didn't have a trace of gold. "Damn disappointing," he said before letting me go with a warning. No sooner did I get a temporary low-paying job turning over dirt on another man's claim—which allowed me to possess a trace of gold dust—than I was robbed by the same masked fellow in the same location, except this time his mask was red and he wasn't so kind (certainly no Red Ranger). He emptied my pockets, told me to tell nobody anything, hit me over the head with the butt of his six-shooter, and left me in a dark alley on a cold fall night. I would have frozen if not for Rufus, who happened along on one of his early-morning jaunts. He had picked up a gambling stake and nearly free room and board from a woman who called herself Virginia Nevada and at the time was helping to run a questionable boardinghouse in Adobetown. Rufus made enough at the assorted gambling houses along the gulch to pay for eggs at $1.50 a dozen, dried apples at 75 cents a pound, and all the whiskey he could gulp. It was far more than I made as a common laborer and left far fewer blisters on the hands, but then I could sleep most anywhere and practically live on bread, the leftovers of other men, and plain old water. In those early days in the gold camps, I didn't touch a drop of anything stiffer.

Things went sour in November when Rufus shot a man who accused him of cheating at cards. The man was a known sharper and suffered only a shoulder wound, so the shooting wouldn't have amounted to anything except on the way out of town he warned someone on the trail about this Virginia City "cheater." The newcomer, Wallace Willingham, promised the sharper to obtain vengeance on the cheater. It seems he had heard the name Rufus Hart before in connection with his wife, none other than Virginia Nevada, real name Varina Willingham. Mr. Willingham had traveled all the way from Kansas to reclaim his runaway little woman and punish any man who might have led her astray. The husband was a solid rich citizen (in farming, not mining) but had an unforgiving nature, a nasty temper, and a shotgun; he tried to shoot Rufus but shot his horse instead. So, Rufus ushered me out of the boardinghouse at midnight and we caught the next A.J. Oliver & Co. stagecoach to Bannack, a former boomtown along Grasshopper Creek seventy-five miles away. I was plenty glad to be leaving the dangerous, overcrowded gulch and headed to Bannack, which had lost a good chunk of its population to Virginia City but which had an actual sheriff by the name of Henry Plummer.

Rufus was nervous as we boarded the coach because he suspected that an old prospector named Tex Crowell was a spy for the possessive Wallace Willingham. The other passenger was equally nervous, because he was obviously a miner carrying gold and thought Crowell might be in cahoots with road agents.

"You know that old man?" the wary passenger whispered to Rufus and me. "They call him Tex."

"Never been to Texas," Rufus said. "Don't know anybody who's been there."

"Look at him, sizing me up. He's *too* curious."

The old man watched us all board, but he stayed behind rubbing his whiskers.

"Better you than me," Rufus replied, pushing against me with his hip to give himself more space on the seat.

"I see you're armed," the other passenger said, smiling. "I can count on you if there's trouble ahead, can't I?"

"Trouble? What trouble?"

"You must be new around these parts. There's a certain outlaw element that . . . you know."

"You don't know me, mister, and I don't know you."

"Leroy Southmayd's the name. I figure you'd want to protect that young good-looking redheaded lad next to you, Mr. eh . . . I didn't catch your name."

"I'm Woodie Hart," I volunteered, pushing back my hat to show off more of my hair. "That's my older brother Rufus . . ."

"Shut up," Rufus said. "You talk too much, bub. We don't got any gold, mister. No cause for us to worry."

At our first stop, the Laurin Ranch on the Stinking Water River, Mr. Southmayd grew more uneasy when we encountered a talkative ranch hand named George Ives who had been in at least one shooting scrape and had a reputation as a drunk and a bully.

"All on your way to Bannack?" Mr. Ives asked.

"Maybe, maybe not," said Mr. Southmayd.

"No matter to me. I'm riding ahead to Cold Spring Ranch. Aim to meet up with Tex Crowell there."

Mr. Southmayd looked like he wanted to turn pale, but his face was too crimson for that. And the miner stayed nervous all that night we spent at the Beaverhead Rock way station. Turned out there was good reason. Three masked men draped in blue blankets appeared, all calling out "Halt!" and all hoisted guns to back up the order. It didn't take much imagination to figure out that the man in charge was George Ives, and after instructing everyone where to stand by waving his shotgun, he kept the barrel pointed between Leroy Southmayd's eyes.

One of the other robbers, whom Mr. Southmayd identified later as Bob Zachary, disarmed Rufus and did the collecting, but he got only $400 in gold dust from the miner, a few small pouches from the driver, and virtually nothing from Rufus and me. He sighed and handed the Army Colt back to my brother after removing the caps. "Damn disappointing," said the third robber, and as soon as I heard his gravelly voice, I knew he was the same man who had held me up twice on Virginia City's

Wallace Street. Mr. Southmayd figured out down the road it must be "Whiskey Bill" Graves. When Mr. Southmayd took a long last look at the trio as he climbed back into the coach, George Ives shouted, "If you don't turn around and mind your own business, I'll shoot the top of your head off." Rufus hesitated at the coach door.

"You want to get it, too, bummer!" Mr. Ives yelled.

"You bet," Rufus said. "Who doesn't want to get his hands on gold."

"What? You must not have high regard for the top of your head."

"Sure, I do. I like my ears, too. I'd like to hear about your organization."

"Organization? What organization!"

"You the brains of the outfit?"

"What? You think . . . My advice to you, bummer, is simple: Don't think! Now, get up and skedaddle."

I pushed Rufus in the back to keep him moving and gave no thought to doing anything foolish, such as looking back or thanking the road agents for not shooting us. Rufus didn't try to reload his Colt; he had no more caps or balls.

In Bannack, Sheriff Plummer stepped out of the express office on Main Street, acted as concerned as a mother hen, and questioned Leroy Southmayd and the driver to get every last detail of the holdup. Rufus had nothing much to say and indicated that I had been struck dumb by the shock of the robbery. For some reason that caused the sheriff, a slender man with a mild, comforting voice, to reassure me that the danger was past and that I deserved three pats on the top of my red head.

Something mighty curious occurred when Henry Plummer was doing the patting. A fiery-eyed bearded man named Gaylord Bissell pulled Mr. Southmayd aside and began whispering in his ear. Rufus worked his way over to have a listen. It turned out that the sheriff, despite being recently married and highly respected by most folks in Bannack, had somehow raised suspicions in Mr. Bissell, a Virginia City doctor who presided over the miners' court there.

"You think you know the identities of the three robbers," Dr. Bissell said. "Well, if I was a betting man, I'd wager that Plummer does, too. Furthermore, I figure he is better acquainted with them than you, Leroy. Best to be on the safe side and *not* name names."

"I don't understand, Gaylord; those men need hanging and if the sheriff knows it, too, then . . ."

"I don't understand, either," Rufus interrupted. "They deserve to be arrested if everybody knows who they are. But when did robbery become a hanging offense?"

Dr. Bissell and Mr. Southmayd looked at my brother as if he were crazy, but then just shrugged and did not continue their private conversation.

"I think I can tell you who it was that robbed you," Sheriff Plummer said. "George Ives was one of them."

"I know," said Mr. Southmayd. "Whiskey Bill and Bob Zachary were the other two."

"I'll keep that in mind. If you'll excuse me, gentlemen—and you, too, Red—Electa is expecting me to bring home a ham hock and fresh vegetables."

I wasn't partial to being called "Red," but I found nothing menacing in the sheriff's tone or manner. Dr. Bissell saw otherwise. He insisted that the three robbers would soon know that Mr. Southmayd knew who they were. "Leroy," he added, "your life is not worth a cent."

Rufus, with a hand on his belted Colt, volunteered for a minimal fee and some ammunition to be Leroy Southmayd's bodyguard while the miner was taking care of some business in

Bannack, and nothing happened to either of them the next three days. Mr. Southmayd breathed easier, but as he prepared to take the stagecoach back to Virginia City, he noticed Sheriff Plummer's deputies Buck Stinson and Ned Ray climbing aboard. The miner borrowed a shotgun from the express office to take along, and as added insurance hired Rufus at an increased fee to accompany him in the coach. When the coach reached Cold Spring, none other than Bill Graves and Bob Zachary, fully armed, were standing there as if they owned the place. Deputy Stinson addressed them as road agents but didn't try to arrest them. Rufus dutifully drew his six-shooter and waved it around in front of the deputies. The two robbers retreated into the ranch.

"Who are you, stranger?" Buck Stinson asked.

"Just a man with a gun, protecting my interest," Rufus replied.

"Friend of Mr. Southmayd's?"

"He's the one paying me."

"No need to worry. Ned and I are both duly appointed deputies."

"I'm not worried. I loaded five of the cylinders of my Colt and Mr. Southmayd has a load of buckshot in that shotgun pointed at your belly."

"What made you pass such a remark?" Ned Ray asked.

"The stranger must be confused, Ned. Don't you know we are lawmen, Mr. Southmayd?"

"I know one can't be too careful on this road," the miner said.

"Gentlemen," Buck Stinson said as if addressing a congregation. "I pledge you my word, my honor, my life, that you will not be attacked between here and Virginia City."

Mr. Southmayd grunted and turned his shotgun to the side. That seemed to inspire Deputy Stinson to start singing a song better known in saloons than churches. Deputy Ray joined in.

The loud duet disturbed Mr. Southmayd, who whispered into Rufus's ear that he thought the two deputies were letting any road agents out there know to leave this particular stagecoach alone. Regardless, when the two deputies showed no sign of shutting their mouths, Rufus joined them in song all the way to Virginia City.

Anyway, that's how Rufus told it to me later. He had left me back in Bannack in good hands—those of Lucia Aurora Darling.

"If you'd look after my kid brother, Miss Darling, I'd sure appreciate it," Rufus had said, though I was certain he didn't know much about this quality lady, except what everyone knew—that she had taught back in Ohio and had opened a school in her Uncle Sidney Edgerton's comfortable home the previous month, and now the children of miners, along with Sidney and Mary's own four children, were filling up the makeshift desks and chairs every day. "You see, I got to go to Virginia—the city that is—on business. He won't cause you no trouble at all. I'll be back directly."

"He looks harmless enough," she replied. "Hardly resembles you, Mr. Hart."

She started taking care of me right away. I got a particle of dirt (it surely wasn't gold dust—that was all gone) in my eye as I was waving goodbye to Rufus in the stagecoach, and Lucia took enough time removing it for me to nearly keel over from experiencing her clean hands, fresh scent, and overall closeness to my dirty face and dusty body. She even commented on my "curious green eyes." I had never experienced anything like it before or after leaving Washington, D.C. Now, Amanda Wadsworth on the wagon train had showed me more tenderness than my own mother ever had, but Mrs. Wadsworth was motherly and old. Lucia Darling at twenty-four was practically a girl, and while she was acting nice like my sister, Lucy, I didn't have a single brotherly thought.

"There," Lucia said. "I got it. All better now?"

My tongue felt twisted inside my dry mouth. She *had it* all right. All I could do was murmur.

"Rufus tells me you've been sleeping in one of the stables for three nights. Poor boy."

I nodded my head, a bit like a smart horse, I suppose.

"Anyway, you'll have a bed tonight."

I gasped, but she ignored it, took my hand, and led me to her uncle's large log house beside the Grasshopper Creek footbridge that led to the main cluster of miners' cabins at Yankee Flats. Sidney had done much carpentry work, putting up partitions as walls so that the family of seven (including Lucia) could have four separate bedrooms. My new quarters would be a spare room in back with an actual spring bed filling up most of the space and bookshelves taking up the rest. Lucia showed me where to wash up and then introduced me to her uncle and aunt and their four children, the oldest being thirteen-year-old Martha who went by "Mattie." Mr. Sidney Edgerton happened to be a former congressman from Ohio who was now chief justice of the territory of Idaho, appointed by none other than President Lincoln. At dinner, I told them all I once lived next to the president but said little else after that because they looked at me as if I didn't have a brain in my head. Lucia confirmed that afterward by sizing me up from head to toe and telling me I wasn't too big for her classroom. I sized her up, too, and figured there were plenty worse places to be. I knew I had much to learn about young women, and my mind became agitated imagining all the things she could teach me.

"Is something bothering you?" she asked in the doorway of the spare room.

I wanted to thank her but only managed to shake my head and squeak.

She patted my red hair as if I were a pet dog or a favorite hog. "Sleep well, Woodrow," she said. "Tomorrow you'll need to put on your thinking cap."

I issued a last murmur, and as I made my way to the spring bed, I heard the door shut behind me. Unfortunately, she was on the other side of it.

Of course, as is usually the case, nothing played out the way it did in my head. The next day Lucia Darling found out I could read well, add and subtract, and recite from memory the first paragraph of old neighbor President Lincoln's Emancipation Proclamation. She told me I was a natural in the classroom just like her and then proudly revealed she had begun teaching school in Akron, Ohio, at age fourteen. I went from oversized student to teacher's assistant faster than Pickett's Charge at Gettysburg. But I didn't see it as a defeat, because now I would be able to repay her kindness every day and she could concentrate on teaching me other things after school. Another miscalculation on my part. Yes, I was her teaching assistant, but she never let me forget that I was fifteen, nine years her junior, and only two years older than Mattie Edgerton. "Nearly three years older," I said in desperation because Mattie struck me as a silly, overprotected child still waiting to achieve the female form.

Once I couldn't help myself when Sidney and Mary Edgerton were at a social gathering with some of Bannack's better class of people. I plopped down on the spring bed, pounded the pillow against my shaky knees, and called out in desperation for darling Lucia.

The teacher dutifully reported to the spare room.

"What's the matter?" she asked. "You'll wake the little ones. Are you feeling under the weather, Woodrow?"

I had thought of things to say, but only muttered nonsense and squeaked.

"You don't look peaked," she said, peering at my cheeks and forehead but not touching any flesh.

"Neither do you," I shouted, grabbing her wrists and pulling her on top of me. I raised my head to try to find her lips and nearly knocked myself out against one of her sharp elbows. I thought of how, despite her delicateness and gentle tongue, she had almost no discipline problems in her classroom. She didn't yell at me now, let alone thrash about or strike me with a fist. I withdrew my hands from her back and she immediately sprang off the bed. But instead of bolting from the room, she smoothed out her blue dress while listening to my profuse apologies.

"I must have a fever," I said. "It made me delirious."

She dared put a soft hand on my forehead. "Not too hot," she said, smiling at my ridiculous excuse for displaying pent-up passion. "A little red, but not as red as your hair."

"Could I sleep here just one more night and then go back to the stables tomorrow?" I asked rather pathetically.

"Don't be silly. You've learned something tonight. I taught the same lesson to Rufus a few nights ago. You aren't as different from your brother as I believed at first."

It didn't sound like a compliment. I apologized once more.

"Bannack is tumultuous and rough," she said. "It is the headquarters of a band of highwaymen. Lawlessness and misrule seem to be the prevailing spirit of this place. I hope my uncle will be able to do something about it. But don't you worry, Woodrow. I won't say anything to him about your behavior tonight. You seem out of place in this gold-hungry land. Your innocence is still showing, young man. However, these sorts of things, rest assured, happen even in civilized places."

Chapter Three

Lucia Darling didn't boot me out of the spare room and said only favorable things about me to Sidney and Mary Edgerton. I showed my gratitude by acting like the perfect gentleman—rather the perfect servant, since I washed dishes, cleaned floors, made beds, read bedtime stories to the younger Edgertons, abstained from liquor and tobacco, ate moderately, attended to the underdeveloped minds and sometimes foul tongues of the dozen schoolchildren, and averted my eyes whenever Lucia caught me looking at her in or out of the classroom. Rufus showed up irregularly, having become involved in various ventures—gambling or otherwise—over in Alder Gulch that allowed him to support himself but not his kid brother. On one visit he admitted he had been spending time with George Ives and his disreputable crowd, which worried me to no end, especially when Rufus made further inappropriate advances to Miss Darling after school. But next time he came to town, he left Lucia alone and said I had nothing to worry about because he had taken a position as one of Sheriff Plummer's deputies in Virginia City. I still worried, though, because I overheard Sidney Edgerton and his nephew, Wilbur Sanders, who lived with his wife, Hattie, and their two children in a small cabin nearby, whispering to one another that perhaps the sheriff himself had close ties to the gang supposedly terrorizing the gold camps.

As for myself, I felt safe enough inside the Edgerton home and doing my level best to stay off the tumultuous and dangerous streets of Bannack ("Like any respectable woman," teased Rufus). At night, I heard the sound of falling water from the miners' sluice boxes and saw their flickering lights on the mountainside, but I never caught even a touch of gold fever or wished to labor in the dirt again for some stingy gold panner. It was enough to be warm and within arm's length of Lucia Darling. Never mind that distortive novelist W.A. Phillips would later write how my character (soon-to-become Red Ranger) hit pay dirt time and time again in Bannack and like a "golden knight of olde" gave away all his riches to disabled miners, orphan children, widows, and especially "that supremely gorgeous but gentle local schoolteacher who had eased our young hero into the many splendors of the male-female union as if teaching a prize student to reach out beyond the A, B and C's of the classroom."

In the middle of November, the Vail family (Henry Plummer had married Martha Vail's beautiful younger sister, Electa, but she had gone East for reasons unknown) decided to host a Thanksgiving dinner for other prominent families. Sheriff Plummer himself delivered the invitation to the Edgertons and Lucia Darling, telling them they couldn't refuse because he had ordered a $50 (in gold) turkey from Salt Lake City for the occasion. No matter what Judge Edgerton secretly thought of the sheriff, they accepted the invitation, as did Lucia on the condition she could be accompanied by their respectable houseguest, Woodrow Hart (she might not have been loving me but she was always looking out for me, especially my stomach). Wilbur Sanders, a lawyer who served as his uncle's unofficial secretary, also attended with his wife, probably because he wasn't yet prepared to offend Henry Plummer, whom he referred to as "the most conspicuous citizen of eastern Idaho." Indeed, the sheriff sat at the head of the table, his blue eyes flashing from guest to guest, as if he didn't want to leave anyone out, not even unimportant me. He gave thanks for his official position in the community, his good health, his friends, and even the "splendid Christian woman" who had married him but had left for "more civilized climes." Perhaps the sheriff, having doubts about his future, was trying to show the people who mattered that he was a good man doing his best to serve justice as well as what Mr. Sanders called "delicacies that had never before graced festal board in Bannack."

The diners were gorging on pumpkin and apple pies made by Lucia and other decent women when I excused myself and went outside to visit the necessary. On the way back, I was surprised to see Sheriff Plummer stomping about on the porch, waving his hands at the moon and biting down hard on a cigar that had gone unsmoked since his wedding day.

"Enjoying the show?" the sheriff asked me, tipping his black hat.

"Eh . . . everything tastes wonderful," I said, thinking he must have meant the food.

"Edgerton and Sanders talk out of both sides of their mouths. They're all die-hard Republicans. I'm a Democrat. They can't stand me, want to get rid of me." He removed his hat, only long enough to run a hand through his sandy hair. And then, without the help of his fingers, adjusted his cigar and took a big chomp on it.

"I don't know anything about politics. I do like Abraham Lincoln. I guess he is one of those Republicans, but more than that he was a neighbor back in . . ."

"I know, back in the capital of the so-called Union. Whose side you on, Woodie?"

"How'd you know that about me?"

"We were introduced by Miss Darling, remember?"

"She told you I was from Washington, D.C.?"

"No, but your brother did. I made him a deputy over in

Virginia City, you know. Rufus is a good man, like me. You disagree?"

"It's not that. I . . . I . . ."

"Forget it. No need to tell me whose side you're on. Lucia Darling's side! Am I right or what? No need denying it. Bully for you. She's the best-looking woman in town ever since my Electa departed."

"I . . . I . . . I'm sorry."

"You know what, Woodie? I believe you are sincere, damn sincere, not like those men in there who can look you straight in the eye and lie like the devil. Well, I'd better get back in there. They might think I'm holding you up or something."

I forced a smile, not sure if he was joking or not. His manners were so pleasing, his complexion so fair, his blue eyes so *sincere,* it was hard to believe he could be anything but an honest lawman.

"A gold nugget for your thoughts, Mr. Hart," the sheriff said.

"I . . . I was just wondering how Rufus is doing, you know, enforcing the law for you over there in Virginia City."

"Well, I tell you, son, about as well as I'm doing right here in Bannack."

Henry Plummer put an arm around my shoulders and gently encouraged me to walk with him toward the back door. "Still wondering about me, aren't you?" he asked, but he didn't wait for an answer. "Don't hardly blame you, living among the Edgertons and Sanders like you do. If you haven't learned it yet from your Abe Lincoln or your Lucia Darling, there's one thing you ought to know and keep mind of as you proceed through the course of your life here and wherever else you might happen to go—the whole damned world is two-faced."

I nodded my head as if I was worldly enough to know what the sheriff was talking about. By the time we got back inside the Vail house, dessert was over. Sheriff Plummer went into what passed as a drawing room to join the other men in smokes (mostly pipes), drinks (though I knew Wilbur Sanders, for one, was a teetotaler), and talk (no doubt *not* about politics once the Democratic sheriff entered the room). I sat alone at the dinner table eating a slice of apple pie, saved for me by Lucia Darling.

"What was the sheriff saying to you, Woodie?" Lucia asked.

"Nothing much," I said, knowing that Lucia was kin to Mr. Edgerton and Mr. Sanders, neither of whom had ever talked to me as much as Henry Plummer had on the porch. "I think he misses his wife."

"Electa is a devoted Christian woman not suited for such a rough settlement. Even he once admitted that neither he nor Bannack were fit for her."

"It's not half bad here."

"Sure. Here. But out there in the saloons, on the roads . . . you don't know the half of it." She pressed against my right shoulder with both hands and added in a whisper, "Don't let the sheriff fool you. He is a dangerous man."

I might have argued the point had Lucia not smelled so sweet and my mouth not been so full. I reflected for a moment or two on that word Sheriff Plummer had used, "two-faced," but then only thought about Lucia's one lovely face. After picking the last crumb of crust off the plate with my fingers, I dared turn my head and gaze at her, not even averting my eyes when she stared back, dimples flashing, and wiped my mouth with a dinner napkin.

"Sorry, Woodie" she said. "That was the last of the pie."

In the next few weeks a robbery occurred west of Bannack and another between Virginia City and Bannack. I paid them little mind. Sidney Edgerton and Wilbur Sanders suspected that Henry Plummer was the ringleader behind both, but that was old hat for them. Their suspicions were based on hearsay and presumption of guilt. Besides, I had my mind on other things—

yes, Lucia Darling and her baked goods but also the local Indians. They hardly resembled the powerful and painted Sioux and Northern Cheyenne warriors who were making travel on the Bozeman Trail all but impossible. Drab and spare, they camped among the sage bushes on the outskirts of town, where they were largely invisible, but on their regular begging trips to Bannack they became pests, at least to Sidney and Mary Edgerton and other prominent people who went out of their way to avoid them.

"They're terrible nuisances," Mrs. Edgerton complained one afternoon in her kitchen. "Scavengers—all!"

"They're hungry," Lucia replied.

"In our town, we pay in gold for our food."

"They have no gold, Aunt Mary. They aren't allowed to mine."

"We aren't miners either, my dear, but we manage."

"I wasn't managing too well until you all took me in," I admitted. "I used to be hungry all the time. Day and night I would wish for . . ."

Mary Sanders, as was her way, patted me on the head as if I were a simpleton. "You can't expect Chief Justice Sidney to support the entire tribe of beggars. They should all go away from our town and find a place to grow corn and gather nuts to support themselves."

"That wouldn't be right," Lucia said. "They are Bannocks. They were here before us."

"None of them were growing or gathering or even hunting anything along Grasshopper Creek before John White discovered gold here in July 1862."

"How can we ask them to leave, Aunt Mary? We named our town after them."

Mary Edgerton scratched her head. It was as if that was news to her. She circled the kitchen twice in silence before speaking again. "We spell our town B-a-n-n-a-c-k. They don't spell, but they are called the B-a-n-n-o-c-k-s, with an 'o' instead of a second 'a.' As a schoolteacher, you *should* know how to spell, my dear."

"The town was B-a-n-n-o-c-k until we got a post office a year ago," Lucia said. "When the name was submitted to Washington, D.C., the 'o' was inadvertently taken for an 'a.' "

"That can happen," I agreed. "The Potomac used to be the Patowmack. Anyway, in my hometown they got a lot more to deal with these days than just spelling."

"And the white men are too busy killing other white men to worry about *our* Indians," Lucia said as she took a loaf of piping hot bread out of the tiny oven. I moved closer to better take in the heavenly scent, and Lucia swatted my nose as if I were a badly mannered mutt.

"All the more reason, we should do something ourselves about those . . . those Bannocks," Mary said, wagging a finger at both Lucia and me. "They pick off all the dead chickens and old bones and bits of meat the hogs don't get and take them to their wickiups for a feast. Do you think you could eat with them, Lucia? I know Sidney and I couldn't. Furthermore, I don't like to have the beggars come into the house; they are so dirty, and I worry about the children."

Lucia bit her tongue and shoved another bread pan into the oven. Her aunt liked to have the final word in any conversation, so Lucia let her. Mary Edgerton gave me another quick pat on the head and excused herself to take a nap before the evening meal.

"Talking about unpleasant things is terribly exhausting," she said on the way out.

No sooner was she gone than two Bannock noses pressed against the kitchen window, with the smaller nose well above the larger nose. Lucia left the oven for a closer look and saw the open-mouthed red face of a small boy who was sitting on the shoulders of a taller boy with sunken eyes. She turned away when she heard a tapping at the back door.

"Would you see who that is, Woodie?" she said.

I hesitated, still being afraid of Indians of all types, but after a gulp of air, I cautiously unlocked the back door and swung it open. Two Indian women of indeterminate age and unbecoming dress practically tumbled inside.

"Naingi," they said at the same time, touching their puckered lips with their fingers.

"Howdy," I blurted out.

"They want to eat," Lucia said. "That's one Bannock word I know." She gave them each a loaf of bread and then held up a finger for them to wait a moment. She opened a cupboard and produced four soda biscuits. "For the boys," she said. And just like that the old women scurried out the door and the two noses disappeared from the window.

"Won't be serving bread to the Edgertons tonight," Lucia told me. "They'll have to settle for veal potpie. I did save a soda biscuit for you, Woodie."

"Thanks, but I'm not hungry," I said, half believing it but knowing in my belly I was lying through my teeth. When I was fifteen, I was always hungry down deep. "You should have given it to *them*," I added, pointing at the closed door.

I would have similar encounters with Bannock Indians in the days ahead—not exactly comfortable but always peaceful. Of course, it is different in *The Man from Montana: How He Escaped the Noose*. The Bannocks seek revenge against the Bannack miners because fishing is no longer possible in Grasshopper Creek. These "dog-eating digger Indians" ally themselves with the powerful Blackfeet Nation, described as "villainous black knights who ride rampant through their Montana fiefdom." In a joint raid, the united warriors haul off all the bags of gold they can carry and three golden-haired girls—two soiled doves from Skinner's Saloon and the reputable schoolmarm, Lucinda Darlington (an elaboration of Lucia Darling). The young Red Ranger, who always maintains his red mask and red cape to hide his identity from territorial Republicans and Democrats alike, trails the raiders all the way to Hell Gate Canyon on the Clark Fork, where they have camped for the night. With great stealth and resourcefulness, he rescues Lucinda just before the savages can subject her to a "fate worse than death" and also takes away three bags of gold dust (enough to buy happiness but not so much as to overload his trusty steed, "Gold"). "Our red-masked hero did not pass judgment on the two soiled doves who, despite his entreaties, rejected his offer to save their immoral souls," writes W.A. Phillips. "As incredible as it may seem to Christian churchgoers, Nugget Nan had taken a shine to the tall, heavily muscled half-naked Blackfeet chief, and Assay Annie was willing to try anything new, including eating dog with the Bannock squaws, rather than return to her debauched and misbegotten life in the hell town called Bannack."

There isn't a word of truth in any of that tale. W.A. Phillips mined my life story and then embellished it until it became Red Ranger's story, unrecognizable to me. I never fought Blackfeet or Bannocks at fifteen or any other age. In fact, I began to identify with the Bannock boys who had pressed their noses against the kitchen window. Like them I had grown up in poverty while my rich neighbors (albeit Washington politicians rather than Bannack miners) acted as if I were invisible or at most a hungry mutt looking for a bone. And like them, in my current time of need I turned to the kindly Lucia Darling for nourishment and nurturing.

That said, I forgot the Bannocks soon enough once they were out of sight. Road agents, even though their numbers have been exaggerated, were a far greater threat than Indians to whatever peace existed in the community. More alarming to me, however, were the vigilantes, who rose up from the town's creaky floorboards like little Gods, stamped their feet, and bellowed, "Vengeance is mine, I will repay." Their targets were not only road agents but also hard cases, drunks, cheats, and anyone else who had a questionable character and/or questionable associates. In the latter category, so the vigilantes contended, was none other than Rufus Hart, who, while absent from yours truly, had become better known in Virginia City as "Rogue Hart."

Chapter Four

With no Indian war forthcoming in the last weeks of fall 1863, the good citizens of Bannack and Alder Gulch turned their knitted brows toward the unrighteous white men amongst them. The concerned citizens engaged in secret late-night talks, although I overheard a few of these while stretched out in bed in the backroom of the Edgerton home. The subject was crime, lawmen acting badly, and the necessity for the kind of vigilante-style justice that had supposedly cleaned up criminal behavior and political corruption in San Francisco the previous decade. Sidney Edgerton, as the territory's chief justice, thought it best not to be directly involved in any extralegal doings, but nephew Wilbur Sanders did enough talking for the both of them. Not that Mr. Edgerton ever saw it necessary to make the trip to Lewiston to be officially sworn in as chief justice. He genuinely feared the natural and manmade dangers on the trail west but more than that was set on heading in the opposite direction to convince President Lincoln and the U.S. Congress to create a new territory east of the Bitterroot Mountains.

"Must you go, Uncle?" Mr. Sanders said one evening at the dinner table. "I mean all that distance at a time like this. Don't forget there's a war going on in the East."

"Can't think of a better time," Mr. Edgerton replied, patting his belly with both hands. "I hate to say it, but I'll feel safer in Washington than I do here. I'm sure you can get the movement going and, you know, take care of things."

The chief justice lowered his voice to a whisper, which only made his wife roll her eyes and ask if he wanted another helping of bread pudding. I knew all about the kind of movement he wanted to get going in gold country, but I just stared at the checkered tablecloth trying to look as dumb as he thought me to be.

"Can't you, as the chief justice of the territory, do something about the situation here?" Lucia asked the man at the head of the table as he dug into his second helping.

"There is no situation here," Sidney Edgerton firmly replied. "You make a fine bread pudding, Lucia."

"That's right," Wilbur Sanders said. "Don't you know, cousin Lucia, that our uncle wants to be appointed governor of the new territory if—or I should say *when*—it is approved." The loyal nephew then leaned toward Sidney Edgerton. "Once you go face to face with the president, there's no doubt in my mind that you will win him over."

"You're gonna see Abraham Lincoln?" I blurted out.

"I believe he is still president," said Justice Edgerton. "You want me to say hi for you, Woodrow?"

Sidney Edgerton had always struck me as stern and humorless, so I had trouble gauging his words. But I managed to nod my head and smile. "I'd like that," I said.

Everybody at the table laughed. I was taken aback, being someone who never intentionally tried to be funny.

As it turned out, Sidney Edgerton postponed his trip to Washington because he determined that traveling east was just as dangerous as traveling west. The road agents were everywhere, watching, listening, scheming, and ready to pounce on any traveler worth his weight in gold. And the chief justice would have been worth a ton because he had planned to have gold nuggets and ingots sewn inside the lining of his greatcoat and the bottom of his valises to dazzle the eyes of the congressmen and let them know that a new territory east of the Bitterroots would be a mighty rich one.

"You are wise not to go, Sid," Mary Edgerton said one afternoon in mid-December when her husband was having second thoughts about staying put.

The chief justice only grunted. For someone who wanted to be a mover and a shaker, he often had trouble moving. I had heard him say to Wilbur Sanders that very morning how he feared that snow would soon be blocking all the passes, causing him to be stuck in Bannack all winter long. Yet he still couldn't budge himself.

"You know I'm right," Mrs. Edgerton continued. "There's nothing Sheriff Plummer would like better than to get the territorial chief justice out of the way. You can bet that his henchmen are on the outskirts of town ready to waylay you."

"Mary is absolutely right," said Mr. Sanders, who got in the middle of things whenever he heard the name "Plummer," whispered or otherwise. "The robbers are anxious to know when you expect to leave Bannack and how much company you will have when you do go."

"Somebody going somewhere?" I asked, innocently enough, having just stepped out of Lucia's classroom.

"No," shouted Wilbur Sanders, pointing a finger at me. "You were listening, weren't you?"

"Not really, but even when I'm not listening, I hear."

"How long were you *not really* listening?"

"Never mind the boy," Sidney Edgerton said. "He's completely harmless."

And also mindless, the chief justice most likely was thinking.

"Don't forget his brother is Rufus Hart, one of Plummer's deputy sheriffs."

"I know. I know. Cain and Abel were brothers, too. Anyway, the older Hart is over in Virginia City."

"Where the situation is just as bad as it is here."

"What situation?" asked Lucia as she emerged from the classroom.

Although Chief Justice Edgerton remained in place, he sent his nephew to the Alder Gulch communities the week before Christmas to drum up support for creation of a new western territory. While Wilbur Sanders was there, somebody found the frozen body, pecked over by magpies, of a missing young German immigrant, Nicholas Tiebolt, and a posse brought into custody George Ives—a usual suspect whenever a foul deed was committed in the area. Some thought immediate hanging would serve the community best and allow the good citizens to quickly get back to their more important business of finding gold. But those in favor of a trial in Nevada City won out. Mr. Ives could afford four good lawyers, thanks to his illegally earned gold, but nobody stood up to prosecute the case. Mr. Sanders had a wife and two small children back in Bannack ready to celebrate their first white Christmas in the Rockies, but instead of catching a stage home, he took on the job as the people's attorney. It made perfect sense to him and to the people, since he was the nephew and secretary of the territorial chief justice.

"I'm going to push the prosecution with the utmost vigor," he told my brother Rufus, who was supposed to be a witness against George Ives the next day at the trial. "If the guilt of the accused be ascertained, I will see to it that retribution is swift and absolutely remorseless."

"You're so sure George is guilty, Mr. Sanders, why not just string him up right now."

"Don't be impertinent, young man. I must do my duty and so must you. You must testify that you saw the boy purchase two mules from Ives with gold dust and then saw Ives ride after him, his intent clearly robbery and murder."

"I didn't see nothing."

"You were there when the transaction took place, and you saw Ives go after the boy, and you saw him come back with the sold mules."

"It was none of my business."

"None of your business, Mr. Hart? Aren't you the duly sworn-in deputy in Virginia City?"

"Not exactly. I'm assistant deputy to Deputy Sheriff Buzz Caven."

"Caven is a coward. He should have gone after Ives. What about you?"

"I ain't no coward. But I ain't no informer."

"That's right. Sheriff Plummer hired you."

"What if he did? A sheriff is supposed to hire deputies."

"And isn't it true, you were assigned to look after things in Nevada City, which is near where Ives shot young Tiebolt in the head?"

"You seem to have all the answers already, Mr. Sanders."

"I'll be asking you things like that during the trial, Mr. Hart."

"You ain't gonna get answers. I know nothing."

"Caven is a coward. That's one thing. But talk is you could be an accomplice to murder. That's a thousand times worse."

"I didn't see nothing. I know nothing. And I didn't do nothing. I'm innocent."

"Like Sheriff Plummer?"

"Leave him out of this. Leave me out of it."

"You like being referred to as Rogue Hart?"

"I been called worse. If you want to hang George Ives, innocent or not, it's really no skin off my neck. You is barking up the wrong tree, Mr. Sanders."

"You know, Rufus, it really is a shame you aren't back in Bannack going to school every day with your brother. He is honest, diligent, and obedient, and should grow up to be a fine citizen one day."

"And poor as potatoes."

"You aren't too old to learn, son, or to change your ways."

"I know enough not to snap to judgment. But you, Mr. Sanders, got a stubborn streak one-hundred miles wide. You don't even listen to George's side of the story. Why, you're about as stubborn as one of his mules."

"You mean the mules young Tiebolt bought and paid for and which your friend Ives reclaimed after he shot down the innocent Dutchman in cold blood?"

"I ain't talking no more."

"It would be in your best interests, young man, to answer all my questions at the trial as forthrightly as possible. You should know that both I and Chief Justice Edgerton believe in law and order, but, if necessary, here and in the other gold camps, there shall be order without law."

A three-day trial would take place directly on and to the east of Nevada City's Main Street. The snow was too packed to clear it away from the outdoor courtroom. It was said that Wilbur Sanders got into it with Buzz Caven, whom he supposed was a Plummer man, over jury selection. Mr. Caven wanted George Ives's friends and sympathizers from Virginia City to decide the accused man's fate, but Mr. Sanders refused to back down and even offered to give the deputy sheriff a duel to the death after the trial was over. Rufus wasn't there. Some present said he got cold feet and bolted from Alder Gulch to tell Sheriff Plummer about Mr. Ives's arrest and to warn him that if too many people talked at the trial, Prosecutor Sanders might come after the sheriff next. I don't know about my brother's actual intentions, but I do know he returned to Bannack and, despite the swirl of unsettling events, tried in his own crude way to court Lucia Darling.

It wasn't until Wilbur Sanders finally returned home and gave a thorough report to his uncle that I heard the details of the George Ives case. Rufus Hart's testimony hadn't been needed because a sad hard case named "Long John" Franck spilled the beans on the accused, possibly to save his own hide. But it was more than that, because some in the crowd expressed the opinion that Mr. Franck was an unreliable witness who deserved hanging as much as George Ives. Mr. Sanders brought to the surface other facts that wouldn't have been allowed in a conventional trial, specifically that the accused had engaged in previous crimes, including robbery of the stagecoach that had first carried me to Bannack. Passenger Leroy Southmayd had lost the most in that particular holdup, and a six-shooter he had owned turned up in Mr. Ives's possession. Most of the other evidence was hearsay. Wilbur Sanders insisted that victims of George Ives's other crimes were reluctant to speak because they feared "exposure to the vengeance of Ives and his partners in crime." Regardless, most of the good citizens in the crowd, according to Mr. Sanders and an England-born newspaperman named Thomas Dimsdale, were convinced, especially after George Ives chose not to testify on his own behalf, "that the worst man in the community was on trial."

Whether from Rufus or somebody else, Sheriff Plummer got word in Bannack about the Ives trial, but he didn't go to Alder Gulch to officially take the accused into custody or otherwise interfere with the proceedings. According to Wilbur Sanders, the sheriff figured he was in enough trouble already and that the good folks interested in order and justice would soon come for him. To his credit, though, Sheriff Plummer didn't run in the opposite direction—to the territorial seat in Lewiston or back to California, where seven years earlier he had seen vigilantes in action. On the third day of the trial, December 21, 1863, Prosecutor Sanders said in his summation that George Ives was a known stagecoach robber, bully, and mean drunk who "belonged to the criminal classes, and that his appetite for blood had grown until it became a consuming passion."

Much to the prosecutor's relief, a twenty-four-man jury agreed with him, but the verdict of guilty came with a lone dissenter who said that the prosecution had not proved beyond reasonable doubt that Mr. Ives had killed Nicholas Tiebolt. Regardless, at Mr. Sanders's urging, the accused was condemned to death. Mr. Ives spoke of his mother and sisters in the States and asked that his execution be put off until the next morning, promising he would not try to escape or allow his friends to attempt a rescue. The crowd suddenly turned sympathetic and the prosecutor thought he would have to honor this last request, but as darkness set in, one of the prisoner's guards, a squat man of great energy named X (short for John Xavier) Beidler, shouted, "Sanders, ask him how long he gave the Dutchman!" Local lawmen not associated with Sheriff Plummer then found a suitable gallows—a dry goods box inside an unfinished log building. With a noose around his neck, the condemned man said, "I am innocent of this crime" and then placed the blame on someone else—not Long John Franck but one Aleck Carter, who had made himself scarce as the trial wound down. "Men, do your duty," somebody shouted (Wilbur Sanders insisted it wasn't him), and the box was kicked out from under Mr. Ives's feet.

The trial/hanging of George Ives has made it into various historical accounts that are probably mostly true. And, of course, it is described in W.A. Phillips's *Man from Montana: How He Escaped the Noose* in largely fictional fashion, as if the actual events that occurred before Christmas in Nevada City weren't dramatic enough. In that dime novel, Red Ranger has captured "Evil Ives" because all the lawmen for a thousand miles around are too corrupt to do their duty and nobody else dares buck Ives's many murderous friends, who are members of "the most vicious and horrific criminal organization in the Old

West—the Plummer Gang." Prosecutor Sanders, renamed "Banders," comes across as a timid, wobbly-kneed teetotaler who backs down to the forces of evil, including "Plummer, the two-hatted, two-faced earthly manifestation of Satan." It is left to young Red Ranger, with a double-barreled shotgun in each hand, to hold back the misguided mob and allow the one-eyed, seven-foot executioner, Mr. X, to carry out the sentence.

Later, Red Ranger would learn three things—that he had been misinformed about how satanic Sheriff Plummer really was, that the legality of the Evil Ives trial could be questioned, and that hanging was *not* the solution to every alleged crime in the gold camps. "Did Ives get what he deserved?" W.A. Phillips asks. "Red Ranger thought so then, before the rise of the vigilante enforcers, but it still left a hollow feeling in his washboard belly, a sadness in his big red heart, and a crick in his sympathetic neck." The actual hanging is described in some detail, with "the fall being too short and easy to crack Evil Ives's thickly muscled neck, causing the condemned man to trip the light fantastic at the end of the frayed rope like dance-hall girl Juanita of California Gold Rush fame and to do so for so indeterminately long as to cause the crowd of impatient miners to start taking bets as to when Judge Lynch would finally declare the murderer dead and defunct."

Chapter Five

His success in seeing the George Ives case through to the end was reason enough for Wilbur Sanders to feel proud of himself. But there was far more to tell; in the immediate aftermath came an event more rewarding and significant—the formation of a vigilante organization. To most of the miners and merchants of the Alder Gulch communities, justice had arrived like an early Christmas present with the hanging of Mr. Ives, but the cost in time and trouble had been too much to stomach. A more efficient method of dealing with the outlaw element was required, for George Ives wasn't even the tip of the illegal iceberg. For starters, Aleck Carter, the man Mr. Ives had pointed to as the true killer of young Tiebolt, was somewhere on the loose, as were the executed man's other accomplices and the road agents operating out of Bannack.

Wilbur Sanders was very much involved in the creation of a Vigilance Committee that had rules, regulations, and officers to guide its mission to investigate all serious crimes and dish out one and only one punishment to the guilty—death. Such formalities as indictments and drawn-out trials would no longer be necessary. But this was no lynch mob, Mr. Sanders insisted, and Justice Edgerton later unofficially concurred. Vigilant men, beginning as early as December 23, 1863, signed oaths of honor to secretly but righteously carry out the necessary punishments with the blessings, if not the direct assistance, of the Good Lord. One would have thought that Wilbur Sanders, with his set jaw, repeated bending of the brow, and uncompromising severity, would have been the logical choice for president. Instead, the vigilantes elected one Paris Pfouts, who no doubt was more personable and politically adept than Mr. Sanders and thus a better recruiter of good citizens to combat the ne'er-do-wells. If Mr. Sanders was disappointed or jealous, he hid it well. "The committee is in good hands and growing steadily," he told his uncle. "I did not seek the position of president, though urged to do so by some of the most upstanding members, who congratulated me on my courage and initiative. I let everyone involved know I wished to return to my new home in Bannack and spend more time with my family. That said, if called upon, I am well prepared to do my duty at the drop of a hat."

Even before Wilbur Sanders returned, my brother had become persona non grata at the Edgerton household, not so much for his close connection with Sheriff Henry Plummer as for his effort to corrupt the morals of Lucia Darling. On the night before Christmas, Rufus, drunk to the gills, showed up at the house dressed in red wool cap and American flag and claiming to be Santa Claus. The four Edgerton children were already in bed, and their parents were not about to allow them out to see this shameful imposter.

"Yes, I'm Santy," he said to the gawking Mary Edgerton and her frowning husband. To emphasize the point, he jumped on the kitchen table and struck a pose with his arms spread wide. "Can't fool you all. You like my Stars and Stripes?"

"You aren't supposed to be here," said Sidney Edgerton, still wearing his nightcap.

"Sure I am. It's Christmas Eve and I'm bringing you all a gift—me!"

"You've been on a spree, Rufus Hart," said Mrs. Edgerton. "You're as drunk as David's sow."

"Yes, ma'am. But I'm *still* Santa Claus. And I ain't no

Confederate Santy. You all are damn good Yankees, and Santy is for the Union, including the coloreds, the red savages, the white scoundrels, and the yellow dogs. I'm from the north, by Jiminy, way up north."

"You're from Washington, D.C.," I said as I stepped out of the backroom.

"Well, that's north of the South, brother."

"You once told me Rebels were more your type."

"Yes, but *not* Santy's type."

"If it isn't the Rogue Hart," said Lucia, who appeared in a loosely cut linen nightgown without any frills, ruffles, or lace. Her arms were crossed, her lips pursed, her eyes cold. Not a dimple in sight. Still she was alluring to the uninvited guest, whose eyes bulged to such a degree that I stepped between the two of them, with my back to her, blocking his vision.

"You can call me Kris Kringle if you prefer," Rufus said, stepping around me with only a slight stumble. "Or Father Christmas, children."

"We're not amused," Mary Edgerton said, her lips quivering. "The children, thank goodness, are sound asleep in their beds."

"Bah, we are all children of . . . something or other."

"You are addressing your elders," Sidney Edgerton said. "This is my home, Rufus Hart, and I demand respect."

"Better yet, call me Saint Nick," Rufus continued. "Who would ever hang a saint? You wouldn't, would you Sid old boy? You like my beard, Lucia dear girl? I grew it for you."

"Old boy? How dare you. And I'll ask you *not* to address my niece."

"She ain't wearing no dress, Mister Chief Justice, kind sir, Yankee Doodle Dandy, would-be governor of the next bloody new territory, Bosom Friend of Christ the Lord, Husband of the Virgin Mary, Uncle of the Undressed Adventuress."

"Mind your tongue, Rufus Hart," said Mrs. Edgerton.

"Don't mind at all, ma'am." My brother blew past me like a blast of north wind and with tongue out and arms extended he met Lucia head-on.

For the first time in my life, I attacked Rufus, that is to say, I jumped on his back. My noble intention was to protect Lucia Darling's honor, of course, but all I succeeded in doing was knocking both my brother and my true love over, with my brother landing flat against her, bosom and all. I yanked on Rufus's hair with one hand and pounded his shoulder blades with one fist until he reluctantly rose off his soft, long-haired human cushion, took hold of the collar of my nightshirt, and slapped my face as red as my hair.

"Stop!" screamed Mrs. Edgerton. "He's just a boy, your own little brother."

Rufus, as was his way, drunk or sober, persisted.

"Yes, cease," agreed Mr. Edgerton. "You want me to call the sheriff?"

Clearly the chief justice didn't realize what he was saying.

"Why not," Rufus replied, and he paused for a moment in his attack on my face. "Henry Plummer is my friend."

When Lucia struck Rufus over the head with *McGuffey's Pictorial Eclectic Primer* he dropped to the floor like a sack of potatoes. The Edgertons immediately retired without a word. Lucia and I took one arm apiece and dragged my brother to the backroom, where we managed to pull him up onto my bed. Then she led me out by the hand, closed the door behind us, and told me to stand guard in case the prisoner tried to escape.

"Good night, Woodie," she said. "You're a good boy. I can always count on you."

Tongue-tied as was often the case in those days, I watched her go to her own room, her nightgown flowing behind her. She moved how I thought a ghost might move, a female ghost. I expected her to turn around and check on me, so I stood at attention outside the door of my own room. But she never looked back. I wanted to ask her how long she expected me to stand guard, but the only way to do that now was to go to her room, and I never did that. I didn't stay at attention long, but I did stay standing, slouched against the door hinges, for more than an hour before sliding down into a sitting position. I fell asleep like that and, at some point, tipped over during the night. I woke up before dawn to make sure the door was still closed tight. I pressed my ear to the doorknob and heard my brother snoring as peacefully as a lamb with a stuffy nose. Relieved, I lay back down and fell right asleep again. I don't know if I had done my duty or not, but it was the best I could do.

In the morning, Rufus acted completely innocent; he denied having designs on Lucia Darling, having any connection with gold-camp thieves, and having ever defamed Santa Claus. Before breakfast, he slipped away without any apologies, confessions, or goodbyes. I was too young to be my brother's keeper, but I was plenty worried about him, so I followed him out of the house and down the street as if I were a Union spy. He met up with Sheriff Plummer's deputies Buck Stinson and Ned Ray, who had just come out of the Elkhorn Saloon, and they exchanged pleasantries like men who didn't have time to be pleasant. I got close enough to hear only a few words. They spoke of the George Ives hanging, the sheriff's agitated state of mind, and rumors of a Vigilance Committee forming companies in Alder Gulch. I stepped closer like a cat whose curiosity overcomes its timidity. I was about to start whistling Dixie because Rufus was always partial to the song, if not always the South, and it usually improved his mood. But I wasn't sure exactly where Buck Stinson's and Ned Ray's sympathies lay.

"One of them death companies could come here . . . for us," Deputy Stinson said, rubbing his chin stubble and scrunching his face as if contemplating the meaning of life. "Don't need another close shave."

Buck Stinson, who was a barber before he became a deputy, had reason to be nervous. Before I came to Bannack, he and at least two others had been involved in the Virginia City murder of Deputy D.H. Dillingham, apparently an honest lawman who suspected his fellow deputies were taking part in robberies. In a quick June 1863 trial, Buck Stinson and one of the others were convicted by a public jury. Gallows were built and their graves dug. But the third accused man, who was tried separately and got off because he was splendid looking and stood so upright (according to Lucia Darling), caused second thoughts about the earlier verdict. The crowd was divided on how to proceed, and in the commotion another deputy commanded that the two convicted men be released of their chains. And so they were. None other than X Beidler, who would later become a key figure in the vigilante movement, reportedly posted a sign next to the two empty holes in the ground that read "Graves to Let." Buck Stinson was free to resume his duties as a deputy for Sheriff Plummer, but that, of course, didn't mean anyone saw him as a model citizen. As far as I knew, nobody had bothered to cover up the two holes, and Buck Stinson's designated grave still awaited his presence.

"I know Plummer ain't been himself," said Ned Ray, taking hold of his fellow deputy's arm as if to settle a trembling hand. "If his cover has been blown, then we ain't got no safety net. I've been thinking about growing a beard and making myself scarce until I can slip out of town and . . ."

"And what?" Deputy Stinson shook the arm free of his partner's grasp. "You ain't good for much on your own, Ned. You'd be caught for something and shot or hanged before you could say Jack Robinson. Either way you'd be as dead as George Ives. Nothing for you and me to do but ride it out with the sheriff."

"That how you see it, Hart?"

I jumped backward as if someone had shot at my feet, but then realized Ned Ray was addressing my brother, not me. My sudden movement didn't attract his intention. I wore no hat to hide my flaming top and it felt as if my entire body was trembling, but he didn't so much as glance at me. Back in our crowded home in Washington, the folks often acted like I wasn't even there. And now I was getting the same feeling of invisibility in broad daylight on Bannack's Main Street.

"I wouldn't cross Henry Plummer any more than I would you fellows," Rufus said, sweeping a wayward strand of blond hair back under his hat. "As far as I'm concerned, we're all innocent, and that's how I'll play it should Wilbur Sanders and the other too-big-for-their-britches vigilantes throw any accusations in my direction."

Buck Stinson nodded his approval. Ned Ray looked at Buck and then did the same.

Rufus's calling himself innocent sounded like an admission of guilt to me. My brother had never confided with me about his doings in Alder Gulch, but I wasn't so naïve as to believe him a strictly legal servant of the law. He didn't seem worried, but it could have been an act put on for his two scruffy-looking associates. I was worried for him. I hadn't seen George Ives dangling from the end of a rope in Nevada City, but my mind's eye saw it over and over again in vivid detail. Like the late unfortunate Mr. Ives, Rufus was tall, blond, and clean-shaven, looking like a gentleman even when throwing a punch or pointing a gun. I couldn't believe my brother would kill anyone in cold blood, but thievery and intimidation went back to his Washington, D.C., days. It didn't take much effort to imagine Rufus wearing the noose instead of George Ives.

But what could I possibly say to Rufus, especially in such bad company? I felt all choked up inside (visions of that rope extending to my own neck, you know) but didn't dare clear my throat. I prayed that Buck Stinson and Ned Ray would just move on to take care of business, no matter what it was. And I promised myself I would stop following my brother for the simple reason that it wasn't a nice thing to do even if one was invisible and full of good intentions.

At first the two Bannack deputies walked right past me, but then the sun must have hit my red hair just right, because Buck Stinson stopped suddenly, turned around, and called out for "Red." That wasn't my name and I intended not to answer to it, but then Ned Ray grabbed me by the shoulder and spun me around.

"We know you, don't we?" Deputy Ray said. "You been listening, boy."

"*Not* listening and *not* hearing," I said, looking to my brother for assistance.

Rufus, though, said nothing. He started whistling Dixie.

"You was staring," Deputy Stinson said. "What you want?"

"Eh . . . a haircut. I . . ."

"I don't do much barbering these days. Nice head of bloody red hair, though. You looking to get scalped?" Buck Stinson drew a knife from his belt and began wiping the blade back and forth on the front of his shirt.

"That's what happens to boys who stick their noses in places where they don't belong," Ned Ray said. "Either that or we'll put you in chains and lock you in the sheriff's cellar for being a damned suspicious character. We represent the law, you know."

My head started bobbing. Was it best to know or *not* to know? Now I was scared more for myself than for Rufus, who had stopped whistling.

"Leave him alone," Rufus finally said, and I could have kissed him on the forehead. "He don't know nothing at all. Never has."

"How can you be so sure?" Buck Stinson snapped. "I seen him before. He could be spying on us. I wouldn't put it past Edgerton, Sanders, and company to enlist just such a . . ."

"Don't make a mountain out of a molehill, Buckaroo. He's just my dumb kid brother."

"No foolin'? But I'm recollecting now. Don't he live with our so-called chief justice?"

"And with the chief justice's niece, Lucia Darling. Ain't Woodie one lucky son of a bitch!"

Chapter Six

Rufus was right. No matter what I knew or didn't know, I was harmless. I wasn't about to provide any information to Sidney Edgerton, Wilbur Sanders, or any other execution-minded vigilante. I didn't want to see my brother strung up, of course, but it was more than that. Any kind of necktie party didn't sit well with me. What was wrong with good old-fashioned *banishment*? Why didn't they build more jails in gold mining country? Why couldn't they put convicted thieves on work details? Why didn't Sidney Edgerton, as chief justice, demand legal justice? Why didn't someone ask Abraham Lincoln what was the best course of action to achieve law and order and form a more perfect united community? Why did the Bannock Indians seem more honest and peaceful than the residents of Bannack? Why didn't I dare pose these questions to anyone but myself?

W.A. Phillips later wrote about what he called the "winner-take-all, rope-and-shotgun, life-and-death struggle between Chief Sheriff Plummer's Ostensible Gang of Cut-Throats and Thieves and the Presumptuously Vigilant, Unwavering, Unapologetic Vigilantes." Most other writers have sided with the "just and fearless" men who stepped up to take a strong stand against the rampant lawlessness in the mining camps. W.A. seems to do the same at first in *Man from Montana,* but then changes his tune in mid-sentence midway through. After that both sides come across as wrong and pigheaded, but the vigilantes are more often portrayed as the worse of two evils.

The only constant is heroic Red Ranger, diligently bringing as much fair play and justice as possible to those turbulent times.

Of course, historically, Red Ranger did not exist, but W.A. Phillips did not cut him totally out of whole cloth. Red Ranger's "true, secret" identity is revealed as "W. 'Red' Hart" in the introduction of *Man from Montana: How He Escaped the Noose* and again at the end in the moralizing conclusion. Through all the pages of redundancy, inconsistencies, and falsehoods, the author has Red Ranger roaming the territory and beyond with one motto in his "lionhearted mind": "No crime deserves to go unpunished but *not* every crime deserves a hanging and sometimes orchestrating a hanging is a crime." Phillips once or twice heard me—meek, unheroic Woodrow Russell Hart say those very words. I had the red hair but was the opposite of fiery. I was weak, like a campfire all but smothered by a dozen bootheels. Red Ranger, on the other hand, was like a controlled prairie fire. This formidable figure—who always wore red buckskins, red cape, red mask, and white hat with a red hawk feather sticking out of it—fingered twice as many lawbreakers as all the vigilantes combined. That made him the No. 1 enemy of Chief Sheriff Plummer. On the other hand, he mostly disavowed capital punishment and saved many a condemned man, believing in rehabilitation and second chances since there was "a little good in the worst of us." That made him the No. 1 enemy of Mr. X, described as "the vilest of the vigilantes, a monstrous one-eyed seven-footer who would have strung up his own grandfather for stealing a glance at somebody else's gold pocket watch." In other words, Red Ranger was caught in the middle but, being a superhuman hero, never allowed himself to get caught.

In retrospect, "W. 'Red' Hart" (the plain and simple me) does have one thing in common with Red Ranger (Phillips's fictional hero, inspired at least in part by me): an abhorrence for seeing a rope attached to a man's neck. Of course, Red Ranger wasn't really there or anywhere, and while I was there, I wasn't actually involved—not in the outlaw activity going on nor the vigilante action meant to curtail it. But there was a Red very much entangled in the whole shebang, namely Erastus "Red" Yeager. I never met the man. All I had in common with him was that we both stood five foot, five inches from our bootheels to our mops of glaring red hair.

After the George Ives hanging, members of the newly formed Vigilance Committee set out on an expedition from Virginia City to capture the man he had accused on the gallows—Aleck Carter. But somebody warned Mr. Carter, and he disappeared into the Rocky Mountains. That somebody was Red Yeager, who worked as a bartender and handyman at the Rattlesnake Ranch, said to be a place where road agents could find refuge. On January 2, 1864, Captain James Williams, executive officer of the vigilantes, arrived with a small party of stern-faced men at Rattlesnake Ranch, on Rattlesnake Creek east of Bannack. The captain was greeted at the front door by the barrel of a six-shooter, held in the shaky right hand of Buck Stinson. When Deputy Stinson saw the armed men backing up James Williams, he sighed heavily and lowered his weapon. Ned Ray, Buck Stinson's ever-present sidekick, then appeared with his hands slightly raised to show he wasn't holding a pistol.

"They found us," Deputy Ray whispered. "Didn't think it would be so soon."

"Shut your bone box," Deputy Stinson replied in what must have been a loud whisper.

"You boys expecting trouble?" Captain Williams asked.

"Never can be too careful," said Deputy Stinson. "You gents want something here?"

"I'm not after you two, if that's what you mean. Anybody else inside?"

"Anybody in particular you got in mind?"

"Whoever else you got inside better show himself."

"Here I am," said my brother, stepping between the two deputies and clear out the door. His arms were crossed and his feet spread wide. He and James Williams engaged in a staring contest. "You want me?"

"I don't even know you, stranger," said Captain Williams.

"Name is Rufus Hart. I'm a deputy, too."

"I'll keep that in mind."

"Fine and who are you?"

"That doesn't matter."

"I recall seeing you in Virginia City."

"That could be."

"It was at the Ives trial."

"I was there all right. You were an interested spectator—Rufus is it?"

"Mildly interested. Didn't stay for the hanging."

"It went well. Nobody else inside? We're looking for a much shorter man with red hair."

"Huh? You mean my brother Woodie?"

"Look, I don't know your brother either. But if he's inside, he should come out, too."

"He ain't inside. He's in Bannack."

"I see. Yet another deputy?"

"No. Just a kid in Lucia Darling's school."

"Well, I have heard of her. But we don't have time for all this jabber, friend. The man we want is Yeager. He's known hereabouts as *Red*."

"What you want him for?"

"Questioning. You know his whereabouts?"

"Nope. Never heard of him."

Captain Williams had run out of patience. He gave Rufus a little push to clear space and then jabbed a finger into Deputy

Stinson's chest. "What about it, Buck? Your luck can't hold up forever. It won't hurt your case to tell me where Yeager is. Now!"

Deputy Stinson immediately squealed. The wanted man was several hundred yards up Rattlesnake Creek in a one-room hut. As soon as Captain Williams and his men headed in that direction, Deputies Stinson and Ray saddled up and galloped in the opposite direction—toward Bannack. Rufus stood his ground. After a while the captain and his men returned with Red Yeager in custody. He hadn't put up a fight. It was cold and dark, so they all spent the night at the Rattlesnake Ranch. My brother actually did know Mr. Yeager, who was nervous but resigned to his fate, whatever it might be. He said there was no point trying to escape, not that Rufus knew him well enough to help him in that regard.

"What'd you do to rile these boys up?" Rufus asked during a quiet moment when James Williams and most of his men were off snoring in other rooms and both guards were half asleep in chairs a little too comfortable.

"Reckon I handed Aleck Carter a message of warning when they was looking for him," Red Yeager replied. "George Brown give it to me. You know old George?"

"I know he was a witness for the defense at the other George's trial . . . George Ives."

"That was real dumb. Trying to provide an alibi for Ives only cast suspicions on his own self. He didn't even like Ives all that much. And at the end or just before the end, Ives fingered Carter for the Tiebolt murder, so these fellows went after him."

"So, Brown must have liked Carter, right, wanting to warn him and all?"

"Never give it much thought. I just give Carter the written message."

"Did you read it?"

"Sure. I can read. It say, 'Get up and dust, and lie low for black ducks.' "

"The black ducks being the vigilantes, right? No need to answer that. But if delivering a message is all you did, then the vigilantes can't . . . Don't answer that either."

"Right. I done some things, just like you, Hart. None of us is truly innocent."

"Shut up. I mean that's what I'd do if I was you. That Williams don't look like a merciful man. He and his boys have enough rope to hang you ten times over. Don't admit to nothing when they question you. It's your only chance to get out of this alive

"Maybe. Maybe not. Sometimes you just got to tell a fellow like that what he wants to hear."

"Don't be a fool, Red."

"Don't worry, Hart. I kinda like the cut of your jib. Won't say nothing bad about you. Promise."

One of the guards broke up the conversation. He might have learned some valuable information had he listened to what Red Yeager and Rufus Hart were saying, but he wasn't that smart. He just figured it was late and everyone was tired and the prisoner shouldn't be talking . . . at least not until he was subjected to James Williams's intense questioning.

In the morning, Rufus wished Mr. Yeager good luck, and he must have felt pretty lucky himself—the executive officer of the vigilantes didn't want him. When Captain Williams and his men took their prisoner away, supposedly only for questioning in Virginia City, Rufus had the whole Rattlesnake Ranch to himself for a while. He made himself some flapjacks, stretched out on the best bed in the place, and slept all morning like an innocent child.

What happened next to Red Yeager has been well recorded in Montana history books and even more dramatically in *Man from Montana: How He Escaped the Noose,* thanks to W.A.

Phillips's limitless imagination. Mr. Yeager never made it to Virginia City in reality or fiction. The Williams's party stopped off at Cottonwood Ranch where George Brown happened to be tending bar. W.A. has Red Ranger, a one-man posse who always gets his man, there as well, but Red Ranger hasn't made a prisoner of Mr. Brown yet because, being a hero with compassion, he is reserving judgment on the bartender. Instead he is listening to George Brown's hard-luck story about how he has never amounted to anything because Comanches scalped his dirt-farmer parents, teachers and lawmen beat him mercilessly, and he never found a friend until Red Yeager came along. For reasons known only to him, W.A., unlike the historians, gave Brown a past and perhaps a reason for readers to feel a touch of sympathy for the poor loser. No doubt it was total fabrication.

The fact was the posse now had under the same roof Brown and Yeager, the two men who had teamed up so Aleck Carter could escape the vigilantes. The pair wasn't much and nobody much cared about their upbringing or the fact they were only minor participants in the current crime wave. James Williams and all his men voted for hanging. The lone dissenter changed his tune when his comrades leveled shotguns at him, but the captain must have had a few second thoughts. He had the vigilantes, now with two prisoners, continue on toward Virginia City. In W.A. Phillips's untrue telling of the story, Red Ranger demands the vigilantes release the so-called outlaws into his custody. "For their *criminal interference,* give them ten lashes apiece or better yet banish them from gold country!" Red Ranger shouts at the vigilantes. "It is cruel and unusual punishment to hang two human beings who have done nothing more than write a message and deliver it." The vigilantes reply in unison, "It ain't unusual punishment for us!" When Red Ranger protests too much, they knock him silly with the butts of their shotguns, tie him spread-eagle to a wagon wheel, unmask him, stuff his red mask into his mouth as a gag, give him ten lashes, tell him to banish himself, and ride off "laughing as diabolically as the red devil."

The party, in true accounts as well as in W.A. Phillips's book, stopped at the Laurin Ranch, a few miles short of Alder Gulch, and resumed talk of a double hanging. Sobbing George Brown hardly said a word there, but Yeager, resigned to his fate like a mouse under the paws of a feral cat, talked his head off. "I don't say this to get off," he told his executioners. "I don't want to get off." Call it a death wish, and it came true. Williams and his men took the pair to a tree on the banks of the Stinking Water River and hanged them side by side by their necks until dead . . . and for some time after that, too, with hand-lettered signs pinned to their backs—one reading "Red! Road Agent and Messenger," the other "Brown! Corresponding Secretary."

In *Man from Montana*, it's different. Red Ranger frees himself from the wagon wheel and drives the wagon like a Roman chariot racer to the hanging tree. He arrives just in time to save the "likable, quietly praying, barely culpable" Brown by cutting the rope, and he can save Yeager, too, except Red waves Red Ranger off and issues these *unrealistic* last words: "Ya know this world ain't big enough for the two of us. The bad Red must die. The good Red must range across Montana righting wrongs and protecting society from injustices committed not only by outlaws like me but also by all those so-called *just* men who play God as easily as Jesus did." Red Ranger flattens six or seven vigilantes with his mighty fists (preferring not to waste lives or cartridges unless absolutely necessary) and safely transports Brown to Salt Lake City, where Brown becomes a model citizen, converts to Mormonism, and takes a couple of understanding wives. The consequences are dire for his savior: the vigilantes now consider Red Ranger a wrongdoer, "the most marked man in Montana," never mind that it was still Idaho Territory.

Yeager, in real life, showed no inclination to save himself or protect the other alleged members of the road agent gang. That Red, with his designated noose dangling nearby, provided a full list (well, as many names as he could remember before his time ran out) of miscreants sounds fantastic, an incredible stroke of luck for the vigilante crowd. W.A. Phillips thought so, too, and couldn't figure out a way to make Red's final scene any more fantastic or dramatic. Yeager named Sheriff Henry Plummer as chief of the closely knit gang and Bill Bunton, who was one of the partners running the Rattlesnake Ranch operation, as second in command. The late message writer George Brown (who only escaped hanging in Phillips's book) was indeed the secretary. Ned Ray—who I had thought of as nothing more than a sidekick to Buck Stinson, who in turn was Henry Plummer's sidekick—held the position of "council room keeper" at Bannack (which I guess was the No. 4 spot in the pecking order, though it sounded as if he might only be a glorified housekeeper). The other nineteen men on the list were "roadsters." Buck Stinson was on it, as was the late George Ives, escapee Aleck Carter, and the two men—Bob Zachary and Whiskey Bill Graves—who held up the stagecoach that Rufus and I were on when we first traveled to Bannack. I didn't recognize any of the other names. What about Rufus Hart, you might ask? Well, Red Yeager didn't mention him, either because he made good on his promise to my brother or simply because he hadn't been given enough time to remember and reveal all the "lesser badmen" on the list.

The executioners hurried to Alder Gulch to tell President Pfouts and the other vigilantes the good news. Two more road agents had been eliminated as a threat, and the Vigilance Committee, thanks to Red Yeager's flapping tongue, could now proceed at full speed with its mission to enforce order in Virginia City, Bannack, and the rough roads in between. At the head of the committee's most wanted list in early January 1864 was Sheriff Henry Plummer, of course, and right behind him were his trusty if thickheaded deputies, Buck Stinson and Ned Ray.

Chapter Seven

Rumors about Red Yeager's naming names reached Bannack soon enough. Rufus was mostly grateful to the dead informer for leaving him off the blacklist, but there were moments, he told me, when he felt he had been disrespected. He wasn't about to abandon his friend the sheriff, who always acted pleasant and agreeable to him without making it seem like an "act." Nevertheless, Rufus swallowed his pride and took a regular job clerking at Francis Thompson's dry goods store on Main Street. He also rented a room in back, and mostly lay low to avoid running into Henry Plummer or any person associated with him on the public streets.

"I guess I just don't rate," my brother told me a week into the new year when I went to Thompson's to pick up some flour, salt, baking soda, and more pie pans.

"Your work here is that bad? At least it is honest and not as dirty as . . . eh . . . mining."

"I didn't come west to be a shopkeeper, having to work long hours at low pay with a dull-witted smile on my face as not to scare off paying customers. But I wasn't thinking about work."

"Oh," I said. I hadn't seen him smile yet. "Still, it's a *good* job, right?"

"I took it, but it's not in my line."

I wasn't privy to his exact line, and I didn't ask. "You're better off here than, you know, out on the road. It's safer."

"A need to be safe all the time is a coward's way."

I suspected he meant my way, but I let it pass. "You should be ecstatic not to have made Red Yeager's list."

"Don't you go throwing out them big words you learned from Lucia, little brother. She still baking all them pies, I reckon?"

We both knew the answer to that, so I shuffled my feet and said nothing. Sometimes any little thing you said could set off Rufus, and it was best to keep your mouth buttoned if you didn't want to get a fist in the jaw. At least that was my experience.

"Keep your voice down, bub," he said anyway. "I got this job because Thompson is a close friend of Plummer's, but now Thompson is suspicious of Plummer and of me. He's a banker, too, you know."

I guess Rufus was saying that Francis Thompson was an honest man on the side of law and order because he was a banker. But that didn't explain Henry Plummer, the sheriff.

"I try not to judge anyone," I blurted out.

That made Rufus laugh so hard that he tipped over an open sack of flour, spilling whiteness across the counter and onto my coat. He kept laughing. I didn't ask him what was so funny, but he told me anyway.

"Good you don't judge me, little brother," he whispered, as he leaned in close to brush the flour off my coat. "You know damn well I ain't innocent. I'm as much a roadster as Whiskey Bill and most of them other fellows."

"Never knew for sure," I whispered back, hanging my head as if I was the guilty one. "This is the first time I ever heard you confess. Even back in Washington that wasn't exactly your strong suit."

"I never killed nobody," he shouted, grabbing me by the coat collar and glaring at me with his old death stare, which he had already perfected in the nation's capital.

"That's damn good, Rufus."

Rufus let me go. "You swore," he said, laughing again, but it was forced this time. "That's damn funny."

Francis Thompson came scurrying out of the backroom holding a pen in his hand. He first pointed it at me but then waved it at his employee.

"Anything the matter?" he asked, suspiciously eying the spilt flour on the counter.

"Don't worry, Mr. Thompson," Rufus said. "The customer is only my kid brother."

That seemed to satisfy the banker/store owner. He gave me a piece of rock candy, patted me on the head, thanked me for my business even though I wasn't doing the paying, and extended his good wishes to the Edgerton and Sanders families even though he admitted not always seeing eye to eye with them about every little thing.

"Oh," I said, thinking that the two families might have had problems with him over the high prices he charged for basic goods. "I'm sure they'll square their account with you, sir."

"It's not that, my boy. It's really nothing. Just tell your benefactors that no matter what they say and no matter what others are saying over in Virginia City, I still contend that the sheriff is *all right.* You might also mention that the incident in my store on New Year's has been forgotten. Yes, Henry and that driver for the Oliver stage had words, and I had to shove Henry out the back door to keep him from pulling his heavy sheath knife. But that wasn't at all like my friend. He's under immense strain lately at having to deal with the rumor that he was a secret part-owner of the Rattlesnake Ranch and all the other careless talk floating in from the gulch. Regardless, he afterward returned to my store and apologized for engaging in the quarrel."

"That's true," Rufus said. "I witnessed it. The sheriff was

most apologetic for letting his temper get the best of him. He also was appreciative of the way Mr. Thompson led him out the back door and thus saved the life of that rascal driver."

"Never mind that part," Mr. Thompson said, addressing me, not Rufus. "Henry is at heart a peaceable man. He wouldn't kill anyone . . . except, as any good man would do, in self-defense."

"He never hanged nobody either," Rufus offered, but that only made his boss frown and suggest that Rufus clean the flour off the counter.

"No need to say a word about *anybody* doing any *hanging,*" Mr. Thompson told me as he ushered me out the front door. "Pretend your brother didn't mention it. Mum's the word, right boy?"

He had me totally confused. Was I supposed to say something when I got home or not? "Got it," I said, forgetting all about the flour, salt, baking soda, and pie pans.

When I got to the Edgerton place empty-handed, Lucia Darling suggested I must have been hit over the head and robbed. I told her it was nothing like that—that I'd just gotten into a long conversation with my brother and forgotten all about why I had come to the store. She didn't believe me, saying that my brother wasn't capable of having a long, civil conversation. I lied and told her Rufus and I had got to talking about the good old days in Washington, D.C. That seemed to upset her even more because I think she was missing her good old days in Ohio or someplace like that. I offered to go back to Thompson's and get the goods, but instead she sent me to bed without supper. She had a way of making me feel like a dumb kid even more than Rufus did. Later, though, Mary Edgerton brought me a plate of leftovers from dinner, and all was forgiven. With a full stomach, I couldn't hold a grudge against lovely Lucia.

I did go back to the store the next afternoon. Rufus was sweeping the floor as if he had something against the floor. He was in a state because suspicions about Sheriff Plummer kept mounting. A freighter named Neil Howie captured a man called "Dutch John" Wagner, who had tried to rob a freight wagon caravan and had gotten a gunshot wound to the shoulder and then frostbite for his trouble. The sheriff said Mr. Wagner deserved a trial, telling Mr. Howie: "This new way our people have of hanging men without law or evidence isn't exactly the thing. Its time a stop was put to it." But Howie refused to give up custody, telling the sheriff he would hold the prisoner himself until a people's tribunal decided on his punishment.

"It's bad enough what they're saying about the sheriff in Virginia City," Rufus said, pressing down so hard on his broom that the handle cracked. "Damn! If everyone in Bannack turns against him, too, then . . ." Rufus paused to inspect the damaged handle. "Then, by God, everything is ruined for him and . . ."

"But not for you, right? Red Yeager didn't name you and you have this job and . . ."

"I don't want to hear all that again." Rufus spun me around, ordered me to pick a piece of straw off the floor, drew back the broom, and swatted me on the backside so hard that I flew forward and ended up on my belly breathing floor dust.

Francis Thompson immediately showed himself, looking distraught, annoyed, and angry—all at the same time.

"What now!" he shouted.

It wasn't really a question, but Rufus answered his boss anyway. "My dumb little brother broke your broom, Mr. Thompson."

It wasn't like Red Yeager naming names, but I was damned displeased at being the only name on Rufus Hart's list. Of course, I said nothing in my defense. I only requested the goods I had forgotten to take home the day before. Francis Thompson retrieved them himself, said not to worry about the broom, and sent me on my way with a mild swat to the seat of my trousers. At home, I soon forgot about the swats and everything else. Lucia, wanting to make up for her previous severe behavior, greeted me at the door. She said she was pleased as punch that I had gone out to fetch her pie pans and such without any prodding. And she showed it in the Edgerton kitchen by kissing me on the forehead and then giving me a friendly pat on the rump when I bent down to put the sack of flour in its proper place.

What sweet dreams I had that night. All took place in a Bannack that had no outlaws or vigilantes, no gold miners or storekeepers, no chief justices or sheriffs, no Rufus Hart, no anybody but Lucia and me and the school children for a while. When Lucia sent them outside to play with their tops and hoops, we were alone together and she began kissing me, starting with my forehead and then working her way down with the kind of passion I suspected was absent from any actual schoolhouse. It was a rude awakening indeed the next morning when four men from Virginia City and Wilbur Sanders came into the house and whispered so loudly that they dashed my dreams. Mr. Sanders made the introductions to his uncle. The leader of the contingent from the gold towns to the east was businessman John Lott, who had convinced Wilbur Sanders to prosecute George Ives and knew nobody in Bannack could be more trusted to see things his way than the bold lawyer. Sidney Edgerton didn't say much, but I recognized his grunts and throat clearings and an occasional "pshaw." Mr. Lott said a lot, and none of it good for the sheriff and his deputies. Plummer's troubles with Neil Howie were nothing compared to the troubles John Lott had brought.

"Red Yeager said it before we hanged him, Justice Edgerton, and now we all can say it," Mr. Lott said, no longer bothering to whisper. "The sheriff commands a crime ring. His deputies double as road agents. The suspicions about them are true."

Sidney Edgerton did *not* "pshaw" that. With my ear pressed to my partly cracked door, I got worried all over again about my brother because Lott hadn't said how many of Plummer's deputies he thought doubled as road agents. I hoped he meant only Buck Stinson and Ned Ray. After all, my brother had been a very low-key assistant deputy over in Virginia City and was now working in a Bannack dry goods store for the honorable Francis Thompson.

"I would like to meet with you and the other most trustworthy leading citizens of Bannack to present the evidence against these duplicitous lawmen," John Lott continued. "The sooner the better. Our Vigilance Committee, of which your nephew is one of the founders, strongly believes that their executions are in order."

Sidney Edgerton grunted, but it seemed like a positive grunt.

"Of course, after we convict them . . . that is to say when and if they are convicted," said Wilbur Sanders.

"Of course," said Mr. Lott. "We'd like the cooperation of your good citizens because we feel our jurisdiction must be extended to your fair city. Can we meet this afternoon?"

"Whatever my nephew wishes," Sidney Edgerton said. "I trust Wilbur to handle these matters. It's early yet, and I need my coffee. Have you gentlemen had your breakfast?"

A "secret" meeting was indeed set up for late that afternoon in some miner's cabin at the edge of town. Sidney Edgerton told his wife that he could not even tell her which cabin and added, ominously, that he doubted he would be home for dinner.

"Be careful, Sid," she told him. "Plummer men are everywhere."

"Never fear, Mary dear," he replied. "We'll get them before they get us."

I, of course, was not invited to the meeting, no doubt because these important citizens considered me too young and unimportant. I hoped it had nothing to do with the fact that I was the brother of a suspicious character named Rufus Hart who had once been employed as a lawman by Plummer. I thought about following Mr. Edgerton and Mr. Sanders to the cabin, but as curious as I was, I didn't really want to spy on them any more than I wanted to spy *for* them. Either way it seemed pretty dangerous business.

The next day, Mr. Edgerton disclosed to his wife in a roundabout way—with me only having to pause in my mopping of the kitchen floor to hear—that some of the Bannack leaders were not yet ready to throw their sheriff to the wolves. Tiptoeing around the official law in Bannack was one thing but putting a noose around the sheriff's neck was something else, something a little too permanent when there was still uncertainty among men with scruples. John Lott had then taken some of them into town to interrogate Dutch John Wagner, hoping the prisoner would implicate Sheriff Plummer the way Red Yeager had. But Mr. Wagner apparently failed to deliver.

"What next?" Mary Edgerton asked.

"Hard to say, and I don't think I should say anything more," said her husband, glancing toward the kitchen where I had resumed my mopping with greater intensity. "But Wilbur does have another idea."

In the early hours of Sunday, January 10, Wilbur Sanders did show up to discuss his idea with his uncle. I must say that I had put off extended sleep to have a listen. Everyone in the household tended to believe that I slept like a baby, but if eavesdropping is a crime, I must plead guilty. As they whispered in the dark kitchen, I was crouched behind the kitchen door with a stuffed nose and ears open. Temperatures had dropped to as low as thirty below that week. The two stoves in the house couldn't produce enough heat to make things comfortable, and I didn't feel at all well. Still, I was more worried about the necks of Henry Plummer and my brother than my own neck, so to speak.

"You have yourself a plan, do you?" Sidney Edgerton asked Wilbur Sanders. "Not too loud now. We don't want to wake the women."

"Yes. But others *must* participate. It isn't something I *can* do alone."

"You need a mob, a lynch mob?"

"No sir, nothing like that. No hanging is involved."

"I see. You want to get rid of the sheriff some other way."

"Exactly. We get someone to go to Plummer and tell him if he doesn't leave town immediately, he will be executed in the morning. So, of course, he will go to the stable for his horse."

"Oh, so your intention has changed, and you only want to run him out of town?"

"No, no. Banishment won't work with the likes of him. He'd only gather up his gang and fight us tooth and claw."

"I don't understand, Wilbur. It's late. Won't he just mount up and ride away? Doesn't sound like much of a plan to me."

"But you see, he won't get the chance to mount up. There will be men concealed in the stable waiting to kill him."

"With pistols? Or clubs and pitchforks?"

"Six-shooters and rifles would work best. We'd want to make sure he was dead."

"Enough firepower to awaken the town?"

"We'll make sure the stable doors are closed."

"I see. Your plan in essence is an assassination plot?"

My nose began running and I couldn't help but sniff. A pause in their conversation had me holding my nostrils shut. But then I couldn't breathe properly. I snorted once or twice. I thought of dashing to my backroom, but then Mr. Sanders resumed talking. Maybe he believed his uncle's house was full of sniffling mice.

"He must be killed," the agitated nephew said, stamping his foot so hard it rattled some pots and pans. "You know that as well as I do, Uncle Sid."

"I'm not arguing that point. But I ask you, wouldn't shooting him down in cold blood make us as guilty as his band of outlaws?"

"Yes," I said before Wilbur Sanders could answer. I threw myself into the kitchen like a defendant throwing himself at the mercy of the court.

They looked as if they were seeing Henry Plummer himself or the ghost of George Ives. Clearly, my early morning appearance had startled them both into silence. They had been worried about waking the women, maybe the children, not about rousing me. They usually thought of me as invisible, since I was not only unimportant to their lives but also usually as quiet as a mouse, albeit one who had the sniffles. They had no reason to be fond of me or to hate me. When out of sight I was out of their minds. But I had spoken—just one word but a word charged with emotion, *yes!*—and now I was there, body and soul, before them, no longer any less visible than their wives or Lucia Darling.

"Pardon me," I muttered to break the silence.

"Who's that?" asked Mr. Sanders. "Friend or foe?"

"Woodie."

"Woodie?" said Mr. Edgerton. "Oh, Woodrow. It's you. Thank heaven."

I heard a joint sigh. And then one of them lit a lamp.

"What are you doing here?" Mr. Edgerton asked as he looked me over with one eyebrow raised.

"I live here," I said.

"I meant here in the kitchen."

"I . . . I . . . I got hungry for pie."

"He loves Lucia's pies," Sidney Edgerton explained, licking his lips.

"And his last name is Hart?" Wilbur Sanders said, rubbing his temple as he studied my red hair.

"Yes, that's right—Hart. Spelled without the 'e' I believe. But you knew that."

"I had forgotten. I've had much on my mind, uncle."

"I understand how that could be a burden."

"Now I remember. He has a brother over in the other camps. Virginia City. Some kind of lawman. Rufus Hart."

"Rufus is hanging his hat in Bannack these days."

"Is he now? How interesting. Another Plummer man to deal with."

"No, no," I protested, and then I proceeded to protest too much. "He is innocent. I mean, the sheriff hired him but . . . but that's as far as it goes . . . went. He has another job now, a steady one at Mr. Thompson's dry goods store. Really. I know him. He's my brother. He wouldn't do anything . . . you, know, really bad. We grew up together and . . . and we traveled here together from Washington, D.C. We lived near Abraham Lincoln. Your uncle knows that. And . . ."

"He tried to seduce Lucia," Sidney Edgerton said.

"This boy did *that*?" Wilbur Sanders said, noticing me again as if I had left the kitchen and just come back.

"No," Mr. Edgerton said. He also looked me over again, and this time it was his other eyebrow that was raised. "His big brother, that Rufus fellow. I forgot that he had been some kind of lawman over there . . . inconsequential, I believe."

"Totally," I said. "Like me."

"I don't like this," Mr. Sanders said. "Him being Rufus Hart's brother and living right here under your nose. He heard our plan."

"*Your* plan, Wilbur. And I think the plan is best abandoned."

"Wait. We can tell the Hart boy to go warn Plummer that the vigilantes will come around to hang him in the morning. That will seem believable coming from the boy. And when Plummer goes to the stable, I'll have Mr. Lott and several of the more adamant citizens waiting in the stalls with loaded shotguns."

"No, Wilbur. All the vigilantes must agree about the sheriff. He'll get his just deserts in due time."

"What about the boy?"

"Lucia says he is an admirable lad. I would say he is *genuinely* innocent. What say we just leave him alone."

And so they did. I went ahead and had my late-night dessert, a thin slice of Lucia's apple pie, which I hoped would confirm my status as an innocent and allow me to go back to being largely invisible.

Chapter Eight

After the pie, I went to bed bundled in my warmest clothes, including a holey wool hat that Sidney Edgerton had discarded (I was surprised to learn we had the same head size) and a scarf Lucia had given me when she first heard me sniffling. My door was completely closed, but I heard footsteps and the front door open. I told myself it was just Wilbur Sanders going home, ignoring the fact, in my growing sicker state, that I heard more footsteps than one man could make. I also heard the wind blowing so hard that the house shook, and at any minute I expected a pile of snow to come crashing through the ceiling and bury me alive. Fact was, I couldn't sleep but couldn't bring myself to get out of my bed again. So, I just lay there, coughing, sniffling, and wondering if I might not die before the vigilantes could hang anyone else.

Somehow, I must have dropped off into dreamland because I visited a summer place where the sun brightened my red hair, a warm breeze off the ocean tickled the hairs on my bare chest, and my toes kept digging in the golden sand in search of the perfect seashell. When Lucia rapped the heel of her hand against my door, I sprang out of bed with surprising energy as if I was late for something extremely important. At breakfast, Sidney Edgerton's chair at the head of the table remained empty, and Mary Edgerton excused her children to go play in the snow even before they had finished eating. Mattie and the other three decided to go back to their beds instead because it was too cold for outdoor fun. Mrs. Edgerton only shrugged. Between bites of her scrambled eggs, she talked about snow accumulation and how her husband had been away all night, involved in a "dark affair."

"It's not what you think," Lucia whispered to me, as if she could read my mind.

"Yes, it is," I whispered back. "Vigilante activity is in the air."

"You know more than you let on, Woodie."

"Not as dumb as I look . . . perhaps."

"One would think it was too bitterly cold for such unpleasant activity."

I must admit at that moment I forgot all the troubles of the mining camps and started thinking about pleasant activity with Lucia, a love affair—the age difference be damned!

"Whatever you two are talking about, please stop," said Mary Edgerton as she clanked her fork down on her not-quite-clean plate. "There has been all too much whispering around here lately. Sid, I'm afraid, has become involved in some nasty . . . let me just say disagreeable business not often conducted by a chief justice. But enough, Mary!" She held the tip of her own tongue for a second before wagging a finger at Lucia and me. "And no more whispering from you two! It isn't a topic for breakfast conversation. In fact, it is nothing the three of us need concern ourselves with at any time."

"You're so right, Aunt Mary," said Lucia. "Shall we talk about the weather instead?"

"No!" snapped Mary. She seized her fork off the plate and uncharacteristically used her fingers to help gather up the last bit of egg. "It is *just* as nasty."

We completed breakfast in silence. As we finished up, the three of us heard hooting from the side of the house. Mary Edgerton said it must be a snow owl. I knew better. The hoot was a signal my older brothers used back in Washington when they wanted to call to each other but didn't want our parents or policemen or other enemies to hear names. As far as Rufus Hart was concerned, the other members of the Edgerton household were now his enemies. In the old days none of the older Harts hooted for me, and I couldn't help but feel pleased to finally be on the receiving end of a hoot.

I excused myself, bundled up again, and went out into the cold. Rufus wasn't dressed for the weather. He wiped a small icicle off his nose with his bare hands as he shuffled his feet in the snow. He commented that the mercury had frozen in the bulb of the Edgertons' thermometer. But that was it for small talk. Rufus wanted to know if I had seen Sidney Edgerton and Wilbur Sanders doing anything suspicious before breakfast. I told him I hadn't seen them at all this morning.

"I knew it," Rufus said, blowing on his hands and then squeezing his nostrils to break the ice forming inside. "They're out swearing in more Bannack men as vigilantes. The end is coming damn soon."

"The end for whom? Surely not for you, Rufus."

"Hell if I know, bub." With his tongue, he swished saliva around in his mouth for half a minute and then thrust his jaw forward and spit. I was sure I saw the spit freeze before it hit the snowy ground. "But one thing is for damn sure, little brother. I ain't gonna make it easy on them by freezing to death before they can do me that way." He rubbed his blotchy red neck and then borrowed my scarf before I could offer it to him. "I better go to work like it's a normal day. Come on, let's go."

We ran through snow higher than our ankles to Thompson's dry goods store. Francis Thompson had a hot fire going, which wasn't as welcome as it might have been because he was chatting in front of it with Sidney Edgerton. As soon as they saw Rufus their conversation came to an abrupt halt. I did all the talking for a minute, something new to me. It was all nervous talk about freezing fingertips, freezing mercury, and freezing spit. Even as I rattled on with chattering teeth, the store owner and chief justice looked right through me at Rufus, who stood there with my scarf over half his face like a bloody road agent.

"Didn't I tell you Rufus would be here," Francis Thompson finally said. "He's a good worker. He's all right."

Sidney Edgerton gave his usual grunt. I hoped it was a grunt of approval, but I wasn't sure. Rufus did at least take off the scarf and move closer to the fire. First, he warmed his hands and then he turned around to warm his backside.

"I was just telling Sidney what a nice breakfast I had this morning with Henry Plummer," Mr. Thompson said, but his tone was such that I suspected he hadn't enjoyed breakfast at all. Both he and Justice Edgerton studied Rufus as if they expected some kind of reaction. Rufus, though, kept a stone-cold face. He started to cross his arms but then changed his mind.

"Henry, however, was feeling somewhat out of sorts, under the weather, if you will," Mr. Thompson continued.

Rufus shifted his weight and then took a step forward. Just getting too much heat from behind, I thought. But then he bit his lip and rubbed his neck, a bit too much like a man facing the gallows.

"Me, too," I said, trying to break the tension. "I was coughing most of the night. Feel better now. Miss Darling made eggs this morning and . . ."

"Seems to me," Francis Thompson said, drumming his fingers on his chin, "an unusual silence is brooding over our little settlement this morning."

"But the wind was sure howling last night," I said.

"I best get to work; I hear customers," Rufus said. "If you'll excuse me."

"Certainly," said Sidney Edgerton, stroking an eyebrow.

The customers weren't really customers. Buck Stinson and Ned Ray had come in out of the cold, ostensibly to warm themselves in front of the fire. They took chairs and made awkward small talk with Francis Thompson about the weather and whether wagons carrying canned goods and other supplies from Salt Lake City could make it over a snowy pass. Sidney Edgerton silently stood over them, like a hawk waiting for a couple of voles to poke their heads out from under the snow. He was obviously making the two deputies nervous. They also excused themselves to go to work, though what kind of work they would be doing on a morning like that they didn't say.

"How innocent do they look now?" the chief justice said after the deputies had departed.

Now it was Francis Thompson's turn to grunt.

"Tell Mrs. Edgerton, I'll be home soon," Sidney Edgerton suddenly said to me.

I was enjoying the fire, but I recognized my cue to leave. I said my goodbyes, but nobody said goodbye back.

"You'll be all right?" I asked Rufus on my way out. He had picked up a broom and carried it to the front door but wasn't putting it to work. He held it like a rifle over his shoulder as he stood straight and still, looking every bit like a Yankee soldier guarding headquarters.

"Sure," he said, looking straight ahead. "For a while."

I stayed inside the warm Edgerton house the rest of the day, mostly helping the chief justice find some missing legal papers, helping his wife hang new curtains, and helping Lucia prepare her Monday school lessons for the children. Mary Edgerton deemed the weather too foul to venture out to the A.J. Oliver & Co. stagecoach office where Sunday worship services were held. Just as well, Francis Thompson said when he showed up at dusk. The services had been cancelled. Mr. Thompson still wanted to escort Mary, Mattie, and Lucia to the Sanders cabin to join Hattie Sanders in their usual Sunday evening choir practice.

"The girls will not be going," Mrs. Edgerton said. "And neither shall I."

"Too cold this evening for you ladies?" he asked.

"That's one way of putting it, Mr. Thompson. Too deathly cold."

Francis Thompson practically invited himself to stay on and keep the Edgertons company, but nobody even tried to be good company. Mrs. Edgerton put the children to bed early but couldn't sit still and kept looking in on them to make sure they hadn't been swallowed up by the night. Lucia, flitting like a moth, served tea and tea cakes, but Francis Thompson let his tea get cold and Sidney Edgerton had no appetite. Conversation was sporadic at best. Mr. Edgerton was in one of his grunting moods. I went back and forth between my bedroom and the kitchen until I finally confined myself to the latter. I began pacing, like a condemned man in his jail cell, I thought. Lucia complained that I was constantly underfoot and should just go to bed. I told her I didn't want to be alone tonight.

"Don't start that again, Woodrow," she said.

"But don't you feel it?" I said, taking her by the hand because I was frightened by my own feelings. She totally misinterpreted my action. I wasn't thinking of her at all—well, just barely.

"Nothing has changed," she said, pulling her hand away as if she had just touched a glowing ember. "I don't feel anything."

"I feel it. The tension. The strain. The apprehension."

"Maybe you should step outside and cool off, young man."

I left the kitchen but had no intention of going out into the cold night until I heard a creak on the snowy path outside and then a louder sound—an owl-like hoot. I grabbed my wool hat and scarf, two pairs of mittens (one pair red and belonging to Lucia), and one of Mr. Edgerton's coats (as it was handiest, and I was filling out to be almost his size). Once out the front door, somebody grabbed me, threw me down on the snow, and dragged me to the side of the house. When I tried to rise, I felt a hand pressing hard against the small of my back. I was able to glance up and see Rufus kneeling in the snow, staring off into the night with a wildfire in his eyes. It was rude treatment from a brother, but I offered him a pair of mittens anyway. He took Lucia's red ones without so much as a thank you. I had a vision of one unusually cold winter in Washington when Rufus and some of the ruffians he ran with bombarded me with hard snowballs just because I had refused to relieve myself on the White House lawn to make yellow snow for President James Buchanan.

"What's going on?" I finally asked.

"Shut pan," he said, pressing my face into the snow for emphasis. "It's happening."

I heard the stamping of men's boots, so many that the footbridge across the Grasshopper creaked and groaned from the weight. I raised my head and started to count boots in pairs, reaching thirty and still counting when Rufus pushed my face into the snow again.

"Quit that," I said, raising up and spitting snow. "They after you?"

"Not me . . . not yet."

After maybe seventy men had crossed the bridge, they formed a close circle for a moment, but it wasn't to stay warm and it wasn't for long. Somebody in the middle of the mob made a slashing movement with his arm and the men divided into two groups and continued on with increased vigor.

"Now don't make me eat any more snow," I said, with my lips trembling, twitching, shivering, and every other involuntary thing lips can do. "Where they going, brother?"

"It ain't to no church social."

"I can see that. Who they after?"

"One group's going for Plummer, the other for Stinson. A third group already seized Ned Ray. He was conveniently passed out on a faro table."

"And nobody else?"

"Ain't that enough! You have any idea what these vigilantes got in mind?"

I had an idea, but I wasn't going to put it in words. "We should go inside. It'll be safer."

"Next to Sidney Edgerton?"

"Francis Thompson is in there, too. He likes you."

"He liked Henry Plummer, too. He could have warned him, could have helped him escape. Instead, he soured on him. No, we ain't going in there. Come on, little brother."

I thought he would make a run for it away from the vigilantes and wanted me to come along because sometimes a frightened man can't bear to be alone and settles for bad company, even kin. But Rufus didn't act like he was frightened. He pulled me off the ground and then pulled me along as we ran across the footbridge, where boot prints had worn the snow practically down to the bare wood.

"That you out there, Woodrow?" I heard Sidney Edgerton shout from the doorway of his house.

"Stop, Rufus," yelled Francis Thompson. "That's none of our business."

I didn't answer and I couldn't stop. Rufus kept tugging on my arm, and I managed to keep pace with his long-legged strides. We reached a patch of white sagebrush and Rufus yanked on my arm until I had crouched like him. We were in the rear of the Vail cabin, which was now surrounded by vigilantes. It appeared that one of them was knocking on the door with no particular urgency, like a neighbor making a social call.

"Maybe Plummer will come out with his pistol blazing and then throw his knife for good measure right in the heart of that sonofa . . ." Rufus cut himself off when Martha Vail answered the door. A minute later the sheriff emerged unarmed and showing no signs of resistance. His sister-in-law seemed agitated at first, but Plummer must have said something soothing or reassuring to her because she quietly went back inside. Vigilantes then bound the sheriff's hands. Rufus now changed his tune. "That was real smart of Henry. If he showed any fight at all they wouldn't have any doubts he was guilty."

"They don't seem to have much doubt now," I commented at the risk of being thrown facedown in the snow.

But Rufus only grimaced and punched me lightly on the shoulder. "Come on, bub. The boodle is pulling foot again."

The vigilantes were headed back toward the bridge and had to pass the Sanders cabin, which was dark. Henry Plummer yelled for Wilbur Sanders to show himself and then stumbled up to the front door like a drunk coming home to the wrong house. A couple of his guards scurried after him but stopped before reaching him, while the other vigilantes froze in place, suddenly not so eager to go where they were going. The sheriff's hands being tied together, he knocked with both of them. The wait seemed endless.

"Maybe he's not home," I whispered to Rufus as we found another good crouching spot behind a snow-topped mound of dirt and community refuse.

"I bet he is," said Rufus. "Like his uncle. Letting others do the dirty work."

Suddenly and briskly Mr. Sanders emerged. Immediately he gave a command in good imitation of an Army officer: "Company! Forward march!"

The two guards instantly responded, each taking hold of one of Henry Plummer's shoulders and directing him back to join the procession. But the sheriff wasn't going silently, perhaps realizing Wilbur Sanders was his last hope. Rufus and I couldn't make out everything Plummer was saying, but one of them was "You men know us better than this." I wasn't sure who he meant by "us," unless he was thinking of his deputies Stinson and Ray, or why he was addressing all the "men," while seemingly making an appeal directly to Mr. Sanders. The sheriff said a few more things, some of which sounded like he might be begging for mercy. Rufus showed his displeasure with my interpretation by shoving me with one red-mitten hand into the odorous pile. I nearly cried out but muffled myself by putting one of my own mittens over my mouth and nose. Rufus showed no appreciation, giving me another slight push.

"It is useless for you to beg for your life," Wilbur Sanders was saying, but I certainly didn't dare tell Rufus *I told you so.* And then Mr. Sanders made things plain enough for everyone present: "This affair is settled and cannot be altered. You are to be hanged. You cannot feel harder about it than I do, but I cannot help it if I could."

That immediately brought to mind the time my father said something similar before taking a switch to me for something (I never was quite clear what it was) one of my brothers had done: "Your mother saw you do it. You are to be punished, Woodrow. You can bet your bottom, son, this will hurt me more than it'll hurt you. But it cannot be helped." I could have argued that my mother was blind to most everything I did, especially the good things; that my father had consumed a cup too much to feel any pain; and that it could have been helped by getting at the truth. But I just took my punishment, like a boy not a man. I cried my innocent head off.

Rufus's mind remained in the present (worried about Sheriff Plummer) and maybe the future (worried about himself). He started biting both ends of the red mittens at the same time while rocking back and forth on his haunches. Meanwhile, the procession continued toward the bridge, merging with the second detachment of vigilantes, which had captured Buck Stinson, still wearing his Sunday best, without incident at another cabin. On the other side of the bridge, they continued down Main Street until they came upon the third detachment, with Ned Ray in tow. This mass of humanity, which also included interested citizens who didn't qualify as vigilantes, next climbed a hill. Rufus and I, and I guess everyone else, too, knew the next stop—the gallows.

Nobody paid any mind to the Hart brothers, though we were tailing close enough now to hear the sheriff both reasoning and arguing with his captors. He insisted he was innocent (something all the road agents claimed), but in his next breaths he said he was willing to serve an extended sentence on a bread-and-water diet in his own jail, be chained up in a dark cellar, or be banished from the gold camps forever. I don't know what Deputies Stinson and Ray were saying, if anything. All eyes and ears were focused on the sheriff. Torchlights illuminated his face, creating flickering shadows that sometimes made him look like the devil himself but other times like just another poor soul feeling sad and alone in a crowd.

At the foot of the gallows, having made no headway with the vigilantes, Sheriff Plummer asked for a jury trial, for time to get his business affairs in order, and for a final visit with his sister-in-law, Martha Vail. These requests were rejected. Jury trials were not the order of the day, and there wasn't time for old business; the new business was a triple hanging. He mentioned his wife, Electa, but everyone knew she hadn't been able to live with him. I didn't see any known respectable women in the crowd, and no female of any kind was there to shed a tear for the sheriff. A woman Rufus only identified as Madam Hall sobbed for her sometime lover Ned Ray, and when John Lott called for the deputy to be brought forward first, the madam made a mad rush to get to his side. A dozen male hands held her back. Ned Ray wasn't asking for a last word or a last kiss with her. He was too busy cursing Mr. Lott and his other captors.

The curses continued even after someone placed the noose around his neck, and two of the vigilantes tried to quickly shut him up by lifting him high in the air and then dropping him. It did not go smoothly. Ned Ray had managed to reach up and slip his fingers inside the noose, which kept his neck from snapping on the drop. But that didn't help him, nor did it help my state of mind. He dangled there, desperately gasping for breath as his face and body contorted for what seemed like minutes. Next up was Buck Stinson, whose stream of oaths and epithets suggested he was trying to do his fellow deputy one better. His hanging was said to be "cleaner," but I missed it, having turned my head and shaken it severely to try and undo the vision of Ray's midair struggles. Certainly, the second hanging was shorter because when I next looked up at the gallows Mr. Stinson was stiller than the man who had been his partner in both law enforcing and law breaking.

"Bring up Plummer," somebody ordered. But it didn't happen right away. The sheriff asked a friend or two—but not Francis Thompson, who had stayed at the Edgerton house—to intervene and then asked for time to pray.

"Let him leave the country," Rufus said, practically under his breath. I was probably the only one to hear him, which was good. I was about to request he say nothing more but didn't have to; he suddenly had a coughing and sneezing fit. Maybe he had caught something from me or some other sick person in the crowd on that frigid night, or perhaps his intention was to create an excuse for not speaking up.

"I can't watch," I said, turning away from the gallows, ready to stampede like a crazed lone buffalo through the ring of observers.

Rufus didn't try to restrain me, but he nudged me with his elbow and said, between coughs, "Would you look at that? That's Joseph Swift."

I didn't know Joseph Swift, but I turned around in time to see the young man shoving his way through the crowd, falling to his knees before Henry Plummer, and reaching out as if to grab the sheriff's wobbly legs. A few men held his arms back. "Let him live," Joseph Swift pleaded. "He is my friend." Friends of the vigilantes dragged Mr. Swift away. Seeing this, the sheriff quickly removed his scarf, thus exposing his vulnerable neck, balled up the scarf, hurled it, and exclaimed, "Here is something to remember me by, Joe." At least that's what I heard, but my focus was on the young man, who broke free of his escorts, threw himself on his belly, and began melting snow by squeezing it in his fists. "Let him live, let him live, let him live!" he screamed, and then he just wept.

"What a sickening display," Rufus said, his voice loud and clear. "He's a twenty-seven-year-old man and he's crying like a child!"

I didn't see anything wrong with that. Joseph Swift, it was plain to see through my tears, was sensitive, compassionate, and sympathetic all rolled into one. What's more, I suddenly saw myself as just like him, though he had been a total stranger two minutes ago. I might have gone to the prone fellow, patted him on the back, and totally shared in his sadness. Instead, moved beyond reason and practically blinded by my tear-shedding, I stumbled along in the opposite direction. I had become Joseph Swift's replacement, taking over where he had left off. I collapsed at the feet of Sheriff Plummer, and, though by no stretch of anyone's imagination could I have been called his friend, I clutched his calves and kissed his ankles. Rufus later told me that he couldn't watch. I had "out-sickened" Joe Swift. All Rufus could do was pretend I wasn't his younger brother and just walk away whistling Dixie.

And what did Henry Plummer do? He merely looked down on me. Actually, while looking down at me he said something that in retrospect seemed beneath him: "Is this the best idea anyone could come up with to save me? You aren't helping me by a damned sight, kid. Save it for your brother. His time is coming!" Resigned at last to his cruel fate, the sheriff, like a perfect gentleman, stepped over me to have his arms pinioned.

"Give me a good drop, boys," he said.

I suppose they did. I did hear a crack when the sheriff's neck broke. When I recovered enough to stop groveling, I stood up and wiped away my tears—real ones for sure but perhaps not all shed for the late lawmen. If Plummer had struggled, it couldn't have been much. Now he just dangled there in the frigid air next to his two deputies. Nobody could say they had been *good* lawmen or particularly *good* men, but how bad they had actually been, I couldn't say. Somehow this trio terrified me more now than they had in life. I suspected they would haunt me forever. Still, I stared at the bodies—I couldn't take my eyes away. I had no idea if these men deserved to die, but I also now knew—having only suspected it during my childhood in Washington, D.C.—that we all *must* die and likely won't manage to do it quietly in our sleep.

Most of the crowd, the vigilantes and the non-vigilantes alike, drifted away to their homes. It had been a long Sunday night. Most would try to get some sleep—if they could. I knew I couldn't sleep. And beside that I had no wish to return to the Edgerton home, not even should Lucia Darling allow me to cry on her shoulder. A few armed guards stayed on as if it was their job to protect the dead—from vultures, bats, wolves, the devil, and who knows what else. But they, too, departed, leaving the bodies to hang on the gallows till morning.

"Go home, fellow," one of them said. "Can't you see it's all over?"

"Right," I replied, but I stayed on till dawn. It felt natural to be a man alone—well, except for those dangling bodies—in the cold darkness. At one point I stepped on the scarf that Plummer had hurled toward Joseph Swift. It hadn't reached the young man, and nobody had picked it up to give it to him. I quickly scooped the scarf off the snow, brushed it off, and folded it as if it were fine linen. Maybe I had planned to find out where Joe lived and deliver Henry Plummer's gift to him. But about ten minutes later I started coughing and sneezing again. I wiped my nose with the back of one of my mittens and then carefully wrapped the scarf tightly around my nervous neck.

Chapter Nine

If you wonder how W.A. Phillips handled the execution of disgraced lawmen Plummer, Stinson, and Ray in *Man from Montana: How He Escaped the Noose,* the best word to describe it is *badly.* Somewhere in that contrived narrative, Red Ranger comes to realize that Plummer is *not* the epitome of evil that Mr. X and the other vigilantes make him out to be. "Sheriff Plummer," Phillips has Red Ranger saying, "has a decent side deep inside him and with the proper handling I can extract it and turn him into a lawman who not only obeys the law but also upholds it." Mr. X puffs up and says, "Ain't I seen you before?" as if anyone else would be running around dressed all in red challenging vigilante authority. "I'll hang you, too, if you interfere with justice!" But, of course, Red Ranger refuses to be intimidated. And here is how the author sums up the big hanging night in Bannack: "And so once again, thanks to his cool daring under extreme pressure, Red Ranger had saved the day—this time by riding under the deadly cold-blooded gallows, cutting the hangman's knot that was tightening on the misunderstood sheriff's stiff neck, and carrying off this intended prize victim of the vindictive Montana vigilantes to get a fresh start slaughtering buffalo on the Great Plains. Yes, our red-masked hero arrived too late to save the two cursing if not cursed deputies, but the duo was of small matter compared to the effervescent and charismatic Henry Plummer, who would go on to help the equally misunderstood Wyatt Earp bring law and order to discombobulated Dodge City, Kansas, without so much as a single gruesome illegal lynching!"

And to think he based the sheriff-saving Red Ranger on redheaded me! In reality, as I've written, none of the Bannack trio's lives could be saved by anyone, and I only made a spectacle of myself by pleading for the controversial sheriff's life. I was a mouse, Red Ranger was a man, albeit a fictional one. He had gotten away safely after his dramatic rescue and given Plummer new life but in short order would gallop back to the goldfields to again be in the thick of the breathtaking action, that is trying to save the cold breath of not-quite-innocent condemned men. You see the vigilantes weren't done, not by a long shot.

When I finally returned to the Edgerton house after being the last man standing at the gallows, the sun was up and Sidney Edgerton, with a rifle in hand, was heading out on important Monday morning business with a group of other honorable and determined citizens. They were going after José Pizanthia, called "the Greaser" and judged an unsavory character, mostly because he might have been the only Mexican in all of Bannack. Rufus told me that he had once seen Señor Pizanthia bust a saloon window with a pistol butt and that he, like many others, considered the Mexican a general nuisance the way he strutted about town boasting about his rich Spanish blood and how his ancestors used to eat tortillas with the Aztecs. The chief justice had stayed home when Henry Plummer, Buck Stinson, and Ned Ray received the noose, but he apparently couldn't say no to this latest invitation. I didn't see how in the world it could have been an invitation to another hanging. But, knowing I would never get to sleep now, I tailed after the group to José Pizanthia's cabin on the hillside behind Francis Thompson's dry goods store.

The cabin was dark and Señor Pizanthia didn't emerge when

summoned. Two men went in anyway, and after some gunfire, they both came out announcing that each had been shot. For the one who got it in the chest his wound was fatal, and I thought that was a better way to go than by hanging. The other one, Smith Ball, got it in the leg, but that barely slowed him down. He tied a piece of cloth around his wound and kept firing at the cabin with the others, though I think Sidney Edgerton was keeping his rifle quiet to save bullets. Maybe the Mexican hadn't done much in the way of lawbreaking in the territory in the past, but he had now, and nobody was going to show him any mercy. Some of the shooting seemed reckless; indeed, I heard bullets thumbing against the side of Mr. Thompson's store below.

"Let's blast the Greaser out!" shouted one shooter as he reloaded his rifle.

"I thought that's what we was doing," said Smith Ball. "Somebody give me more shells. I'm plum out."

"I mean a big blast! Where's Mr. Edgerton? Everyone knows he keeps a small howitzer under his bed."

Not exactly true. I didn't know it, and I had been sleeping in the spare room at the Edgerton home since November. Of course, I had only set foot in Sidney and Mary Edgerton's bedroom to sweep the floor and make the bed. I had never thought to look under the bed.

Sidney Edgerton was immediately besieged with requests to borrow his howitzer. He gave his consent, and several vigilantes told the chief justice he could take a load off his feet because they would gladly fetch the "trusty cannon."

"Thanks, men," Justice Edgerton said. "Just tell Mary I sent you."

Those eager fellows were good on their promise. They soon returned, using a rope to haul the howitzer uphill. A couple of other men borrowed a wooden box from Thompson's store and set it down about thirty feet from the windowless side wall of José Pizanthia's cabin. Once the howitzer was mounted and the barrel aimed, nobody wasted time warning the Mexican he best surrender or be blown to bits. I felt bad for him all right, but I wasn't about to go inside and tell him that or to stand with my back against the outside wall with arms and legs spread and say something stupid like "If you want him, you'll have to go through me!" I had learned my lesson about creating a spectacle.

The first two shells broke through the wall, but there was no explosion. The third shell did the trick, striking the chimney and exploding. The shattered chimney and part of the roof fell into the cabin, the front door toppled inside as well, and the vigilantes moved in for the kill, if one was still necessary.

They had to lift the door off of Señor Pizanthia. He might have only been unconscious because I thought I saw one of his legs twitch. But it didn't matter because Smith Ball, bandaged leg and all, plowed ahead and at point-blank range fired six revolver shots into the prone man's body. The crowd wanted something more. A few of the most eager fellows took the same rope used to haul up the howitzer and secured it around the Mexican's neck. They dragged him to a pole, where I believe I once saw an American flag attached, and strung him up, even though he was past caring—or so I hoped for his sake.

"Bastards!" said a familiar voice. It was Rufus, come out of hiding.

"I'm glad it's not you," I muttered inanely.

"The vigilantes think hanging him will make it all official and proper."

"I guess if I had a choice I'd rather be hanged after I was dead."

"It ain't over, little brother."

Rufus was right. For the next five or ten minutes, the mob—for that was what it had become—riddled José Pizanthia's red and white plaid shirt with bullets. Rufus, for lack of anything more productive to do, began counting rounds fired—more than one hundred. At one point, some of those who lacked guns or had run out of bullets set the cabin on fire. I couldn't see what purpose it served except to keep the living warm on a terribly cold morning.

I turned away from the dangling human target to look at the blaze but soon turned my back on it. Maybe it was only to get more heat on my backside. But the timing was just right to catch sight of another familiar figure practically at arm's length. He was scurrying away from the action, dragging a rifle more than carrying it.

"Mr. Edgerton," I said. "That's you, isn't it?"

The man stopped in his tracks but then took half a minute before he turned to face me.

"I'm afraid it is," he admitted. "I wish you weren't here to see this . . . to see me. You shouldn't be here. You're just a boy. I shouldn't be here. I'm the chief justice of the territory for God's sake."

"I didn't see you shoot, sir."

"That's right. That's right. I only watched. Tell my family that if they ask, won't you? Tell them I witnessed the horrible scene from high above. Don't look at me like that. It's really not a lie, Woodrow. Maybe you better not say a word. Don't tell anyone you were here or I was here. Let's call it, our little secret."

"But lots of other people saw you here, sir?"

"Right. Right. And my howitzer."

"I didn't see Mr. Sanders here, though."

"What? No, no. Wilbur had another engagement. Fortunate for him. He didn't have to see this. But he couldn't have stopped this. No man could have stopped this."

"You might have," said Rufus, who had finally turned around and was now in Mr. Edgerton's face. "You didn't even try."

"Oh, it's you. All I can say to you, Rufus Hart, is you should have picked better friends."

"He wasn't my friend. The Greaser didn't make friends. He certainly wasn't part of any outlaw gang. He didn't like outlaws or vigilantes or anyone sitting on the fence. He pretty much hated all of us, and I don't blame him."

"Well, I don't have time to discuss it. You should take your little brother away from this awful place. I know I'm leaving. It's about time for the chief justice to be elsewhere."

After Sidney Edgerton had left the scene—though the same thing would have happened had he stayed—members of the mob cut down José Pizanthia from the pole and tossed the body into the flames as if they were just adding another log to the fire. The cabin and its owner thus became ashes together, and thanks to the bonfire, nobody froze to death. I must say I didn't mind the heat, though everything else that had happened that morning was eating at my head. A few men had the sense to pull the howitzer away from the flying embers. Somebody brought a guitar and, on the spot while strumming away, composed in his head and then sang vociferously "The Ballad of the Greaser." I would have left in the chief justice's footprints, but I didn't want to desert Rufus, who kept staring at the dancing flames as if they contained the mysteries of life and death.

When the fire died out, a dozen men stepped into what was once the cabin's interior and poked around with sticks and the toes of their boots. I couldn't figure it out, but it was no mystery to my brother.

"Looking for gold dust, bub," Rufus said and then he snorted his contempt. "These are the same law-abiding citizens who would hang a man for stealing a single half-full pouch from an overburdened traveler."

I figured that was something my brother had done, at least once. "Keep your voice down," I said. "They aren't all after gold. Some of the others might be after another victim."

"You got something there, little brother. Never can tell what a mob will do."

"I reckon not. They don't look too civil."

"They're people, same kind that's fighting a civil war back where we come from. By the way, that's a nice-looking scarf you're wearing. Looks familiar."

"What? Oh, this thing. You want it? It belongs . . . belonged . . . to Henry Plummer."

"You stole it off his dead body, huh?"

"Never did anything of the kind. I . . ."

"Never mind, bub. I know you're too honest to steal anything at all."

It didn't sound like a compliment. I dropped the matter and went back to studying the unpleasant subject at hand. "You really think Señor Pizanthia has any . . . I mean *had* any . . . you know, valuables?"

Rufus didn't answer, and when I turned to him, he wasn't there. I glanced at the large boot prints in the overworked snow where he'd been standing and then quickly looked around. I couldn't see him running away or even tell which way he'd gone. Rufus was fast. That was a good thing. Still, it didn't guarantee nobody would ever catch him.

There was nothing else to do but go back home, that is the Edgerton house. I tried to slip into my back bedroom without being noticed, but none other than Mattie, thirteen and going on twelve, caught me by the arm. Her face was flushed but not from being out in the cold. She'd just heard from her father about the three hangings at the gallows and the half-hanging at the pole. It was nervous energy that had her flushed.

"Papa told me everything," she said.

"Fine," I said. "Then I don't need to talk."

"Yes, you do, silly boy. By everything, I don't mean *every thing.*"

"I'm exhausted. Good night."

"We haven't even had our noonday meal yet. Tell me, was it the most awful thing you ever saw?"

I managed to nod my head.

"Tell me more!" Mattie demanded.

"I want to be alone."

"Pshaw. Look how I'm sweat . . . perspiring. Feel how warm my forehead is."

She took my right hand, which had grown cold during the short walk from the bonfire to the house and flattened it against her forehead. It was indeed hot, so I nodded again and didn't pull my hand away directly.

"I mean," she said. "Such doings don't happen every day."

"Around here, they just might."

"What are you two doing?" It was Lucia Darling and her face was as red as everybody else's. I quickly withdrew my slightly comforted hand from Mattie's overexcited face.

"Just talking," Mattie said.

"Well, stop that!" Lucia said. "You know your father said *not* to talk about it, not *any* of it."

Lucia seemed to be either trying to get her own hands warm or else was wringing them. I remembered my mother's hands doing much the same thing, but it never had anything to do with hangings or shootings—even with rumblings of war and then war itself going on outside Washington. My brothers, with their stealing, fighting, and lying habits, were generally the cause of her worry, and I suppose naïve and innocent me was, too, when she bothered to think of me.

"You best go to your room," Lucia said, as sternly as any mother who wasn't yet a mother could.

It wasn't clear if Lucia was addressing Mattie or me, but it didn't really matter. We went to our separate rooms—Mattie to fret over the unfairness of being too young to be allowed to experience the excitement going on in town, me to just try and get some rest.

That afternoon, Sidney Edgerton took me aside, that is to say he brought me into his bedroom while his wife and their daughters and Lucia were in the kitchen doing things and having conversations fit for females—both women and girls. Mr. Edgerton had me sit next to him on the bed, and it was all I could do to keep from looking under it to see if his small howitzer was back in place.

"Do not judge the vigilante leadership by what you saw today," the chief justice said, putting a hand on my shoulder for perhaps the first time ever. "Will you do that for me, Woodrow? Rather, will you *not* do that?"

He sounded as confused as I was and removed his hand to scratch the back of his neck. I did nod my head, which was always something I was good at when listening to my elders and superiors—which included about everyone I ever met, except maybe those two Bannock Indian boys who had pressed their noses against the kitchen window. I saw them and me as equals.

"Any questions?" he said suddenly, the way his niece Lucia did in the classroom.

"Eh . . . Didn't the vigilante leadership want to hang the sheriff and those two particular deputies?"

"Of course. You saw that, too, did you? That was justice, strict justice, being served. I meant what you saw at the cabin of the Grea . . . Mexican. Things did get a little out of hand there, I confess. But it wasn't the doing of the vigilante leadership. We won't let that happen again."

"You mean the execution of an innocent man like José Pizanthia?"

Mr. Edgerton frowned fiercely. Perhaps two questions were

one too many. But then he softened a little, at least his face grew softer. He almost smiled as he put a hand back on my shoulder and gave a fatherly squeeze. "The Mexican was by no means innocent," he said as if correcting a child too naïve to see the truth. "He was not part of the Plummer gang, but he was guilty of many things." I was about to ask guilty of what, but he now spoke louder and more quickly so I couldn't get in another question or even a word edgeways. "The fact of the matter is the important job of the Vigilance Committee is to punish with death men unfit to live in Bannack, Virginia City, Nevada City, or, well, any community you can name."

I was thinking of Washington, D.C., my hometown, but I didn't name it.

"Rest assured," the chief justice continued, "more bad men will be punished by execution, but in the future, we shall try to make the drops and deaths of the condemned seem simultaneous. It is our desire to hang men efficiently and properly without any of that cruel shooting and disgusting burning. And believe you me, Woodrow, the vigilantes will only hang a man who has confessed to his crimes in an effort to save his immortal soul."

I couldn't rest on the bed any longer. I bolted up and began to pace the room the way I used to see my father do whenever he was trying to solve an impossible problem or make the right decision when all the alternatives he recognized were bad.

"Perhaps I have been talking too long," Mr. Edgerton said. "I have made myself perfectly clear, haven't I?"

I paused in my pacing and nodded. But then I went back to pacing, which seemed to agitate this particular elder and superior.

"Stop that!" he said, again sounding like his niece. "This concludes our little talk. Why don't you run along and see what the womenfolk are cooking up."

I took two steps toward the door but then hesitated.

"All right, Woodrow," he said. "I can tell you have one more question. What is it?"

Actually, I had two. The first: *Did they put your howitzer back?* I decided, though, in the big scheme of things the answer wasn't all that important. Instead I dared pose my second question: "The vigilantes, that is to say the vigilante leadership, wouldn't be considering at some future time executing any other of Sheriff Plummer's deputies?"

"That's hard to say. Plummer did hire a few who have been deemed honest."

"Yes. Good. I mean I'd hate to see an innocent deputy at the end of a rope."

"Anyone in particular you have in mind, Woodrow?"

It has always been hard for me to tell a lie. So, I couldn't bring myself to say no or even shake my head. But I certainly couldn't nod, either, let alone mention my brother when the chief justice hadn't pronounced his name.

"I'm not one to name names, sir," I said. "But thanks for asking and thanks for your explanations about . . . you know, everything going on. And . . . eh . . . Mock oysters. I believe Lucia said that's what's being served for supper."

What Mr. Edgerton didn't tell me was that the vigilantes already had another man targeted for their brand of harsh justice—Dutch John Wagner, who was already in custody. That very night, Wilbur Sanders and other vigilantes went to the German immigrant, promised him his life for a confession, got the confession (he admitted to the failed wagon train robbery), and then executed him anyway but in orderly fashion, so different from how Señor Pizanthia got his apparently just but unsightly deserts.

No, I wasn't there. I was catching up on my sleep at the time, but in the morning of the 12th, Mattie Edgerton came barging into my room, sprang onto my spring bed, shook my left shoulder until I turned over to my other side, and then did the same to my right shoulder until I opened my eyes and acknowledged her presence.

"I know you were fake sleeping," she said.

"That's my privilege in my own room," I said, snapping my eyes back shut.

"In my papa's house."

"All right. I'm awake now. Are you and your papa happy?" I opened my eyes as wide as I could and pointed to one and then the other to make sure the little pest could see.

"No reason to shout!"

"You're the one who's shouting, and so early in the morning."

"It's *not* so early, sleepyhead. Besides I have reason to shout. I know something you don't know."

I didn't ask her what she knew, but she told me anyway. She had heard her father and uncle talking about it after the fact. I must have been really out of it during the night, because the conspiring whispers of Sidney Edgerton and Wilbur Sanders usually were enough to bring me out of any kind of slumber. Mattie talked in her particularly annoying high-pitched, hurried voice, but I must admit her tale made me rise into a sitting position and poke fingers in my ears to try to draw out the earwax.

According to Mattie, when Dutch John learned death was his destiny, he begged and prayed for his life, even suggesting that Wilbur Sanders cut off his arms and legs and then let him go. "How far would he have gotten like that—you know, limbless?" Mattie asked, interrupting her own story. But she didn't wait for an answer to her stupid question. She just kept on telling it. The confessor wanted to write a goodbye letter in German to his mother, but he couldn't hold a pen because his frostbitten fingers were wrapped in rags. A fellow German tried to take down his words but apparently was barely literate in any language. Wagner ended up discarding the rags and painfully forced his cold, hard blue fingers ("as blue as the winter sky," Mattie said because Lucia Darling had taught her about similes) to put his final words on paper. As soon as he had signed the letter—"Lots of love, Dutch John," said Mattie, but I doubted it—the vigilantes force-marched the prisoner to the building where the frozen remains of lawmen Plummer and Stinson were, as Mattie put it, "waiting to go under thawed ground." She said the sheriff's body lay on top of a carpenter's workbench but that Stinson's lifeless body had been left on the floor. At that point in the telling, Mattie paused long enough to allow me one question.

"What about the other deputy, Ned Ray?" I asked.

Mattie smiled the way she did when she anticipated one of Lucia's questions in class. And she delighted in delivering the answer: "Ray's body had been claimed by one of those ladies of ill dispute."

"Ill repute," I corrected, but Mattie was already back to telling the gruesome story.

The vigilantes allowed Dutch John Wagner time to pray while he knelt near Buck Stinson and gazed up at the sheriff gone bad. "He uttered nothing anyone could hear," Mattie noted. "For all Uncle Wilbur knew the bad German could have been cursing to himself instead of praying." The executioner—apparently his name was one thing Mattie did *not* know—threw a rope over a crossbeam and then put a barrel beneath it to give the condemned something to stand on.

Mattie stood up on my bed to utter Dutch John's last words (a secondhand quote, of course): "I have never seen a man hanged. How long will it take me to die?" Wagner did get an answer from a voice in the crowd: "Not long," but Mattie failed to give me the answer for a long time. She went on and on about how she had never seen a man hang either, nor a woman or child, and how it wasn't really fair because she wasn't at all as squeamish as some of the boys she knew and she thought it would provide a life lesson or at the very least something few members of her sex were ever allowed to experience.

"You obviously have been terribly deprived your *entire* life," I told her. "Now please get off my bed, that is if you have finished with your story."

"That's all you have to say? Have you ever heard anything so awful in your whole life?"

I could have reminded her that I had not only heard but also seen something more awful than the German's execution the previous morning—the brutal execution and disposal of the Mexican. But I didn't wish her to prolong her stay in my private space.

"I wonder how many bad men are left for Papa and Uncle Wilbur to hang," she said, but she obviously didn't give it much more thought than that. Like the child she was, she clasped her little pale hands on the sides of her neck, jumped in the air, and gasped as she giggled. She lost her balance upon landing on my pillow and toppled over. One second later came a knock on the door and the appearance of Lucia Darling wearing a floured apron and holding a bowl full of lumpy flapjack batter. I was still sitting up in bed, but now Mattie was sprawled across my lap in what I judged to be a very unladylike position.

"What now!" Lucia shouted.

"Just talking again," Mattie said as she scrambled off the bed.

"She was doing the talking," I said. "I was doing the listening."

"He's an awful listener!" Mattie screamed, brushing past Lucia and running from my room as if she had seen something far more awful than a hanging.

Chapter Ten

Lucia Darling and the Edgertons were none too happy with me. Lucia even stated that my unfortunate upbringing in the nation's capital was starting to catch up with me. She suggested that my trying to lead young Mattie astray was the first *step* in me following in the footsteps of my incorrigible (yes, I had to ask her the meaning of that word) brother. I reminded Lucia—and myself—that I was only two years older than Mattie, that Mattie had a vivid imagination, and that my brother, incorrigible or not, had an honest full-time job at Francis Thompson's dry goods store. That only hurt my case. Apparently, a gentleman didn't tell tales about the opposite sex, and Mattie surely was that, though not in a good way.

The Edgertons didn't close me out of my room and boot me out onto the bitterly cold and just plain bitter streets of Bannack, but they did insist I get out of the house more and start pulling my own weight. In other words, they told me, as Lucia suggested, that I get a job instead of standing idly by in her classroom all day. I suppose I could have hired out to some rich miner who needed a low-wage helper, but I didn't want to freeze my backside off in the elements or to work for greedy, fearful men who judged the worth of a body by how much gold he possessed or how many lesser men he had executed. Early on Wednesday, January 13, I headed over to Thomson's store to see if my brother really did still have his job there. He didn't. Mr. Thompson said that after what had happened to José Pizanthia and Dutch John Wagner, he could not positively assure Rufus that the vigilantes would never come calling for him. He had recommended that Rufus take leave of his employment in Bannack for two or three weeks and not tempt Sidney Edgerton or Wilbur Sanders by showing himself about town. He further suggested that my brother seek shelter in Virginia City with George Lane, who was an honest, generous, and somewhat pitiable boot maker in the Dance and Stuart's Store there, but not to address him by his popular nickname, "Clubfoot George."

"You think good old generous George could shelter two Harts?" I asked. "I'd call him Mr. Lane."

"Why would you leave, son? You haven't done a single thing wrong, or have you?"

"No, sir. I mean . . ."

"I was just funnin' you, Woodrow, though perhaps that is something one shouldn't do in these deadly serious times. Of course, you haven't done a single thing wrong. You are the perfect little gentleman. What's more you are quite fortunate to have your very own private room at the Edgerton home."

"I'm sure I'm fortunate, but . . ."

"But what, Woodrow?"

"Well, they want me to kind of get a job, you know to pay for my food and such."

"You got one, son."

And so, just like that, I became the second Hart to work for Francis Thompson in his dry goods store. I think Mr. Thompson might have been feeling a little guilty for not supporting his old friend Henry Plummer more at the end or for scaring Rufus off to Virginia City and for getting so rich without digging in the dirt a single day in his life. But I did come cheap. And though I would never have thought of myself as a "perfect little gentleman," I did work hard and did *not* go to saloons before or after work, nor did I covet gold or females of any age any longer, not even Lucia Darling.

At the Edgerton house on Friday morning, the 15th, I heard rumors about some enormous vigilante doings over in Virginia City the previous day. Mattie Edgerton had listened at her parents' bedroom but hadn't heard much about it. What little information she did pick up she wished desperately to share with me for it must be "the awfulest yet," but first she needed to complain about how unlucky she was to be a girl in Bannack instead of a man in Virginia City. I would have no part of it. I waved her away from my door, politely declined breakfast, and went to work. Mr. Thompson had heard some things, too. He was relatively close-mouthed, and I didn't press him. I had seen too much of the vigilantes in action in Bannack, and I wasn't some silly girl dying to know about all the horrible ways there are to die. Besides, Mr. Thompson told me the most important thing—none of the five men hanged was named Rufus Hart. One, however, was the unfortunate Clubfoot George Lane, executed for being a suspected horse thief.

I tried to put the latest vigilante action out of my mind, and it wasn't difficult because I had never laid eyes on Mr. Lane, didn't know the names of the other hanged men, and had heard no disturbing details. Mattie Edgerton claimed to have learned more exciting facts, which I did not doubt because I was well acquainted with her inquiring, morbid mind and her abilities as a spy in her own household. I told her I wasn't interested and backed it up by never letting myself be alone with her. The supreme cold weather broke, and after work I'd take long walks in the dark before returning to my room. It wasn't only Mattie I was avoiding. I wanted to show Lucia Darling how much I hated her superior and controlling nature and how well I could do without her righteous thinking and sugary pies. It wasn't easy because, though I never admitted it at the time to this older woman or to myself, I was hopelessly and sincerely in love with her.

As for Sidney Edgerton, I had no wish to have him squeeze my shoulder again or explain his greatness to me. I saw him *not* as a chief justice but as a *chief injustice* for allowing the vigilantes to operate freely and mercilessly across the mining camps. I didn't even want to cross paths with Wilbur Sanders, who often stopped by the Edgerton house to meet with his uncle about the best positions for them to take during this time of unrestrained retribution. Mr. Sanders, as ambitious as Mr. Edgerton, was a lawyer who conveniently skirted the law to punish not only the lawless but also anyone he and his uncle deemed unworthy of citizenship in the territory. I thought more highly of Mary Edgerton, a caring mother (such a contrast to my own mother) who did everything in her power to keep her children from catching cold, getting frostbit, and hearing nasty things out on the street. It was her wish to keep them all bundled up inside where they were safe from the elements (criminal and nature's) and fairly warm as long as there was enough wood to fuel the two stoves. I didn't blame her for that. Still, she was too much her husband's wife, believing everything he said he believed in and, like him, not caring beans for the men hanged by their necks until dead.

I can't say I ever had any heart-to-heart talks with Mrs. Edgerton, whose motherly caring never extended beyond her own children. Not that she was cold to me. I mean if she ever had only one hambone and saw me begging on the doorstep next to a Bannock Indian boy, she no doubt would have thrown the bone to me. Our closest human encounter came on Sunday night, January 17. I didn't have to work that day, but it was practically above zero so I spent most of it outside. In a secluded spot on the far side of cemetery hill, I made myself a life-size snowman that I called "Henry"; I gave him Grasshopper Creek ore eyes, an empty tin-can mouth, a stick nose, and, in a final flourish, Sheriff Plummer's actual scarf. I was half hoping that someone would see Henry and feel a twinge of guilt, but if I had really wanted to be the conscience of Bannack, I would have established Henry at the gallows and at least tried to hang him, as hard as it might be to hang a snowman.

After that, though, I felt my own twinge of guilt for immortalizing, at least until he melted, a two-faced lawman deemed deserving of death by the respected family that provided me with shelter and grub. So, what I did was collect whatever small pieces of wood I could for the Edgerton stoves. Wood of any kind was hard to come by anywhere around town that winter, so I didn't get back to the house with my armful until after supper. Three of the children had already been put to bed, and Sidney had put himself to bed (perhaps not to sleep, I thought, but to polish his howitzer, think about who next to hang in Bannack, or to resume planning for his long-awaited trip to Washington, D.C.). Lucia and Mattie had gone to the Sanders's cabin for choir practice, which made them easy to avoid, but Mary Edgerton had stayed home because she said her throat was scratchy.

When I went to the kitchen to find something to satisfy my belly, I found Mrs. Edgerton at the table alternating between dipping her quill pen in ink and pressing the tip to fine stationery. My sudden appearance startled her, but she composed herself quickly and asked me to sit down next to her. The letter was to her mother and sisters back in Tallmadge, Ohio. She read me the one sentence she had written so far: "The past week has been an eventful one here."

"To say the least," I said. "I mean that's very true."

She was too busy writing again to hear me. I just kept sitting there, my stomach growling and my mind mulling over all the tragic events of the past week. I thought it would be impolite to get up to look for something to eat that didn't need cooking.

"How many *m's* in committee?" she asked without looking at me.

"Two," I replied.

"That's right. But only one *t,* correct?"

"Two *t's,* too."

"And *e's*? Is two too many? It looks like too many."

"No, ma'am. There's two of all three of those letters. But only one *i* and one *o* and of course the one *c.*"

"A capital C is correct. I know that."

"Whatever you think best, Mrs. Edgerton."

She read me another sentence: "I hope the Committee—with a capital *C*—will not have to hang any more men here for I do not like such excitement, but I shall feel that Mr. Edgerton will go much more safely now than he would have gone two weeks ago, for I have no doubts that they intended to rob him." After that she wrote for a long time in silence. I counted the number of times her pen dipped, which seemed politer than trying to read over her shoulder.

"Do you spell Plummer with two *m's* or one?" she asked with a long sigh, and I immediately lost count.

"I'm not sure," I admitted. "I never spelled his name. Red Yeager had 'Plummer' on his list, but I think somebody else wrote down the list."

"Never mind. I'll just say the sheriff of this district was the captain of the gargantuan gang of criminals."

I wasn't well informed enough to argue the point about Henry Plummer, but I did question her use of the word "gargantuan."

"It means enormous," she said, now on a writing roll.

"I know that, ma'am, but how big can the gang really be?"

"I believe thirteen gang members have been successfully executed so far, and Sidney and Wilbur say many, many more are still roaming our streets and roads waiting to waylay and murder anyone with gold who starts for Washington or anywhere else in the States."

I hadn't realized it was quite that many. I only knew some of the names. "Maybe that's the end of the hangings, Mrs. Edgerton," I said. "Maybe there is no need any more for . . ."

"But there is. Like I just put in my letter, the band has committed about one hundred murders."

"What?" I only knew of a few. To me it seemed like far more men had been hanged by vigilantes than killed by outlaws. This was one point I had to at least question. "Excuse me for saying so, ma'am, but how can that be? I mean one hundred men."

"Sidney says one hundred and two. Isn't any wonder the committee has more work to do, is there?"

"He knows the exact number? I beg your pardon, but where are all the bodies? I mean the ground is too frozen now to dig graves. Are they all piled up in various cabins turned morgues? Are you saying Sidney . . . eh, Mr. Edgerton has gone around and counted them all?"

My own questions were making me sick to the stomach. I had lost my appetite. I could see the stacks of remains, whether they were fact or fiction. Mrs. Edgerton was quiet for a minute, and I feared I had brought offense for doubting her and her beloved chief justice body counter. So, it shocked me when she put her nonwriting hand on top of my still cold hand in what could have passed as a comforting gesture and explained things the way she thought they were.

"You see, Woodrow," she said, tapping my knuckles, "these murders have not been discovered by the people here. The victims were murdered and robbed on the roads leading away from the camps. The murderers cut some of them into pieces that they put under the ice; others were burned, and still others buried in remote places."

The outlaws now sounded as bad as the vigilantes. Mrs. Edgerton had put me over the edge. I pulled my hand away from hers and stood up from the table without even excusing myself. I doubled over, scrambled to the sink, and felt like I was about to vomit, but I reckon there was nothing in me to come out. After a while, I said good night, and Mary Edgerton, no longer taking notice of me, dipped her pen in the inkwell and continued her letter.

On Monday morning, my appetite returned but not my desire to rub elbows with any of the Edgertons or Lucia Darling, so I rose early, stole a half loaf of sourdough bread, and went to my job at Thompson's dry goods store. Francis Thompson wasn't there yet, so I sat behind the counter gnawing at the crust and wishing I worked at a store that had canned fruit. When I heard footsteps, I asked if it was Mr. Thompson, and when I got no answer, I asked who was there. When I still got no answer, I thought "robber" and, I am ashamed to say, crawled behind a pile of blankets and hid my entire being under a seven-foot log cabin quilt.

Someone with plenty of heft pounced on me, bounced on me, pounded my shoulders, and worked my head over with both hands as if packing together a snowball. I worried about breathing my last under the quilt and dying without even knowing the identity of my killer. But then my attacker started whistling Dixie.

"Let me up, Rufus, you're suffocating me!" I yelled.

"Don't be such an all-overish baby!" he yelled back.

I realized we had said such words many times before, back in Washington when my brother was in a mood to torment and I was the handiest one around.

"Couldn't you have simply announced yourself," I said after extracting myself from the quilt with almost no help from him.

"No fun in that."

"Suppose not," I muttered. It was dark in the store, but that was fine with me. I had no desire to see his face clearly.

"Speaking of fun, I come into town by way of cemetery hill and I seen someone made a snowman up there. You wouldn't know anything about that?"

"Since when did making a snowman become a crime?"

"Around here you never know. Depends on what kind of snowman, I reckon."

"If you're wanting me to tell you I'm *innocent,* I won't."

"No need to tell me anything, bub. I took something from him, by the way. Here you go."

Rufus handed me Sheriff Plummer's scarf, which I never expected to see again. I started to protest, but he tucked the scarf in the top of my shirt. "You need it more than him," he said.

"I suppose," I mumbled, turning away from my brother.

"I heard you took my job," Rufus said, poking me in the back.

I crawled off a ways but stayed behind the counter. I sat up with my back against the far wall.

"Just filling in till you got back."

"Miss me, little brother?"

"Well, I thought you might be cold as a wagon tire."

"Nope. The vigilantes in Virginia City missed me, too."

It was a mighty close call, Rufus related. When President Paris Pfouts and the executive committee had privately met on Wednesday, January 13, in Virginia City, they came up with a list of six men in immediate need of hanging for being either highwaymen or dangers to the upstanding citizens living along Alder Gulch. Rufus recited the list in dramatic fashion, lingering on the names as if each was inscribed on a monument of fallen heroes—"Hayes Lyons, Boone Helm, Frank Parish, Jack

Gallagher, Clubfoot George Lane, and Rufus Hart—that's me, bub!"

"You weren't on Red Yeager's list," I said. "How'd you get on this list?"

"Don't take much. Remember that Willingham fellow who come to Virginia City looking for his wife Varina who was calling herself Virginia Nevada and who I was familiar with?"

"I know he shot your horse."

"When aiming for my backside. Anyway, Varina told Willingham a week ago she wanted a divorce, and he, blaming me for no good reason, started doing a heap of talking, making me out to be a bad character. It's not like I had anything to do with Varina having a fondness for younger men or leaving the boardinghouse to go work for Madam Featherlegs."

"Madam who?"

"Never mind. That's not important now. I figure Wallace Willingham didn't try to shoot me again because he didn't want to risk getting on no list himself. So, he said words that got me on the short list. But it don't matter. All that matters is that I was on the list and Willingham wasn't. You want to hear the rest or not?"

I did and tried to show a listener's enthusiasm by edging away from the back wall and leaning toward him.

Rufus continued. At dawn on the 14th, armed men surrounded Virginia City to prevent the wanted six from escaping, and then squads of other disciplined men hunted them down. They rounded up five of the accused as easily as sleepy sheep; none resisted arrest. They found George Lane replacing a customer's bootheel at his cobbler's bench in Dance and Stuart's Store. Even calling him "Clubfoot" hadn't gotten his dander up; Mr. Lane thought his boss Walter B. Dance was playing a practical joke on him.

"But the joke was on Georgie," Rufus said. "Hell of a guy.

He never killed nobody, nothing like that. Trouble is the damned vigilantes only recognize one punishment—a good long hard choke on a rope."

"They were looking for you, too?"

"You bet. Like I said, they'd heard an earful from that Willingham fellow."

"And that was all it took?"

"That's right. Oh, and one of the vigilantes recalled I had been working for Plummer and that my whereabouts were unknown during two stage holdups west of the gulch. Ridiculous, ain't it? I could have been anywhere. They got nothing but a circumcised case against me."

"You mean circumstantial?"

"Nothing that big. After they got Georgie at work, they searched his cabin anyway because, you see, informers told them I'd been bunking there. Except I wasn't there when they got there. I know these two gals from the California Exchange—that's a saloon who are sharing this nearby shack. I borrowed a disguise. One of them gals was big enough to fit me."

"You put on a dress?"

"A man gets desperate. But I covered most of the dress with Lulu's big fur coat, painted my face like her, and wore the other gal's hat on account of she is almost skinny but has a large head. I walked with fat Lulu right past the guards on Wallace Street. One or two of them might have admired us, but they never suspected a thing."

"And then you rode off?"

"Not just yet. Didn't have a horse. Me and Lulu watched the vigilantes, led by Captain James Williams, march their five prisoners up Wallace Street. It was easy to spot Georgie; he walks funny on account of his bum foot . . . or he did. In front of the Virginia Hotel, Georgie catches sight of Walter Dance and begs him to set the others straight. Dance won't have no part of it. Where Lulu and I was standing we could hear his excuse, which ain't worth shucks. He says, 'Your dealings with me have been upright, Mr. Lane, but what you have done outside of that I do not know.' Well, I know—Georgie is all right, I tell you . . . *was all right.* But everyone just went on marching till they stopped at a store building on the corner of Van Buren."

"The . . . eh . . . hanging took place inside?"

"That's right. The cold spell broke the day before so it could have been an outdoor event but nobody wanted to take the time to build gallows. Williams had his men throw five ropes over the main crossbeam and set up a barrel under each rope. You never seen nothing like it."

"Dutch John got it that way here in Bannack. But I was sleeping at the time, and there was only one of him."

"Didn't know Dutch. But I knew old Georgie. So, he and the four other boys are standing on the barrels, see, and that dirty little hangman X Biedler has the nooses all adjusted on their necks, see, and . . ."

"How'd you see all this if you were outside?"

"I didn't say I saw it all. I got my own informers. I did hear Williams yell, 'Men, do your duty!' But no sooner did those dirty words come out of his foul mouth than Georgie went flying off his barrel, even before one of them scoundrels could do his damn duty and kick it away."

"He wanted to be first, so he jumped?"

"Maybe. Or maybe he lost his balance on the barrel on account of his clubfoot. In any case, the rope was a mite too long and that bad foot of his scraped against the dirt floor before the noose choked the life out of poor Georgie."

"And then the other four had their barrels kicked away?"

"That's right. But I'd seen and heard enough. By then I had lit out with Lulu."

"You got a horse and left town?"

"Not yet. She took me back to her cabin, and Slanty Sally helped me out of her clothes."

"You mean Lulu's clothes?"

"Right. Lulu's clothes that I was wearing as a disguise. Slanty Sally is the skinny one."

"But it was Slanty Sally's hat you wore."

"That's right. And Slanty Sally got out of her own clothes, too, for the night. Now you got the picture, little brother? Truth of the matter is them two gals—the big one and the little one—made me forget about poor Georgie right quick."

Now I was getting some disturbing pictures that had nothing to do with hangings. I stood up and rubbed the sleep and more out of my eyes. "You rode away the next morning, then?"

"Yup. It was easy. The five bodies were still hanging when twenty-one riders rode out at dawn in search of more men to hang. They were in a big rush to hang as many folks as possible in the countryside because the talk in Virginia City was that a people's court with a judge and jury was on the near horizon. Seems like some of the lawyers in town was grumbling they couldn't make a living unless they had the opportunity to defend lawbreakers, especially those who possessed a lot of loot. Anyway, bub, I rose late that morning, took my sweet time kissing Slanty Sally and Lulu goodbye, and then, without a disguise or a gallop, rode out of Virginia City in the general direction the vigilantes went."

I reminded myself that it was Monday, January 18. I wondered how many poor souls those twenty-one riders had caught up with in the past few days.

Francis Thompson arrived through the front door humming a hymn he might have sung the day before at church. I cleared my throat as not to overly alarm him.

"That you, Woodrow?" he asked.

"Yes, sir," I said. "I was just about to light the lamp."

My brother was now standing next to me, squeezing my right shoulder. "Never you mind," he whispered. "I'll get it."

"Who's that? Who you got back there with you, Woodrow?"

"I . . . I . . . it's just . . ." I couldn't bring myself to say my brother's name. Maybe he was still wanted. Maybe Mr. Thompson wanted him—and not to work in the store.

"Me," sang out Rufus. "I'm back."

CHAPTER ELEVEN

In *Man from Montana: How He Escaped the Noose,* Red Ranger comes back from Dodge City to Virginia City to rescue the five condemned but relatively innocent men (there is a sixth man who escapes on his own, but he isn't named Rufus Hart; as you recall, W.A. Phillips left Rufus completely out of his dime novel). The red-masked hero brings the "Freed Five" to the Virginia Hotel, where he disguises them as helplessly large women and heavily bearded old men, which "totally discombobulates the hangman and hangers-on." The vigilantes, afraid that the American justice system is about to catch up with them and that they will soon be judged by a jury of their peers, decide they, executive committee and all, had better vamoose. They spread out across Montana Territory (in reality still Idaho Territory) from the Big Hole to Hell Gate—clad in black uniforms with golden epaulettes and King of Prussia spiked helmets—looking to find and immediately hang the Freed Five as well as any other political enemies and murdering thieves, collectively referred to as "The Plummers." Red Ranger can't be everywhere at once, but he tries, with what Phillips calls "the loftiest conviction of the most sainted, most muscular cowboy," to ride every which way on his white stallion Gold to "preserve, protect, and propel the criminal justice system and the American way of life!"

It's hard to pick out the hints of truth in the above (and in fact in Phillips's entire body of outrageous work), but there truly were vigilantes scouring the countryside for further "victims." Francis Thompson knew something about them. In the middle of greeting Rufus like a long-lost son, Mr. Thompson told me to collect a bucket of ash from the woodstove and empty it in the privy hole out back to reduce the odor. When I returned from that unpleasant assignment, Mr. Thompson was talking about how two days earlier a party of vigilantes had caught up in the Big Hole River valley with Steve Marshland, supposedly Dutch John Wagner's partner in the botched freight wagon holdup of the previous November. Like Dutch John, Marshland had been shot during the robbery and suffered from frostbite afterward. But unlike Dutch John, young Steve hadn't yet been introduced to the noose. That changed on the evening of January 16. The law enforcers inspected under his shirt and found his bullet wound to the chest and then unwrapped the bandages around his lower legs to find feet black with gangrene. None of the men had medical training, but they figured that the young failed robber might last only a few more days in his current state. Still, they didn't want to wait around to make sure, so they built a fire to get the circulation going in their cold hands and then took him out to the corral and hanged him on a pole.

"Wolves picked up the rotten scent of gangrene and death and came around at a safe distance with their hungry stares," Mr. Thompson said. "The hangmen decided to bury the young man that very night instead of leaving his dangling body at the mercy of the wolves."

"Such kindness," said Rufus. "Such respect for the dead."

"We'll all have our judgment day. I'm not one to pass judgment on anyone."

"I know. Not even on me, right?"

"You've always been right by me, Rufus. You'll be safe here."

"What else did you hear, Mr. Thompson? Did the vigilantes

track down anyone else?"

"That's the only one I know of . . . so far. Last I heard, the main force of hangmen was headed for Cottonwood, still after the elusive Aleck Carter and other wanted men."

"A good place to avoid. What about here in Bannack?"

"Pretty quiet the last couple days. The smell of death still lingers, though."

I quietly blew my nose on Plummer's scarf and then pointed my nose at the ceiling and took a couple of long sniffs. It smelled all right inside Thompson's store. The scent of death was absent, and so now was the scent of Thompson's outhouse.

Rufus, feeling relatively safe, immediately took over his old job in the store. I showed up the next day, the 19th, as an unpaid assistant to the assistant. Before we quit work, Mr. Thompson got word from a man who rode in like he might have been a veteran of the Pony Express. Vigilantes had paid a call on Bill Bunton, said to be Plummer's second-in-command (and perhaps the No. 1 man now that Plummer was deceased), at his cabin behind the combination saloon and grocery store he was operating in Cottonwood along Deer Lodge Creek. Without benefit of a real trial and with a rope attached to an outdoor beam and his neck, Bunton stood on a plank between two cracker barrels from his store and sprang off before Captain James Williams could give the hangman the proper signal. As in the George Lane execution there had been a slight miscalculation: Because the rope was too long, the heels of Bunton's boots scraped the earth.

"He was the only one hanged in Cottonwood?" I asked.

"Can't get enough of that, eh, little brother?" said Rufus.

"No, no. I'm glad. I hope I never see another hanging as long as I live."

"Another fellow, name of Tex Crowell, was held and released for lack of evidence," Mr. Thompson said.

"That must be a first," Rufus said. "Good for old Tex. What about Aleck Carter?"

"Got away again. He and some friends took off to the northwest, maybe headed for one of the passes in the Bitterroots."

"Or Hell Gate. It's one hundred miles to there from Cottonwood. Been there once. They probably figure it's out of the vigilantes' range."

"I don't know about that," said Mr. Thompson. "Captain Williams strikes me as the kind of man who would travel to the ends of the earth to achieve his idea of sure, swift, and secure justice."

"Somebody should stop the son of a bitch," Rufus said. "Maybe it'll be me."

But I couldn't take him too seriously. For one thing, he had a broom in his hand when he said it. And, for another, he was the same fellow who had recently resorted to wearing a dress to escape personal danger. I mean I was darn glad his dress disguise had worked in Virginia City, but the mental picture had stuck in my head and seemed disconnected with the bully brother who used to hand out "manly" beatings to me and even to young strangers back in Washington, D.C.

That evening I broke the news to Sidney and Mary Edgerton that I would no longer be able to pay for my room and board because I had lost my job at Thompson's store to a more experienced worker. I did not say his name was Rufus Hart because Mr. Edgerton and Wilbur Sanders must have heard through Francis Thompson or the vigilante grapevine that the Vigilance Committee in Virginia City had targeted my brother for execution.

The Edgertons shrugged me off, asking no questions and practically running through me (invisible once more) as they scurried about the house like a couple of disoriented field mice.

I wasn't sure what was up until I saw Lucia Darling sewing gold nuggets into the interior of a valise. I remembered how last fall Mr. Edgerton, wanting to talk up the cause of a new territory, planned to take gold to Washington to impress and influence President Lincoln and other political bigwigs. His trip had been postponed then, but now it was full speed ahead. The chief justice was planning to leave the next morning. That's all that Lucia told me. She gave me her "I'm too busy to talk to you" look and then stopped looking at me.

I wondered if there was anything I could do to help, but I didn't know how to sew and I didn't think any of them wanted a nonfamily member handling Mr. Edgerton's gold, though the most I had ever stolen from any of them was half a loaf of bread. I stood dumbly in the doorway of my bedroom waiting for somebody to ask me to carry a bag or to give directions to the White House. Finally, Mattie Edgerton came along. I had shunned her so much lately that a few days earlier she told me—using an unladylike expression she must have picked up from one of Lucia's rowdy male students—that I was "not worth a fart in a chinook wind." But when she knew things I didn't know she couldn't keep from rolling them off her tongue like a child reciting the alphabet.

"Papa is taking a lot of gold with him tomorrow," she said. "I suppose you know that much. But what you don't know is that he'll be carrying $2,000 in cash, all of it donations to the cause by well-to-do merchants and the more successful miners. The cause happens to be Papa working hard with the Republicans in Washington, which is the capital of the United States, to give us here east of the Bitterroot Range our very own territorial stature."

"I think you mean *status,*" I said. "And I do know that Washington, D.C., is the nation's capital. In fact, I used to live there, a few blocks from where Abe Lincoln lives; they call his residence the White House."

"Everybody knows that. I think *you* are mean, Woodrow Hart."

"I guess I know that. But there's lot meaner around."

"You wouldn't mean me, would you?"

"I reckon not, Mattie. You're just young."

"So are you. The mean ones are all the outlaws around. But they're getting just what they deserve." She put both hands on her neck, tilted her head, and made a throaty sound.

"I'm not so mean to wish all the hangings going around."

"Are you saying Papa is mean? And Uncle Wilbur?"

"I wouldn't say that," I said. *Especially when I'm living in your father's house.* That's what I thought but didn't say.

"Good, because they are good men doing what men got to do sometimes."

"Like hanging other men, you mean?"

"Exactly. It makes everything safer. Thanks to the hangings, Papa and other good men can now safely travel the roads. Mama says she doesn't think there is danger of his being robbed tomorrow."

"So why does he have gold sewed into the lining of his coat and the sides of his valises?"

"Don't you know it is better to be safe than sorry?"

Playing it safe was my usual course of nonaction. But I still often felt sorry, usually for some other fellow, like that young man down in the Big Hole who got himself shot in the chest during his first and last robbery attempt, had his frostbit toes turn black from gangrene, and then had his neck stretched permanently. Of course, that wasn't anything I could tell the Edgerton girl.

"I don't know how safe Washington is right now with a war going on," I finally said. "But I'm sorry not to be going there with your father. It would be going home again."

"And you could see your own papa and mama," Mattie suggested in all innocence.

And just like that I fully realized I didn't really want to go home again. My father had died of pneumonia in a drunken state within three hundred yards of the Capitol three or four or maybe five years ago (it wasn't an anniversary to remember), and my mother had never been particularly glad to see me walk through either the front or back door.

"You don't have it so bad in Bannack, you know," I told Mattie.

"I know that," she replied. "Who ever said I did?"

Mrs. Edgerton called Mattie away to help her find Sidney Edgerton's fisher fur cap, the one that kept his head warm in the worst of weather. Nobody asked me to do anything. I felt helpless and went to bed dreaming of Lucia's fingers sewing brains inside my scalp.

In the morning, Sidney Edgerton was raring to go, but he took time to talk to all four of his children and, to my utmost surprise, Mrs. Edgerton's stomach. I was flitting about the house in my invisible state observing with natural curiosity family life. His goodbyes to his children were long, but it wasn't hardly any kind of goodbye to his wife's belly. "See you later," he said as he sat on the edge of his bed with his hands on the hips of his wife, who stood facing him with her belly protruding ever so slightly. I immediately made myself scarce, hoping they hadn't seen my shadow passing by their bedroom doorway.

Later I heard Sidney Edgerton reassuring Mattie not to worry about him during his travels because he had planned everything with one thing in mind—to be safe not sorry. On the trail to Salt Lake City he would be leading a train of packhorses and reliable men, and from Salt Lake he would head east on a stagecoach that had never been held up. Regardless, Mattie called him the bravest man in the world and hugged him around the waist as if she hoped to detain him forever. He then kissed his oldest daughter on the forehead and put on his fisher fur hat, which she had found under one of the old winter coats (the one I usually wore). Mr. Edgerton hugged his wife more gently, probably because everyone was watching and she was expecting, though I wasn't certain how many of the others knew that. He then kissed her on the cheek but was surprised to see how wet it was. Her tears began flowing, and when the children saw the state their mother was in, they all began crying, too, even Mattie.

"What's wrong with everybody?" Mr. Edgerton asked. "You knew I'd be leaving. You all agreed it was the right thing to do, for the family and for Bannack. Everything is set."

"You forgot that tomorrow is Mama's birthday," said Mattie, suddenly turning on her father and glaring at him behind misty eyes.

"What?" Mr. Edgerton took off his fur hat as if he had just entered a church. "Of course, I know it's her birthday tomorrow. January 21—just like it's always been."

"You didn't get her a gift, Papa," Mattie said.

Mr. Edgerton turned his back on his oldest daughter. "I'll not give you a gift now," he told his wife but loud enough for all to hear. "I shall bring you many gifts back from Washington. I won't leave *all* my gold in the White House with Abe or in the House and Senate chambers—just enough to dazzle the eyes of the Congressmen and give them some idea of the great mineral wealth of this section of the country." It sounded more like a political speech than a goodbye.

Mrs. Edgerton wiped one of her cheeks. "The only gift I want, Sid, is for you to return to our home unscathed."

"You can count on it. And with good news about a new territory."

"That goes without saying, my husband."

"Never fear, dear. Wilbur is nearby, and he shall be stopping by every day to check on you and the children."

"Twice a day," said Mr. Sanders, as he gave his uncle two friendly blows to the back.

"Nothing will happen to them," said dry-eyed Lucia Darling, stepping forward and standing before him like a Spartan soldier. "I'll keep a sharp eye on the children."

"As always, my darling niece," he said, smiling at his own gentle cleverness and planting what he might have thought to be his last kiss on her well-carved but partially knitted brow.

"Still, it would be nice if you were with us for at least a tiny part of my actual birthday," said Mary Edgerton, patting her stomach.

"Yes, yes, yes," cried the children.

"Yes, but I . . . All right. All right. A twenty-four-hour delay won't kill me. Lucia will fix a birthday breakfast on January 21 and then I'll be on my way."

Wilbur Sanders had brought up a stout, almost pale, lead horse, with the gold-laden valises already carefully attached to the first packhorse behind him. Mr. Edgerton's traveling companions were all mounted. Mr. Edgerton made his deepest apologies, and everyone assured him it wasn't a *terrible* inconvenience.

"Same time, same place, tomorrow," he said. "Will someone be so kind as to bring my valises into the house."

After Mr. Sanders and the other men had departed, and Mr. Edgerton's family had settled back in their happy home, I remained in the yard studying the sun and thinking how every day it had to go down again and start all over. That took a lot of energy. When I heard Sidney Edgerton clear his throat and address me, I jumped to attention as if I were a Yankee soldier singled out by General Ulysses S. Grant.

"So tomorrow it is, Woodrow," he said as if reassuring himself that he was doing the right thing. "What's one more day after all?"

"Not much, sir," I said.

"I can use the extra day to rest up. It'll be a long time in the saddle."

"Yes, sir." I had never actually seen him ride a horse.

"And I really should make sure I packed everything I'll need."

I wanted to ask if he might pack his howitzer to deal with any as-yet-unhanged robbers and murderers. Instead, I said, "Anything I can do for you, sir?" I was hoping he would say something that would recognize my worth, something like *I'm counting on you to be the man of the house while I'm away, Woodrow Hart. I have all the faith in the world in . . .*

My hoping was rudely interrupted. "Try not to be a burden, boy," he told me. "Be good. Find the correct path in your life and take it. Refuse to follow in the wayward path your brother Rufus has chosen."

I wanted to say something in defense of Rufus or to insist that *I was good,* but I was tongue-tied. I nodded slightly. Before I could manage a *Yes, sir,* Mattie reappeared, hugging her father and expressing her love for him as she guided him back inside to attend to something her mother needed.

"You best listen to Papa," Mattie said when she paused in the doorway.

"Sure. I always listen."

"And do what he says, too."

"I got to go to work."

"You don't have a job anymore."

"Right. Well, I got to go anyway."

"No, you don't. And don't you go telling that awful brother of yours that my papa will be carrying a valuable cargo tomorrow."

She had the last word, and since no comeback came to me, I

bent down and made a snowball. But she slammed the door shut behind her before I could do something *bad.* It turned out I did have to go. Rufus showed up riding the black horse he'd owned (a gift from Sheriff Henry Plummer) since his days as an assistant deputy in Virginia City and was leading a small spotted pony I didn't recognize.

"Hop on, bub," he said. "Mr. Thompson give her to me. She be gentle and used to a saddle. I got food in the saddlebag."

I hesitated, because I was less used to a saddle than Mr. Edgerton, not having ever owned a horse and never having had much opportunity to ride in Washington or Bannack. On the Bozeman Trail I had shared a horse with my brother, but in Virginia City that unfortunate animal took a fatal double load of buckshot meant for Rufus.

"Come on," Rufus said. "You're thinking I stole the pony. I did *not.* It did once belong to a Bannock Indian boy, but he come to the store and traded it to Mr. Edgerton for some blankets during the recent cold spell. His name is Manahuu."

"The pony?"

"No, the boy. Manahuu is a familiar face around here. He's with the Bannocks that come begging in Bannack."

"Yes, I might have seen him pressing his nose against the Edgertons' kitchen window."

"Well, never mind him. The pony is yours now."

"Mr. Thompson just gave it to you?"

"No. To you, little brother, part bonus for your work, part birthday present."

"But he already paid me for my work, and I don't turn sixteen until July 4."

"So, I might have told him you were born on December 25 like Jesus Christ. It don't matter. Now hop on already. Besides the food for us, I packed grain for the mounts and blankets for you and me. We got to make tracks."

"Because you stole the horse?"

"Damn you, little brother. I already told you I didn't steal it from Thompson. The pony's name is Togu, which means dog. He comes when he's called. We don't have all day. Hop!"

I didn't feel like testing the animal or like hopping. "Maybe later," I said. "I'm busy."

"The hell you are. Don't make me get down and put you in the saddle!"

I recognized the color of his face; he was on the edge of rage. It was no time to stand up to him. Besides, the pony nuzzled my arm.

"Steady, Togu," I said as I climbed aboard. "Why the food and blankets? I have time only for a short ride. Where to?"

"Hell Gate," Rufus said, giving Togu a swift swat on the hindquarters.

Chapter Twelve

We rode and we rode, mostly through snow as much as a foot deep. I bounced in the saddle as Togu, with the enthusiasm of a young puppy, followed close behind Rufus's powerful nameless black horse. Of the two four-footed beasts and two two-footed ones, only I wanted to turn back to Bannack. Rufus wouldn't let me. As he told it, the vigilantes would likely come for him soon if he was there, and he couldn't chance it. He claimed that the persistent Mr. Willingham had traveled by stage from Virginia City to Bannack just to see Wilbur Sanders and make his case against the wife-stealing Hart (even though Rufus said Varina was quite capable of hiding without his help). Mr. Sanders had listened well and stated that Rufus Hart was already under observation if not suspicion as a former Plummer man and for acting indecently with Bannack's one and only schoolteacher, Lucia Darling. With two fellow vigilantes as armed backup, Mr. Sanders had gone to the Thompson dry goods store to question the immoral and possibly criminal employee.

"Mr. Thompson hid me," Rufus told me the first night out of Bannack when we camped in a rocky place between two snowdrifts. "He likes me well enough. He didn't want to see happen to me what happened to his friend Henry Plummer."

"The Edgertons are his friends, too," I said, as I debated whether to dig out a place for my sleeping blankets or just lay them out on top of the snow.

"Sure. Mr. Thompson was caught in the middle all right. Not that he could have done much for the sheriff even had he a mind to. While he was hiding me, he admitted he couldn't hold off the vigilantes for long if they really wanted my neck. He advised me to leave town, gave me some extra pay, provisions, and the pony, of course. He promised I could have my old job back when things settle down. Not much of a job, though. I can do better."

"In Hell Gate? That's far away."

"Not as far as it was this morning. We did good considering the snow. I got me some friends there."

"Like who?"

"Whiskey Bill Graves and Bob Zachary for two."

"What! You don't mean those two men who held up our stage when we first left Virginia City for Bannack?"

"Only Whiskey Bill I know of. There be only one Zachary for sure. They've had time to reform."

"I hope so."

"And there's Cyrus Skinner. He opened one of the first saloons when the prospectors came to Grasshopper Creek. His Elkhorn was right on main street next to the Goodrich Hotel. You must know Cyrus. A fun-loving, generous guy. Has knife scars on his face and hands."

"I don't think so. I never set foot in the Elkhorn."

"Someone should teach you how to drink, little brother. Later, when the rush was on at Alder Gulch, Cy and Nellie—that's his woman—moved over there from Bannack and opened a saloon in Virginia City. Last month he sold his Virginia establishment and went to Hell Gate, where he and Nellie are operating a first-rate saloon. We'll be as welcome there as warm weather."

"Wasn't the vigilantes who scared him off, was it?"

"Why should they? Cyrus never done nothing wrong,

leastwise not in this territory."

"I don't know. Something about this Hell Gate place doesn't quite sit right with me." I recollected Sidney Edgerton once dismissing the Bannock Indians as a poor example of their race. In his next breath he mentioned *true redskins,* the fierce and proud Blackfeet, who used to ambush and slaughter so many local Indians in this one canyon that French-Canadian trappers called it *Porte de L'Enfer,* which meant "Door of Hell." The later English translation was "Hell's Gate."

"You always was the nervous type, little brother, from the day you was hatched. The West sure ain't cured you of that."

"With all the killings and hangings, how could it?"

"Look, bub. I'm the one the vigilantes is after and I ain't nervous. And I'll be less so once we get to Hell Gate. For God's sake, would you put your damned blankets down somewhere. We'll be moving on at first light. We want to get there before the snow flies!"

"You know a storm's coming, do you?"

"I feel it in my bones. But not tonight, maybe not for a few days. But it's coming. We can beat it. Now lie down and shut up."

I did as he said, but my eyes soon popped open. I called out good night to Togu.

"Knew you'd like that pony," Rufus said, "despite your usual protests."

"Yes, I like Togu fine, but there's one thing I still don't understand."

"One thing? Tell me one thing you do understand."

"It's mighty cold out here."

"It's winter, Woodrow. Now shut the hell up. You told me yourself you was plum sick of living with the Edgerton family."

"Those weren't my exact words. I said that Mattie sometimes made me ill."

"A real pain in the backside, huh? Like you sometimes."

"Yeah, my backside is sore, too. I'm not used to time in the saddle."

"If that mouth of yours opens again, I'll shove a fistful of snow down it. Now rest easy, brother. We still got at least four more days to go in the snow before we reach Hell Gate."

"That far! I can't make it. I'm not used to . . ."

"Your pony is doing all the damn work. Quit your bawlin'."

"If I'm such a pain, why'd you take me along? That's the main thing I don't understand."

Rufus sat up in his blankets, sized up the moon and the stars, and then threw a snowball that struck me in the left knee. "Same reason I took you west to begin with, bub," he said so softly I had to stop brushing snow off my kneecap to hear. "A brother needs to look after his brother. I got other brothers but I don't know where the hell any of them are. Most are probably dead. You're the only brother I can look after these days. It's for your own damn good us leaving Bannack. You're smart but you got less horse sense than that pony. Them Edgertons never was gonna stop working you like a slave. And that schoolmarm you took such a shine to was never gonna stop turning her nose up at you. We ain't their kind of people. I know you, little brother. You act all worried and afeared. Inside, though, you be achin' to do things; you just don't know how to do nothing by your lonesome. If not for me, Woodie, you never even would have mounted Togu this morning."

I had never heard him go on for so long. I might have preferred a punch in the nose or that fistful of snow down my throat. I suddenly felt as exhausted in mind as I was in body, certainly too tired to argue any of those points he had made about me.

"Good night, Rufus," I said. "Wherever you want to go is fine."

"Who knows," he said maybe ten minutes later. "In Hell Gate, they just might be needing a smart young man without any horse sense to teach school."

It was the nicest thing Rufus had ever said about me. I curled up in my blankets and fell right asleep. I slept well. I didn't dream at all.

Rufus was right. No storm hit during the night. The sun peeked out soon enough and we were back in the saddle. We rode close to the Clark Fork when we could to avoid the deeper snow. The river was frozen, so at times we rode right on top of it. I did fine on Togu, but the ice wailed under the weight of Rufus and his big horse. In the early afternoon it cracked and the horse broke through. Rufus, not knowing how to swim any better than me, elected to stay in the saddle. As Togu carried me to safety on the riverbank, I saw so much thrashing going on that I figured both black horse and brother would go under and never be seen again. I would have thrown my brother a rope, but I didn't have one. Neither did he. We never had much use for them.

The horse must have strained every last muscle, and Rufus must have said every last curse and prayer he knew, but they got out of the river. Still, there was the matter of freezing to death or getting frostbit, which could result in the same end. We made a fire and lost time. I didn't know what rush there was in getting to Hell Gate, but Rufus kept telling me a powerful storm was coming and we'd be warm and safe there. His friends would make sure of that.

Once we got going another near tragedy occurred. The black horse slipped on an icy rock ledge and one of its legs caught in a badger hole. The leg didn't break but some of the flesh around the hoof was scraped clear off. For the rest of the day, Rufus and I took turns riding my pony while leading the hobbled horse. Togu wasn't up to having us ride double, but she took to the challenge of breaking the hard snow. She did better when it was me doing the riding because I weighed less and didn't try to control her every step. We camped that night in what might have passed as a cave and finished the last of the hard biscuits.

We were back on two horses and pushing it again the next day, gnawing on jerky when we could. The snow on the ground thinned out and we made even better progress on the third day. The fourth day was our best yet, our horses' best yet that is, 'cause I was half asleep in the saddle most of the time and Rufus kept complaining about aches and pains and the lack of food. We stopped at a frozen creek in late afternoon and broke the ice for water. The horses were blowing hard, but we gave them the last of the feed Rufus had brought and it seemed to give them new life. Togu, unlike me, was no complainer. Just after nightfall we reached the Mullan Road, which ran right through Hell Gate and then crossed over a pass in the Bitterroots on its way to Fort Walla Walla. I was certain it would be a "starving" camp that night, but Rufus shot us a jackrabbit, skinned it, and cooked it on a stick. It tasted stringy and possibly undercooked, but I didn't complain. Togu and the big black mostly ate snow but seemed content.

"Thank you, Rufus," I said as I picked my teeth. "You're a life saver."

"You got spoiled living like a slave off the Edgertons."

His words didn't quite make sense to me, but I was tired again. "They don't hunt for their food," I said in lieu of just nodding.

"You should really think about getting yourself a gun, little brother."

I really didn't want to shoot anything—rabbit or road agent, vole or vigilante—but that's what one usually ended up doing with a firearm. "Sure might think about it," I replied.

"And tomorrow we'll sup in Skinner's two-stove saloon.

Nothing like good whiskey and vittles after a long trip, bub."

Rufus was right again, because we left our camp well before dawn, our mounts anticipated better browsing ahead, and we didn't run into a storm that could slow us down. Neither of us had reason to mention that Rufus had been wrong about his storm prediction. There wasn't going to be one, at least not one created by Mother Nature.

After we reined in the horses in front of his saloon, Cyrus Skinner had one of his customers take care of the beasts. I thanked Togu and told him I'd see him later. Mr. Skinner then ushered us into his place, which did have two stoves, though the second one wouldn't be fired up unless more customers showed up. We sat down for ham and eggs, and Rufus had two shots of the saloonkeeper's best rye. The wood walls and furniture smelled fresh-cut and his woman, Nellie (wife or otherwise), smelled good, at least as good as the hot meal. Mr. Skinner put an arm around Nellie's waist and, while squeezing her tight, claimed that while Hell Gate wasn't as lively as Virginia City or even Bannack, it was a far more comfortable place to hang his hat. He then boasted he had the best saloon gal (he meant Nellie) and best saloon in the whole of Idaho Territory.

"It could be part of a new territory soon," I mentioned—my only contribution to the conversation during the meal.

"Won't change a thing," Mr. Skinner said. "Not long ago we were in Washington Territory. Meant nothing to me. Who's going to miss Idaho Territory when we're out of it? Not yours truly. As far as Cyrus Skinner is concerned, this is *my* territory. I'm my own boss here. Population here in Hell Gate might be only thirty-two but every last one of them is a damn good customer. And we get plenty of traffic on the Mullan Road. Have another egg. It's damn near fresh. Any brother of Rufus Hart is a pal of mine."

When Nellie sashayed to the kitchen for more vittles and Cyrus Skinner sauntered behind the bar for another bottle of whiskey, Rufus told me that Mr. Skinner might be his own boss but was only the number three man in town. Four years ago, Frank L. Worden and Christopher P. Higgins had used cottonwood logs to build a cabin and, anticipating the Mullan Road reaching them, soon turned it into a store, stocking it with goods brought from Walla Walla on a seventy-six-mule packtrain. The Worden and Higgins store had been going strong ever since, selling goods at reasonable prices to the Mullan Road travelers passing through the Hell Gate Valley, the few white residents who had built cabins nearby, and friendly Indians, mostly Flatheads from the Bitterroot Valley to the south and the St. Ignatius Mission Indians to the north.

"It's still Higgins and Worden's town," Rufus whispered. "There wouldn't be this saloon here without their excellent store; Cyrus buys his stock of whiskey on credit from Worden. But don't tell him that or say anything to Whiskey Bill and Zachary, who I expect we'll be seeing here shortly, them being his most regular customers. I reckon every man needs a place to call his own."

"You bet," I said, thinking it made me sound more manly. I imagined myself owning a little sod-roof log house on the outskirts of Hell Gate and living a quiet, peaceful life with my wife, Lucia Darling Hart. I'd be a schoolteacher like her—well, not quite like her because I would be considerably tougher, handling the young male hard cases and any problem girls (I had Mattie Edgerton in mind). Of course, Hell Gate being a two-schoolteacher town would have to wait awhile, what with there being no children residing in it yet.

I had a second helping of ham and then dozed off in a chair for a moment. Rufus must have done the same, for when I was half awake, I saw my brother stretched out half under the table and both Nellie and Cyrus Skinner standing over him laughing.

Mr. Skinner picked an empty whiskey bottle off the floor and saluted his woman with it.

"I win the bet," he said. "He passed out in under an hour."

"It was part exhaustion," Nellie said as she fiddled with her gold necklace. "The boy had a hard ride. His brother didn't touch a drop and look at him."

"Don't be a sore loser, Nell honey. I'll just collect now."

Cyrus Skinner began to nuzzle her neck and explore her full figure with both hands—a display I had never seen at my boyhood home in Washington or at the Edgerton house. With only one eye open, I planned to watch them proceed, but we were rudely interrupted by a commotion outside. It wasn't enough to cause Rufus to stir, but the Skinners and I rushed to the door to see why there was so much late traffic on the town's only real street. We got there in time to see maybe a dozen horsemen gallop past the saloon and out of town (though, admittedly, that wasn't very far at all) before they reined in their mounts and backtracked. They stopped this time in front of the saloon, dismounted practically as one, and formed a semicircle in front of Cyrus Skinner.

"Throw up your hands!" several of the men shouted, but the one who shouted the loudest was a stern fellow I only knew by reputation—Captain James Williams of the vigilantes.

"You must have learned that from the Bannack stage folks," said Nellie.

I think she meant her comment as a joke, but these were not men to joke with. With faces like rocks, they pulled Cyrus Skinner out onto the street, tied his hands behind his back, and marched him across the street to the Worden and Higgins store. Two men blocked Nellie's path, though she hadn't made a move to follow. One told her she shouldn't attempt to interfere with Lady Justice. The other said tears couldn't save Cyrus Skinner's skin now. Nellie, without a noticeable tear in her eye, crossed her arms in defiance. In the meantime, I quietly strolled to the store—my invisibility having kicked in once more. Nobody stopped me when I entered the store and stood in the corner near both a stove and a shiny safe that sat on a platform for all to marvel over. The vigilantes were interrogating Cyrus Skinner on the other side of the store, and I couldn't hear what was being said. I sat down and pretended I was warming my hands the few times anyone looked in my direction.

After a few minutes, they brought in another man, and I was glad to see it wasn't my brother. It turned out to be none other than Aleck Carter, the big fellow who George Ives had fingered and who had eluded capture until now. The vigilantes now had two men to interrogate, but after finally tiring of that they held what might have looked like a trial in the center of the store, with Captain Williams presiding. I didn't hear too much, but I did catch a loud statement from Mr. Carter that seemed to make sense to me: "You boys are doing this work in such a hurry that you are bound to send some innocent men to the happy hunting ground." But the trial did continue well into the night. The vigilantes led Cyrus Skinner and Aleck Carter outside by torchlight to continue their work at the corral behind the store. I followed in no particular hurry, as not to arouse anyone's attention. When somebody slipped an arm around my shoulder from behind, I nearly jumped out of my shivering skin.

"You're mighty young for a vigilante," the man said, stroking a short beard and looking at me with eyes whose lids seemed half closed. "Where you from?"

"Washington," I said. "Not the territory, the nation's capital."

"Long way to go for a hanging. I'm Christopher Powers Higgins, all the way from Ireland, originally. Folks hereabouts mostly call me C.P."

"I'm not a vigilante, but I'm not an outlaw. I'm Woodrow R. Hart. The R stands for Russell. Some think it stands for Red, but Red is just a nickname, and I don't . . ."

"I can see why you're *Red.* Only thing I ever saw as red as your hair is a dress I ordered from St. Louis for my wife, Juliet. She's back in our cabin down the road. Women and boys don't need to see hangings. The guards are keeping Nellie away. Maybe I should keep you away. Must be past your bedtime anyway, Red."

"I don't want to see any more hangings anyway," I said. "But I'm not sleepy."

"Sure. It's only midnight. But why stand out in the cold. Come on back inside the store, Red, where it's plenty warm."

We stood by the stove. Mr. Higgins caught me staring at the raised vault and boasted it was a first for the territory. He then matter-of-factly stated that it held $65,000 in gold dust. I shrugged and commented how impressed I was with the many canned goods he carried in his store.

"Gold doesn't interest you, Red?" he asked.

"Mostly I'm hungry," I admitted.

He opened a can of peaches for me, and I thanked him with as much gusto as I could muster. "Skinner and some of his unsavory customers have had an eye on that safe since they came to Hell Gate last month. But I wouldn't hang a man for thinking about doing something they oughtn't do."

Another bearded man, but this one with bright wide-opened eyes, came through a back door as if he had just had a nice chat with a neighbor. "Ben Franklin once said 'an ounce of prevention is worth a pound of cure,' " he said. "Skinner needn't worry about gold dust and buying Nellie gold necklaces a second longer. He's hanging at the corral. Carter, too. Quite a large body that Carter has. But the drop was clean enough."

"Fair enough," said Mr. Higgins, who then introduced the other man, Francis Worden, his partner since 1860. They could have been twin brothers—at least they had identical beards.

"This young man is Red Hart, neither a vigilante nor an outlaw."

"A customer, then?" Mr. Worden asked. "No, don't tell me. He is penniless."

"Mostly," I admitted, my mouth half full. "But I have a pony."

"To his credit, Red has no designs on the gold dust in our safe and thanked me for offering him a can of peaches, which he has devoured," said Mr. Higgins.

"I'll give him a can of tomatoes."

Mr. Worden did, and I was thanking him with my mouth full when he asked a surprisingly blunt question: "What the hell are you doing in Hell Gate, Red?"

I didn't really know and got tongue-tied as usual. Under the circumstances, mentioning that Rufus was running from the Bannack vigilantes would be like signing his death warrant. "I . . . eh . . . I came up with my older brother," I said. "We're just passing through."

"On the way to where?" the partners asked at the same time.

"I'm not sure—oh, wait I think my brother mentioned Lewiston," I said because I knew it was the capital of Idaho Territory and I couldn't think of any other place to the west.

"And where is that brother of yours now?" asked Mr. Higgins.

"Last I saw he was . . . eh, sleeping at the saloon across the street."

"Our only saloon in Hell Gate," said Mr. Worden. "He a friend of Cyrus Skinner, the late Cyrus Skinner?"

"No, not really. Like I said we're just . . ."

"I know, just passing through. What's your brother's name?"

"Hart, same as mine. Rufus Hart. He doesn't have a middle name that I know of."

"Never heard of him, have you, Worden?" said Mr. Higgins.

"Nope. Sure haven't, Higgins," said Mr. Warden.

"Good," said I. "I mean he's not a vigilante or outlaw either."

Chapter Thirteen

Mr. Higgins and Mr. Worden invited me to spend the night in their store because I didn't seem like the kind of fellow who would steal them blind. I thanked them but went over to Skinner's saloon to make sure Rufus was all right. He was. He was at the bar consoling Nellie Skinner over her recent loss. Her head lay on his shoulder when I came in, but by the time they noticed me his head was on her shoulder and sliding down toward her ample chest. She immediately pulled away from Rufus and came at me a little too fast for comfort.

"You see it?" she asked, grabbing me by the shoulders and shaking me.

"No, ma'am. I didn't want . . . I mean I couldn't . . . I . . ."

"They told me I could see him later, but when later came, he was already hanging there. Did he say anything at the end? Did he mention my name? Did he die brave?"

"I really don't know. Like I said I . . ."

She shook me again and then let me go and turned her back on me. "It's not your fault. What could you do, a boy?"

"Nobody could stop it," Rufus said. He walked up to her and tried to guide her head to his shoulder, but she jumped back as if he were a man-eating bear.

"You sure couldn't!" she screamed. "You were passed out on the floor."

She marched to the door.

"Hey, where you going?" said Rufus. "What did I do?"

"Nothing. I'm going to the cabin Cy built for me."

"What about me . . . and my brother?"

"You stay here and watch the saloon. Don't let any of those vile men in here to drink Cy's whiskey."

As soon as Nellie left, Rufus began cursing and stamping around the saloon like a corralled bull. It was hard to tell if he was angry at her, the vigilantes, or me. I didn't ask. Finally, he told me to close the front door and bolt it.

"If they want to hang me, too, they'll have to wait till the sun comes up," he said.

"I don't think they do, Rufus," I said. "I think the vigilantes are done in Hell Gate."

"I'm not," he said. But he didn't explain himself. He walked back behind the bar and lay down on the floor, using several bar rags as a pillow. "A tired man can go to sleep if he wants to, can't he?" he said. "He can't be expected to wake up with every little disturbance."

I chose to spend the night slouched in one chair, with my legs stretched across another chair. I kept waiting for someone to pound on the door, but nobody did . . . not till morning.

No eggs for breakfast. Rufus decided to wake up with a glass of whiskey, but I wondered if he just wanted to pass out again. I opened the front door to get some fresh air and saw riders pull up in front of the Worden and Higgins store. Armed men, clearly another set of vigilantes, led a bound man into the store to join Captain Williams and the first set of vigilantes.

"You won't believe it," I called back to Rufus at the bar. "That's your friend Bob Zachary they got."

"Damn," said Rufus, pouring himself another glass. "I'm liable to run out of friends before I know it."

"I'm going to the store to see what's up with him," I said. "You want to come along?"

"No, thanks. I'll venture to guess Zach will be up in the air directly."

By the time I got inside the store, Captain Williams was already conducting a trial of sorts for Mr. Zachary. Francis Worden, if nobody else, saw me. He pulled me over to the sputtering stove and asked if I'd had breakfast. I said I wasn't hungry, that my stomach was too agitated.

"Good," he said. "I wouldn't want to spoil your appetite. Over in the Bitterroot Valley they hung a twenty-one-year-old man in a barn, maybe even before Skinner and Carter got it here. Went by the name of George Shears. Don't know why he was on the list. He surrendered without a fight. Had some memorable last words as I understand it. He asked a real polite question: 'Gentlemen, I'm not used to this business, never having been hanged before. Shall I jump off or slide off?' Somebody told him to jump and he was real obliging. 'All right,' Shears said. 'Goodbye.' Word I got is he jumped like he'd done it before."

"I can't believe it, just two years older than . . ." I cut myself off, still not wanting to throw Rufus's name around more than necessary. "Actually, I can believe it. But why didn't they bring him back here to . . . you know, have a trial?"

"To save time. Result would have been the same."

"But they brought Bob Zachary here?"

"He was a lot closer when they seized him. I don't like his chances. He and his partner, Whiskey Bill Graves, held up a stage and robbed Leroy Southmayd."

"I know. Ru . . . my brother and I were passengers on that stage. They didn't shoot anyone."

"No matter. I'm not sure what isn't a hanging offense these days."

The trial had ended right before our eyes. Mr. Zachary was now dictating a letter to his family. "Drinking, gambling, and bad company have brought me to the gallows," he said. Mr. Worden suggested that the condemned man was warning his younger brothers in Oregon not to follow in his path. The vigilantes took him out to the corral to hang. I did not follow the crowd. I pretended they were just going there to look at the horses. Mr. Worden and I shared a can of peaches, and my half went down with surprising ease.

"Whiskey Bill must have gotten away," I said as I wiped juice from my mouth. "Now the vigilantes must *really* be done in Hell Gate. Don't you think, Mr. Worden?"

"I think almost, Red. Looks like there is room for one more." Vigilantes were carrying a young man into the store. "Wait. That's Johnnie Cooper, Cyrus Skinner's nephew. Aleck Carter shot him during some kind of drunken disagreement, and he was laying low in Skinner's cabin. I heard the lad was on Red Yeager's list, but don't know what he did to get there. You got any theory on the subject, Red?"

"Me?" I couldn't remember anyone ever asking me for my theory on anything, not even when I was in Lucia's classroom as an assistant teacher. "I don't know anything at all," I said, thinking that while Mr. Worden was nice enough, he could, if asked, tell the vigilantes I was just a dumb kid. "And do you mind calling me Woodie instead of Red, Mr. Worden?" I didn't even want the nickname connection with the executed Mr. Yeager.

"Sure, Woodie. And no need for the 'mister' for me or for Yeager. I'm plain Worden to everyone, including my partner, who is plain Higgins, except to them that call him C.P. My name comes first, of course. It's the Worden and Higgins store. Worden and Higgins everything."

I think he was joking, but whether he was or not, he didn't smile and neither did I.

We watched the proceedings, me with my mouth mostly

hanging open but closing regularly for difficult swallows involving an Adam's apple that felt like a lump of coal. Out of the corner of my eye, I saw Mr. Worden alternating between tugging at his beard and rubbing his right eye. I thought he might be shedding a tear because, even though I didn't know this wounded Johnnie Cooper fellow who couldn't even stand up on his own, I started to cry listening to Captain Williams accuse him of belonging to a robber band without specifying any particular crime committed in the territory. The captain did mention a possible murder in Oregon, but Mr. Cooper admitted to nothing except that his uncle was the recently hanged Cyrus Skinner. I was imagining Rufus and even me in Johnnie Cooper's shaky boots.

"Captain Williams and the vigilantes putting on a good show, Worden?" It was Mr. Higgins, who came in from the store's storeroom, holding an open can of peaches.

"Captain Williams looks to be wrapping up—another hanging is inevitable, Higgins," said Mr. Worden.

No sooner had he said it than Captain Williams stopped making a case for the death sentence. No more words were necessary. The vigilantes carried Johnnie Cooper out, put him on a sled, and pulled him toward the corral where Cyrus Skinner, Aleck Carter, and Bob Zachary had gone before him on guided final walks.

"You don't need to see this one, either, Red," said Mr. Higgins, but Mr. Worden had already blocked my path to the door. "Last of the peaches. Eat hearty, Red."

"He doesn't like to be called Red, Higgins."

"What should I call him, then, 'Peaches' perhaps?"

"He likes Woodie."

"Sure. Can't very well call him Hart, what with that other Hart in town. Saw him slip out of the saloon and creep around to the corral—to watch, I reckon."

"Rufus doesn't know Johnnie Cooper, either," I blurted out, accidentally spitting peach juice on my chin and down the front of my coat. I wiped my chin and then one of my wet eyes, which now stung from peach juice. "I don't know why Rufus is outside. I don't know when it all will end." I stumbled over to a table, slammed down the peach can, and collapsed in a chair as if seriously wounded. Well, it felt like I was, the pain running inside my eye socket and up into my brain.

"I'll go out and check on your brother," Mr. Higgins volunteered. "You stay here with our young friend, Worden. He looks mighty sick."

"Sure does, Higgins. A bad case of sensitivity is my diagnosis. Young Woodie doesn't need to *see* what's happening out there to feel all to pieces pained—like someone just kicked him in the head."

"He'll live. Beats getting your neck stretched."

Mr. Higgins buttoned up his coat and left. A minute later I heard a neck snap all the way from the corral, but a half minute after that I heard a neck snap again, so I knew it was all inside my head. Mr. Worden said he didn't hear a thing except the wind howling. It was a long wait. With his help I finished the peaches.

When the vigilantes swarmed inside the store to warm their faces and hands and necks, I caught sight of someone with bound hands moving in the middle of the flow. At first, I thought they had spared Johnnie Cooper, if for no other reason than to let his leg wounds heal before hanging him. I wouldn't have put that past these devout punishers of their fellow man. But the man in the middle moved too well to be the wounded Cooper. I sprang out of my chair for a better look.

"For the love of God!" I cried. "It's Rufus."

The vigilantes brought him to the front counter and turned him around so that he was facing Captain Williams and his other accusers. Mr. Higgins came in last, had me sit back down, and assured me everything would be all right.

"But they have my brother!"

"Just for questioning. He was watching quietly from behind a fence at first. Young Cooper requested a last smoke from a pipe and got it, but while he was smoking, your brother started singing the last verse of 'Dixie' over and over—you know, *I wish I was in Dixie, Hooray! Hooray! In Dixie's Land I'll take my stand, to live and die in Dixie. Away, away, away down south in Dixie.*"

"I know it. Rufus usually just whistles the tune. We're from Washington, you know. Rufus always said that should be part of Dixie. And I heard President Lincoln loves that song."

"Maybe so, but it's no favorite with those vigilante Republicans."

"What did they do?"

"Mostly just bit their lips and listened, I reckon. When Cooper was done with his smoke, they raised him up on a box, same one Skinner stood on. He couldn't put much weight on his wounded leg, so the hangmen tried to get the noose in place quick. But then the condemned got right playful. He waggled and jerked his head, causing the hangmen to miss the mark half a dozen times. Your brother enjoyed the show, clapping, stamping his foot, and shouting, *Hooray, Hooray, In Hell Gate, make 'em wait. Make your last stand grand.*"

"Don't know what got into Rufus. I thought he wanted to make himself invisible."

"He made himself suspicious. But all he has to do now is explain his presence."

"And then they'll let him go? You sure?"

Mr. Higgins turned away to watch.

"Higgins is sure," said Mr. Worden, but he tugged at his beard as if a tumbleweed had blown in with the vigilantes and attached to his face.

The examination wasn't anything pretty or even something bordering on judicial procedure. Nobody bothered to untie my brother's hands. The burly Captain Williams wanted to know why Rufus had been singing "Dixie" and demanded that he confess to any misdeed he had committed in or outside the territory. When Rufus didn't cooperate, the captain poked him in the belly, seized his chin, and slapped his face. "Did you hear what I said?" he kept repeating, but Rufus kept mum.

A parade of vigilantes who didn't give their names and were unknown to me stepped forward to reveal the little they knew about my brother: He was a Plummer man, having worked as a low-level law officer in Virginia City; he was a Skinner man, having received free drinks and eggs from Cyrus; he was an Aleck Carter, Bob Zachary, and Whiskey Graves man, having been seen in their company; he was a suspected holdup man, having been missing from Virginia City both times masked robbers struck stagecoaches outside town; he was a Red Yeager man, even though Red had left his name off the notorious list; he was a Southern man, based on his song selection; he was a Johnnie Cooper man, having encouraged his gallows antics; he was a shiftless man, since he had no gold or known means of support; and most of all he was a problematical man, since he had never joined a vigilance committee or even rubbed elbows with any honest, respected citizen in the territory. Nobody mentioned Wallace Willingham's accusations against him or the fact Rufus had actually once been on another, shorter "death list." But what was said about him sounded bad enough—enough to hang him. After all, the vigilantes had hanged men before without any hard evidence.

Captain Williams looked too pleased with himself. His sharp, self-assured voice whittled away at my self-control. Several times I nearly jumped up to defend my brother, but each time something held me back—either Mr. Higgins, Mr. Worden, or myself, Mr. Cowardice.

"If you have anything to say in your defense, Mr. Rufus Hart, you best say it now," said the captain with what he must have figured to be the final belly poke before he and the other accusers handed Rufus the same sentence they gave most everybody else.

Rufus grinned, grinning in the face of death as I saw it since it was a relatively short walk to the corral. "I reckon you men can't correct all your past mistakes," he said with sweeping hand gestures. "But you better think twice about the mistake you are making now. I happen to be the top hired hand at the Francis Thompson dry goods store in Bannack. Mr. Thompson is more than a boss to me; he's also a damn good friend. Among my other friends are Chief Justice Sidney Edgerton and his nephew Wilbur Sanders, who I'm sure all you gentlemen know and respect as two of the most law-abiding citizens in all the land. My most special lady friend is Lucia Darling, Bannack's much-admired single schoolteacher. What's more, her prize student and the longtime houseguest of the Edgertons is here with us today and can vouch for my good moral character. Gentlemen, allow me to introduce Woodrow R. Hart, my dear brother."

His words, though of course containing only grains of truth, did make Captain Williams and the others think twice. At least the room went silent, which suggested some thinking was going on. I don't know how many of the vigilantes believed what he was saying. Naturally Rufus wanted to live and was desperate, but still it took great strength and smarts to deliver such a speech, perhaps the longest and most eloquent one I had ever heard from him. Regardless, and as much as I wanted my brother to escape the noose, it felt like another kick to the head. Why bring Lucia Darling into this? Why bring me into this? The vigilantes were turning their heads in all directions trying to spot the "dear brother" among them. I was the opposite of invisible now. I slumped in my chair and squeezed the empty can.

"Don't be shy, Woodrow," Rufus said. "These gentlemen would love to meet you."

I suppose Rufus wasn't taking much of a chance, and in any case, he didn't have much choice. He knew I hated to lie and had tried to behave admirably all my life, whether or not parents, teachers, Washington policemen, gold country vigilantes, chief justices, or any other authority figures were around. But he also knew I didn't know beans about any misdeeds he might have committed since leaving Washington and in any case would never betray him.

Mr. Higgins pulled my chair back from the table and Mr. Worden helped me to my feet as if I were seventy-five instead of fifteen.

"Step right up here, son," commanded Captain Williams. He then addressed the other vigilantes. "We clearly can't question his alleged friends in Bannack tonight, so we will have to make the most of what we got. We'll make it a two Hart examination."

The captain directed me to stand next to my brother. With his frosty eyes, he looked us over as if comparing our heights (Rufus was a head and a half taller), our weights (Rufus was much heavier but it was all muscle), our manes (mine was deep red, of course, and Rufus's roughly yellow), and our facial hair (I had some peach fuzz on my chin; Rufus had a heavy three-day beard). He then ignored Rufus to grill me. He asked if Rufus was truly my brother. "One of them," I said. He then asked my age and where I was born. I said, "on the Fourth of July 1848 in Washington, the D.C. one" and volunteered the information that I was born near the White House and was a longtime admirer of my neighbor Abe Lincoln. He said the president wasn't in the White House when I was born and that Lincoln was born on February 12, 1809, on the Sinking Spring Farm near Hodgenville, Kentucky, as if to impress me with his knowledge. I nodded my head but didn't tell him I already knew all that, having looked up all the facts I could about Lincoln when I was seven.

Next, he stated that we were straying from the subject at hand as if it was my fault and asked me my name. I said "Woodrow R. Hart," because that's what my brother had said. He imagined my middle initial stood for Red like the nickname of Yeager. I assured him it stood for a real name, Russell, the name of a peaceful grandfather who read books and never hurt a fly in his life. That answer seemed to annoy him, and he peppered me with questions about the Edgerton and Sanders families and their homes in Bannack. I hadn't needed to lie yet, but then he asked me a challenging question: If Lucia Darling was truly my brother's special lady friend. I hesitated, but when I finally said, "Well, I reckon he thinks so anyway," it made some of the other vigilantes laugh. Captain Williams dropped that line of questioning and paced in front of Rufus and me, no doubt trying to phrase his next question just right.

"I want the absolute truth now, son," he said. "Has your brother Rufus Hart partaken, either alone or with accomplices, in any illegal activities—that is to say robberies, murders, or any other crimes, successful or not."

"You mean in the territory?" I asked innocently enough, but it drew more laughter from the vigilante crowd.

"I mean anywhere," snapped the captain.

"He once stole a knife in Washington."

"Whose knife and what did he do with it."

"It was my penknife and he used it to play mumblety-peg with his friends."

The crowd laughed, and fortunately Captain Williams didn't

question me about any other crimes Rufus might have committed in Washington. The list, even just including the ones I knew about, was long if not dreadfully serious.

"Never mind Washington, son. Since you arrived with your brother in the gold camps last fall, has your brother ever had an inordinate amount of gold in his possession?"

"Not sure what 'inordinate' means, sir, but Mr. Thompson did pay him wages at the dry goods store." When I heard additional laughter from the back of the room, I kind of soaked it in, and couldn't resist saying, "I'm sure every man here possesses fifty times more gold than my brother and me combined."

"Having so little, wouldn't your brother have wanted something more?"

"Don't all those miners want something more, sir? That's why they mine for gold."

"Don't get smart with me, son. Your brother never mined a day in his life, did he?"

"I don't know."

"And if he robbed a stagecoach or two to get gold you wouldn't know about that either, right?"

"I admit I don't know everything, sir. In fact, I don't know much, but I'm learning. I'm only fifteen, not old like you."

"Do you believe your brother is capable of stealing?"

"He stole my pocketknife. But later he carved me a little wooden horse that even had a tail and . . ."

"Never mind that. What I'm asking is if you think your brother could ever take gold that doesn't belong to him?"

"I don't know. Maybe if he found gold in Grasshopper Creek he would take it home."

"I don't mean panning for it or digging for it. I mean stealing it."

"But I already told you. Rufus doesn't have any gold."

"I've had enough of you. You obviously want to protect your

brother and maybe yourself. I suppose you'll tell me you never stole a single thing in your life?"

"Not unless you ask, sir."

"I'm asking. Go ahead and tell me you have never once in your fifteen odd years on this planet taken something that didn't belong to you. I dare you."

"Do you count half a loaf of bread from the Edgerton kitchen?"

"So, you did steal . . ." The captain cut himself off because the laughter had picked up. He looked around the room, and plenty of vigilantes had to wipe smiles off their faces. "Never mind," he said once more. "This isn't getting us anywhere."

Rufus hadn't said a word for a long time, but he had been busy. He had freed his hands from the rope. He patted me on the back and gave me a nod of appreciation for my answers on his behalf. He then stepped forward, going face to face with Captain Williams.

"You've about badgered my little brother to death," Rufus said. "Why not just take me and him out to the corral and string us up. But when Chief Justice Edgerton learns about what happened to the Hart brothers, don't expect a medal, Captain. Why, he might even call you vigilantes a bunch of murderers, if not hang you himself."

Nobody was laughing now. Captain Williams's face went crimson in a second. Both meaty hands formed fists at his sides. With the left one, he pushed Rufus in the chest. He raised the right one as if ready to strike, but Rufus beat him to the punch, and I didn't doubt my brother's mighty blow would have ended most any barroom brawl, not that I had actually seen one of those yet. The wallop to the vigilante leader's jaw flattened him. If Rufus hadn't already gone too far with his words, he surely must have done so now. Funny thing, though, none of the vigilantes moved right away to corral Rufus or to revive their leader. I was as stunned as any of them, but once Captain Williams's neck twitched, I was the first one to bend down, look into his cloudy eyes, and see if he had regained his senses.

Chapter Fourteen

"Let us continue with the examination," Captain Williams finally said after picking himself off the floor without my help, rubbing his eyes, wiggling his jaw, unsuccessfully smoothing his coarse chin whiskers, and clearing his throat four times. Groans and murmurs moved in waves through the room. The captain glared at his followers, churning his fists at his sides as if trying to regain the aura of command temporarily knocked out of him by my brother's fist. "Damn it!" he shouted. "An innocent man wouldn't act like that!" Heads lowered, eyes cast downward. Was it out of shame or embarrassment? I liked to think so, giving these vigilantes the benefit of the doubt that they possessed those human feelings. Of course, these feelings might have been triggered by the awkwardness of their passive defiance of their leader rather than by any distress caused by consciousness of his wrong and foolish examination of the Hart brothers. In any case, I suspect the examination would have indeed continued if not for the two owners of the store.

Vigilantes parted to clear a path for C.P. Higgins and Francis Worden, whose slow-but-steady walk brought them to the front counter, where they needed to say only a few words to steal Captain Williams's spotlight.

"I kick against hearing any more talk," said Mr. Higgins.

"And I kick against any more hangings in Hell Gate," said Mr. Worden.

"Red Hart—I mean Woodie Hart—has his heart in the right

place," continued Mr. Higgins. "No unkind word need be said against him. As of this moment, Woodie has a job working for Worden and Higgins as long as he wishes to remain in Hell Gate. We'll watch over this honest and true young man, and he'll watch over us so that we treat all our customers and trading partners fair and square."

I needed to grasp the countertop to keep from fainting dead away. But when I recovered from the "kind shock," I stood up a little straighter and held my chin up rather high to look out on the subdued faces of the vigilantes. More than anything, they looked exhausted.

"As for Rufus Hart," said Mr. Worden, picking up where his partner left off, "we don't know him as well as Woodie Hart, but nothing was proved against him and we admire the way he stood up for himself and his little brother. We can understand and excuse his sober and not particularly rash act of violence we just witnessed. James Williams seems to have fully recovered, everything except for a bit of his considerable pride, I imagine. I suggest those who don't live here in Hell Gate buy whatever you need in our store and move on."

Captain Williams didn't let that pass. He stepped in front of Mr. Worden and thanked him and Mr. Higgins for their earlier cooperation in allowing the vigilantes the use of their store and the corral in back before delivering a few cutting remarks: "You two are shopkeepers interested in making a profit. The men here are vigilantes interested in justice. We come and we go as we see fit to rid this territory of highwaymen, murderers, and other undesirables. I concede the young Hart is not a criminal at this stage in his life, has been a houseguest in Bannack of our esteemed friend Sidney Edgerton, and knows practically nothing about what is happening in and around our communities. I still, however, have strong doubts about the older Hart, who was at one time suspected of robbery and other criminal behavior in Virginia City and now has no known residence or means of support. I don't doubt many of the rest of you still share these same doubts."

A few of the vigilantes mumbled their agreement, but it was clear the majority was not with him, at least on this point. The captain was smart enough to realize it was not time to call for another rope.

"We'll take him with us," Captain Williams said. "In time we'll have the chance to hear about his character and activities from Sidney Edgerton, Francis Thompson, and other reputable citizens in Bannack and Virginia City. In short, we can determine his fate at a later date."

"He'll be staying here with his brother," Mr. Worden said.

"Yes, that is best," Mr. Higgins said. "He'll work for us."

"You intend to employ both Harts in your store?" Captain Williams asked. "You are more prosperous or generous than even I had thought."

"Woodie will work in the store, Rufus will run the saloon, which we've had a stake in from the beginning. We got Cyrus Skinner started here in Hell Gate. Cyrus left his controlling interest in the saloon to Worden and me, you know? We became friendly from all the times he loafed in our store, mostly sitting on our safe and patting it. He wasn't *all* bad. Anyway, Cyrus believed the saloon would be too much for Nellie to handle by herself."

Captain Williams's mouth flew open, either to make a protest or to reassert his authority in all matters of crime and public safety. But he closed his mouth just as fast and went back to pacing. Clearly, he thought best on the move, so everybody, including Mr. Higgins and Mr. Worden, waited on the captain to make his next pronouncement.

Finally, he stopped pacing and, without even glancing at the store owners or us Hart brothers, headed directly toward the front door, his followers making way for him and then following him. "We got bigger fish to catch," the captain shouted. "Should we require further dealings with Rufus Hart down the road, we know where to find him. Let's go, men, let's go hunting."

They left so fast I thought the store might be on fire. "They going fishing or hunting?" I asked.

"They're gone—nothing else matters this minute," said Rufus.

"I hope they don't want to hang anyone else?"

"They will. That's all they know. It's not trout or buffalo they're after."

"Then they'll need provisions," said Mr. Higgins, running after the vigilantes. "Come back, all you men. We got what you need. And if we don't, we'll order it."

"Don't bring them back here!" yelled Rufus, too late. "They might change their mind about me."

"I doubt they'll be back," said Mr. Worden. "That Captain Williams had fire in his eyes. Must have some other fellow in mind."

"I ain't taking no chances," Rufus said. "Let's go, little brother."

"Where to?"

"I don't know. Out the back door for starters."

"Go across the street to the saloon if you like," Mr. Worden said. "No danger. Captain Williams never allows drinking before a hard ride. Might as well make yourself at home now as later."

"You mean it's no joke—I'm really going to run Skinner's saloon?"

"Why not? Higgins and me have our hands full over here. Besides, drinking and goods don't mix so well, especially when our safe is next to the goods. But don't try changing the name to Hart's—sounds too female—or getting rid of Nellie, at least not right away. She just lost her man, and she might not be too accepting about losing the saloon, too."

"I'm good with Nellie," Rufus said, running to the back door. "It's damn good to be alive."

Rufus didn't ask me to go with him, and I must have seemed at a loss as how to proceed with my life, because Mr. Worden threw an arm around my shoulder and said: "Take your coat off and take a load off your feet, Woodie. You figure to be here awhile, and Rufus will be nearby out of harm's way. Hungry? We're all out of canned peaches right now but we've ordered more, plus we got other canned goods galore. You'll be working for the best store this side of the Bitterroots."

Mr. Worden had opened a can of pork and beans and heated it on one of the store stoves for me by the time Mr. Higgins returned. No vigilantes were with him, which suited me just fine. He said Captain Williams had found all the supplies his vigilantes needed on pack animals that had belonged to two of the hanged men—Johnnie Cooper and Aleck Carter. Apparently the two wanted men had been planning to leave Hell Gate together for safer environs when they drank too much at Skinner's saloon and Mr. Carter ended up shooting Mr. Cooper in the leg and delaying their trip. Well, the pair had no need for the supplies now.

"Nothing to do but get some shuteye," said Mr. Worden, a single man who usually bedded down in the back of the store, not too far from the safe.

"That sounds good," I said. "I mean I had a room at the Edgerton house in Bannack, but I can sleep most anywhere where there is a roof over my head."

But Mr. Higgins insisted that I leave the pork and beans for Mr. Worden to eat and I come with him. He took me down the street past the saloon where, as I saw through the lighted window, Rufus and Nellie were clinking glasses. He showed me into his log home, the largest in town. It smelled wonderful inside because Juliet Grant Higgins, who he had married less than a year ago, was boiling a turkey with oyster sauce. She boiled it to perfection. She told me the oysters she used were from the Chesapeake Bay and canned in Baltimore, not far from my hometown of Washington. "I heard tell oysters are good as gold in that neck of the woods," she told me. "You betcha, ma'am," I said, though that was news to me. I had certainly eaten well at the Edgerton house, with Mary Edgerton and Lucia Darling doing the cooking, but never anything like this. And back in Washington, President Abe Lincoln might have eaten that well at the White House, but at my house two blocks away, I was lucky to get a bowl of watery potato soup if my brothers hadn't slurped it all up ahead of me.

After dinner, I was full and content and helped Juliet wash the dishes while C.P., as she called her husband, smoked a pipe in the next room. I recalled, with a certain longing, washing and drying dishes for Lucia, but then became bothered by the smoke—more specifically by the fact that Mr. Higgins could calmly sit there with a pipe in his mouth despite having recently witnessed Johnnie Cooper smoking a pipe as a last request. I dropped a plate of oyster shells. The plate broke and I cut my finger twice on the shells. She insisted I must be tired after a long day of "unfortunate unpleasantries," and after bandaging my wounds and all but kissing my hand, she said it was time for bed. I thought she would show me to one of the rooms in their substantial home. Instead, C.P. Higgins led me to the employee bunkhouse next door, where an old man in charge of Worden and Higgins's hogs and horses showed me to an unoccupied lower bunk. Two other men were already snoring nearby. Soon I was doing the same, but twice in the next few hours I woke up screaming. The first time I was dreaming that Captain Williams was in Washington handing out a death sentence not only to Rufus but also to my other seven brothers, even the one who had drowned and the one who was missing. The second time I was dreaming of bodies hanging from nooses tied to the posts of ten bunk beds. I was walking along examining each head in a noose and was relieved to see each one belonged to an unknown Confederate soldier—that is until the last one, which had a mop of blood red hair, blinking green eyes, and a tongue tied in a double knot behind quivering blistered lips.

My last screams woke up the old man as well as the other two employees in the bunkhouse. The three of them were bent over my bunk looking at me like I had seen a ghost or was one.

"You was having a nightmare," said the old man, whose own head was so skull-like I thought I was still dreaming.

"I know you?" I asked.

"I put you to bed, boy. Name is Y Callaway. You can call me Y."

"Why?"

" 'Cause that's what my dear mother named me the day I was born, which happened to be the very day Daddy Callaway run off to sail the seven seas." He chuckled for a spell and then, when the other two employees began laughing, the old man started stamping his foot and slapping his knee as if he was at a square dance. I couldn't help but join them in their surprising early-morning revelry and forget all about my bad dreams.

January 26 was a quiet day in Hell Gate. Y Callaway fixed bacon and biscuits for me and the other two employees, both of whom attended Mr. Worden's garden in warmer weather but whose main duties were cutting wood and ice this time of year. Afterward Mr. Callaway took me to the hog pen to introduce me to his "pig family" and then to the Worden and Higgins store, where Mr. Higgins was explaining to an Indian man why there were white men hanging at the corral. The Indian could speak good English. He was a Kootenai who lived and farmed on the Flathead Indian Reservation at St. Ignatius Mission, founded by Father Pierre-Jean De Smet a decade earlier. He now called himself Jean-Pierre as a tribute to his mentor, and he thought the hangings were highly unchristian. I nodded, and said they seemed unfair all right. He asked me if I was a Roman Catholic. I said I wasn't any kind of Catholic and had been raised without religion in Washington, D.C.

"You don't say," said Jean-Pierre, rubbing a surprisingly round belly. "You're in luck. Thanks to the Jesuits I am an educated, baptized savage who tries to bring the blessings of Christianity to those unfortunate poor white settlers whose ramshackle homes and primitive mode of living have made them unrighteous and unjust and kept them in the dark about the power of the Holy Ghost."

He had me scratching my head. Jean-Pierre was a far cry from the Bannock Indians who begged at the Edgerton house in Bannack. For one thing he spoke better English than me. For another, he looked extremely well fed.

"He makes me laugh," said Mr. Higgins. "I don't have anything against any man who puts God ahead of business as long as he doesn't take himself too seriously. I needed a good laugh this morning."

"We all do," said Mr. Worden. "I know they left, but I was hearing vigilante horses all night. Must have been a bad dream."

"No, my friend, they were around," said Jean-Pierre. "Outside of Hell Gate, my young son and I met on the Mullan Road in friendship with white men from Walla Walla packing goods to Fort Benton. Captain Williams and his posse caught up. They wanted the lead packer, name of Tom Reilly, who had been seen in bad company. They accused this Reilly of some misdemeanor on the west side of the mountains and gave him the sentence of death. I think our violent captain was born with a noose in his hand."

"Not another necktie party," said Mr. Worden, throwing his hands in the air.

"Not this time. I told the captain that even if he believes in an eye for an eye, Mr. Reilly has *not* shot anyone's eye out, deserves the benefit of the doubt, and in any case will have to answer to the Lord on Judgment Day."

"And he listened to you?"

"Hell, no, if you'll pardon my English. I'm a savage who can't possibly know right from wrong. The captain judged me a meddler, and his possemen knocked me to the ground with their fists and rifle butts. As they were so occupied, it allowed Reilly's men to rescue their leader and flee back toward the west. I expected the posse to stamp on my red face and perhaps hang me by my red toes, but instead they chased after the Walla Walla men. What happened, I cannot say. But I heard no shooting and assume Reilly has survived to pack again."

"You seem none the worse for it?" said Wiggins.

"I had God on my side. And blood doesn't show so well on my red flesh."

"But where's your young son?" I asked. "What happened to him?"

He had no need to reply. The boy, perhaps five or six, answered with action. From behind the shelves he came, wearing a mountain goat robe like his father, screeching like a bobcat, and swinging a long stick to keep two tin cans rolling along in front of him.

"See here, boy," said Mr. Higgins. "That's no way to treat the goods we're trying to sell."

One of the cans rolled to a stop against Mr. Higgins's bootheel, and the boy, accidentally or not, cracked his stick in half against the store owner's ankle. When Mr. Worden tried to pick up that same can, the boy kicked him in the shin with one of his elk-skin moccasins and then the other. Mr. Worden looked as if he was about to kick back, but Mr. Higgins scooped the boy off the ground and twirled him around in the air by his stubby arms. Once finally set down on his feet, the dizzy and angry boy went on the attack but promptly tipped over and landed on his back. For some reason, perhaps because I never had a little brother to play with, I used half a stick to strike the second can. It rolled ten feet, straight at him, and he lifted his legs so it could pass under and hit him in the rump. He laughed and stood up.

"Open, *titkat,*" the boy said, handing the can to Mr. Worden.

"*Titkat* means man," said his father. "All he really needs is a little *wóo.* That means water."

"That's all right," said Mr. Worden. "The little scalawag wants soup in the morning, I'll give him soup in the morning."

Mr. Worden left with both cans to prepare the soup. Mr. Higgins backed away when the boy came charging toward him, but the boy only wanted to fetch the other half of the stick.

"Woodie, meet La La See, my only son," said Jean-Pierre.

"That's his name?" I said. "I mean no offense, but . . ."

"When he was baptized in Wild Horse Creek, he pointed to the earth bank and said *La La.* The priest said the child was saying 'land land' because he didn't like getting wet."

"I see," I said.

I extended my hand to La La See, but he extended his half stick. I took the challenge, raising my own half stick, and we fenced like a couple of the Musketeers. Jean-Pierre asked his son not to hurt his new friend, me, and then went about his business with Mr. Higgins and Mr. Worden. He traded red ochre his people had collected far to the north and several buffalo robes for bags of salt and flour. No coin or gold was involved in the transaction.

"What the Lord doesn't provide, Worden and Higgins do," Jean-Pierre said to me. "La La See seems to like you, Woodie. You are his first pale-faced friend."

"I'm glad," I said. "He's my first . . . you know, Indian . . . friend."

Jean-Pierre intended to start back for St. Ignatius Mission at noon, but he changed his mind. Instead, he wanted to take La La See and me fishing. I said I couldn't because it was my first day on the job at the store, but Mr. Worden excused me. Jean-Pierre led us five miles down the Clark's Fork River to Rattlesnake Creek (not to be confused with the one east of Bannack), where we fished till dusk. On the way back we traded two freshly caught cutthroat trout for a ride with one of the packtrains using the Mullan Road. A mile short of Hell Gate, though, we were set afoot because La La See had poked our driver in the eye with his fishing pole, and the driver had responded with an expletive-filled tirade about redskins, damn Christians or not. It was Jean-Pierre's decision to walk the final stretch to town.

"Didn't want La La See to hear that man call us one more bad name," Jean-Pierre said. "I've always tried to teach the boy that the palefaces might lack color but are just like the Kootenai—all God's children. I was also a little worried the man might believe in an eye for an eye, if you know what I mean."

Even La La See was worn out by the time we reached the Worden and Higgins store. He handed me his fishing pole, climbed onto one of the empty shelves, and curled up to sleep. Jean-Pierre said he best sleep on the buffalo robes he brought because the boy often dreamed he was being chased by wolves and woke up screaming. I said I was well acquainted with nightmares and volunteered to stay there and let him use my bunk in the company bunkhouse, but he said savages did *not* use beds. I thought he was probably trying to be funny, but I couldn't bring myself to laugh.

When I finally got to the bunkhouse, I had less reason to laugh. Another employee, a freighter, was there, just finishing up telling Y Callaway and the two others a dramatic and tragic bedtime story. He was ready to repeat it for my benefit, in fact insisted on it even though I told him it was late and I was bone tired. "Your ears ain't," the man said. "Anyway, you're going to want to hear this."

The story was actually fresh news. The dramatic event had occurred that very day in the Bitterroot Valley at Fort Owen, a popular trading post run by John Owen and his Shoshone wife. Whiskey Bill Graves had come there to rest and recover from snow blindness. When three vigilantes showed up, he couldn't make out their faces, but he could feel the cold steel of their six-shooters pressed against his chest and belly. They had not come to rest or to trade. They had come for him. The long-standing charge was suspected stagecoach robbery—the coach being the one Rufus and I took from Virginia City to Bannack the previous November. His alleged fellow robbers had already had their necktie parties, George Ives in December in Virginia City, Bob Zachary the previous day in Hell Gate. Whiskey Graves didn't confess to robbing the stage or any other crime but that was of no matter to the three vigorous vigilantes.

My ears were wide awake even if the rest of me felt dead or dying. "They hanged him right there, didn't they?" I muttered.

"Not quite right there," the freighter said.

He let me think about it awhile, but when I didn't ask another question he continued.

"They took him down the trail on a horse and hung him from a tree."

"Oh."

"Not that John Owen would have objected to the hanging happening at his fort, but his Injun wife thought the practice barbaric and would not allow it to happen in her presence. Then there were all the peaceful Flatheads camped as usual near the fort. They're real sensitive to rope burns and such, you know. They would have run away screaming their heads off at the horror of a hanging. A red man would rather be shot full of arrows, filled with lead, scalped, sliced into little pieces, and burned to ashes than have someone stick a noose around his neck."

"Oh," was all I could manage again. I'd only seen Whiskey Bill Graves once behind a mask, if it was indeed him, but the news of his hanging, on top of the quartet the day before, was like getting scalped after being clubbed four times in the head—or so I imagined in my state of exhaustion and stupefaction.

"The three vigilantes was in a rush to tell Captain Williams and others about their good deed. They didn't bother to bury Graves. End of story. Time to find my sack. Good night all."

"Twenty-one," blurted out Y Callaway. "House wins."

"Say what, Y?" the freighter said. "You gambling again in your head, old man?"

"Whiskey Bill makes twenty-one. That be the number of men the vigilantes have hanged in just better than three weeks. That's not counting George Ives, who was strung up before the Vigilance Committee formed in order to justify such final actions. Red Yeager was the first on January 4 and Graves got his today, the 26th."

"I didn't know you was keeping count, Y."

"A man gets tired of counting only hogs . . . and sheep. I'm turning in, too."

"Game over, huh?"

"That'll be the day. I'd say the vigilantes are still dealing."

I followed the lead of the others and went to my bunk. I usually slept on my side but became too aware of my heart pounding as if it intended to break out through my ribs. I settled on my back with my eyes wide open. At some point I finally fell asleep, but not for long. I was dreaming the same dreams as that wild Kootenai boy in the store. I woke up screaming. The pursuing ravenous wolves had just about caught up to me.

Chapter Fifteen

So how did W.A. Phillips handle this gruesome chapter in the life of my far-fetched fictional self, Red Ranger? *Outrageously* comes to mind first, quickly followed by *inconsistently* and then *libelously*. Not that I ever considered suing the woolly chaps off him or anything like that. For one thing, this scribbler of subterfuge revealed his hero's real name as "W. 'Red' Hart" and not many readers could tie that name to me. For another, he dedicated the book "To Dearest Laura, the shining light of my existence," instead of using the real name of my sister, Lucy Hart. I suspect Lucy's politically powerful ex-husband, William Penn Norton, had threatened legal and/or physical action if W.A. intimated having had a relationship with Lucy. In any case, I've never had any use for lawyers, though I suppose they don't look as bad as vigilantes to criminal types.

In *Man from Montana: How He Escaped the Noose,* as I previously mentioned, W.A. has Plummer escaping the vigilantes with the help of Red Ranger to hunt buffalo on the Plains and then serve with Wyatt Earp in Dodge City and later Tombstone (where Plummer, as the "fifth" man, fights alongside the three Earp brothers and Doc Holliday against the Clanton and McLaury brothers in the middle of the O.K. Corral). In the book the reformed Plummer "never once thinks twice about his old appalling pals back in Bannack and Virginia City," which makes some sense since in reality Plummer was dead. Red Ranger, though, knows that there is more heroic work to be done in Montana Territory (yes, still actually Idaho Territory). He saves from the gallows ten "largely innocent" men—Cyrus Skinner, young Johnnie Cooper and Whiskey Bill Graves included—and they all have a drinking contest afterward in Skinner's Hell Gate saloon, with Red Ranger emerging as the victor since he "can hold his liquor better than any man, good or evil, who bellies up to a bar for a glass or twenty of tarantula juice."

Despite Red Ranger's well-executed, last-minute salvations, W.A. Phillips's vigilantes are far more productive than their real-life counterparts. Instead of hanging *just* twenty-one men in January, they manage to execute two men a day for a record monthly total of sixty-two. "Damn glad we didn't wait until the undersized month of February to get the show on the road," the monstrous Mr. X tells his fellow vigilantes. All sixty-two "vigilante-inflicted fatalities," are men, since, as gallant Red Ranger tells one hurdy-gurdy girl, "I wouldn't permit any man to string up a member of the fairer sex no matter how manly she looks or how many hombres the she-devil mighta done in." Seventeen of the men hanged are half-breeds or full-blooded Indians, whether Bannock or otherwise is left unsaid. "The only good red fiend is a red fiend hung until he is *dead, dead, dead,*" Mr. X tells his disciples, who are, as the not-so-witty Phillips puts it, "hanging on his every word." W.A. then has Mr. X make a two-page speech, but the gist of his (rather *their*) opinion of Indians comes in the first paragraph: "We can't have them savages running wildly amok, killing and scalping our civilized citizens, and we don't have the time or the inclination to build all the jailhouses needed to contain those hordes. Hanging, therefore, is the best solution. It teaches the heathens hard lessons they all need to learn and is not without its good effect upon the neighboring tribes."

In the book, Red Ranger learns that one William Hunter,

wanted by the vigilantes, is sick and holed up in a cabin in the Gallatin Valley. Phillips's hero "hunts for Hunter" to determine if the man deserves hanging or salvation. But he is delayed when a party of "extra wild savages" steals his horse. Red Ranger is forced to run the rest of the way through ten-foot snowdrifts, erupting geysers, boiling mud pots, and "enormous *horribilis* bears awakened from hibernation by stampeding gold miners." Phillips adds that "No man or beast had ever run faster through beautiful but obstacle-filled Yellowstone National Park except perhaps speedy mountain man John Colter in 1807." Alas, Red Ranger has expended all that energy running through the park (which, by the way, wasn't officially born until 1872) for naught. He finds Hunter dangling from a tree limb and no vigilantes in sight.

Red Ranger lets out a heroic sigh and makes a speech to a great horned owl perched on a higher branch of the hanging tree: "It's over now, wise old Mr. Owl. Hunter was the last of Henry Plummer's band, though Henry is alive and well as a new man with an honest occupation—shooting great buffalo on the Great Plains. How many members of his band truly deserved their fate? Most were unsavory ruffs and thieves, I'm sure, but were they all cold-blooded rascals who killed for gold instead of for food like you do, Mr. Owl? I think not. Yet, it is not for me to judge the outlaws, though I did my best to save the best of them. And to achieve balance, I shall not judge the vigilantes either. They can't all be as vengeful and unforgiving as Mr. X. Perhaps good will come from this wave of deadly territorial activity. With the grisly work completed, all the white men, fair women, and growing children in our growing settlements can not only behave themselves but also display high morals and good manners to such an extent that the Vigilance Committee need not rise again or cause others to rise again at the end of a hangman's knot. If this should be the new order of the gold camps, so be it. And I, Red Ranger, shall happily run, or ride if I can obtain another mount, to a more backward territory where I can answer the cry for justice the same way you, Mr. Owl, answer the distant hoot of another owl of your type!"

But enough about that poor excuse of a book, that worthless dime novel, that incompetent compendium, that trash! I can tell you there really was an alleged bad man named William Hunter. And he really was hanged in the Gallatin Valley on February 3, 1864, eight days after Whiskey Bill Graves. What's more, when Y Callaway heard the news he retired early to the bunkhouse and did some refiguring. He emerged many hours later and hurried over to the saloon, though he was not a drinking man. It was close to midnight before he returned to the bunkhouse, still sober and full of apologies. He admitted he had miscounted the vigilante victims by including Rufus Hart on his list, when in fact Rufus Hart was alive and more than well tending bar in the saloon of the late Cyrus Skinner with the assistance of Cyrus's widow. So, Mr. Graves was only No. 20 while Mr. Hunter was the real No. 21. I asked Y Callaway why it mattered, and he acted all together annoyed, saying he just wanted to get the number right so he could correct his list. I told him I could have told him my brother was alive, but that made the old man wrathy.

"You're too young to comprehend," Y told me. "Getting the list right happens to be more important than anything I ever done in my life. In two hundred years, people aren't going to care a lick about how many hogs I butchered. They're going to look at my list and nod their heads in appreciation. They're going to say: 'God almighty! They sure were a bloodthirsty lot in them days—the hanged no doubt but more so the ones who done the hanging. We can thank Mr. Y Callaway for providing this highly legible and comprehensive list. This gentleman must have been one of the few sane, intelligent, and forward-thinking men amongst them.' Now you go to your bunk, Woodrow Hart, and ponder on it. If we don't get history right, what do we have to show for our existence? Nothing, I tell you. Not a damned thing."

"Whatever you say, Y," I told him, even though it sure sounded as if he had done at least some drinking to go along with his thinking when he visited my brother's saloon. "Sleep well, you hear."

I didn't sleep well myself. That is to say, I hardly slept a wink. I kept thinking about Y Callaway's corrected list. I asked myself, "Did that really make anything better?" I decided it did a little. I didn't want people two hundred years from now to think the vigilantes had eliminated my brother in their usual fashion. At the same time having a correct list didn't help anyone on the list. The names belonged to actual human beings, most with families somewhere. And their real deaths had been painful—to varying degrees, depending on how well the hanging was executed. Even as I thought such thoughts, a voice inside me kept saying, "In two hundred years nobody living today will even be alive, so why in the hell does any of this dying and thinking about dying matter!" By that time, I had been sweeping the floor, stocking the shelves, and helping to unload the freight wagons at the Worden and Higgins store for better than two weeks. I dragged my exhausted body and mind through my work the next morning.

"We working you too hard, Woodie?" Mr. Worden asked.

"Haven't taken to the bottle, have you, Woodie?" Mr. Higgins asked.

I assured my two bosses that I was a hard worker and that they weren't working me too hard; in fact, I could handle more work if they wanted to give it to me. I also assured them that no whiskey had passed through my lips and that I hadn't even gone to visit my brother in the saloon during my second week in Hell Gate.

"Blood is thicker than whiskey," Mr. Higgins said. "Why not pay your respects to Rufus. He's doing a fine job running the saloon in the absence of Cyrus."

Permanent absence, I thought. And my brother seemed to be doing a fine job with the widow Nellie as well. Twice I had gone into the saloon the first week to say howdy. Once Rufus had said that a nonpaying, nondrinking boy like me was bad for business. The second time he was too busy to see me, even though the only other living soul in the saloon at the time was Nellie; they were doing more than talking, I could see that much. I didn't say any of this to my bosses. I just smiled and returned to my sweeping to show what a hard worker I was. At least Rufus seemed to be staying out of trouble. I was glad about that. He had always liked being in charge of things, but there never had been much he could be in charge of until the saloon job opened up. Serving up whiskey to others and himself must have been his ideal job, and he apparently functioned better in his cups than our father had back in Washington. As for his relationship with Nellie, well, Cyrus Skinner wasn't in any position to object, and I didn't care to think about it too much.

"Go ahead now," said Mr. Higgins. "The regulars don't get there this early. Take as long as you need with your brother. We can manage without you for a while."

"I'm good," I said. "Rufus hasn't much been in a talking mood lately. He doesn't need to bother about his little brother."

"What our young friend needs is a little trip," said Mr. Higgins.

"Right you are, Higgins," said Mr. Worden, who snatched the broom from me and put an arm around my shoulders. "Bannack or Virginia City? What's your choice?"

"You don't like my work? You want to get rid of me?"

"Just the opposite, Woodie," said Mr. Higgins. "We want to

keep you. A little trip will do you good. We know at this point in time, Hell Gate doesn't have much to offer a teetotaler with no mother figure or female companion in the picture."

"Notice how Higgins looks at me when he says those words," said Mr. Worden, his arm growing heavier. "We'll have wagons going both places soon. So, what is it, my boy, Bannack or Virginia?"

Mr. Worden released me and went off with the broom so I could go to the stove and think without any pressure. In Bannack, I could pay my respects to the Edgertons and my old boss, Francis Thompson, and of course lay my eyes on Lucia Darling again. I hadn't been thinking about her all that much, what with multiple hangings, a new home, and a new job taking up most of my thinking time. Not that any woman had taken Lucia's place in my head. The only females I had seen lately were Mr. Higgins's wife and Rufus's whatever. Neither compared with Lucia. Was there any woman in the whole territory who could compare? And to think I used to live in the same house as her.

"Virginia City," I announced with a loudness that even surprised me. "I could go there for a while and then come back and work harder than ever, if that's all right."

"Excellent choice," said Mr. Higgins. "Our man Hank will be leaving tomorrow to bring goods to several merchants there. We get so much traffic passing by the store, we can charge lower prices than they do in Fort Benton, Lewiston, or Salt Lake City. And our transportation costs to Virginia City are negligible. You can ride in the wagon with Hank but tie your horse to the back so you can stay a few extra days to take in the sights. All expenses paid."

I hung my head because I felt ashamed that my two bosses were so good to me, especially when I was thinking about a certain bordello on Wallace Street that Rufus had mentioned a time or two. That's right. I figured that my chances with Lucia Darling in Bannack were about the same as me getting hit by lightning in the middle of winter. Soiled doves of all sizes and shapes were fluttering inside my head. Nobody knew me in Virginia City, either. I'd be freer there, and I sure wanted to become a man before I turned sixteen in July.

"He's all choked up about it," said Mr. Worden, happily twirling the broom over his head with one hand. "Go ahead now to the saloon, Woodie. See if your brother wants to make the trip with you to Virginia City. I'd say both Hart brothers are deserving of some leisure time in the big city. What say you, Higgins?"

"I surely do say the same," said Mr. Higgins. "Y Callaway can help Nellie run the saloon for a few days while Rufus is away. We know old Y won't be drinking up the profits."

"I don't think my brother would want to leave now. He and Nellie . . ."

"What the heck," said Mr. Higgins. "Take Nellie along, too. Business is good now that the temperatures have moderated some. We're feeling generous, aren't we, Worden?"

"As generous as Mr. Lincoln the day he freed the slaves, Higgins," said Worden. He then danced with the broom right up to the stove, pointed the broom at the front door, swatted me on the backside with the broom, and commanded, "Git to the saloon, boy, time's a-wastin'!"

I couldn't very well object to the generosity of my two bosses, so I bundled up and marched across the street as if I was just following orders. Once inside the saloon I didn't see anyone, but I heard Rufus and Nellie making lovey-dovey sounds somewhere out of sight. To kill time, I weaved around the tables pretending to be soused and feeling no pain. I wasn't about to call out and be a bother, and I was feeling some pain. Finally, I decided they were taking too long, and, being a working man, I rushed to the door. But a woman's voice called out to me.

"What you doing, little Hart," she said, stepping out from behind the bar, buttoning up things in no particular hurry. "You coming or going?"

"How long you been there spying on us?" Rufus said, popping up like a weasel.

"I wasn't spying. I was . . ."

"I know you wasn't looking for no drink. What you want?"

I came right out with it to get it over with. "I'm accompanying Hank tomorrow on his run to Virginia City. You want to come or not?"

I suddenly remembered how Rufus had run into trouble in Virginia City the previous month. He hadn't been on Red Yeager's list but had gotten himself on some other "men to hang" list. He had somehow escaped, something to do with donning women's clothing. I couldn't recall the details; the multiple hangings since then were running together in my head and clouding up all my January memories.

To my surprise, Rufus didn't hesitate one second. He wanted to come along, no questions asked. But Nellie asked how we were able to leave work, when would we be leaving, why exactly we were leaving, and what would we do while we were away. Rufus called her a real nag, but I tried to answer her questions. First off it was the bosses' idea. Rufus liked the part about how going there was only kind of like work in that we would be helping Hank, and that after we got there, we'd have a few days to "kick up our bootheels and raise a little Cain."

"For crying out loud," Nellie said. "You run a saloon. You can kick up a storm right here. And anyway, Cain raised up and slew Abel. They were brothers you know."

Rufus and I knew that much. He turned his head askance, looking at her and then me. "If I was going to kill Woodie," he said, "I would have done it long before this."

"You tired of me already, Ruf? You wasn't pawing me back

there like you was."

Rufus grimaced but then grinned. "It ain't till tomorrow. Tonight, I'll show you how *untired* I be."

"You know gals in Virginia City, do you?"

Rufus kept grinning without answering. I could tell he was doing some thinking on the subject, probably about the runaway wife Varina and then maybe her vindictive husband Mr. Willingham because the grin suddenly vanished. After a while, he frowned and bit his lip. No doubt he was thinking on those vigilantes who, inspired by the harsh words of the same Mr. Willingham, had seen fit to put him on their death list. "I don't have to go," he said, tapping his Adam's apple.

"You want to go, I know."

"Look, no gal means anything to me there. I won't go."

"I want you to go," she said, pushing his shoulder.

"What made you pass that remark? You can't be tired of me."

"We'll miss each other a few days. It's not the end of the world."

They stared at one another, not quite knowing how to proceed with their conversation.

"You can come with Hank and us, Mrs. Skinner . . . eh, Nellie," I said. "Mr. Higgins said so." I selfishly wanted Rufus to come along but didn't necessarily want her to come, too; she occupied too much of my brother's time. But I wasn't going to keep that bit of information from them.

"Somebody has to stay here and run the saloon," Nellie said. "I'm not going to turn over the job to Y or one of the other Worden and Higgins men."

"It's settled then. Neither of us will go tomorrow."

"You don't think I can run the saloon myself? Cy wasn't always around you know, and the regulars kept buying drinks."

"It ain't that. I got me an enemy or two in Virginia City."

"If the damned vigilantes didn't hang you in Hell Gate, they won't hang you down there. Go, goddamnit—'less you're too fearful."

That struck a nerve with Rufus. He turned his back on her to hide a sneer.

"Come back in the morning," he said to me. "I'll be champing on the bit to go. Now git. I got a saloon to run."

"Right," I said, but I started to seriously worry about what Mr. Willingham or the vigilantes might do to Rufus in Virginia City. "Should I tell Hank you'll both be going?"

"Haven't you been listening, boy," Nellie said. "I'm staying."

I nodded and left. As I walked out, the first customer of the afternoon walked in, a Mullan Road traveler who looked thirsty enough to help business.

Chapter Sixteen

Hank said little, and when he did open his mouth it was usually to lambast the four mules pulling the freight wagon. He didn't like to be crowded, so only one of us Hart brothers sat next to him at a time. The other would ride alongside the wagon—either Rufus on the big black horse or me on my Indian pony—when the trail allowed, mostly chatting about what lay ahead. Rufus planned to get a haircut, shave, and a bath, then walk down Wallace Street viewing the sights, including the promenading girls of easy virtue, before settling into a night of drinking with old friends and dancing and romancing with the hurdy-gurdy gals. I said it sounded right fine, which made him laugh. He said I probably wouldn't need a shave until I was eighteen, might have a beer and a half at most in one night, and would be too shy to ask for a single dance, even if I could pay for it. I told him I might not settle for a beer and a dance. He laughed at that, too. I took no offense. Coming from my mouth, it must have seemed like a big joke. It felt good to be traveling along with Rufus again and sitting Togu some of the time, though my pony seemed skittish around the bulky wagon.

We unloaded the wagon at three places in Virginia City—a mercantile, a saloon, and the Pfouts and Russell dry goods store on Wallace Street. Paris Pfouts was the president of the Vigilance Committee, and Rufus refused to go inside his store. Hank, who was all business, moved on to a hotel he knew in Nevada City, leaving Rufus and me and our horses behind with not more than a grunt for goodbye.

"Ain't it a joy to see all these people again," Rufus commented as he watched a woman with an exaggerated wiggle pass by, escorted on each side by a strutting man. "In Hell Gate you keep seeing the same faces over and over."

"Like Nellie Skinner?"

"I already forgot about her. A fellow can see new faces here every day, almost as many new faces as you'd see in Washington."

I hadn't heard him mention our hometown but once or twice since we arrived in the territory. But now wasn't the time for him to get homesick or careless.

"I'm worried that the wrong kind of person will see your *old* face here and . . ."

"You mean like Pfouts? I ain't worried. Captain Williams didn't hang me in Hell Gate and he's a far greater bastard than Pfouts."

"Mr. Pfouts is the president of the vigilantes. And I noticed you didn't go inside his store."

"Just being cautious, like you want me to be, little brother worrier. I doubt he would even recognize my face."

"What about your name? You told me you were . . . you know, on that one list, right?"

"He didn't make the list himself, maybe never even saw it. But no reason to tell him our names, is there, bub? Let's forget those damn vigilantes. How 'bout it? We're just two law-abiding visitors who've come to see the sights in the big city."

We soon witnessed two violations of the law that made us think we had come to the wrong place. First, right at the hitching post in front of Pfouts's place, two unarmed fellows only a few years older than me were arguing about something downright silly—whether a person suffered more pain freezing to death or burning to death. They seemed reluctant to get physical, but they got to cursing up a storm, each trying to top the other one with colorful insults. Rufus found it amusing and interjected that hanging to death was the most painful way to go.

The young men stopped for a moment to stare at Rufus and then one of them said: "How the hell would you know? You ain't nobody."

"Could be I'm a vigilante."

"You ain't. I know all . . ." The one young man stopped talking when the other one signaled him to button his lip. They gave my brother a closer look.

After a while Rufus grinned. "You're right. I ain't."

They backed away from the hitching post to what they thought was a safe distance and started cursing Rufus. My brother didn't do a thing, but the pair backed right into some kind of badge wearer who clearly knew them. "No warning this time," the badge wearer said. "That'll cost you where it hurts most. Empty your pockets."

The badge wearer was no holdup man in disguise. He was fining the two young men—for cursing.

"Damn," said Rufus, heading up Wallace Street, with me at his heels. "What kind of madness is that." He suddenly had a bright idea and took Van Buren Street to Cover Street and over a few blocks to the Gilbert Brewery. "We'll have a few beers to warm up before we go get sheared, little brother," he said. "Gilbert beer is the best in town."

"I'm . . . eh . . . not ready for that," I admitted. "I thought it was a haircut, a shave, and a bath first."

"The list wasn't writ in stone. Look, the Gilberts got a home right next to their brewery and there are more than a half dozen little Gilberts running around. While I'm drinking, I'm sure you can find someone to play with."

Rufus couldn't rile me. I had been hearing such insults from him my whole life. But he didn't get his beer. Outside the brewery we saw a man emptying a crate of broke bottles into a snow pile on the corner of Cover and Hamilton Streets. Rufus was about to hail the man when a second badge wearer appeared. "Got you again, Sam," the badge wearer said, reaching down to carefully pick up a particularly lethal-looking piece of sharp glass. "That'll cost you. Second offense."

Rufus changed his mind about *not* following the order of his things-to-do list, and he forgot about the beer for the moment to lead me to the tonsorial parlor. The bald barber had nothing to say about Rufus's shaggy and dirty yellow hair, but he went on and on about my red locks. As he trimmed them, he said he would save some of my fine hair but didn't elaborate. He switched to another topic—those strange badge wearers. They were new deputies, hired to help maintain the new public order in Virginia City.

"Whose order?" Rufus asked.

"There was a miners' meeting two Sundays back," the barber said. "They voted on some laws to keep things more civilized. It is now against the law to discharge a firearm within city limits, to litter the streets, to curse in the open air, and to frequent houses of ill repute."

That last one got to me. I didn't own a gun, didn't litter, and cursed infrequently under my breath. I didn't frequent houses of ill repute, either, but I was wondering if it was against the law to visit one of those places one time. I didn't dare ask, of course.

"All hanging offenses," Rufus said, straight-faced, but I'm sure he must have been kidding.

"Fines, fines, fines, nothing but fines."

"And that's fine with the vigilantes?"

"We have a people's court with Judge Alexander Davis presiding. Our vigilantes have done their job, quite efficiently I might add. But that's done with. They have dispatched the truly evil men. William Hunter, No. 21, was the last hanging on February 3, and that was up in the Gallatin Valley. We haven't had a hanging in Virginia City since January 14. We are becoming more moral. We are learning to behave."

"Thanks to those persistent badge wearers."

"They are only temporary, I'm sure. People will be enforcing themselves before you can say Jack Robinson. It's all about morals and manners now."

"That's a hell of a note, barber man. Has anyone broken the news to James Williams or X Biedler? They don't have morals or manners, as far as I'm concerned. They are rulers of the mob."

The barber said nothing. He made a few snips behind my back and then began collecting the red strands to save on a tin plate. It was hard to tell if he was a friend of the vigilantes or not. Maybe he thought them a necessary evil. I wasn't going to ask questions, and I hoped Rufus wouldn't state any more of his opinions on the subject. Even if the hangings were finished, saying bad things about the vigilantes might be a violation of the new code. Nothing came cheap in the Virginia City establishments. Us Hart brothers had no gold and probably not enough money to cover the fines if we also wanted to drink and eat and sleep with roofs over our heads.

"Give me a damn shave, barber man," Rufus said as he replaced me in the chair. "My little brother don't need one."

"He will. Give him some time. Bet it will be a fine red beard—that of a Viking."

I liked the barber. He was a knowledgeable man. But I still couldn't bring myself to ask him about the legality of a one-time bordello visitation. Those two badge wearers weren't much, but they still had me on edge and fearful.

The barber lathered up Rufus's face before addressing him again: "I can count my blessings for one thing, mister. No matter what the local law does or doesn't do, there will still be plenty of men around who need a shave and a haircut."

"As long as we don't all go bald as a musket ball like you."

The barber chuckled. "Stop by again in a month," he said. "I may be wearing a red wig next time."

"Not likely we'll be back, barber man. I'm a businessman, too. I got me a saloon up in Hell Gate, where cursing is every man's goddamn right."

"Fine, fine. Good luck with that. Enjoy your stay in our fair city. You boys behave yourselves, hear?"

I did my part. We returned to the Gilbert Brewery, and I had my one beer for the night. Rufus had two and then moved on to the saloons. We went our separate ways shortly after he met up with someone far more interesting than a kid brother—a living legend by the name of Jack Slade. He'd made his reputation out of the territory as a no-nonsense stage driver, superintendent, and division chief for the Overland Stage. Four years earlier he killed a man who done him wrong and cut off the man's ears, which he still wore on his watch chain. I caught a glimpse of the rotting appendages and got a strong whiff of them before I slipped away unnoticed. On my own and without asking directions, I discovered two of those houses of ill repute. I walked between them several times and spent considerable time at each—that is to say outside the establishments, watching from various hiding places as the lights in the windows went on and off for reasons I could only imagine. When I saw what I think was a badge wearer coming in my direction, I retired with the two horses to a livery. Sleeping with the horses wouldn't bring an extra charge and by not taking a room at one of the boardinghouses, I could save money for better use. Yes, I was bound and determined to actually enter a bordello, moral code or not, the next night. Anyway, a man could do worse than sleeping next to a fine pony like Togu.

I have no idea where Rufus slept that night or whether he slept at all. I wasn't going to travel from saloon to saloon searching for him, but I did keep my eye out for him in the morning as I toured the town with clear, wide-open eyes. I saw only a slight amount of litter. A bakery interested me most. To keep me going but not waste money I bought a half loaf of nut bread to serve as both breakfast and the noonday meal. I bit into it as I walked. I stopped in at the tonsorial palace to hear what the smart barber had to say today but didn't stay long because three waiting customers were arguing about iron pyrites with the man in the chair, a miner whose grizzled beard resembled a magpie's nest. I got a sudden craving for canned peaches to top off my nut bread and headed to the Pfouts and Russell dry goods store. I didn't go in, though. I just leaned against the hitching post thinking how it would show a lack of loyalty to Rufus to buy anything from a vigilante leader and also disrespectful to Mr. Worden and Mr. Higgins to get my cans of peaches from anywhere but their store.

All hell suddenly broke loose on Wallace Street. It was a one-man show. He appeared on horseback out the front door of one of the saloons, cursing the bright sunlight and man's love of gold while tossing a gold scale into the middle of the street. A disheveled barkeep, cursing the man, followed him out, but he was soon silenced when the rider produced a six-shooter. In the rider's other hand was a bottle of rye. He took a long swig and then dismounted to share the bottle with his reluctant mount. When the barkeep cleared his throat as if to register some kind of complaint, the man fired a shot close enough to an ear to cause the barkeep to duck back through the swinging doors. The conspicuous drunk whooped, swigged some more, shattered the bottle in the street, remounted, whooped some more, and galloped in my direction while recklessly firing his six-shooter in the air. He had committed at least three violations of local public decorum laws that I knew of, but no badge wearer was foolish enough to show himself.

"Watch me take the town," the drunk hollered in my direction, but I doubt it was me he was addressing or even saw. Behind me, Paris Pfouts had stepped out of his store and stood with his hands on his hips and scorn written on his face deep enough to cause permanent furrows. The rider tipped his hat, which was black with a white flower where the brim met the crown, and fired a parting shot at the "Pfouts and Russell" sign atop the building. Down the road, a fearful woman in front of a meat market dropped her wrapped bundle of fresh cut, screamed, and fell over backward into the arms of a young man. At that point the rider must have entered another saloon or store without dismounting, but I'm not sure. My attention was now directed toward the man who had caught the woman. He was clean-shaven with closely cropped blond hair and a fine glow to his cheeks. It was Rufus.

The clatter of horse's hooves again redirected my attention. The rider was back on the street coming toward me again from the other direction. He was whooping with his hands off the reins. He waved his flowered hat in one hand and his pistol in the other as he galloped past the meat market. The horse looked as if it was intent on plowing either me or Mr. Pfouts over, but at the last second, the rider dropped hat and pistol to the ground and with both hands yanked on the reins, causing his horse to stop and rear back on its haunches.

"You can have your town back now, Mr. Paris France," he said before he fell off his horse and cracked his bare head against the hitching post. He lay on his back, completely still.

"That's Slade of the Overland!" said Mr. Pfouts as he stood over the drunk legend's body. The vigilante president then began muttering into his mustache, but I was close enough to hear. "You say you support the work we've been doing to rid this town of riffraff and then you go on another drunken rampage. Tomorrow you'll repent, if you haven't killed yourself. Damn you, Slade. It might be for the best." Mr. Pfouts then bent down and felt his pulse. "He's alive," he announced to the crowd that had gathered around the unconscious man.

Rufus arrived with the woman. She had one arm linked to his while the other arm clutched the meat package. She was wearing the drunk's flowered hat and a red dress and green jacket that together made me think of a Christmas tree I saw men bringing into the White House. I was real young then; Franklin Pierce was president.

Rufus seemed to point a six-shooter at Mr. Pfouts for a second before flipping the gun around and handing it to him butt first. "He dropped this," Rufus said.

"Lucky he didn't kill anyone," said Mr. Pfouts.

"No harm done."

"He frightened the . . . eh . . . lady."

"She's seen worse."

The woman, still linked to his arm, smiled broadly at the vigilante president. "Much," she said. "Haven't seen you around much lately, Paris. Have you stopped drinking and playing draw poker?"

"I don't let those activities get the better of me, ma'am," he said, before half turning his back to her and pressing the six-shooter to his chest. "Slade a friend of yours?" he asked Rufus.

"We were elbow to elbow in the Pay Dirt saloon last night. He was friendly and gentle before his first bottle."

"That's Slade all right. Seems like I know you?"

I stepped up, almost between them. "You don't know us," I said. "Me and my brother are from out of town, way up in Hell Gate."

"That right? Heard there was quite a bit of action up your way last month."

"Nothing to do with us. We're just honest working men who . . ."

Rufus pushed me aside. "Shut up, little brother. I can speak for myself. But he is right. We're the Hart brothers." Rufus paused, and fortunately Mr. Pfouts showed no sign that he recognized that name. "I know who you are. How's business?"

"Store is doing fine. Excuse me. I think Slade might need a doctor."

Mr. Pfouts walked away, but only two steps. He told a bystander to go fetch a particular doctor who usually had a beer in the Pay Dirt this time of day. Meanwhile Rufus grabbed Jack Slade's hat off the woman's head, plucked the white flower from the hat, tossed the hat on the chest of Mr. Slade, who was starting to stir, and then opened the woman's jacket so he could pin the flower to her red dress.

"Aren't you going to introduce me to your little brother, Rufus?" the woman said. "He's cute. How come he got the red hair and you didn't?"

"Not positive we had the same daddies," Rufus said. "His name is Woodrow. And this beautiful lady who is about to cook me up a medium rare steak is Varina."

"Better known hereabouts as Virginia Nevada. You like steak, Woodrow?"

"Well . . ." So many thoughts were churning in my head that I couldn't make a second word come out of my mouth.

"Rare, I bet, plenty of red showing?"

"He already et. Let's go, Varina. Show me where your new place is. I'm hungry enough to chomp on a sow bear."

"Nonsense. The boy needs more meat on his bones. You come along with us, Woodman. No need to say a word. I won't take no for an answer. And that is that."

But suddenly I could speak. "Thank you, Mrs. Willingham, I only had some nut bread."

"Thunderation!" shouted Rufus. "Won't you ever learn to keep your dumb mouth shut!"

Chapter Seventeen

Varina told me not to worry. She was Mrs. Willingham in name only. She had gotten rid of Mr. Willingham "permanently" two weeks ago with the help of Madam Moll Featherlegs and the tough hired man who enforced the code of decorum in Moll's bordello. She held my right arm close to one side of her and Rufus's arm close to her other side as she led us to her private quarters above the Pay Dirt. I carried the package of meat in my left arm, squeezing it too tightly each time Varina's left hip bumped against my right elbow. I must admit the whole way I thought of her working in Moll's place, one of the bordellos I eyed but didn't visit the previous night. Even in my imagination, though, I allowed her to keep her red dress mostly on.

"A penny for your thoughts," she asked me as we climbed the outdoor stairs behind the Pay Dirt.

"He's thinking about you and me," Rufus told her.

"Was not," I protested as I squeezed my nostrils. I had never been anywhere before where the scent of perfume slammed me in the face and nearly overpowered me.

"All right then, he's thinking of you and that bastard Willingham."

"That right, Woodman?"

"I . . . I . . . did wonder about him, ma'am."

"My mother sold me to him when I was thirteen," she said, and then paused to see how I took it. Thirteen was the age of Mattie Edgerton. I couldn't image this woman ever being the age of Mattie.

"Our mother would have sold my little brother back home in Washington, but she couldn't get a penny for him," said Rufus. "She couldn't afford to sell me. I was the breadwinner, you might say, after the old man drunk himself to . . ."

Varina ignored Rufus and resumed talking to me. "He must have been pressing thirty already. He made me call him Mr. Willingham and beat me regular like I was one of his plow horses. Owned with his brother the second biggest farm in Kansas. When I got to be fifteen, I dared to call him Wallace, and he knocked two of my teeth out, said the honeymoon was over, and made me marry him. I shudder to think of my ruined girlhood when I had to live with such a . . . such a . . . husband. I ran away a half dozen times, but he caught me every time, even after I became Virginia Nevada and helped run that boardinghouse in Adobetown. That was before I learned how much more gold a gal could pocket by showing lonely men a good time at Moll's place. I just learned the other day what the name 'Wallace' means. It means 'stranger.' "

"*Strange* be better," said Rufus. "*Loco* better still. Remember how he tried to shoot me but plugged my horse instead when we first come to the territory, Woodie? All because I was fornicating with a girl who'd been working horizontal for . . ."

"Hey, you son of a bitch, you're talking about me, the lady who was gonna make you steak."

"I call a spade a spade."

Rufus wasn't big on offering apologies. I was thinking that she got married at fifteen and that I was fifteen right now. I couldn't see myself married, but I could see myself doing some of the things married people did.

"I'm sorry," I blurted out. That made Rufus cackle.

And it made Varina laugh—a deep throated laugh that sounded as if it were coming from some secret female place below her neck. "What you have to be sorry about, Woodman?"

My thinking, for one thing. But I didn't say anything.

We were inside now. She had two rooms, one dominated by a black walnut high-back bed that she said was a gift from Moll Featherlegs; the other little more than a closet full of dresses as bright as the one she wore so recklessly.

"What you thinking now, Woodman?" she asked, and for a moment I thought that among her other imagined talents, she could also read minds.

"There's no oven," I said.

"Of course not, silly," she said.

I was still gripping the package of meat too tightly as if it contained a live animal that might escape. She took it from me now, but it took some doing.

"I didn't mean for you to hold it forever," she said.

"I'm sorry," I said, sniffing the white flower pin.

"Stop apologizing, Woodman. I know you didn't learn that from your son of a bitch brother." Regardless, she bent down and kissed Rufus full on the lips while giving him a squeeze below—between his legs, as far as I could tell. "They let me use the kitchen below," she said. "You boys make yourself at home."

Rufus tried to follow her out, but she kissed him again, pushed him back inside, and shut the door in his face. I pretended not to notice. I stared at myself in the mirrored washstand, covering my beardless chin with both hands, trying hard as I could not to look fifteen.

"What do you think?" Rufus asked.

"I guess whiskers will come in time," I replied.

"Not about yourself, stupid. What do you think of her?"

"Virginia Nevada, you mean?"

"No. Queen Victoria."

I turned away from the mirror and looked for a place to sit down. The only place was the bed, so I kept standing. "She's nice," I said.

"Not how most men describe her, I suspect. And I'm *not* talking about the queen."

"Right. Virginia Nevada."

"Don't call her that. That was her name when she was over there in Moll's fancy house. She's here now. You might say she graduated, schoolboy. And never ever call her Mrs. Willingham again. Her name is Varina. Got it?" Rufus didn't wait for an answer or even a nod. He flopped on the bed and lay on his back, hands locked behind his head, boots kicking on the quilt.

"But is she still married to him?" I asked. "You know, Mr. Willingham?"

"As much as I want to know him. It don't matter. She was with him on and off for ten years. That's enough. Lincoln freed the coloreds. White women must be freed, too."

I did the addition. Varina was about twenty-three, which was at least a year younger than Lucia Darling. I never would have guessed it. Some living situations and some lines of work clearly aged a body faster. "They're divorced then?" I asked

"Divorced. Separated. Detached. Disunited. Split. Severed. Give me time and I'll think up some more good words. Or have a go at it yourself, schoolboy. Wait. *Set apart!* That tells it best. What's it to you anyway?"

"I was just wondering and . . ."

"Worrying needlessly like a nervous hen."

"Foxes do get in henhouses, don't they?"

"Look, little brother, maybe it will ease your mind to know that a few weeks ago Moll's hired man gave Wallace Willingham a taste of his own medicine—beat him senseless. Moll then used Willingham's own money to pay a freighter friend to haul him off to a Fort Benton steamer for shipment back to Kansas. She pinned a note to Willingham's shirt that said, 'Return to Virginia City and you're a dead man.' Moll always was one to protect her girls. She had a particular liking for her prize dove, Varina, who goes back now and then to have high tea with Madam Featherlegs."

"I see," I said, fighting my imagination gone wild. "So that's what . . . eh . . . Varina meant earlier when she said she had gotten rid of Mr. Willingham *permanently*?"

"Of course. Moll and her strong-arm man aren't vigilantes. They didn't hang the bastard."

I paced the entire room for a few minutes, pausing each turn at the mirror to see how I looked to someone who wasn't me. But I knew I must be irritating Rufus with my worried ways, so I sat down on the edge of the bed and studied the brown and red triangular patterns in the quilt. I finally glanced at Rufus because I heard him snoring. His eyes were shut. At that moment I believed he didn't have a worry in the world. He had some money in his pocket, a bed made for sleeping in and more, his next meal being delivered, a younger brother who had taken care of the horses and knew not to be a bother, a fine saloon and widow woman waiting for him up in Hell Gate, and no angry husband or vigilante snapping at his heels.

"Quit watching the door," Rufus said without opening his eyes. "It won't make her come any faster with the grub."

I closed my own eyes but did not lie down. Rufus was snoring again, though the sound of my own breathing drowned it out.

When Varina returned, she came with plates, forks, knives, a bottle of wine, and three steaks. Her appetite was as large as that of Rufus. She didn't mind showing it off as the three of us ate right there on the bed. She said the bed, that particular one, was her favorite place in the world. She and Rufus ate lying on their sides, using their hands to help themselves and each other chew. I was on my own, being careful not to spill any of the bright red juice. Once I did, but it didn't make her mad.

"It isn't blood," she said, taking a drink straight from the bottle. "And it adds color to my quilt."

When we were done, I realized they were just beginning. They had each other for a lengthy dessert. I asked if I could take the dirty dishes down to the kitchen. Varina told me to just shove them under the bed, and then, though it was still afternoon, she asked me if I had a place to sleep. I assured her I did and headed for the door, which was for the best because Rufus was looking all together irritated again.

"Leaving so soon, Woodman?" Varina called out.

"He's not Woodman," Rufus said, correcting her on my name for the first time. "He's just a dumb kid."

"Thanks so much for the meal," I told her as I touched the cold door handle.

"My pleasure. No charge. Never a charge for a Hart."

"See you later, Rufus."

"Much later," Rufus said.

On the steps down, I bumped into a small man in a greatcoat and fur hat who was on the way up. His face was red but perhaps not from the cold.

"I was told Virginia Nevada lives at the top of these stairs," he said.

"Yes, that's one of her names, but . . ." I wanted to tell him to go back down, that she was busy, that she had someone with her, another customer but one she didn't charge. The words wouldn't come out. He was looking me over from head to shoes and it made me uncomfortable. What's more he extended a hand across the stairway to the opposite railing, constraining my forward movement.

"You look too young. Your name Hart?"

I didn't want to answer him now. I could sense something wasn't right. When he asked again, I might have nodded slightly. Maybe I should have lied for a change. He pulled a handgun out from somewhere inside his greatcoat. It could have been another Army Colt. I wasn't up on the kinds of weapons men were using in the West, but I suspected it had six chambers. All I knew was that I could feel the muzzle against my full belly and that he would need to empty only one of those chambers to do the job.

"I am unarmed," I said because I had heard that mattered to some men who toted weapons. "And I'm not one of her . . . eh . . . customers. I am only fifteen."

Perhaps I sounded cowardly but at that moment I didn't care. And the man did pull back his revolver slightly so that it no longer pressed into my gut. I looked at his face more carefully now but could not see a single cut or bruise. And he had taken the stairs without a limp.

"Someone else is up there with her, right?" he said. "What's your full name?"

"You aren't a customer either, are you?" I replied.

"That's right. Your full name unless you want a belly full of . . ."

"Woodrow R. Hart"

"And the R doesn't stand for Rufus, does it?"

"Nor Red. It's Russell after my grand—"

"But Rufus Hart is up there, right?"

I knew better than to answer that or to nod. I got bold. "Who are you?" I said. "Why are you pointing that gun at me?"

"Go on down the stairs, boy. I don't want you."

He took a step up as he gave me a nudge in the back to go down. His revolver was now pointed to the closed door. His back was practically to me. He wasn't tall or wide. I could have jumped him from behind and wrestled the weapon away from him . . . maybe.

Instead, I asked another question. "You can't be Wallace Willingham, can you?"

"No. What do you know about Wallace Willingham, boy?"

"Nothing. He's a stranger."

"I figure you're lying. We both know Wallace Willingham and what happened to him."

"I'm not lying. But do you know Mr. Willingham?"

"I should. I'm Walter Willingham, Wallace's brother."

The man waved his revolver at me and ordered me to the bottom of the stairs unless I wanted to get it in the back. I didn't want it in the back any more than I did in the belly, so I raced the rest of the way down, taking two steps at a time. I then ducked behind the railing where I found an empty whiskey bottle—clearly a Virginia City littering violation by one of the Pay Dirt customers. I raised up and hurled the bottle. Could be I meant to hit this Walter Willingham, but the bottle flew past his fur hat and shattered against the door.

"Watch out, Rufus!" I screamed as I ducked again, expecting the man to fire a shot at me.

No shot came. I heard his footsteps, going up. And I heard Varina's door swing open. The hinges squeaked, by design or otherwise. I wasn't sure if it was Walter Willingham who had opened the door or somebody from the inside. But when the footsteps and squeaking stopped, a shot did follow. Walter Willingham toppled head over heels back down the stairs landing dead on arrival at my feet.

I didn't stick around to check his pulse or anything. The blood soaked through his shirt to stain his greatcoat, right over his heart. I ran up the stairs, and the first man to step out the back door of the Pay Dirt yelled to the others: "There he goes. Look at him run, the murderer." Inside Varina's room I was breathing hard, as if I had run to Nevada City and back. Varina was holding the smoking gun, though the six-shooter belonged to Rufus, and he took it back as soon as he saw me.

"I done it," Rufus said.

"I did it and I'm not the least bit sorry," Varina said. "He was as mean as his older brother, just didn't hit as hard. Walter always thought highly of Wallace. They were two of a kind—the kind that will knock you to the ground, kick you for just lying there, and spit on you for good measure."

"He won't kick nobody no more. I shot him in self-defense."

"He was trying to shoot me. He was out for revenge. I was defending myself."

"His brother missed me earlier, so he gave it a try."

"I told you it was me he was after. He knew I had his brother beaten. A *wife* isn't supposed to treat a husband that way. Now he knows how I can treat a brother-in-law. He deserved what he got."

"From me," insisted Rufus. "We best keep our story straight. I did it. You got that, Woodie? I did it."

"Don't believe it, Woodman," she said. "Your brother is just covering for me."

I didn't know what to believe. I knew Rufus had lied plenty of times in his life, but I had never known him to be noble. "I didn't see it, the shooting I mean. That's the truth."

"Damn your truth," Rufus said. He looked as if he wanted to shoot me.

"I did it, so you both tell them I did it. They won't hang a woman."

"I wouldn't put it past them. It's my Colt, and I'm the man. He was gunning for me, but I outgunned him. That's the way it is out here on the frontier. Man against man. I don't want to hear anything different."

Nobody knocked. The noisy door swung open, a crowd poured in, Rufus's gun was seized, and questions flew at us from all directions. A few of the intruders—mostly vigilante types, according to Rufus—gave what they thought to be the correct answers without even asking any questions. The answers were the same as accusations. The man who saw me run up the stairs continued to accuse me of bloody murder, but somebody else accused him of being too drunk to see straight, and someone else suggested I was too young to be a killer even if I did have fiery red hair.

Varina was ruled out as the killer. True, she was a lady of ill repute, but she was still a woman of uncommon beauty. Nobody had ever seen her handle a derringer, let alone such a large six-shooter, and nobody thought she was capable of shooting so straight and true. "Got it right in the middle of the heart," declared one of the later arrivals. Still later a doctor arrived to confirm it. Rufus, on the other hand, was deemed rugged enough to kill in cold blood, and, as more than one concerned citizen noted, he was found holding the murder weapon, which fit his belt holster like a glove.

"I remember you," said a man, waving a black gloved hand in front of Rufus's nose. "I been in Virginia from the beginning. I seen you before. You was a Plummer man."

"I was a lawman, mister." Rufus protested. "Maybe I arrested you."

The man stepped back a pace or two and began to bite the knuckles of his glove. But he recovered quickly and took a giant step forward, waving both hands this time. "That don't mean a thing. Plummer was an underhand sheriff."

I heard onlookers passing on the word to those who hadn't heard it: *The killer was a friend of the hanged Sheriff Plummer.*

"Seen him with wild man Slade last night in the Pay Dirt," said a man in spectacles. "They busted furniture and noses, shot out a mirror, and made miners lick the dirt off their boots. Saw Slade again today. He was lying dead drunk in the street, and this fellow was standing there telling Paris Pfouts he better leave his friend alone or else. A friend of Plummer, a friend of Slade!"

I was starting to get the nerve to challenge that ridiculous account when an English gentleman came forth with a "jolly good" and claimed he saw me on the street at the same time and suggested that the "dangerous duo" might actually be a "treacherous trio." That remark inspired others to push, shove, and punch me. Rufus got the same treatment. We were in the hands of a mob that so far could think of nothing beyond manhandling us. Nobody said a word about the dead man at the bottom of the stairs; he probably hadn't been in town long enough to tell anybody his name. That didn't keep someone from crying out: "Ain't none of us safe. They killed a stranger." Of course, that made no sense unless the fellow believed Rufus and I had squeezed the trigger at the same time or maybe Rufus had steadied the six-shooter while his lover Varina had done the squeezing.

A badge wearer stepped forward to declare that this was a matter for the law, but only I seemed to pay him much mind. Besides the cheap badge, I noticed his oversized bearskin mittens saturated with snow. I suspected this was a man experienced only in issuing fines for littering and whose voice was too high-pitched to carry weight in this crowd. But then a far more forceful man barged into the room, panting and chanting about the need for public safety. He still had enough energy to push his way through the mob and fire off a derringer into Varina's ceiling. The room became so quiet you could have heard a glove or mitten drop.

He spoke in a clear voice, but one *not* as deep as might be expected from the mouth of such a bulldog of a man. "In case you don't know me, friends, my name is Williams—Captain James Williams of your Vigilance Committee. These killers are now in my custody."

Chapter Eighteen

Captain Williams, with a little help from his friends, escorted Rufus, Varina, and me to the back of Paris Pfouts's store. The captain made the disturbing point that as long as innocent men could be shot down on the streets—or outdoor stairways—of Virginia City, the Vigilance Committee must continue to be vigilant. Even more disturbing, though I suppose not really surprising, President Pfouts agreed. Varina—who as Virginia Nevada had shifted from a bawdy boardinghouse to a bordello to her own boudoir—was a familiar figure to the two men. Mr. Pfouts remembered meeting us Hart brothers on the street earlier when Jack Slade was on a spree. James Williams, of course, knew us all too well from the interrogation at Hell Gate during which I stood up for Rufus's imagined innocence and Rufus got away with knocking the captain to the floor.

"And so we meet again," said Captain Williams, barely glancing at me before standing nose to nose with Rufus. "I was counting on it."

"You going to knock me over with your bad breath," said Rufus.

"Want to take another swing at me, mister? I dare you."

I could see Rufus was considering it while the captain reached down for his pistol. I quickly shuffled my feet, trying to get between them. Both men pushed me away at the same time, causing me to crash into and turn over a barrel of molasses. But at least there was no shot or punch.

"Fine," Captain Williams said. "I'd rather hang you than shoot you."

"Now, now," said Paris Pfouts. "Let's not get ahead of ourselves. Let's hear from him, from all three of them."

We each gave a statement, agreeing on three points—the man's name was Walter Willingham, he had stormed up the stairway intent on murder, and was shot in self-defense. Varina said she did it, Rufus said he did it, and I said I didn't do it and didn't know who did. Captain Williams said straight out that he believed Varina was protecting her latest lover and I was protecting my brother. He double-checked a copy of Red Yeager's list of alleged outlaw gang members to make sure the name Rufus Hart wasn't on it.

"You mean you didn't hang everyone on the list?" said Rufus, with jaw thrust out.

I didn't think it was a very smart thing to say under the circumstances; it was lucky that the captain didn't remember the later short list that did include Rufus's name. Rufus's comment made Captain Williams grin—a false grin but a grin just the same. "Some got away—some, not many," he said. "You know I never forget a face. I saw you before that time in Hell Gate, didn't I?"

"How should I know."

"Now it's coming back to me. It was at the Rattlesnake Ranch when we captured Red Yeager. You were there with Buck Stinson and Ned Ray. We didn't take them that day either, but their day would come soon, once we had Red Yeager's list. Now, it looks like your day has come, mister. You won't get away this time."

"I'm not trying to get away. I shot the son of a bitch in self-defense."

"And now something else is coming back to me. You once were a Plummer deputy just like Stinson and Ray. You've shaved and cleaned up since then, but . . ."

"Assistant deputy and not for long. Buzz Caven, for one, served under the sheriff, and you didn't hang him."

Captain Williams appeared to be pondering that point when Paris Pfouts spoke up. "True enough," the president said. "That shows our Vigilance Committee is a responsible body that examines the evidence against any man before deciding whether or not he is guilty and/or incorrigible. We examined Mr. Caven, and, as you noted, he remains a member of our community. He has musical talent, plays a fine fiddle."

"I don't play no instrument," said Rufus.

"Let's stick to the specifics of this examination, shall we?" Captain Williams said, rolling his hands and then his entire arms.

"By all means," said President Pfouts. "Please continue, Captain."

James Williams immediately got in Rufus's face again. "The man you murdered was named Willingham, right?"

"The man I killed in self-defense was a Willingham all right."

"I know the name Willingham. But I never saw his face before, him being a total stranger to Virginia City. That doesn't add up."

"Can't help you," Rufus said. "I never saw him before, either, and my brother can tell you I never was too good at addition."

"Or subtraction," I blurted out, but that didn't sound right. "I mean it was self-defense. The man ran up those stairs with his gun out and pointed. I saw him."

"Why would he do that? Why would he want to shoot somebody he didn't know?"

"He knew me," said Varina. Despite Rufus's protests, she explained about the two cruel Willingham brothers, how she had married and left the one named Wallace, how he had come to fetch her in Virginia City several times but she had refused to go back to Kansas with him, and how the one named Walter had come to kill her because he judged her a sinner who had not lived up to her sacred marriage vows.

"No question you're a sinner," Captain Williams said matter-of-factly. "I know you called yourself Nevada Virginia when you were one of the fallen angels at Moll Featherlegs's establishment."

"Virginia Nevada."

"No matter. It's a fake name, and fornication is the work of the devil."

"The devil does get around town . . . the entire gulch, actually, and over to Bannack."

"Fact is, Virginia Nevada . . . or should I say Mrs. Willingham . . . there's a strong possibility Walter Willingham came here to bring you home to your rightful husband, not to shoot you or Rufus Hart. Tell me the truth now. Didn't Rufus Hart, him being a sinner himself, shoot your brother-in-law on your behalf?"

"He didn't shoot him at all. I keep telling you that. I took Rufus's gun and . . ."

"It was either him or me," said Rufus. "I beat Walter Willingham to the draw."

"Even though his gun was out and pointed like your brother said?"

"That's right. I reckon they do things mighty slow in Kansas."

While Captain Williams was completing his examination and clearly hoping for one confession instead of two, X Beidler burst into the room with news. Wallace Willingham, he found out, had been seen several weeks ago at the Moll Featherlegs's bordello looking for his wife and had suffered a severe beating at the hands of Moll's bodyguard, Curly Winters.

"The husband came back for revenge and for Virginia Nevada," concluded Mr. Beidler. "Got himself shot dead for his trouble. Oh, howdy, Mr. Pfouts. Didn't see you standing in the corner."

"The dead man is the husband's brother, X, not the husband," said Captain Williams.

"But his name is Willingham, and Moll told me that Willingham was the one who Curly beat and . . ."

"Yes, they are both Willinghams, X, being brothers and all. As far as we know the husband, the one beaten, is back in Kansas now and alive."

"Oh." X Beidler was a short man, and when he sank down in a chair, he looked even smaller. But soon he straightened up, and his eyes brightened. "Reckon, it don't matter which Willingham was murdered. The murderer got to pay. Which one done it?"

"That's the burning question," said Paris Pfouts.

"It wasn't murder," snapped Varina, glaring at X Beidler as if he was a customer who refused to pay. "I shot the son of a bitch in self-defense. He aimed to kill me." She smiled a little too wide, touched Mr. Beidler's arm, and softened her voice. "Moll and Curly are well, I hope. I mean, before he came to my place looking to shoot me, Walter Willingham didn't go over there and, you know, try to do anything to them out of a desire for vengeance?"

"Desire for vengeance?" repeated Mr. Beidler, lips curling. "I don't reckon men go to Moll's out of that kind of desire. You admit you did the killing, huh? Never did hang a female, Captain Williams."

"No need for that kind of talk, X," said the captain, and Paris Pfouts nodded his head. "Women lie for a variety of reasons. I'm positive Rufus Hart shot him. I have a nose for sniffing out killers. That would be the taller of the two Hart brothers."

"Good, good." The veteran hangman pressed his stubby fingertips together and looked to the ceiling as if giving thanks.

"You can't be positive," Varina insisted. "You can't be sure it wasn't me."

"I sniff out liars, too."

"I'm not saying he did it, mind you, but even if it was him, you can't hang a man who was only trying to protect his life and mine. It was . . . I mean, it would be . . . sort of noble. Any one of you gentlemen in similar circumstance would do the same. Am I right?"

The vigilante leaders ignored her. They had heard enough. She crossed her arms and turned her back to everyone.

"What about the kid?" asked Mr. Beidler, who seemed to be staring at my neck.

"He wasn't even in the room when the shot was fired," Captain Williams said. "He couldn't shoot a man in the chest if he was standing behind the man. The boy can't help having a brother like that. And he sure doesn't come across as a sinner. He's shaking because of a bad case of the nerves, not because of any guilt."

"I trust your judgment, Captain," said Mr. Beidler, who now turned his full attention to my brother.

To me, it looked as if the notorious X was now mentally measuring Rufus's height and weight and the thickness of his neck. It made my toes squirm as if my shoes were too tight. But he must not have remembered Rufus's name being on the short list, either, or else he would have mentioned it.

"Self-defense must count for something," I managed to mumble. "This is the West."

"You didn't see the actual shooting, boy," Captain Williams said. "You said so yourself."

"I know, but . . ."

"You don't know that it was self-defense. If anything, he was defending her."

"Well," I said, speaking louder now. "Doesn't defending a

woman count for something?"

"Maybe. Maybe not. Depends on the woman. Nobody has ever called Nevada Virginia innocent."

"Damnation," said Varina. "It's Virginia Nevada. Can't you get anything right!" She put her hands on her hips, pursed her lips, and loudly let her breath out. "Besides, I'm called Varina these days. That's my *real* name. V-a-r-i-n-a."

"Very well, Varina," said Paris Pfouts. "But that doesn't help us get at the truth."

"We know the truth," insisted Captain Williams. "She—whatever she calls herself—is protecting her murderous lover."

I began to pace the room, and the vigilantes let me because I was no longer a suspect.

After listening to my pounding heart compete with the sound of my own footsteps, I worked up the nerve to ask a plain question, directing it to Mr. Pfouts in the corner instead of the other two vigilantes because I figured I'd like his answer better and he was the president. "You going to hang my brother?"

"Not now," President Pfouts replied, waving me off with the back of his hand. I thought he was letting me know he was *not* taking questions. But a moment later, he added, "These things have to run their course."

I wasn't exactly reassured. "Look," I said, and all three vigilante members did look at me, which made me regret saying that word and started me wishing I was invisible.

"What is it, young man?" the president said. "If you have something to say, you best say it now. You might not get the chance later."

"I . . . I just wanted to say that hanging him is wrong . . . that is to say, it isn't the best solution when there is so much doubt about . . . you know, motives and everything. And . . . gentlemen sirs, there is an alternative."

"And what would that be? You'd have us let him go scot-free,

I presume."

"No, no. Not exactly, sir. Why not banishment? We both live in Hell Gate. Rufus runs a saloon there for two honorable men—Mr. Worden and Mr. Higgins. And I work for the same two gentlemen in their excellent general store. In fact, we mostly only came to Virginia City to deliver important goods. That's the honest truth. You could banish us to Hell Gate. We'd never come back to Virginia City or Nevada City or . . ."

"People like your brother and Jack Slade always come back," said Captain Williams. "It's in their evil natures. Maybe they just can't help it. But that's no excuse."

"Please," I said. "You can't hang him for protecting a . . ."

"Look, young man," interrupted Paris Pfouts. "This matter isn't entirely in our hands. Besides the Vigilance Committee, we have a people's court presided over by Judge Alexander Davis. All the evidence will be weighed and . . . Regardless, don't worry about your chickens until they've hatched."

I wasn't sure what he was talking about. I had never in my fifteen years ever owned any chickens. I was ready to beg for mercy, for my brother. I didn't get the chance.

X Beidler and James Williams took Rufus out the back door to an undisclosed location despite loud protests from Varina and me. Rufus went quietly, tipping his hat to her and nodding his head toward me.

"I'll see you later," I said.

"Sure, bub, sure," said Rufus.

After my brother was out the door, Paris Pfouts made a small effort to reassure Varina and me by confirming that the vigilantes had recently agreed to submit future cases of alleged criminal wrongdoing to Judge Davis for public trial.

"And the future is now," he said like a Washington politician. "This will be a test case, with the vigilantes working in conjunction with the people's court to reach a fair verdict based, as I said, on all the evidence."

"What do you mean a test case?" I asked.

"He means he knows it will fail," said Varina.

"I know no such thing." As he spoke, Paris Pfouts seemed to puff himself up like certain birds. "I maintain an open mind."

"They'll hang Rufus even though I shot Walter Willingham in self-defense. And if Wallace Willingham ever dares to come back to Virginia City, I'll shoot him, too."

"That isn't the kind of thing you'll want to say at the trial, ma'am. I'll pretend I didn't hear that. You best go about your business now. I have my own business to take care of here."

"Where's Rufus? I want to see him again."

"And so you shall, Mrs. Willingham. At the trial. You are free to go, both of you."

Paris Pfouts moved to the front of his store and started to look busy, so Varina and I left through the back door. To take my mind off all the unsettling events of the day, I paused to look at the six horses in the Pfouts and Russell corral. I wouldn't have swapped Togu for any two of them. Varina showed no interest and motioned me to come along. She was a people person.

Neither of us had much to say to each other without Rufus around. Plenty was going on in my head, though. I wondered if she had really shot Walter Willingham and whether she would say so at the trial. I also wondered if anyone would believe her, and if anything said by anybody at the trial would convince Judge Davis and the people's court that the shooting was justified. More than anything else I wondered if the vigilantes would hang my brother no matter the verdict of the court. She didn't offer a penny for my thoughts, and she didn't reveal what was going on in her head, either. She looked up and down Wallace Street as if she might be wondering where they were holding Rufus or else looking for a new customer.

"You hungry?" she asked.

I shook my head. Not even another steak sounded eatable at that moment.

"Me neither. I can't go home. I need a drink, somewhere other than the Pay Dirt. You want to come along?"

"No, thank you. I . . . I . . ."

"I know you don't imbibe, Woodman. And if all this hasn't driven you to drink, hell if I know what would. You have any place to go?"

"I'll go see Togu, that's my pony."

In the stable, I gave Togu a long, hard brushing, and he showed his appreciation by nuzzling my arm. For the second night in a row I slept in the same stall as my pony, and I slept well considering how many thoughts had awakened as I lay in the hay. Togu wasn't restless or a kicker, but in the morning, he nudged my back with a hoof in a pushy way. I told him I agreed with him. I was starting to get a suffocating feeling in that stall. I needed to go somewhere as much as he did.

I rode him to Nevada City because I wanted to see if Hank was still at his hotel or had already taken the freight wagon back to Hell Gate. The clerk said he had checked out the day before, which somehow made my spirits sink even lower, though I knew the old mule skinner couldn't have done a thing about Rufus's plight. I got the idea to ride to Bannack to ask for help. Chief Justice Sidney Edgerton was in Washington, but Wilbur Sanders had plenty of influence with the vigilantes. Sidney's nephew had never shown much interest in me, and I doubted he cared a lick about my brother, but I was prepared to plead my case, rather Rufus's case. It wouldn't take much for me to start weeping at his feet. Trouble was it was 140 miles round trip, totally out of the question. There was no telling when the people's court would go into session. That thought threw me into a panic as the pony and I were finishing our bread breakfast.

"We got to get back, Togu," I shouted. "I need to testify. Run,

Togu, run. Like the wind."

Togu galloped the whole way back to Virginia City, and I was lucky to stay in the saddle. He barely slowed down on Wallace Street, and I worried that he might run somebody over or I might be mistaken for a drunken rider in the same vein as Jack Slade. I tied up in front of the Pfouts and Russell dry goods store and panicked again when I saw Mr. Russell there but not Mr. Pfouts. Mr. Russell had no idea where Mr. Pfouts was, although he said his energetic partner often met with his fellow Freemasons in their lodge or else tried his hand at draw poker in any one of a number of saloons. I didn't know where the lodge was and didn't ask. I didn't visit any of the saloons either. I went up those bloodstained stairs and listened at Varina's door. I heard a female voice singing, so I knocked. A brawny bald man with a jagged scar running above his forehead answered, and I staggered backward. I might have tumbled down the stairs, but one of his strong arms reached out and clamped on to my left shoulder.

"What we got here?" the man said as he yanked me inside the room. "You want me to keep this tadpole or throw him back?"

I was afraid but also angry. I knew Varina had worked at Moll's bordello and was most likely still in the same profession as an independent, but I had seen her as Rufus's lady, however imperfect she might be. And now, with Rufus being held in captivity while awaiting trial, she was "entertaining" another fellow. Maybe business was business, and perhaps she needed the money to buy all those steaks, but I wasn't going to pretend to like it.

I stepped right past the big guy and crossed my arms in front of Varina, whom I now noticed was fully dressed. Her dress was black. "If you're done with him, I'm here on important business," I said.

"You have news of Rufus?" she asked.

"No. I . . ." I suddenly wasn't sure what important business I had with her.

"Curly has brought news."

"Who?"

The large scarred man came at me, and I raised my arms to protect my face, but he only wanted to shake hands. His grip was surprisingly mild. He knew his own strength.

"That's me," he said. "Curly Winters."

"Curly wasn't scalped by an Injun," Varina said, maybe because I was staring at the long scar. "A few years back a hard case at Moll's cut up one of the girls and then when Curly came to her defense . . . well, he got Curly good before Curly redirected the knife into the man's heart."

"Gives me personality, don't it?"

"Oh," I said, forcing myself to take my eyes off his forehead. "You're the one who beat up Wallace Willingham."

"Anything to help the ladies. Didn't count on him having a brother. Too bad the brother didn't come for me instead of Miss Varina. I would have crushed him."

I didn't see how he could have made Walter Willingham any deader, but I nodded and thanked him.

"Curly's news is good, Woodman," Varina said. "He has talked to half a dozen men on the Vigilance Committee and convinced them to push hard for banishment."

"For you?"

"No, silly. I'm not on trial. For your brother."

"Oh. How'd he manage that?"

"The six are all regulars at Moll Featherlegs's house. They all admire Moll and the way she runs a nice clean and peaceful business, with the assistance of Curly here."

"Like I said, I always try to help the ladies." Curly leaned in close to Varina without touching her and took a long whiff of her perfume. "They're all so darn sweet."

"And in this case, it'll be helping your brother, too," said Varina.

I had great difficulty imagining the likes of President Paris Pfouts, Captain James Williams, and hangman X Beidler consorting with soiled doves, but then I really didn't know the trio well and could only assume not all vigilantes were cut from the same irreproachable cloth.

"If you can help Rufus, I thank you, Mr. Winters."

"And I'll testify that Rufus shot Walter Willingham to keep Walter Willingham from shooting me," Varina said. "I'd hate to see Rufus banished from Virginia City, but there's no reason on earth I couldn't go visit him—and you, too, Woodman—in Hell Gate."

I couldn't bring myself to thank her. Earlier she had said she'd tell the truth at the trial—that she was the one who pulled the trigger. I didn't mention that, though. I figured the best that could happen at the trial was banishment, and it was fine with me if my brother got banished instead of her. I had no wish to make another trip to Virginia City myself.

"When do you think the trial will take place?" I asked, thinking the sooner it happened, the sooner Rufus and I could mount up and head for Hell Gate. Togu would be rarin' to go.

"Curly's vigilante contacts say as soon as tonight but probably tomorrow," said Varina. "It won't be long, Woodman. Patience. It will all work out for the best." She now touched my shoulder as if she were my big sister. But she wasn't. I wished the hand belonged to Lucy, who nobody had ever said was soiled, fallen, or of ill repute. It seemed like a long time since I had thought of Lucy. That was wrong. Lucy had always had a genuine concern for me. Her final words of advice before my departure from the East came back to me: "Woodie, Washington is your home. Let Rufus do what he wants. Doesn't mean you have to do what he wants. You're your own person, and a good person you are. Don't go West, young man, don't go West."

"It's Woodrow, not Woodman," I said, maybe a little too forcefully.

Curly Winters had to get back to his paid job at Moll Featherlegs's place, and Varina wanted to take a hot bath somewhere. I said my goodbyes and walked slowly down those outdoor steps. I suppose I was feeling somewhat better about Rufus's fate, but for some reason it still felt as if I was descending from the gallows. I wasn't convinced that Mr. Winters, though obviously strong and a fighter, could sway the entire Vigilance Committee to his (that is to say Varina's) way of thinking. Furthermore, I remained skeptical that Varina could help Rufus's case no matter what she said.

I walked to Pfouts and Russell's store and peeked in the window. Mr. Pfouts was looking at a list handed to him by a female customer, and Mr. Russell was sitting on a barrel casually talking to a couple of miners in need of socializing. The peaceful scene pleased me. I was a dry goods veteran now, at least in my mind, having worked briefly for Francis Thompson in Bannack and for Mr. Worden and Mr. Higgins in Hell Gate. I could even imagine working for Mr. Pfouts, since I had never shot or robbed anybody and was the opposite of a carouser. But that could never happen, I reminded myself. I'd be leaving Virginia City soon.

After several people on the street joined me at the window because they were curious what I was looking at, I went to the hitching post to get my pony. I rode Togu slowly across town and then back again a little faster. I wondered how Rufus was doing and whether anyone had mentioned "banishment" to him. Sitting in the saddle was not calming my nerves, so I took Togu back to the stable and put him in our stall. He was the only real friend I had in Virginia City. I wrapped my arms around his neck and held him close for five minutes. That was all he could stand before he broke free of my grasp, whinnied, turned his head, and either tried to bite me or remove my hat.

"I'm sorry, boy," I said. "I know you want to ride more—I mean be ridden—but I'm afraid to go anywhere. I got to stick close by for Rufus's sake."

At dusk, I walked out of the stall when Togu wasn't looking and wandered about. I paused for a while in front of Moll Featherlegs's place in case Curly Winters came out, but I saw no sign of him and moved on to the Pfouts and Russell store. It was closed for business and dark. I peeked in the window anyway but only saw shadows of stocked shelves. I wished he was in there taking a nap or meeting with the Freemasons at their lodge. But what if he was in neither place? I started to take a deep deliberate breath, but a question cut it short. *They wouldn't start the trial tonight without me, would they?* I hurried to Varina's room to see if she'd heard anything more. I knocked on her door until my knuckles were sore, but she didn't answer. I sat down on the top outside step and waited. Over and over I imagined myself at the bottom watching Walter Willingham, bleeding like a stuck Kansas pig, come tumbling down toward me. I had witnessed more than my share of hangings, and I wouldn't forget them, not even the ones I only heard about. But at that moment and for the next half hour, my mind's eye was closed to everything but the shooting and the subsequent fall.

Varina finally showed up. She had taken the first step on the stairs when she noticed me. She stepped back to the hard ground. She looked as if she was about to slip away into the Pay Dirt. But I called her name and she froze.

"Where were you?" she asked.

"What do you mean? I've been right here. Before that I was at the stable, waiting."

"I went to the stable. I only saw horses."

"You went there? What for?"

"To tell you the people's court was in session."

"What! Where?"

"The Gilbert Brewery. The Gilberts and their ten children went to visit friends, and Judge Davis set up court."

"I was afraid something like this might happen. Let's go."

"No point now. It's over."

"Over? How can it be?"

"It was a public trial but hardly any of the public was there, except the vigilantes of course. When I couldn't find you, I went there alone. I was the only witness called. It all happened so fast."

"But I needed to be there. I saw Mr. Willingham fall down the stairs. I could have been a witness, too."

"Yes, but you didn't see the shooting itself. Everyone knew that. Only I did, besides Rufus, of course. Paris Pfouts said there was no reason for you to be there. Judge Davis agreed. They said you were just an overly sensitive and nervous boy too much under the spell of your big brother to say anything bad against him and would only start crying and pleading for his life. They didn't want that kind of display."

"God! What are you talking about! They banished him, right?"

"A few of the vigilantes, just as Curly said, mentioned the word—you know, banishment."

"Good. What happens now? Rufus and I ride off to Hell Gate pronto?"

"I'm afraid not, Woodman, I mean Woodrow, Woodie. The people's court ruled otherwise."

"What do you mean otherwise?"

"Judge Davis accepted the verdict. The vigilantes, except for one or two men, concurred. At least it wasn't unanimous."

"What are you saying? You can't be saying . . ."

"Yes. He was sentenced to hang. There's nothing to be done

about it. I'm sorry. I did my best. I tried to tell them about Walter Willingham, but they wouldn't listen to me. They said they couldn't excuse Rufus just because nobody knew the stranger, only that he was the brother of my husband and had every right to come to Virginia City to bring me back to Kansas to be with the man I wed."

"I can't believe this," I shouted, but I believed it more than anything, including my own name. "When will it happen? When will they hang Rufus?"

"Right away. It could be happening as we speak. It might even be over with. Those men belief in swift justice."

"I know, damn it. Where? Where are they doing it?"

"I'm not sure. I didn't ask. You don't want to see it. Come inside with me. It's horrible, I know, but we can comfort each other."

Varina took one step up, but that was as far as she got. I raced down the stairway and, accidentally or not, bowled her over. She landed on her back and lay very still, but I didn't stop to help her to her feet. I didn't feel much like being a gentleman. I took off down the street and for some reason it occurred to me for the first time how this was Wallace Street and the man who had triggered all the trouble by relentlessly seeking his strong-willed runaway wife also had the first name of Wallace. At some point as I neared the Pfouts and Russell store, I realized where I was going. I had seen enough vigilante action in Hell Gate to know a most likely spot for a hanging—the corral in back.

Chapter Nineteen

I didn't hear a sound as I came around the side of the store, and I half hoped nobody would be back there. If it wasn't here, though, it would be someplace else. The Vigilance Committee didn't need gallows or even trees to carry out its organizational purpose. I halted in my tracks when I saw men sitting or standing at the corral fence as if waiting in awe to watch a daring rider break a mustang. Torches and lanterns provided enough light for me to make out faces. I saw the grim profile of Paris Pfouts and recognized James Williams and X Beidler from behind. Above them, a noose dangled from a crossbeam atop two extended fence posts. I gulped the night air, like a fish out of water. Seeing no neck in the noose at least allowed me to catch my breath. When Captain Williams and Mr. Beidler each stepped aside to create a path, I saw a dry goods box beneath the noose. I realized the path wasn't opened for me. Other vigilantes marched the struggling condemned man to the box, and he promptly kicked it. Only after they had pinioned his hands behind him and boosted him onto the box did Rufus speak.

"Where's Judge Davis?" he said, his voice cracking. "He promised me you'd wait until someone fetched my little brother. I need to speak with him. Ain't right, ain't right! Let me live long enough to see Woodie one last time. For the love of God!"

None of us Harts were raised with any religion to speak of. I had never heard Rufus mention the love of God before. And I had never heard him mention my name this way, as if he had some kind of love for me. Or maybe he spoke out of fear. He hadn't wanted to go west alone and now he didn't want to die alone. It didn't matter what made him do it. *Woodie,* he said, and he kept saying it: *Woodie, Woodie, Woodie.* My tears ran as I stood there, and when I trudged toward the corral, they flowed harder with every step. Nobody noticed me at first.

"This ain't fair!" Rufus cried out. "What kind of men are you!"

"The kind that hang men like you," said Captain Williams, holding his jaw as if he could still feel Rufus's long-ago punch. "X, would you do the honors."

X Beider climbed on another box so he could reach the noose.

"It wasn't murder!" my brother screamed.

A well-dressed mostly bald man with a trim white beard and mustache excused himself several times as he worked his way through the crowd. "You had your trial, son," he said almost too softly for me to hear. He wasn't short like Mr. Beidler, but he still had to look up quite a bit since Rufus was on the death box. "This is Judge Alexander J. Davis speaking."

"I can see you, and right through you."

"I have nothing to hide. A moment please, X. He is entitled to his last words."

"Whatever you say, Judge," said Mr. Beidler, who was about to fit the noose over Rufus's drooping head. "It's best not to drag these things out."

"I'll say when."

"Just doing my job, Judge." Mr. Beidler let go of the noose, crossed his fingers, and started twiddling his thumbs.

"I'll have you know I once refused to join the Vigilance Committee," Judge Davis said to Rufus. "I am *not* a member to this day. I have *not* agreed with some vigilante actions in the past. But a people's court has heard your case. You chose not to be represented by a lawyer, as is your right. I presided, as you well know, and I must abide by the decision of the court, which just happens to be the same decision reached by President Pfouts and his valuable committee."

"Thank you, Alex," said Paris Pfouts.

"You know damn well it wasn't murder," Rufus persisted. "Everyone knows."

"No matter the circumstances in which you shot Mr. Willingham, I'm afraid you were already slated to be executed." The judge bowed his head.

"So true," said Captain Williams, now caressing his chin. "You can't talk your way out of this, Rufus Hart. I found the list with your name on it."

"As you duly testified to when we held court," Judge Davis said. "That was important evidence we all took into consideration."

"Absolutely right, Alex," said Mr. Pfouts. "We can't tolerate repeat offenders."

"Damn that list," Rufus shouted. "Damn Red Yeager's list, too. Damn all lists. I'm innocent!"

"Did I hear you say 'when,' Judge?" asked Mr. Beidler, who was on his toes on the hangman's box to better reach the noose. Anticipation had him drooling like a dog.

"Wait!" screamed Rufus. "You sent someone for my brother, didn't you, Judge? I want to say goodbye to him. Bub has nobody to look after him now. I'm his only relative in the whole wide West. He's helpless. You promised."

"We'll say goodbye for you," said Captain Williams. "Do your duty, X."

"Just a minute," Judge Davis said. "I mean he does have a point. We can wait another minute to see if his brother does show up."

"No need," I called out, drying my eyes with my coat sleeves.

"I mean I'm here now."

Everyone saw me, for better or for worse. The vigilantes and other onlookers cleared a path for the pathetic little brother. I walked right up to the execution box.

"Glad you could make it, bub," Rufus said. "Wanted a last word with you."

"I appreciate it," I said. "But it doesn't have to be a last word. Did you tell them the truth—that Varina Willingham did the shooting."

"No, but I can tell you it's no use."

"Please . . . tell them."

"Hey, all you damned vigilantes. You want the truth? I'll tell you the goddamn truth. Varina, well known to many of you as Virginia Nevada, pulled the trigger on Walter Willingham. Not that any of you should blame the distraught lady for shooting the bastard. It was in self-defense as sure as I'm standing here before you this evening."

There was only a minor buzz in the crowd.

"We heard that in court from the very woman you speak of," said Judge Davis. "The people don't believe it. And frankly, neither do I."

"I do," I said, slapping at my head as if my hair was on fire. I'm a person."

"You're a brother."

"It doesn't matter," said Captain Williams. "We've made that abundantly clear. The condemned should have been hung already for his earlier crimes. He knows that. There is no mistaking it. His name is right on the list."

"Not Red Yeager's list," Judge Davis said. "Explain it to the boy, Captain, if you would be so kind."

"That's correct, Judge. It's the shorter list with only six names plain as day—Hayes Lyons, Boone Helm, Frank Parish, Jack Gallagher, Clubfoot George Lane, and Rufus Hart. The other five were hanged right here in Virginia City on January 14 of this year. Rufus Hart somehow escaped our grasp that day, and the list was laid aside and forgotten. It's like I said in court. This murder brought the list to light again. We are fortunate to get this second chance."

"Well said," said Judge Davis. "I just wanted the brother to know about this particular list that was exhibited as evidence during the trial."

"I heard about it," I yelled. "It's bogus!"

"Try to control yourself, son," the judge solemnly advised.

"But it *is* bogus. Your people's court is bogus. Everything is bogus."

"The rope is real and this is real justice," proclaimed Captain Williams, "We've dragged this out too long. You wanted to have a last word with your brother, Rufus. Well, here he is. Have your word or forever hold your peace. You have fifteen seconds."

Rufus cleared his throat but didn't say anything. Perhaps he had become tongue-tied. I knew the feeling. His hands had worked free and shot up to his neck, and he seemed to hang on for dear life. He squeezed the flesh too hard, forcing out choking sounds.

"You can't cheat the hangman," said X Beidler, as he slipped the noose over Rufus's head. "Better talk fast before you meet your maker, who might just be the Devil."

"No call for talk of the Devil," Judge Davis said. He then put a gentle hand on my shoulder while addressing Rufus. "Your brother has arrived as promised. Now say something."

Rufus began whistling a subdued "Dixie."

"What can I do?" I asked him.

"Not a damn thing. Well, one thing, little brother. Remember me forever."

"You know I'll do that. You think I could forget you?"

"Hell, no. But everyone else will. I'm thinking of Varina and Nellie and all the other females I ever knew, including our not-so-dear mother. And of course, Judge Me Not Davis, President of Pain Paris Pfouts, Captain Calamity James Williams, and the Devil X won't remember me any more than they will the god-damn Willingham brothers."

"We don't need to hear any more of this blasphemy." Captain Williams said. "Time's up! All's ready, X?"

"At your convenience, Captain. Just say the word."

"When, Mr. Pfouts?" the captain asked.

"When, Alex?" the president asked.

"Now," the judge said.

But Rufus kept on talking, causing a slight further delay. "I tell you, Woodie, with you remembering your big brother, it'll be like a part of me is still alive on Earth."

"As long as I'm alive anyway. Count on it."

"I am, bub. You're a good dumb kid. You'll live a long . . ."

Rufus couldn't finish. Williams gave his familiar order, "Men, do your duty." Many resolved feet kicked away the death box, none harder than the captain's own.

Out of something beyond desperation, I lunged forward, grabbed hold of the edge of the box, and attempted to pull it back so that Rufus could again put his feet down on something solid. Hands, many hands, shoved me out of the way, and I saw Rufus's feet dangling as I slammed against the other box, the one X Beidler still stood on. The hangman spread his legs and braced himself, trying to retain his balance as a lumberjack might riding felled logs downriver. But his box toppled onto its side and Mr. Beidler landed on his back on the hard ground. He wasn't moving, and the hands in my head applauded loudly. I crawled toward him, prepared to ring his neck or at least spit in his face, all the good having been temporarily knocked out of me. I didn't quite get there. Another knock, this one with a gun butt to the back of the head, flattened me good. I was out cold but somehow would later remember hearing a combination of whistling and choking from the hanged man and sobbing and moaning from me, along with a final word from Judge Alexander Davis: "It's for the best."

What happened after that I don't know. In fact, the next three weeks were lost to me. All that time I was in a coma or a stupor, whatever you want to call it. I later learned that a doctor present at the corral that night declared Rufus dead and then tended to me. That is to say, he took my pulse, placed a cool compress on my head, waved a candle back and forth before my eyes, and had me transported on a makeshift stretcher to Varina's two rooms above the Pay Dirt. She had only the one bed, though, and sleeping with an unconscious boy not only was no fun but also was bad for business. I was apparently there for just two nights before she had Curly Winters transport me in a wheelbarrow to his room at Moll Featherlegs's bordello. Curly had just the one bed, too, but he didn't mind giving it up even though he hardly knew me. He had other places to sleep on the nights when he tired of sleeping on the floor next to me. The bordello had many small rooms on the second story. Later, the big joke among the good-time girls (what they liked to be called instead of the many other names customers used) was that they made me a man while I was "stupefied from head to toe."

Because of my unresponsive condition, I didn't witness the big doings at Moll's on the night of March 8, only heard about them when I snapped out of it three days later. Jack Slade was on one of his sprees that night and brought along two good drinking friends. Mr. Slade, wearing only red long johns and his gun belt, entered the parlor on a bucking horse. His pals followed on foot wielding shotguns and ropes. They knew the layout of the place and stopped first at Curly Winters's room, where one held a shotgun on the house guard while the other one tied him to the bedpost and gagged him. I imagine they were quite drunk because, despite my condition, they tied me to another bedpost. Meanwhile, Mr. Slade either dismounted or else fell from the saddle (depending on who told the story) and proceeded to mount Moll Featherlegs herself either with his long johns on or them bunched at his ankles (again depending on who told the story).

For maybe half an hour after that the trio went from room to room, roping and whipping customers and forcing the good-time girls to drink cheap whiskey and listen to two crude songs they crafted—one called "Moll the Mother Doll and Her Naughty Barefooted and Bare-breasted Children" and the other titled "Moll's Fresh Doubts About the Philanderer Pfouts." Moll finally untied Curly Winters, and he went on to subdue the three house invaders without any trouble. Mr. Slade's two pals had lost track of their shotguns and needed rescuing, as they were being slapped and punched by female employees and male customers alike. Mr. Slade had already run out of energy and had fallen asleep on the stair landing while clutching Moll's lace unmentionables.

Moll brought assorted charges against the three men, specifically accusing the drunken Mr. Slade of "assault with attempt to seduce." Paris Pfouts, angered over the dirty song that linked him with Moll, agreed that this was inexcusable behavior. "He has gone too far," the vigilante president told the bordello owner, according to Moll. "You've seen his wife? Maria Slade is a well-formed black-haired beauty of graceful carriage with pleasing manners and . . . Anyway, for him to behave in such barbarous fashion with you when his wife is clearly . . . What I'm saying, Madam Featherlegs, is that what occurred here tonight is concrete confirmation of what so many of us have already said many times: The man is incorrigible."

Two days later, Mr. Slade got into more trouble with another drinking companion, Bill Fairweather, one of the founders of gold at Alder Gulch. Sheriff Jeremiah Fox arrested Mr. Fairweather for drunken rowdiness and brought him to Judge Davis's new courtroom, where they were joined by Mr. Slade. Mr. Fairweather produced a six-shooter that frightened Fox away and caused Mr. Slade to cheer. Judge Davis calmed the two drunks down and said they had best depart before the vigilantes came around. Mr. Fairweather sobered up fast enough to leave not only the courtroom but also the town. Mr. Slade took a different approach, sticking around and pulling a derringer to take the judge hostage to thwart any vigilante action. A bystander came along waving two six-shooters and freeing Judge Davis. Mr. Slade put away his derringer and issued his usual apologies. But it was too late. "Slade you are my prisoner," said a stern voice. Captain James Williams had arrived.

I heard all this from Moll Featherlegs when I woke up from my obliviousness the following day, March 11. First thing I did was ask if Rufus was all right. Obviously, I wasn't clear on the events of February 17, and Moll didn't make anything clearer. And when I asked where I was, she only said her name and that I was safe and warm and in good hands. She told me I'd have all my questions answered in due time. Right then, though, as an underdressed young lady spoon-fed me milk and mush from a bowl, Moll was intent on giving me every last bit of Jack Slade news.

"When I made my charges against Slade for his violent indiscretions here, Sheriff Fox should have locked him up," she said as the younger woman wiped mush escaping from my lips. "Then there wouldn't have been the scene in the courtroom and the attempt to capture Judge Davis at gunpoint. And if those things hadn't happened, Slade would be alive today."

"What, Mr. Slade is dead?" I said, spitting mush and milk.

"Hanged by the neck last night," said Moll as she fiddled with a string of pearls around her fleshy neck. "For all the havoc he created in my house, I didn't want a permanent solution. Poor bastard! He was a demon when in his cups, but he never killed anybody that we know of. Not even Judge Davis thought Slade deserved his fate."

I waved off the young lady feeding me, and she took the bowl away. I couldn't help but notice how freely her backside moved as she walked slowly to the door. I was temporarily distracted and full of regret, more from dismissing her than from Mr. Slade's dying.

"I didn't complain, mind you," Moll continued. "Some of the most dedicated and secretive vigilantes are regular customers." She paused and sighed, and I nodded my head to show she hadn't lost me.

"I saw him laid out in a blanket in the Virginia Hotel," she continued. "Maria Slade was weeping and telling everyone it was indecent to hang him instead of shooting him. At least they quickly cut him down from that crossbeam at the corral instead of leaving him dangling as they often do."

I bolted up in bed so suddenly that the startled Moll Featherlegs accidentally snapped off her pearl necklace.

"Corral!" I shouted. "You mean the same one where they . . . Rufus!"

"Yes. It's right behind Pfouts's store. Convenient. I wasn't sure how much you remembered. That was better than three weeks ago."

"Where's my brother now?"

"Underground. There was a thaw and the men could dig. I'm sorry, but it was best they put him under as soon as they could. And Doc wasn't sure if you ever would . . . you know. How about a second helping or a glass of a Hot Moll—that's half whiskey and half hot water with a touch of honey. My girls all drink it and never catch cold."

"No, thank you. I . . ."

What I did next was foolish. I pushed off the blankets and got out of bed. I'd been there too long; I had missed seeing my brother's last living moments and being able to mourn his passing in timely fashion. I wasn't thinking clearly. I was wearing a small nightshirt and drawers that didn't even have a button, but, like a sleepwalker, I just kept on walking. Out the door I went. In the hallway I saw so many partially clad women, young and old, I thought I'd also died in Virginia City and gone to heaven. They were all giggling openly or with their hands over their mouths. They were all staring at me and not just at my face, but I didn't know why and I didn't care.

"Hi, Woodie," the skinniest girl said. "Glad to see you upright. You must be feeling a mite better."

She tried to touch me with her long white fingers, but I pushed her aside. I pushed aside the others, too. "Where's Rufus's Army Colt?" I demanded to know. "I need a gun."

"That ain't what you need, sweet thing," the skinny one said even though I had pushed her. Strands of her dirty blond hair draped her right eye.

"I need it. I need it bad. Got to shoot the captain, the president, X, and all the rest."

"You can't get them all," shouted Moll Featherlegs, trailing me down the hall. "And the survivors will hang you."

"The ones I don't shoot, I'll hang myself. And I'll leave them hanging. Won't bury them no matter how soft the ground is."

Moll caught up with me and put a hand on my shoulder. What I did next was shameful. I spun around and punched her in the jaw. I had never struck anyone before like that, man or woman. All the good-time girls gasped as one. Moll didn't even go down, though. She staggered back and three or four of them caught her. I licked my knuckles and kept moving toward the front door like some common hard case.

"It's all right," Moll said. "He doesn't know what he's doing.

Curly! Come quick. Where are you, Curly?"

Curly Winters had been upstairs, but he came racing down, taking three steps at a time. He was brandishing a six-shooter that looked like the one Rufus used to carry. He cut me off on my path to the door, and I knew I could not get past this strong, wide body. But it pleased me at first.

"You brought me my gun," I said, reaching out for it.

"What you want me to do?" Curly asked, twirling the six-shooter as he pulled it away from my quivering fingers. "He's been sleeping in my bed all this time. I can't just shoot him."

"Of course not," Moll said. "Put that thing away. Just take him back to bed."

"Yes, ma'am."

"And where's my pony?" I shouted. "What did you do with Togu?"

"Your horse is still at the stable," Moll said. "He's being taken care of. Now let us take care of you."

"I'm healthy as a . . . a horse," I said, as I made another feeble grab for the six-shooter.

Curly tried to put the revolver in the waistband of his trousers, but I took a deep breath, lunged for the weapon, and somehow knocked him off balance. Next, I threw another punch. I missed his jaw and connected with his Adam's apple. Curly screamed in pain, and then some of the good-time girls screamed in sympathy for their male guardian. I think all that screaming snapped me out of my walking stupor, because I became aware what an out-of-character fiend I had become. I started to apologize to Curly, Moll, and every last one of those young girls whose mouths hung open. I hung my head in shame and was staring forlornly down at my buttonless drawers when Curly elected to raise the butt of the six-shooter and bring it down on the top of my head. Unlike on the night Rufus was hanged, I saw it coming. But I couldn't move in time. And for the second time in what was supposed to have been a short stay in Virginia City, I passed into obliviousness.

CHAPTER TWENTY

In *Man from Montana: How He Escaped the Noose,* Red Ranger is twice shot and left for dead but is never hit over the head. The first time he is shot, it is in the belly while trying to rescue from the gallows an unnamed innocent man (since Rufus is excluded from W.A. Phillips's book) who was suspected of being the vengeance-minded brother of the late Red Yeager. Red Ranger is brought to the home of the pretty schoolmarm Lucinda Darlington, who nurses him back to health. But then the schoolmarm is set upon by monstrous Mr. X and other lustful vigilantes, and Red Ranger is shot again, this time in the head, while trying to arrest Mr. X and put him in the jail of the sheriff, Sylvester "Sly" Fox. The vigilantes vote against hanging Red Ranger and, instead, bury him—dead or still barely alive doesn't seem to be a concern—in a shallow grave. But Lucinda digs up his "barely breathing red-caped body with her lovely bare hands and re-nurses him to become a whole good man, not so he can wreak violent vengeance on the vicious vigilantes but so he can become a Red Knight who ranges the often cruel Wild West to rescue and befriend broken and damaged wives from their bodily and mentally abusive husbands, whether white or red or half-breeds." Red Ranger takes half a year to recover from his bullet to the head, and upon regaining his full senses he sees Lucinda waiting there in a straight-back chair, where she seems to have been sitting for six long months. He then goes out to "save the wives in dire need of saving," but still finds time to wreak some vengeance on vigilante types in Montana.

Yes, W.A. Phillips had an active imagination, but he really was influenced by true life events. It took me a long time to recover from the second gun-butt blow to the head—not half a year like Red Ranger but nearly four months. When I regained full consciousness in Virginia City there was no local schoolmarm named Lucinda waiting for me, of course. Lucinda was fictional. And there was no Bannack schoolmarm named Lucia waiting for me either; Lucia Darling was in Bannack and had been mostly waiting for Uncle Sidney Edgerton to return from Washington. But there was a woman at my bedside in Virginia City in July when my eyes finally opened wide and clear. It was Lucy Hart, my sister, and she was not alone. Standing in the corner chatting with a couple of underdressed girls was a slight man with a large curling mustache that seemed to tug upward, causing his chin to stay raised as he sniffed about the candlelit room.

"You seem to be in good hands, Woodie," Lucy said once I recognized her.

"I'll say he is," said the man, stepping away from the girls and gliding up to a position directly behind my sister.

"Lucy," I said. "Lucy, Lucy, Lucy."

"Yes, it really is me. I was hoping you'd come around and be in good enough condition to celebrate your 16th birthday. May I be the first to say happy birthday to you, dear brother Woodie."

"Happy what? What date is this?"

"Friday, July 1. I got here four or five days ago, and you've been drifting back and forth between unresponsiveness and a state of confusion."

"In the year 1864," added her companion, who, to see around Lucy, stood on the toes of his boots, which I noticed had star-shaped leather inlays. "Summertime. With your double dose of head trouble, you pretty much missed the entire spring. For your information, the Civil War continues to take a heavy toll back in the States this summer. Or perhaps that is something even those in full possession of their faculties don't pay a mind to way out here in the remote wilds."

"Pay him no mind," Lucy said to me, waving away her companion. "Your birthday, which also happens to be the nation's birthday, is just around the corner."

"How time flies when you're half-conscious at best."

"Do you know where you are?" Lucy asked, concern written all over her face, which was still pleasing enough, though showing far more lines than I remembered.

I nodded and smiled even as tears formed and the pair of underdressed girls giggled. Lucy smiled back, mostly with her eyes, which seemed kinder and more attentive than ever, perhaps because of the well-defined wrinkles around them. It was the one face I remembered fondly from my Washington days—well, her face and that of President Abraham Lincoln. At some point during my slow recovery, Curly Winters had carried me up to my own little bedroom at the end of the upstairs hall and reclaimed his own bed downstairs. Possibly it was all the noise—squeaking springs, screams, moans, ejaculations—from the active nearby rooms that brought me out of my stupor.

"You went in and out of consciousness many times, but now, Madam Featherlegs and the doctors all agree, you have decided to stay with us for the duration, fully aware of the people and things around you, except during times of natural sleep, of course. You are aware of the onetime Capitol Hill dandy at my back and the two young ladies of the house over in the corner?"

"I am."

"Excellent. It pleases me considerably that you are alive in this strange western land, Woodie. Remember how I worried so when Rufus took you off on that train into the deep unknown and . . ."

eard about our brother . . ." I blurted out.

n peace . . . with all the others."

any months ago, yet I . . . I have lost track

?" Tears multiplied quickly, a combination

py ones, and they flowed quickly to my

ed them with my tongue. Life tasted bit-

to show it, not to Lucy anyway.

ng my forehead. "Hanging is hard. Back

g some deserters but mostly shooting

civil war. Here, there is peace, but not a

nd."

gue me," said her companion. "Can't

ad. Same might be said of Rufus, I

net the man. Lucy says he was bad,

igue me as well, Woodie. You have a

m and don't judge people."

e fiery tempers," Lucy told him.

iet and sweet."

ns." He tapped my forehead. "You

il without regard to your personal

outside the context of war, a genuine

where all that was coming from, but

, he interrupted me by shaking my

a rag doll rather than a flesh-and-

roduce us before, but I don't think it

loudy head. Name is Wilberforce Ana-

er gave me 'Wilberforce' because it was

te lover. My father gave me 'Anaconda'

born on a South American sailing ship

snake. I was beaten up too many times

t by Anaconda until I was old enough to

more poisonous snake than my grand-

father. I had to overcome a miserable upbrin
Lucy—and you, too, it figures. That's one of th
Lucy and I have in common. I had one good bro
Spencer, who was hanged as a Yankee spy in R
year. Lucy had one good brother, too, and h
somehow surviving in what I surmise to be the wi
in the whole West. Lucy and I are a perfect match
husband who wanted to control everything about h
her breathing at night, and I've been looking my wh
woman like Lucy, who holds my utmost respect an
under control by simply caressing my . . ."

Lucy slapped Wilberforce Anaconda Phillips
mouth, which shocked me. But it also stopped him
and put a silly grin on his face.

"Ain't she wonderful," he said. "I was only goin
neck."

"Nice to meet you . . . eh . . . Wilberforce."

"I only go by initials now. Call me W.A.—every
Wilberforce and Anaconda no longer exist; I've cre
identity. I am an adventurer and a writer, not necessa
order."

"You write true adventure stories?"

"He hasn't written anything yet," said Lucy. "He's
talker."

"And a listener, my dear," he said, shaking his lef
"As for who you are, Woodie Russell Hart, I've heard
you, feel like I know you better than my own dead goo
who wasn't actually a spy but had only infiltrated t
lines to . . . All right. All right. Lucy is rolling her ey
take a hint. I'll shut up now, Lady Lucy, and go see
gals are cooking up for supper. You can slap me again l

"He's a friend," Lucy said. "Just a friend."

"And bodyguard," he added, patting her on the sh

"We all know how dangerous it is out here in the untamed West."

"We all know I can take care of myself."

"No *body* I'd rather guard. Luce knows she can always count on W.A."

W.A. Phillips kissed Lucy on the left cheek, winked at me, and then backpedaled to the corner. He left the room with an underdressed girl on each arm and his chin raised as if totally pleased with his initials and his clever, under-control self.

"He's an unusual man," Lucy said when he was out the door. "Good, I suppose, in his own way." She did not explain further; she changed the subject. "It was no surprise to me when I heard Rufus was dead. Not that I wished that upon him. What matters now is that you are alive. We must keep you that way."

She sat down on the bed, which still smelled like one of the good-time girls despite my extended stay. In the next few minutes she told me about the rest of the Hart family, and it made me understand why she hadn't taken Rufus's execution too hard. Our alcohol-soaked father had curled up against the Washington Monument one cold night and died of what was called "exposure." Our mother held back her tears and was now being kept warm at night by a one-armed Union soldier who was an officer in the Invalid Corps. Of the nine Hart sons, six were known dead, two were unaccounted for, and only I was known to be living. Before leaving Washington, I had known about my two "Forty-niner" brothers—Adam drowned in the shallow Platte River, as reported by Hiram, who told us so in the only letter he wrote home before disappearing somewhere in the Sierras. I had *nearly* witnessed Rufus's death on February 17, 1864. Lucy told me about the others—Clement was missing after running off to Canada with two runaway slaves; Jacob chose suicide (he hanged himself) rather than fight for either the North or the South; our two Union soldiers, Irwin and

Franklin, both died at Payne's Farm during the Battle of Mine Run in Virginia; and Samuel, after contracting malaria and obtaining enough quinine to control his symptoms, accidentally took a fatal dose of same.

I told her it was a miracle that she was neither deceased nor missing, and we both had a nervous laugh in memory of my old detectable sense of humor that had seemingly deserted me during my western ordeals. I could have dwelled on all the deaths in the family and in the territory, but it was my turn to change the subject. I didn't quite manage it.

"Your Mr. Phillips mentioned you had a husband who was not him," I said. "This husband isn't dead, is he?"

"Only to me," Lucy said. "He would still *have* me. W.A. was right when he said my husband tried to control my every movement. He forbade me from seeing mother, not that I wished to see her after the overbearing one-armed officer took command of her life. But my husband, who actually has much in common with that one-armed officer, also forbade me from seeing people I liked or from tending the wounded and sick at Mount Pleasant Hospital."

"I'm sorry. It must be hard to love a man."

I hadn't meant that as a joke, but her nervous laughter returned for several seconds. "I might have loved him once, before we were married. You know him, Woodie. Soon after you left for the West, I married William Penn Norton."

"Oh, right, the big-talking railroad man who wanted to get rid of Rufus and me."

"Have you heard it said you only regret the things you don't do?"

"That's mostly true in my case. I don't do much."

"You do more than you think. I mean you *think* more than you *do,* but you still do a lot."

"I don't really think so. I . . ."

"In any case, I very much regret marrying William Penn Norton—the biggest mistake of my life. But there's no do-over."

"That bad, huh? I'm sorry."

"I should have read the signs, like how he demanded I see the world—everything from railroad building to Manifest Destiny to the gold standard to military draft evasion—exactly as he did. Plus, he never had any use for a single member of our family. But then neither did you, did you, Woodie?"

"I wouldn't say that. There was always you, Lucy. I don't know what I would have done in those childhood days without you and Aunt Clementina."

My sister bent down and planted five kisses on various parts of my face. "And I'm here for you again. You're the brother I always liked best."

"But how'd you get here? How'd you know I was even here?"

"Pure luck, or call it fate. William Penn Norton dragged me to this party on Capitol Hill that countless significant and useful—to him—government officials and businessmen were attending. He even told me what dress to wear, who to talk to, and how much food to put in my mouth. I planned on having a simply miserable evening, but then I happened to meet someone you know and, well, it was delightful and rewarding. Can you guess who?"

"Abe Lincoln?"

"Try again."

"Walt Whitman?"

"No, no. I mean somebody you really know and who is not a member of our family."

I couldn't think of a single name. "I don't know anybody there. I give up."

"He wasn't from Washington. He came from far away. One more guess."

"Ulysses S. Grant? Robert E. Lee?"

"Now you're being silly, not that silliness is a bad thing after what you've been through."

I recalled how Lucy liked to play "Guess Who?" when we were children. Me giving up didn't always end the game. "I don't know," I said. "And furthermore, I don't care."

"Of course, you do. The fine gentleman's name was Mr. Sidney Edgerton, a most significant and useful—*to you*—figure in Montana Territory."

I was stunned, of course. Somehow, two worlds that I had seen as completely different had come together. My mind spun with questions, but the first one that actually came out of my mouth was, "Did you say Montana Territory, Lucy?"

She had. And it was. Lucy explained that on May 26, 1864, Abraham Lincoln, my hero, had signed the bill creating Montana Territory into law. Bannack and Virginia City—and, yes, little Hell Gate, too—no longer need answer to the Idaho territorial government in Lewiston on the far side of the Bitterroots. Lucy said that Mr. Edgerton had worked diligently to get the job done after arriving in Washington at the beginning of March. Among his allies was none other than Francis Thompson, who had also made the strenuous trip from Bannack. The two men displayed gold dust and nuggets in the Capitol, and members of the House of Representatives and Senate were duly impressed by the glitter. Gold reserves could surely help the Northern cause. Virginia City miners were extracting at least $600,000 a week. The congressmen also learned of the summary executions by the vigilantes but showed no shock and expressed no criticism. After all, a much greater horror, a bloody civil war, was ongoing at their doorstep. What's more, they understood the vigilantes to be mostly Republicans from the North and the men they hanged to be Democrat secessionists.

One senator, Charles Sumner, objected to the name "Montana" because it sounded peculiar, as if it was "borrowed from some novel." He would have preferred to give it a "good Indian name" but was unable to think of one and knew no American Indian who might suggest one. Even after the name passed muster, the Montana bill stalled over such matters as Negro suffrage, even though black men were as scarce as upper-class Bostonians in the Montana gold camps. Lucy said that her new friend Sidney Edgerton became anxious not only because he wanted to be made governor of the new territory but also because he missed his family, which was about to grow as soon as his wife completed her pregnancy. In the end, Congress approved a bill that gave the vote in the new territory only to white men. Sidney Edgerton shrugged that off.

After the president put his John Hancock on the dotted line, Sidney Edgerton visited President Lincoln in the White House. Lucy wasn't there, of course, but she said Mr. Edgerton told her all about it afterward. He was not shy about asking what he wanted—to be appointed governor of the new Montana Territory. Abe Lincoln, though, had heard opposition from several senators who objected to the fact that Mr. Edgerton had neglected his position as chief justice of Idaho Territory and as a result of that neglect no courts were established and more than twenty men, supposedly guilty of criminal acts, were unlawfully hanged. Mr. Lincoln was a sensitive man, so those hangings even amid the horrors of the war must have touched a nerve. He told Mr. Edgerton he would need to think over his request.

"Sidney packed his bags without knowing if he'd have a job when he got back to Bannack," Lucy said. "And I packed my bags. I would accompany him. I told him William Penn Norton need not know. I told him my husband was like an enormous black cat who keeps a white mouse in its claws to tease and torture but not to kill, at least not for a long while."

"Mr. Edgerton went along with that? I mean, he let you go with him?"

"I'm here, aren't I? He thought I'd make a delightful traveling companion. As not to give the appearance of impropriety, Sidney and I agreed there must be a chaperone who could also double as a bodyguard for both of us."

"Don't tell me, W.A. Phillips?"

"Who else? He was from a poor family barely making ends meet on Capitol Hill and was dying to go west. In fact, he said he would die if I went without him."

"How terribly romantic."

"No romance was involved. I had met him on the public grounds reading a book; it was *The Black Avenger of the Spanish Main,* by someone named Buntline, but we talked and he knew lines from Macbeth—that's Shakespeare."

"I heard of him. Shakespeare that is."

"Yes, well, W.A. and I decided that William Penn Norton was like Macbeth, you know, consumed by ambition. Not that W.A. doesn't have his own ambitions."

"I don't know much about ambition."

"W.A. was the only one I could talk to about my marital difficulties, and he had become quite fond of me. He would do anything for me. I wanted him as a chaperone *only.* He only pretended to be a bodyguard. He had never fired a gun before. He lost every fistfight he had ever been in, either as Wilberforce or Anaconda. He's not a large man."

"No, he didn't appear to be."

"All his battles as W.A. have been verbal, some oral but most written. He has some experience as an independent newspaperman and has written many letters to editors. I find him entertaining and easy to talk to, so different from William Penn Norton."

"The three of you traveled all that way together?"

"Yes. It was funny during our stay in Salt Lake City in June. Several Mormon elders were aghast, believing I was a woman with two husbands. The truth, of course, was that neither man was my man in that sense, and my actual husband was back in Washington, no doubt seething over my secret departure from his ironclad grasp."

I immediately thought of Varina Willingham, who I had been trying to forget. I couldn't see Varina and Lucy having anything in common except that each had run away from a no-good controlling spouse.

"The trip was safe, then?" I asked.

"Safe and good. Not a sign of a red savage. W.A. didn't have to fire his new rifle one time. Oh, and something else happened when we were in Salt Lake. Sidney received the telegram he had been hoping for from the White House—friend Abe had answered his dreams and appointed him governor of Montana. I'm happy for him. It beats being chief justice in Idaho."

"So, he made it. Good for him."

"And good for the new territory, I'd say."

"And so you have. You met Mr. Edgerton's family in Bannack?" I was mostly wondering what Lucy thought of Lucia Darling.

"What, oh we didn't stop there. Out of Utah Territory, we rode with freighters who said Bannack was too far out of their way. They were eager to reach the richer communities at Alder Gulch. Sidney and I said our goodbyes a few days ago. I imagine he's arriving at his Bannack home about now and seeing his baby girl for the first time."

"Mary Edgerton gave birth, did she? I knew she was . . . you know."

"Expecting?"

"Right. I saw Mr. Edgerton talking to her . . . you know . . . stomach."

"We heard it happened on May 23. She called the young thing 'Idaho.' Isn't that funny? Montana Territory was carved out of Idaho Territory just three days later. Idaho should have been called Montana, little girl-wise."

"I reckon," I said. "But neither Idaho nor Montana sounds like a suitable name for a baby girl."

Moll Featherlegs entered the room and had something to say about that. "Idaho is supposed to be an Indian word meaning 'gem of the mountains,' but it's fake Indian, made up by some white politician. Montana, and I got this from a highly educated customer, is derived from the Latin word *'montaanus.'* That set plenty of the girls a-giggling and repeating the Latin version up and down the hallways. Monta-ANUS. Hardly ever hear *asshole* around here anymore. The girls got educated."

I kind of squirmed in the bed. I didn't think Lucy should be hearing such things.

"Interesting, Moll," said Lucy. "Sidney Edgerton told me that Montana came from the Spanish word *montaña,* meaning mountainous."

"That must be the polite version. So how you two Harts getting along?"

"Better than most brothers and sisters, I imagine," said Lucy, patting my cheek and then giving it a slight pinch.

"And your friend with the smiling mustache is getting along famously with my girls."

"Hope he doesn't talk them all to death."

"Amen, sister. But he asks questions and listens to the girls, too. I even saw him writing down some of their words like that schoolteacher turned newspaperman Thomas Dimsdale. If he stays on much longer, he'll have to pay for all that talking."

Lucy started to apologize for W.A. Phillips's brazenness but was interrupted by Curly Winters, who politely knocked before entering the room and then looked down at his feet as he apologized most sincerely for cracking me over the head with his six-shooter way back when. Moll spoke for him, too, saying her strong-armed house guard had never killed a man in his life and all the men he'd ever struck before with fist or weapon only stayed blacked out for an hour or less.

"Hell," said Curly, whose face was dripping with what I figured was nervous sweat. He glanced at Lucy. "I mean *heck,*" he said softly. "I didn't mean to hit you so hard, Mr. Woodie. I thought I knew my own strength, but I must have been carried away by the moment."

"Me, too," I said. "I must have been out of my head before you knocked me cold."

"I don't know about that."

"He was protecting me and my girls," Moll Featherlegs said. "Just doing his job."

"Too damn—darn—well, I reckon. I'm mighty sorry."

"Sure." I had only lost about four months out of my life, but I was still young.

"It was madam's notion for me to move you up here," Curly continued. "You could have slept in my bed forever. I didn't want you to die. You're a nice fella, and, as you know, them vigilantes don't show much toleration for men that kill other fellas, even by accident."

"It wasn't so bad being in bed and I'm fine now," I told him. I sat up and thought about swinging my legs off the bed and standing up. But there was the question of whether my legs would fully cooperate. Also, I wasn't exactly sure what I was wearing under the blankets.

"You sure?" Mr. Winters said, wiping his forehead with one of his large forearms.

"Sure, I'm sure. And they can't hang you if I don't die."

"I'm not so sure about that. You might recall that Jack Slade never killed . . ."

"He's done enough recalling, Curly," Moll Featherlegs told her house man.

"Yes, ma'am, but I also wanted to apologize to him about his horse. He run off some weeks ago . . . got tired of waiting for you to recover."

"Togu's gone?" It hit me hard that I had lost my horse and that I hadn't inquired about him sooner.

"Back to his people, I'm thinkin'," Mr. Winter said. "You know, the Injuns. I'm real sorry."

"Bannocks," I said. "I hope they're not so hungry they have to eat him."

"You've made your apologies. Curly," said Moll. "Now have one of the girls draw you a bath. You're perspiring like a pig on a spit."

"Sorry again, Mr. Woodie," he said as he awkwardly shuffled toward the door. "And sorry to you, Miss Lucy, for, you know, perspiring like . . . I'm plum sorry all around."

"Don't hold it against Curly," Moll said when he was gone. "He means well and is a good man at heart, which I can't say for the majority of men who've passed through my pearly white doors, present company excepted."

I nodded in appreciation, but my mind was elsewhere—first on Togu, but I told myself the tough little pony was better off without me since I had been so immobile, and that allowed my thoughts to shift again. "He mentioned Mr. Slade. I started to wonder."

"I told you about his hanging. You don't recall?"

"I recall all right. What I was wondering is how many men have been suspended in the air since Mr. Slade and while I've been recovering from my broken head?"

"I can count the number on my pinky," said Moll, holding out her right hand. Three of the four fingers on her left hand had rings on them, all golden. Only the pinky was bare.

"Well, that's good news, isn't it? Judge Davis and his people's court must have taken over from the Vigilance Committee."

"Not hardly. The judge quit because of the Slade hanging, and his people's court faded away. The committee headed by Paris Pfouts was still in command. His vigilantes were ready to act again, and they did last June when a Nevada City saloon owner named Brady shot a miner named Murphy. Everybody thought Murphy would soon die. Captain Williams and his many associates decided to take care of the murderer earlier."

"Same old thing, right? Another hanging."

"Yes. I believe it happened outside of Nevada City. Don't recall the details. I do know that Murphy recovered from his wounds."

"What a disappointment that must have been to the captain that the murdered man didn't cooperate and actually die. Of course, the captain probably would have hanged this Mr. Brady anyway—attempted murder not being so different from murder."

"Many folks in Alder Gulch saw a difference. They began questioning, loudly or not, the hasty actions of the vigilantes. Coincidence or not, there hasn't been an execution since, not in Alder Gulch, not in Bannack, not in Hell Gate, not anywhere."

"A peaceful summer in Montana Territory . . . so far," said Lucy. "How terribly nice."

Chapter Twenty-One

The blowout in the bordello seemed like the biggest thing to hit Alder Gulch since gold was discovered, but most folks didn't know about it, or if they did, they couldn't get past Curly Winters guarding the pearly white front doors. It was a private affair. It all centered around me—the "delightful, distinguished guest," as Moll Featherlegs called me—just because it was my 16th birthday and because, as I was shocked to learn later, Lucy Hart Norton had paid for everything using money that had once been locked in William Penn Norton's personal safe behind the portrait of John W. Garrett, president of the Baltimore & Ohio Railroad. "Some might call it robbery," she told me. "But I would say he owed me. Same way a field slave might leave the cotton plantation with a pair of the master's shiny black boots."

I suppose it was naïve of me to have thought Madam Featherlegs would shut out her regular customers, including more than a few vigilantes, just to give a party to a burdensome boy who had never emptied his pockets for her or for one of her faithful employees. Back in Washington, the Hart family had gone through too many darn birthdays and too little spending money to make any anniversary special. "None of my babies was born with silver spoons in their mouths and they ain't about to get none after the fact," our mother once told Lucy when her young inquisitive only daughter wondered about this happy birthday tradition she had heard about on the street.

"This, hopefully, will make up for some of that," the older and wiser Lucy told me when she presented me with my best sixteenth birthday present. "It isn't silver, but I hope this will do." It was a gold spoon, and it did just fine when I used it instead of a fork to dig into the cherry pie she made and the Indian pudding some of the good-time girls concocted.

The working residents of the house enjoyed this break from their daily routine by dressing up in their finest clothes, which meant they wore more clothes than usual. Moll Featherlegs wore a voluminous white dress with a small white collar of lace that was closed at the neck by a large brooch; tight on her head and hanging loosely over her shoulders was a hooded red cape. The good time girls started calling her "Little Red Riding Hood," which amused Moll for at least four reasons—nothing was the least bit "little" about her, it made her feel young, she once had a patron she called the "Big Bad Wolf," and she liked to think of her life as an adult fairy tale. "You look good enough to eat, Madam," W.A. Phillips told her, turning away, at least for five minutes, from the more available morsels all around.

I must say, though, that the celebration got out of hand. I mostly blame W.A. Phillips, who drank so much grog that he did a fair imitation of the late Jack Slade. To make a sordid story short, he sloshed his way from girl to girl asking for free party favors since there weren't any other customers in the house. At least he didn't carry a whip or a rope, although he did use a newly acquired fountain pen for both pricking and writing on bare flesh until the madam of the house confiscated it. As for me, at Phillips's insistence—and backed by the girls he hadn't yet offended too deeply—some of that grog more than touched my lips. For the first time in my life I became "three sheets to the wind," as Moll Featherlegs referred to it, she having been acquainted with countless drunken sailors during her early days in the business at assorted Atlantic Ocean ports. In fact, one of the more generous or more drunk sailors gave her that red satin cape without asking for anything in return. At one point late in my birthday celebration, according to W.A. Phillips, a yellow-haired, yellow-toothed good-time girl named Little Gold Bit initiated me (though possibly it was my second initiation) into another realm of manhood in the room next to mine. I don't remember a thing about this rite of passage; I may as well have been unconscious again.

The next day, I wasn't about to ask Lucy, Moll, or even Little Gold Bit if they knew what I might have done or had done to me in my drunken state on my birthday night. I avoided looking at any of them in the eye or anywhere else above their ankles. But in the afternoon, when I stepped out into the hallway, Little Gold Bit put a hand on the small of my back and told me I shouldn't feel bad or guilty.

"I . . . I don't," I replied, but my skull had started pulsing again. "I mean not too much." I didn't ask her why I *shouldn't,* but she told me anyway.

"Good because I wasn't expecting anything," she said, flashing those yellow teeth. "Your sister already paid me in full."

"I'm just glad it's over," I said, which didn't sound right. "I mean my sixteenth birthday. My head still hurts. I never drank so much in my entire life. Truth be known, I really never drank any grog or red-eye before. Rufus—that was my brother—could never get me to have a glass of whiskey even when he ran a saloon up in Hell Gate. He would have laughed at my performance last night. I can tell you one thing, Miss, I won't be doing that again. Never."

"What about the other? You should try it again sometime when you ain't so lushy."

Sensing my face was reddening fast, I turned away. I suppose if I had been older and more experienced, I would have given her a firm squeeze and a smart verbal response. As it was, I waved one of Lucy's white handkerchiefs at her without looking at her or saying another word.

"You'll need a bag of gold dust next time, mister," she called out to me. "I don't come cheap."

I was exaggerating some when I spoke of the blowout in the bordello. I mean it was a big deal to me because of the drinking and the "other." But the real action was outside the pearly white doors of Moll's place. It was Independence Day after all. Up and down the gulch, folks were saluting the flag, parading, making bonfires, shooting off muskets, and feasting on summertime fruits and vegetables brought up from Salt Lake. I reckon it wasn't all the folks though. Virginia City certainly had its share of Union loyalists, but there were plenty of people who were still counting on Confederate General Robert E. Lee to emerge victorious in the state of Virginia and save the South. I reckon if Rufus had still been alive, he would have been one of them, although he wanted no personal involvement in the Rebel cause. Lucy was the opposite, hating with a passion slavery and anything else the South stood for with its own passion.

As for me, I was an Abe Lincoln man, plain and simple. His ways were inscrutable, but his honesty, sincerity, and conscience showed through; sometimes he had trouble being decisive; often he grew weary of the divided world around him; and he was, as he admitted, "rather inclined to silence." I could relate to those things. Not that I compared myself to the great man. He was many things I was not—deeply intelligent, energetic, earnest, enduring, persevering, generous, bearded, and tall. Anyway, I was in no condition to think about President Lincoln on the birthday of the nation and myself, but he was much on my mind in the days that followed when I said my goodbyes to the bordello and Virginia City.

I adapted for my own resolve on the road ahead some of the words he used in his famous address at Gettysburg the previous

November: *all men are created equal . . . from these honored dead we take increased devotion to that cause for which they gave the last full measure of devotion . . . that these dead shall not have died in vain . . . shall have a new birth of freedom . . . shall not perish from the earth.* In short, I was looking ahead—like the preamble to the U.S. Constitution said and Mr. Lincoln believed in wholeheartedly—to the formation of a more perfect territory that established "legal" justice for all, ensured some kind of domestic tranquility for me somewhere, provided for my defense from both robbers and vigilantes, promoted my general welfare (I needed to get a job again), and secured the blessings of liberty to me (so I could act a little freer) and to Lucy (so she could stay free of her husband).

"Give me a penny and I'll tell you what you're thinking," said W.A. Phillips, on the eve of our departure by stagecoach to Bannack. He held out one hand as if I had a one-cent piece to give him. He kept his other hand behind his back.

"I know what I'm thinking," I snapped. I was plenty annoyed with him because he kept egging me on to carouse with him in or out of Moll's place and, even more disturbing, to seek "luscious revenge" against Captain James Williams and the other men who executed my brother.

"You are thinking ever so deeply about how much you'll miss every bit of Little Gold Bit in the weeks and months to come. Don't deny it. I can see it in your green eyes. They are turning blue."

"Wrong. I was thinking of the preamble to the Constitution and new Montana Territory. Before that, about President Lincoln's Gettysburg address."

"You don't say. Strange but I know you as a rule don't lie. Maybe your eyes are turning red and white as well as blue. And speaking of red, look what Mother Moll donated to my cause." From behind his back he brought out the red satin cape she had worn at my birthday party. "The only thing she asked in return was for me to include her in my book about colorful characters in early Montana Territory."

"I didn't know you were writing a book."

"You haven't been paying attention then. I told you W.A. Phillips was a writer. That's what writers do—they write."

I nodded. I couldn't recall ever referring to myself in the third person. "How many pages is your book so far, W.A.?" I asked.

"I'm in the note-taking stage now. I want to write something with backbone. That takes time, you know."

"Oh, so you haven't started yet?"

"The undertaking has begun. Don't rush me."

"Sorry."

"For your information, my good man, I intend to write many books. Hell, I might even include you in one or two of them. Care to try on the red cape, Woodie? Moll gave it to me, but I'm giving it to *you.* It's the right thing to do. It ain't meant for me. With your red hair it will make you even more colorful."

"No thanks. Why would anyone put me in a book?"

"I'm *not* just anyone. I'm W.A. Phillips."

"Sorry. At least you have ambition."

"Damn right I do. Now, try on the red cape."

I pulled away from him instead. "It's meant for a girl, isn't it?"

"Could be. So, you're thinking of Little Gold Bit again."

Actually, I was thinking mostly about getting away from all the soiled doves, Madam Moll Featherlegs, and Curly Winters. No matter how kind and understanding they were, I felt out of place, somewhat unclean. Outside the bordello walls it was worse, considerably dirtier, what with the vigilante citizens, Captain James Williams, X Beidler, and Varina Willingham strutting about Virginia City's Wallace Street and other ugly roadways. I knew every last one of them would be burrowing inside my head like pocket gophers until it was my turn to be buried, but at least I could put some physical distance between *them* and me. Soon my sister was hankering to move on herself. I could have kissed her for getting the same urge as me.

I had wanted to go back to Hell Gate, and maybe I would have had I still owned a horse. It was Lucy's idea to go to Bannack, where she could see her friend Sidney Edgerton and the place where I once was a houseguest. W.A. Phillips would go anywhere Lucy wanted to go as long as it was west, not east. The gallows where Sheriff Plummer and Deputies Stinson and Ray had swung intrigued him. He insisted that even ghosts could be colorful. We went by stagecoach, which naturally brought to mind that first trip to Bannack with Rufus. It was clear rolling, though—no interference from any road agents along the road or at the Point of Rocks stage stop, even though a couple of other passengers were carrying gold, Lucy was carrying Eastern money, and I was carrying a gold spoon. Lucy had wrapped her greenbacks in handkerchiefs and sewed them inside the folds of her traveling dress. She didn't mind being lumpy in places, even though W.A. Phillips kidded her about it until she threatened to make him ride on top with the driver.

"You think the vigilantes eradicated the outlaw element or were we just damn lucky?" W.A. Phillips said when we pulled safely into Bannack. He sounded disappointed. I was anxious to rid my mind of ghastly images, particularly the one where Rufus was hanging high, his legs kicking at the clouds, his neck cracking with every shift in the wind. The would-be author, on the other hand, wanted to see ghastly things to write about, since in his book ghastly translated to colorful. "Maybe the bad men were afraid to tangle with you, Red," he added, trying to show off his dry wit. But he couldn't keep a straight face. I had an easy time *not* smiling with him.

That was the first time he called me "Red." My hair being the way it was, I suppose it hadn't taken much imagination on his part. Of course, I had heard it before from people far wiser and kinder than him, such as Mr. Worden and Mr. Higgins up in Hell Gate. It was more annoying coming from him.

"It feels deader than Virginia City," I said, brushing off the front of my shirt as if the dust was death itself.

"Now, now, your gloominess won't do," Lucy said. She tried to take a large optimistic breath but ended up coughing. "Plenty of gold dust around," she said.

"Not as much as there was," I said. "Not that it matters to me."

"I said to stop it, Woodie. Lose the long face. We both lost a brother, you know."

"You never approved of Rufus. You . . . never mind. I'm sorry, sis. I'm tired from the stagecoach ride, I guess. I'm glad I'm here with you."

Lucy smiled and brushed dust off the back of my shirt, not even bothering with the cloud hovering over her own clothes. "Goodrich Hotel," she said, reading the sign on an otherwise not particularly inviting building. "This looks like the place to stay. There won't be room for all of us at the Edgertons. Grab the luggage, W.A."

"There she is," said W.A. Phillips, pointing over the top of the hotel and past a few cabins on the hillside. "That's where they hung the sheriff. The high point of the town no doubt." He looked ready to bound up the hill to the gallows, but Lucy shoved the biggest bag in his path.

"And over there on that hill to the east is where somebody finally buried the sheriff," I said. "Bannack's cemetery. I used to spend some time up there."

"Nice place to visit but wouldn't want to reside there, huh?" said W.A. Phillips, now scanning this other hill. "We'll go up there as soon as we get the baggage inside. Graveyards tell a lot about a place."

"We'll get our rooms and then go to the Edgertons," Lucy said. "It's the polite thing to do. And no talk about gallows and cemeteries from you two. Sidney is the governor of a brand-new territory and is full of optimism about Montana's future. Let's share in that optimism."

"Sure, Lucy dear," W.A. Phillips said. "But everyone has to die."

"Not now, W.A. You sound like Woodie."

"How many dead you've seen out here, Red?" he asked me.

I suppose I had started counting in my head when Lucy told him to shut up and raised a threatening hand.

"Anyway," he continued. "There's bound to be more gold and some honest sheriffs down the road. Hell, in another five or ten years, they might even stop lynching folks."

Lucy elected not to slap his face, settling for a not exactly polite shove to his chest, causing more dust to rise.

Once we were settled in the Goodrich—W.A. Phillips sharing a room and a bed with me, Lucy in her own room with a bigger bed and better view of gallows hill—my sister renewed her insistence that we pay a call to the governor and his family. She made me and him put on fresh clothes, comb our hair, and wash whatever flesh showed.

We were all surprised when Governor Sidney Edgerton answered the door himself. He scarcely recognized me; maybe I had grown some, maybe I looked cleaner than he remembered. He recalled my last name but called me Rufus by mistake and then apologized without any of us mentioning what had happened to my brother in Virginia City. He gave W.A. Phillips a hardy handshake and told him how good it was to see him again somewhere other than "the open road." After letting us into his home, the governor ignored me but also W.A. He and

Lucy shared two hugs and rapid, unstrained conversation. She asked him how it felt to be governor. He said it felt great, but he was still a little lonely. Apparently, there were no other office holders yet; he alone was the Montana Territory government.

Still, he had his family to fall back on. Wife Mary soon came in carrying her less-than-two-year-old fifth child, whose name I supposed was still "Idaho," and hadn't been changed to "Montana." Mrs. Edgerton said how much she had heard about Lucy Hart from her husband, and Lucy quickly scooped up the babe and showed all the motherly instincts she had picked up from women other than our own mother. The four older Edgerton children drifted in one after the other and all stood politely and patiently for introductions.

Mattie, the oldest but still looking plenty underdeveloped, approached me cautiously. I thought she might be tempted to give me a seriously hard hug, so I took a step backward. That caused her to stop in her tracks and rethink our reunion. She told me she thought for certain I was dead but said nothing about being glad that I was still breathing. Finally, she extended her limp hand, palm down, as if she meant for me to kiss it. I let her hand dangle at the risk of appearing to all as something less than a worldly gentleman. I figured that beat giving her ideas about me and her. She scowled, rolled her eyes, shook her head, curtseyed to W.A. Phillips of all people, and excused herself from the room. The other children except for the babe, who was not yet capable of such action, then scattered.

The adults talked and I barely listened. It was all I could do to keep from asking the whereabouts of Lucia Darling. I got it in my head that she was hiding in her room, wishing I had never returned to Bannack. That turned out to be presumptuous of me. She wasn't thinking of me at all. Mary finally mentioned that Lucia was over at Wilbur Sanders's house teaching his five-year-old son, James, how to read something other than a book of law or the Bible, which were both too hard for him. The Sanders family was about to move to Virginia City, where two-thirds of the territorial residents now lived. Mary Edgerton didn't want to go through all the work of pulling up stakes, and Sidney Edgerton was fine with that because across Grasshopper Creek from his house was "Yankee Flats," home to loyalists who supported him and the Union. Since Sidney Edgerton was in Bannack, it became the territory's first capital, but not even the governor figured that "honor" could last.

Lucy committed us to staying for the evening meal. Mrs. Edgerton with the help of Mattie had a hearty dish of calf's head already in the works. Mattie delighted in explaining to me the cooking process—and worse, showing me. The head, minus the brains, along with the heart, feet, and lights had already boiled for an hour and a half and now it was time to put the thoroughly washed brains and a pounded cracker in the pot to boil with the rest. "You notice we left the windpipe on," she said as she did so. "That's extremely important. You see if you permit the windpipe to hang out of the pot while the head is cooking, all the froth will escape through it." After another half hour the brains were sufficiently boiled, and little Mattie mashed them fine with a knife before peppering, salting, and buttering them. I left during the peppering, quickly excusing myself from dinner and bolting from the kitchen and then the house. I made it to the creek and vomited into it. W.A. Phillips had trailed me there, and I was on my knees when I heard his laughter behind me.

"You can stomach a hanging or twenty but not a home-cooked meal," he said.

"Leave me alone," I replied.

"You think they killed the calf by hanging it?"

"How'd you like a fist in your face?"

"I like your fighting spirit, the way you stand up for the calves of Montana Territory."

But I didn't stand up. I vomited a second time.

"Here you go, Red." W.A. bent at the waist and tapped his jaw, which he had thrust at me. "I invite you to take a swing at me. I want to see what you got."

"It's not worth it," I said, splashing creek water on my face.

"Your restraint is admirable."

"Go back and eat. I'm going for a walk."

"To the Sanders's house?"

"What makes you say that! I have no love for Wilbur Sanders. He helped get the horrible hanging spree started by making sure they strung up George Ives in Virginia City."

"I see, but I got you all figured out, Red. You're going there to see Lucia Darling. I heard she shines like a gold nugget."

"You didn't hear that from me."

"Sure I did, Red. Didn't anyone ever tell you you talk in your sleep?"

"You're wrong," I insisted, now standing and spitting into the creek. "I'm not going there at all."

"To the gallows then, or the cemetery? I'm game."

What happened next about tore my heart and brains out. I may as well have been a calf ready for the slaughter and the carving. Lucia Darling appeared, shining in the evening light as she ambled up the street toward us. She carried an 1850 edition of Charles Dickens's novel *Oliver Twist,* which W.A. Phillips happened to have read. I thought he was lying to impress her, but they were already discussing the plot and characters before I reluctantly made the polite introduction. Afterward, as we walked right past the Edgerton house, where she was supposedly heading for dinner, they talked about her teaching and his novel writing, even though he hadn't written even part of one yet.

Was she glad to see me again? If she was, she hid it well. She didn't ask about what I had been up to while I was away, only congratulating me for having befriended and spent time with such a well-educated, eloquent man—W.A. Phillips. Yes, she called him a *man*, not a young man, which was the best she ever called me back when I was the Edgertons' houseguest. Yes, I was sixteen and Phillips claimed to be twenty-one—which, if true, made him only three years younger than her—but it still bothered me to the point where I *really* wanted to sock the next presumed Charles Dickens off his feet.

When he told her his full name was Wilberforce Anaconda Phillips, she laughed—but not at him, with him. They both agreed, she would call him W.A. instead of Wilberforce or, almost as bad, Mr. Phillips.

"And you can call me Woodie," I blurted out after letting myself fall behind them in Yankee Flat.

"That's what I've always called you, silly," Lucia said. "What do you want me to call you now? Mr. Hart?" She laughed and he laughed like it was their private joke.

Why the heck not, I thought. I've been with a real grown-up woman. Her name doesn't matter, but it happens to be Little Gold Bit. And she didn't just shine. She sparkled! What I said, though, was this: "You could call me W.R. Those happen to be my initials."

"Well, W.R.," Lucia said, her hand half covering her grin, "I got a question for you."

"It stands for Woodrow Russell. That's what goes with Hart."

"That isn't my question. What I want to know is where you've been hiding W.A. all this time?"

Her question didn't deserve an answer. I thought about telling her about my ordeals—how I had been knocked out twice for extended periods of time—but I was afraid to in case she thought I was too stupid to waste sympathy on. By the time we had circumnavigated Yankee Flat and were approaching the

Edgerton house again, he had slipped his hand into the crook of her arm and she had let him keep it there. At the front door, with darkness setting in, he gave her a peck on the cheek and then she turned her head in such a way that their lips met as if by accident. Their lips stayed pressed together—which was no accident. I watched from a dark shadow.

It was W.A. Phillips who finally broke the kiss. I got the impression she would have kept their lips locked for hours.

"I'm hungry," W.A. said. "How 'bout we head inside to see if they saved a little calf's head for us?"

"Sounds wonderful," replied Lucia Darling, the first female I ever thought I loved. "That's absolutely my favorite dish."

No, I didn't go in with them. I didn't say good night to them either.

"He's no doubt headed for the Goodrich Hotel," said W.A. Phillips as I walked away. "Red needs his rest."

"You're wrong again," I shouted, and I didn't look back.

Truth was I did intend to go to the Goodrich and sulk on a too hard bed. But to prove Charles Dickens Jr. wrong, I—now thinking of myself as something of an Oliver Twist–like figure—walked right past Cyrus Skinner's old saloon and then the hotel without so much as a full glance. I tramped up the easternmost of the two hills behind the Goodrich. I told myself, and even convinced myself, I was eager to see how the nearly full moon looked from the cemetery.

Chapter Twenty-Two

W.A. Phillips and I continued to share a room and a bed at the Goodrich Hotel. He also continued to see much of Lucia Darling. But not in the hotel. Since my sister Lucy was paying for the room, I had no qualms about telling W.A. that our room must never be used for any disreputable activity.

"The Goodrich isn't a bordello," I told him one hot night in late July when he complained that I spent too much time cooped up in the hotel.

"How dare you besmirch the reputation of Governor Edgerton's niece!" he snapped back. "Every female of age is *not* like one of *your* girls at Moll Featherlegs's place in Virginia City. To mention Little Gold Bit and Lucia Darling in the same foul breath is an outrage. You may as well compare a White House maid to the first lady." I wanted to protest that Moll Featherlegs's girls were far more *his* than mine, that I had never compared Lucia Darling to one of them or to anyone else, and that the last thing I ever wanted to do was besmirch the lovely schoolteacher or her reputation. But I felt too sick in the stomach and too dizzy in the head to protest. I lay awake a couple of hours that night before I woke him up and insisted he shake hands on an agreement: Neither he nor I must ever again mention in this room the name "Lucia Darling" or refer to her as "Governor Edgerton's niece," "Bannack's schoolteacher," or anything else whatsoever. He knew I was extremely envious of his time with Lucia and quoted somebody I never heard of from one of William Shakespeare's plays that was not *Romeo and Juliet:* "Beware, my lord, of jealousy; it is the green-eyed monster which doth mock the meat it feeds on."

I didn't quite get it, but I nodded with my own green eyes open wide. By nature, W.A. was a man who loved to talk, tease, taunt, and boast, but he agreeably shook my hand and then turned in our bed so that his back was to me. The silence soothed me . . . for a while.

"We are agreed, so let me get my sleep," he said just when I was finally starting to doze off. "She is about far more than standing or sitting around in a stuffy classroom dispensing knowledge and wisdom to the dirty-faced tykes of this very fair city or lying in her bed reading between the lines of Billy Shakespeare. She likes to do so many different things both inside and outdoors and she knows what she likes, as you can imagine. I need to be well-rested indeed to keep up with the lovely, lively Lu . . . Miss Anonymous."

Maybe W.A. turned to Lucia Darling because he couldn't have Lucy Hart the way he wanted her, but at that time it never crossed my mind. All I knew was the big-talking writer-in-waiting now represented my biggest obstacle to everlasting happiness, never mind that Lucia had spurned my feeble romantic advances long before W.A. came to town. While I stewed in my own juices and W.A. carried on with *my girl,* Lucy checked out of her room at the Goodrich. The new occupant was a substantial (in size if not in wealth) miner who snored up a nightly storm. Montana still had no territorial secretary because President Lincoln's choice for that position had declined for health reasons. Governor Sidney Edgerton filled the gap by hiring a personal secretary, my sister. She now received free room and board at the Edgerton home. In fact, she occupied my old room there.

"With the money I am earning and saving, the least I can do

is cover the cost of your room at the Goodrich for the time being," she told W.A. Phillips and me. How could I object? W.A. wanted even more. He broached the possibility that, considering her situation, she might contemplate providing separate rooms for her bodyguard pal and her melancholy brother. He got nowhere. I doubt Lucy was considering how Lucia Darling fit or didn't fit into our living arrangements. My sister was generous but was not about to become extravagant. She felt she needed to be more careful with her own earnings than she had been with the money absconded from her Washington-based husband, money that was about run out.

As for Lucy and Lucia, they, according to my sister, got along famously. Since I didn't allow W.A. Phillips to talk to me about my true love in or out of our hotel room, I got all my Lucia information from my sister. The two women had much in common, sharing books, cooking, mending, and the Edgerton family for sure, and W.A. only to a certain degree. Lucy encouraged Lucia to pursue romance freely and without guilt since her own relationship with the mustachioed word-loving romantic, despite all the time spent together, had never been anything but good, old-fashion friendship. "I haven't a jealous bone in my body," Lucy assured her new friend. "My love for W.A. is just as sincerely platonic as my love for the governor. I'm as glad for you and W.A. as I am for Mary and Sid."

Lucy had always been the noble one in the family. I said nothing to her about what Lucia Darling meant to me and never asked her the question that burned inside my brain: *"Don't I deserve Lucia's love more than W.A. Phillips does?"* In August Sidney Edgerton asked Lucy to accompany him to Virginia City, for he "governed those people, too" and needed her at his side—with her abundance of charm and Washington savvy—to make sure he did all the right things to win them over. W.A. Phillips didn't wish to go along since he had that busy romance in Bannack; I wished to go along to get away from *that* romance and the damned Goodrich hotel room.

The night before I left, I threatened him, or at least tried to, since threatening anyone wasn't second nature to me. I got tongue-tied while making a fist in bed. We were each lying on an edge of it, as far apart as humanly possible.

"What you muttering, Red?" W.A asked. "Or is that green-eyed monster raising its ugly head again?"

"All I'm saying is when I'm gone, don't bring her here or I'll . . ." He knew I couldn't finish the sentence, let alone strike him, or embarrass both of us with too plain talk.

"Calm yourself," he said, but he didn't sound calm. "I know the difference between a bordello and a cheap hotel."

"It's not so cheap, but you wouldn't know, seeing as you aren't the one paying."

"Neither are you. But don't worry. Red. I wouldn't bring her . . . Miss Anonymous . . . here even if this were the four-poster bed of the Royal Highness Queen Victoria herself."

"All right then, but I don't like you calling me *Red.*"

"All right then. Now get some sleep, Red. We both have a busy day tomorrow—you traveling, me doing whatever. Do watch out for Lucy, just as I would if I was going."

I wished he was making the trip with the governor, Lucy, and me. It was my humble opinion that Lucia Darling needed a good long break from his bad company. Of course, if he had been going, I told myself, I would have stayed behind to keep Lucia entertained. "Right," is all I said.

Returning to Virginia City presented its own set of concerns, the two main ones being it was the site of Rufus's mockery of a trial and brutal execution and also the home to the people who made that happen, including Varina Willingham, President Paris Pfouts, Captain James Williams, and right down the long vigilante line. Yes, it was stuck in my head that Varina was at least partially responsible, that she had had it in her power to convince the *bastards* that she was the one who shot her husband's brother. Not that I would have wanted her hanged instead of my brother, but I was also certain she would have had the power to convince all those *bastards not* to hang her by her pretty neck even if they viewed her as a wanton murderess. It was amazing how many people I was now calling *bastards,* at least in my own head—but never a woman.

I could not actually talk myself into giving Varina a dressing down in her rooms above the Pay Dirt saloon or entering the Pfouts and Russell dry goods store to give the vigilante president a piece of my mind. I did circle around to the corral behind the store and drop to my knees. It wasn't exactly praying. I hoped that Rufus was still able to whistle "Dixie" wherever he was, and I asked *somebody*—even if it was only one of the other late Hart brothers or Sheriff Henry Plummer—to watch over Rufus and make sure he didn't get into further trouble. Somehow it made me feel better, but rage rose in my head the next day, August 19, 1864, when the big bugs of Virginia City came out for a rally to welcome the new governor. I glared at their sweaty brows and chubby red cheeks and silently condemned them to fates worse than death.

Apparently, a band serenaded Sidney Edgerton but afterward I admitted to Lucy I never even heard the music. I did hear the governor speak. He called Virginia City beautiful and Montana Territory the "Switzerland of America." He hailed the vast riches of Alder Gulch and assured everyone that these magical resources would lead to continued growth and a greatness not imagined even one year ago. The words may have poured from the governor's mouth, but Lucy was the one who thought up the Switzerland comparison, the phrase "magical resources," and most of the pleasant adjectives about Virginia City. It was also her idea to leave the capital city of Bannack out of his speech. "Any recognition of your adopted town could very well cause this crowd to turn on you, Sid," she wisely advised the governor.

Most important, though, was what he said about law and order. "Rule of law must prevail here," he cried out, right in the faces of Paris Pfouts, James Williams, and X Beidler. "I pledge my word that the laws should be executed." He didn't go so far as to use all of Lucy's words; she had wanted him to say *I pledge my word that the laws should be executed rather than the marginal men on flimsy evidence.* But I think even the most dunderheaded vigilantes got the message. And it sure beat the alternative of thanking the Vigilance Committee, including his nephew Wilbur Sanders, for all its hard work. Thanks to my sister, my rage subsided.

It would rise again before we left for Bannack. As early as the next day, I saw posters tacked about town that warned Virginia City citizens against careless discharging of firearms and creating public disorder or else face "summary punishment." The posters were all signed: "The Vigilance Committee." I didn't doubt that the vigilante leaders were behind it, if for no other reason than to remind Sidney Edgerton that when he was doing nothing as chief justice of Idaho Territory, the vigilantes were enforcing laws and fighting crime, and that now as governor of Montana Territory, he *must* recognize that their important work was not done.

Very soon the vigilantes had the opportunity to show just how active and relevant they were. Somewhere in Idaho Territory on August 21, road agents struck a stagecoach headed from Virginia City to Salt Lake City, taking nearly $30,000 in gold dust from the four passengers. Within a week, Captain Williams led his vigilantes west to track down the robbers. They braved rainstorms, skimpy bedding, and little grub before catching one Jem Kelly in a haystack near the Snake River ferry on

September 5 and accusing him of the stage robbery. Kelly got an immediate trial and then a unanimous death sentence. The vigilantes cut a notch in a Balm of Gilead tree and rigged up some kind of ingenious scaffold. The only witnesses beside the vigilantes were a group of Shoshone warriors who were so disgusted by what they saw that they ran off before Kelly stopped kicking. Williams's men, now the Montana Territory vigilantes, had struck again, and even though it was beyond the Bitterroots in Idaho Territory, the folks back home took notice. Paris Pfouts not only gave the captain and his possemen pats on the back but also $1,000 to pay for their travel expenses.

"It does demonstrate a certain dedication and persistence," Governor Edgerton told Lucy after hearing the news back home in Bannack. "I can't say I entirely approve, but at least it didn't occur *in* my territory."

"But all the executioners were from Montana," Lucy reminded him.

"All from Alder Gulch. Well, anyway, we can't change what has been done. I don't doubt for a minute that this Kelly fellow was guilty. It wasn't his first crime. That's fact. It's just too bad his accomplices in the robbery weren't apprehended."

"Yes. From what my brother tells me, *our* vigilantes prefer a good multiple hanging."

Anyway, that's how Lucy told it to me. She proved a good influence on the governor. He named a sheriff and a justice of the peace who had no connection to the vigilantes, and his most powerful county commissioner, James Fergus, spoke out against the Kelly hanging and suggested the vigilantes had outlived their usefulness. In fact, in a letter written to the vigilantes, Mr. Fergus stated that only tyrants would deny American citizens "the right to be tried by the laws of their country, in open court and by a jury of their countrymen." Lucy earnestly approved; in fact, she apparently fed the commissioner some of her notions about how no man or woman should be allowed to set the laws of the land aside, though Fergus left women out of his letter.

"Only Fergus could get away with something like that in the face of the Montana vigilantes," Sidney Edgerton said. "He's the most fearless unarmed man I know."

"You could be just as fearless, Sid," said Lucy. "You know he's right."

"So you keep telling me, my high-minded public servant. And I do appreciate your own fearlessness. I wouldn't have it any other way in a secretary of mine. But I'm governor. I can't write a letter like he did and have all those Virginia City Democrats angry and wanting to . . ."

"Hang you?"

"Now, now, Lucy. Not that. But they might want a new governor."

"Or for you to at least move to Virginia City, make it the capital, and govern from there."

"Mary is against it. My wife, believe it or not, likes me to stay home all the time."

"I know that. She's a lucky lady indeed."

Lucy had that awful husband William Penn Norton back in Washington, but she told me even had she been legally free, she would have had no designs on supplanting Mary Edgerton. Lucy had an admirable record of honesty with me; there was no reason for me to doubt her. She had high expectations for anyone in political office, and not even Sidney Edgerton could live up to those. It was beyond him to demand that the vigilantes coil their ropes and put them in a closet. He admired fearlessness in James Fergus and Lucy Hart, but he was somewhat shaky when it came to personal courage. Lucy conceded that the governor was trying to appease the vigilantes when he appointed a Vigilance Committee founder, John Lott, territorial auditor and failed to object when freighter turned sheriff Neil Howie named as his deputy the notorious hangman X Beidler.

Because of my continued reluctance to visit the Edgerton home, Lucy came to the Goodrich Hotel for most of our conversations. W.A. Phillips only appeared in the room to sleep, and he didn't seem to sleep much. At least he hadn't yet been out for an entire night. One evening in early September while Lucy and I were sitting on a bench in front of the hotel I finally admitted to her how much the Phillips-Darling romance gnawed at my overworked brain.

"Lucia is a wonderful woman with a good head on her shoulders," Lucy said. "She knows that even if W.A. was the marrying kind, she would turn him down. She just needed a little something more than her books and her students and all that cooking and cleaning and sewing for the Edgertons."

"Aren't I a little something more?" I asked, rather pathetically I must admit now.

"You're young. She wouldn't want to hurt you by showing an interest in you and then abandoning you . . . well, it's complicated."

"I'm hurt now, what with her carrying on so with *another* man. I mean W.A. isn't exactly mature or wise, is he?"

"He has been a good friend. I have no reason to speak ill of him simply because he can be frivolous at times. He's fun to be around, and that is something Lucia needs right now."

"And I suppose I'm no fun," I said, hanging my head.

"You are a good brother. If you need a female friend, that is besides your dear sister, have you thought about Mattie Edgerton? She isn't so much younger than you and seems bright enough and . . . Oh, I know that look. Well, there are other fish in the sea."

"We're a long way from any sea."

"You can come with me back to Washington when I'm ready to go."

"You're actually thinking of going back to Mr. Norton?"

"To obtain a divorce. But not just yet. The governor and I still have much work to do in Montana Territory."

What I needed was more to do. My idleness led to overthinking, and my thinking was usually morbid (Rufus and the vigilantes), disheartening (W.A. Phillips and Lucia Darling), or depressing (doubts about my future in Montana Territory or anywhere). Lucy never complained about supporting me, perhaps because my lifestyle (no drink, no gambling, no women, minimum food, shared bed with W.A. Phillips) was extremely moderate. Still, I knew I must start paying my own way again. A word from Lucy to Sidney Edgerton's friend Francis Thompson, who like Mr. Edgerton had lobbied in Washington for a new territory, also did the trick. She told him that I was at wit's end since the death of his former employee Rufus Hart. It must have helped that I had experience in the dry goods clerking business working briefly not only for him but also for Mr. Worden and Mr. Higgins up in Hell Gate.

Mr. Thompson was still Bannack's leading banker and the owner of the well-supplied dry goods store, but he now operated the territory's first steam-powered sawmill, which he had shipped up the Missouri River from St. Louis to Fort Benton. Selling lumber had made him as prosperous as the most successful gold miners. I went back to clerking for him, but he noticed how pale I was and suggested I should spend more time outdoors. Next thing I knew I was outside helping to unload the logs from wagons, as well as "limbing" (cutting branches off tree trunks) and "debarking" (removing bark from the logs). Maybe I wasn't a true sawyer, as it wasn't my job to stand behind the saws and control the levers that moved the log carriage back and forth, but it still felt like rugged man's work.

That is to say it beat stocking shelves and sweeping floors or doing nothing but thinking. I took pride in every blister and callus I developed, even showing them off to W.A. Phillips, that idler, on occasion.

"It feels good to put in a day's work," I told him one night in early September after I was certain he and Lucia had been a-sparking. "You should try it some time."

"You're a fool, Woodie," he said. "Wood isn't gold, least not to the common laborer."

"It's work. It pays for this room. I earn my keep."

"I have a job, looking after your sister."

"Right—as if she needs looking after."

"I know how to fire a firearm. Just because I haven't shot anybody, doesn't mean I can't."

"Well, please don't start here."

"I've also started to do a little prospecting."

Hand in hand with Lucia, I thought, but I stayed away from that forbidden topic. "Let me see your hands," I demanded. He held them up in my face. I poked one of them. "They're soft," I said. "Have you ever held a pick or shovel in your entire life?"

"Mostly I'm thinking and writing. That's where my life is leading me to—the world of literature. Writing is a different kind of work. It can be very hard on the brain. But if you write good enough, your hands can stay soft and nobody will criticize you."

"I don't know about that. Have you *actually* started writing something?"

"I'm primarily in the note-taking stage. Once I have accumulated enough interesting things, I shall write a great tale of the West—the *Moby Dick* of the frontier. The American prairie after all is a sea of grass. The mountains are here for the conquering like great white whales. You'll see."

"I don't know about that. Maybe I'll believe it when I see it."

"What you need is a little faith, Red. You should really read *Moby Dick* sometime."

"Maybe I have . . . parts of it anyway. Isn't it more about obsession than faith?"

"I possess faith, which is a good thing for a writer to have. Captain Ahab was obsessed to the point of insanity."

"There is no crazed Captain Ahab or whales of any size in Montana Territory to write about."

"True. But there is a crazed Captain Williams and vigilantes of all sizes."

CHAPTER TWENTY-THREE

Captain Williams was at it again in mid-September 1864. In Alder Gulch, a man known as John "Hard Hat" Dolan stole $700 from a miner he shared a cabin with and then bolted. Instead of going out of the territory and collecting saddle sores, the Vigilance Committee hired a private detective named John McGrath to track down the thief. Mr. McGrath went all the way to Salt Lake City to get the vigilantes' man and return him to Nevada City. On Saturday morning on the 16th, the vigilantes gave Hard Hat Dolan a trial in which he confessed to the robbery while drunk. That was good enough for the captain and his many supporters. They intended to hang Hard Hat that night, minus his hat, of course. But there were protestors, which prompted Captain Williams to raise his voice and probably a weapon as well. "It has been said that you will rescue the prisoner, don't try it on, for fear of the consequences," he warned. "What is to be done has been deliberately weighed and determined, and nothing shall prevent the execution of the malefactor."

And soon Dolan was dangling as so many before him had, all for the "safety" of a community where life and gold were so much exposed, as John Lott said, addressing the divided crowd. The vigilantes marched off in companies, and the crowd, protesters and all, dispersed without incident. Back in Bannack, Governor Edgerton essentially shrugged off the latest vigilante action in Alder Gulch. He was busy fixing up his house, scraping the mud off the roof and walls and replacing it with lime. I know because I was doing much of the dirty work as a favor to Lucy, who said the governor needed all the help he could get. W.A. Phillips was not available, of course; he had gone off with Lucia Darling to pick late summer flowers on cemetery hill. All I heard the governor say about the latest execution was that enough money was raised on the spot—on the grounds near the hanging—to repay the miner victim the full amount that the late Hard Hat had stolen from him. "The proceeding might have been unpleasant," Sidney Edgerton said before sending me off to take a bath, "but it goes to show that good, honest folks were doing their best to make everything right." I couldn't even muster my usual nod of acceptance. Everything wasn't right—a point that a month later was brought much closer to home.

In early October, Lucy volunteered to move back to the Goodrich Hotel because of the arrival of Montana Territory's first chief justice, Hezekiah Hosmer, who brought along two children from his first marriage and a second wife. They couldn't all quite squeeze into the lime-coated Edgerton home, so Lucy reclaimed her Goodrich room. It didn't lessen her enthusiasm for helping Governor Edgerton and Chief Justice Hosmer campaign for a Republican ticket in the new territorial legislature. The governor's nephew Wilbur Sanders had his eye on becoming a delegate to the U.S. Congress. With Election Day a week away, the three men and Lucy traveled to Virginia City for an October 17 political rally. Lucy invited me to come along to rally with them, but I didn't want to leave my sawmill work for Mr. Thompson, and anyway I had no intention of ever returning to a place where Captain Williams and his vigilantes still reined.

I'm not sure how many words Lucy contributed to the speeches made that day, but the male trio lashed out against the Democratic Party and its support for Jefferson Davis, that "bloody traitor who headed the Confederacy." My sister blamed herself for not gauging the crowd better and bringing aboard the Democrats who did support President Lincoln's war effort. While the new legislature was evenly split between the parties, Mr. Sanders made a poor showing, losing out to a rotund, hard-drinking lawyer deemed by the Republicans to be an inferior intellectual specimen. Sidney Edgerton was happy to go back to governing from Bannack, where he had more supporters and less copperhead and vigilante agitation.

Late morning on Friday, October 28, I was debarking at the sawmill when a man rode in on a swayback mule, slid down the animal's hindquarters, landed on his back, and ended up lying in the sawdust as flat as a flapjack. Instead of shoes or boots, he wore bandages and cut off moccasins. I propped him up against a tree stump where I usually ate my noon meal and shared a biscuit and cold succotash with him. I gave him water but he wanted whiskey. When I asked him to come over and meet some of the sawyers, he refused. He said he had only one friend in town, a French-Canadian saloonkeeper name Mitty Bessette. I admitted I wasn't acquainted with him or any other saloon-keeper in Bannack, but quickly added that my brother was once a saloonkeeper up in Hell Gate.

"Never got that far after they banished me," he said, picking crumbs out of his ragged beard. "My mule got lame and I wasn't in no shape for walking. Still ain't." With his back against the stump, he raised his legs and wiggled his misshapen moccasins high in the air. "In case you was wonderin', fellow, I ain't got no toes and only a small amount of feet—the heels."

"I . . . I'm sorry," I said.

"It ain't your fault, 'lessen you be one of them. No, can't be. You ain't got no rippling growth on your chin, nor cruelness about the eyes, nor scoffing tongue."

"I'm not one of anybody. I'm me, Woodrow Hart."

"That's good, real good. Me, I'm one of their victims. Rawley's the name. Call me R.C."

"Call me Woodie. Might I ask one of whose victims are you, Mr. R.C.?"

"The vigilantes. You must be acquainted with them."

"We aren't close, if that's what you mean, Mr. R.C." I found myself staring at his thin, fleshless neck.

"No rope burns," he said. "They didn't try to hang me. Like I said, I was banished—me and my mule. I believe it was for public drunkenness and not having any gold to make me the least bit acceptable. I reckon the old mule was my accomplice. Her name is Eunice. She ain't no looker but she been faithful to a fault."

I patted the mule's head and thought of Togu, my lost pony.

"It happened last winter when the vigilantes were just getting started and hadn't yet decided to hang everybody. Nothing I could do but roam the cold countryside. My mule stepped in a prairie dog hole and fell. After that I roamed on foot with my mule limping behind. Got frostbit. That is, I did. Mule just got hungry. Would have died—maybe the mule, too—if not for some Bannock folk coming along and taking me into their camp. Them be Indians."

"I know, Mr. R.C. I'm sorry. I mean about the vigilantes, not the Indians."

"Don't want no pity, fellow. And there ain't no *Mr.* with the R.C. It's plain R.C. It don't stand for nothing. I'm just R.C. And I'm back in Bannack for only one solitary reason, well two actually. For a taste of Mitty Bessette's whiskey and for revenge."

I rolled that word over and over on my tongue—*Revenge!* I must have thought about it previously, but I couldn't recall exactly when or exactly how serious the thoughts might have been. Not that thinking about revenge took much courage, but actually seeking it for real sure did.

"The vigilantes hanged my brother Rufus," I blurted out.

"You don't say! Tough luck, fellow. But I bet you fate brought us together. I was a victim. Your brother was a victim. Of course, I lived to tell about it and he didn't. But you did, Woodie Hart. You were meant to find me. Now it's the two of us out for revenge. Two is better than one! What's to stop us!"

I thought of a lot of things. Revenge was sweet all right in theory. The odds against it, in fact, remained overwhelming; there were hundreds of vigilantes still operating over in Alder Gulch. What's more, he was a cripple with a crippled mule. And I was a coward without any kind of mount. It didn't look as if he possessed a rope or a gun, and of course I didn't want to put my hands on either of those bloody items. It was a darn shame about his feet, but revenge couldn't bring them back—nothing could. At least his neck and the rest of him seemed pretty much intact. I wanted to tell the poor guy that the best course of action was to just wait it out until the time came when Governor Edgerton and Chief Justice Hosmer were presiding over a territory with a full complement of lawmen, lawyers, judges, jails, and courthouses. As I went over my words in my head, I realized how lame they were. Hell might freeze over before all those elements were in place. I couldn't say anything except repeat how sorry I was.

"Stop saying that," he snapped. "And stop standing over me like some superior being."

I immediately dropped to my knees and buttoned my lip to keep from apologizing yet another time.

"You think revenge is wrong, friend?" he asked.

"I don't know. I . . ."

"I think it is only natural, especially when you ain't got no feet to stand on."

I gave him a hardy nod.

"So we're friends. A friend is one who has the same enemies

as you have."

I kept nodding. I couldn't believe it. President Abraham Lincoln had said the very same thing—not to me, of course.

I had to get back to work. I stood up but not completely straight as not to look too superior. I had trouble shaking a vision of R.C. Rawley springing off his mule, wrestling Captain Williams to the ground, and, with my help, tying the captain in place on the log carriage. With the pull of a lever, the vigilante leader would then be on his way to having his feet sliced off at the ankles and a lot worse. I let out a small scream but wasn't sure if it was a scream because I could feel the captain's pain or a scream for joy.

"You got to go?" he asked.

"Yes. I'm sorry. And I'm sorry I didn't have more to give you to eat."

"It's a drink I'm after, and . . ."

"I know. Revenge. Can I help you onto your mule?"

"No thanks. I'll wait."

Once I was peeling off bark again, I was able to think of things less stressful than revenge. Whenever I looked back, though, he was still seated at the stump, the mule picking through the sawdust beside him. I was hoping he'd give up and ride off in search of that glass of whiskey, but he was still there when my workday finished at dusk.

There was nothing else I could do but bring him into town. He directed me to the saloon where his friend Mitty Bessette was saloonkeeper. I wanted to wait outside with the mule, but my new friend insisted I help him get to a table. It took the barkeep a minute to recognize him, since his banished comrade had become so thin and raggedy, but then Mitty brought us a bottle of his best whiskey, and words, laughter, and drink flowed freely. I swished a little in my mouth before taking a hard swallow. I must say it wasn't bad. It made me wonder why I had avoided hard liquor all these years. I took a full glass and then another. At that point I was ready for revenge myself.

Mitty Bessette now brought us a large sheet of paper and a pencil that the saloonkeeper sharpened with his folding knife. "I'd help R.C. myself 'cept my English writing ain't passable," he said, handing the pencil to me.

R.C. Rawley immediately grabbed the pencil from my unsteady hand. "I can put the words down if you tell me the right words and the right spelling," he said. What he had in mind for revenge was an anonymous letter addressed to the vigilantes that he would post in a prominent place in town. As it turned out, he had trouble making his letters legible, so I took over and found, despite being as dizzy as a goose, I could do better. Together, we crafted the following:

To All You Sons of Bitches—

You know who you are. You're reading this, aren't you? You vigilantes and relatives of vigilantes and friends of vigilantes are ALL GUILTY. I'm a drinking man but a peaceful one. Drunk or sober, I never harmed a hair on any man's chest and never beat a woman or kicked a dog or voted Democrat or anything else in any election. You booted me out of your town like I was a Negro or a redskin or a cussed criminal. Set me and my old mule out on the coldest damned day of the year, you did. Told me to never return. I proceeded to lose my feet from frostbite. My old mule came up lame stepping in an iced-over hole. We near froze to eternity. Well I'm back, with my mule but without my feet, and I aim to tell you what I think of you. You're all no good. You're mean, greedy sons of bitches who wouldn't offer the likes of me as much as cold coffee. You forgot about me sure enough, but I remember you all. First one of you who says "How's Your Poor Feet?" I aim to pull myself up by a rope and spit in your face.

—A Victim

P.S. You sons of bitches also hanged the brother of a good friend of mine.

R.C. Rawley wasn't too good at reading what I "wrote," so I read it over to him four times and once to Mitty Bessette.

"You call them sons of bitches three times," said the saloonkeeper.

"Not enough, huh?" said R.C., pouring us all another drink. "We'll fit in one or two more. Where's the best place for more sons of bitches, fellow?"

"Anywhere you damn please," I said. "While we're at it, we'll put in my brother's name, Rufus Hart. That's spelled R-U-F-U-S. Hart is spelled like heart without the 'e.' Don't want the bastards to ever forget old Rufe. Oh, and we might call them *bastards,* too!"

It was the whiskey talking. Mitty Bessette wisely reminded us that we wouldn't remain unanimous for long if we told everyone who our brothers were.

"I ain't got a damn brother," said R.C. Rawley. "I ain't got nobody in the whole world to stand up for me but you two fellows."

He began to sob, but he cheered up fast when I suggested that we should mail a copy of the letter to Virginia City since that was where more vigilantes lived and was where they hanged my brother. But then we made toasts to Rufus and all my other brothers and to all the brothers R.C. Rawley didn't have and to Mitty Bessette's brothers back in France and even one to my sister. The tip of the pencil broke, Mitty cut himself unfolding his knife, and I threw up on the only other clean sheet of paper anyone in the saloon could locate. Anyway, the copy was never made. We did tack up the original on the saloon door but removed it after a half hour when Mitty surmised that it could lead to trouble for him even though he hadn't written a single word. I re-tacked it on the front door of the Goodrich Hotel

"Grasshopper Creek ain't dry," the miner snapped.

The door was open just a crack, but I managed to slip inside. Upstairs in the hallway, I literally ran into my sister, practically knocking her over. I apologized profusely until she told me I had done so enough. Then she asked me if I was sick. I told her I was fine, but I tried to open the wrong door, felt dizzy, and quickly sat down because it felt as if I would topple over anyway. Lucy looked at my tongue and smelled my breath.

"If I didn't know you better, I'd say you'd been drinking," she said.

"If I knew myself better, my head wouldn't hurt so much," I replied.

"I don't even know what that means."

"It means I had a few last night, and today I'm unable to deal with any parts of trees."

"Won't they miss you at the sawmill?"

"It's Saturday."

"I thought you worked six days a week."

"Not this week. The bark will still be there to peel on Monday."

"Missing work doesn't sound like you either. Is W.A. behind this?"

"I didn't have a single drink with the bastard."

"And that sounds even less like you."

"I reckon I can't keep sounding like myself forever, Lucy. I'm growing up."

Lucy helped me to my feet, into my room, and onto the bed that W.A. Phillips had failed to make.

"Will you be all right without me?" she asked.

"Sure. I'll just be resting right here."

"I didn't mean just today, Woodie. I mean in the long run?"

I was in no mood to try to answer such a question. I curled up on the bed and closed my eyes. She said we'd talk about it later, kissed me on the temple, and left. When she exited the hotel, she would see the commotion and no doubt read the anti-vigilante letter. Perhaps she would recognize my handwriting, although she hadn't seen much of it over the years. No matter. Lucy would never say anything to endanger her younger brother and nobody else could possibly connect the letter to me—that is, unless R.C. Rawley or the French saloonkeeper talked. But they wouldn't do anything like that. They weren't out to get me. I had done something—written a letter—and I regretted it. I was wishing the whole thing would just blow over. Drinking was one thing (like W.A. said, virtually every man in Montana Territory did it), but speaking out against the vigilantes was another matter (few dared do it). I hadn't grown up that much.

Chapter Twenty-Four

I spent the Lord's Day in bed recovering. Come night, I felt better but certainly not well enough to pick up where I had left off in Mitty Bessette's drinking establishment. W.A. Phillips pretty much left me alone the little time he spent in our room. He may have actually been showing consideration, since he had been in my state a time or two dozen, or he may have had other things on his mind—like his next outing with Lucia Darling.

I rose early Monday morning and was hardly surprised to see no letter on the outside of the hotel door. In its place was a messy X carved into the wood. I took it as some kind of warning. I saw nobody on the street and heard only a sign rattling in the breeze and the periodic bark of a distant dog that I imagined was as hungry as I was. I started down Main Street, hoping to find one of the town's three bakeries open. I soon changed my mind when the dog howled as if talking back to a wolf or a coyote or a ghost. I followed the sound, slowly climbing the hill behind the hotel with my head down and knowing in my heart that the X back on the door was more than just a warning.

Upon reaching the gallows where Sheriff Plummer had been hanged, I came upon the dog, a scruffy creature with sagging face and droopy ears. The animal was quiet now, content with sniffing at the bloody bandaged stumps of a man in rags who hung from the crossbeam like so much spoiled meat. I slowly lifted my eyes upward, following his slight form to his lifeless face, where they fixed on his purple protruding tongue. The dog paid me no mind, not even when I dropped to all fours and released a forlorn howl of my own.

At some point I flattened out on the ground, shut my surprisingly dry eyes, and tried not to breathe. The dog eventually sniffed me and left. I lay there all day breathing softly against my will until Mitty Bessette showed up with a burying crew. *"Dieu vous garde!"* he said, before he cut his friend down. As his associates carried to cemetery hill the vigilantes' twenty-seventh victim of 1864, the saloonkeeper provided the translation, "God keep you." He then resorted to French again, calling the vigilantes everything from *"les chiens sales"* (dirty dogs) to *"meurtriers qui ont tué in cold blood"* (murderers who killed in cold blood). He told me he had learned of the hanging from the dog with no name that often showed up behind the saloon for bones and bread crumbs. I could not make my tongue work until Mitty led me away from the gallows. All the way to his saloon, I mumbled, "Twenty-seven, twenty-seven, twenty-seven . . ."

At a table inside, I drank, ate a plate of bread and beans, and drank some more. I passed out, only to be awakened by two men, each shaking one of my shoulders. Another man put a pencil in my shaky hand and made me write my name four times on the back of a copy of the *Montana Post.* A fourth man closely studied my handwriting, muttering "The same, the same," and passed the newspaper on to the next man, who said, "Agreed, agreed."

"You wrote the posted letter to the vigilantes," said one of the quartet; it wasn't a question. "We knew the cripple couldn't write worth beans."

I was too far in my cups to keep from nodding my head as it lowered itself to the tabletop. Since I would not be wishing myself dead so strenuously the next day, it was fortunate that Mitty Bessette intervened on my behalf. He told the fearsome quartet that I had only been the transcriber of the words on behalf of R.C. Rawley and had been too inebriated at the time to understand the meaning of the words.

"As you can plainly see, he doesn't know what you're saying now, either," Mitty pointed out, and it was hard for the vigilantes to argue the point, but they did. The saloonkeeper practically stopped them dead when he added, "This boy can't be guilty, for if he *is*, you hanged the wrong man last night."

After much thought and even more pacing the saloon, one vigilante finally replied: "We have never hanged what you'd call an innocent man. It is my belief that this man you call a boy was in fact a disreputable drunk in cahoots with Rawner."

"Rawley," Mitty Bessette corrected. "And this boy had never taken a drop of whiskey in his life until the other night. I blame myself for giving him . . ."

"Save your breath, barman. We know you can't help who comes into your saloon. We'll have to take this fellow in, though, to face the music."

Funeral music, I supposed. Two of them began shaking my shoulders again while ordering me to sit up. I pretended not to hear and didn't budge on my own. It wasn't so much that I was afraid at that moment (though no doubt I was); my head was just too damn heavy.

"That, friends, would be a mistake." A new voice had entered the mix, and I recognized it instantly. I raised my head just enough off the table to confirm that W.A. Phillips was doing what he did best—talking.

"Who the hell are you, mister?" said a vigilante.

"I've seen him around," said another. "He's the fellow who's been courting Governor Edgerton's niece, you know, the schoolteacher."

"That's right, gentlemen. I am W.A. Phillips, writer and sometime bodyguard to the governor. You have been manhandling Woodrow Hart, a hardworking, traditionally sober and innocent young man who happens to have once been the governor's houseguest and is the brother of the governor's personal secretary, Miss Lucy Hart. Sidney Edgerton won't appreciate the way you four have been tormenting and intimidating this . . ."

"We haven't been doing anything of the kind," one vigilante insisted. "We . . . we were just leaving. Transcribing another man's words isn't necessarily a crime, and anyway, this Hart doesn't have a record of behaving badly and I'm sure he'll watch what he puts down on paper in the future . . . let's go, boys."

"Shouldn't we at least issue a warning?" asked another.

"Not now. Maybe when he's sober and can hear us."

"I wouldn't do that," W.A. Phillips warned. "You wouldn't want the governor to hear about your persecution of this . . ."

W.A. didn't have to finish his sentence. The four vigilantes quickly filed out. I now sat up, thinking I should feel better, at least well enough to thank my bunkmate. But as I watched Mitty and W.A. shake hands, my head only grew heavier and finally dropped again like a falling tree. I heard it bang against the tabletop and then heard nothing at all.

In the weeks that followed, I resumed my day work at the sawmill but did not shy away at night from my favorite saloon or my new best friend, saloonkeeper Mitty Bessette. I learned from Lucy that Sidney Edgerton was none too pleased with the vigilantes' extermination of a helpless, relatively harmless fellow like R.C. Rawley and mistreatment (guilt by association) of a totally helpless and harmless young fellow like me. W.A. Phillips hadn't said anything directly to the governor, but my ordeal had come up in one of Mr. Edgerton's casual conversations with Lucia Darling, who had then mentioned it to Lucy, who in turn had ascertained the facts from me and filled in the governor with most of the details. I'm not sure how Lucia referred to me, but Lucy called me her "poor, misguided little brother." At least the governor didn't argue the point. Their concern pleased me to some degree, but it didn't keep me from seeing poor, unfortunate Rawley hanging around, literally, in my bad dreams or me from drowning my specific and general sorrows each night in my chosen saloon.

Sidney Edgerton continued to govern from his home in Bannack, but Chief Justice Hezekiah Hosmer moved out, taking his family to Virginia City and setting up a courtroom in a hotel. The governor immediately invited Lucy to return to his unoccupied guest room, although she delayed leaving the Goodrich for a week because of her concern for me. Finally, upon tiring of lecturing me each night about my drinking, she did depart. I must admit I was *not* sorry to see my favorite Hart go. For better or worse, I began to see much more of W.A. Phillips in our room and at Mitty Bessette's saloon. I didn't ask about any falling out between him and Lucia, but he hinted that she was too demanding of his time and thus keeping him from emerging as the great American novelist of the 19th-century West. Fact is, though, I had yet to see W.A. writing anything. His sleeping and drinking (often matching drinks with me at Mitty's) expanded.

It was W.A. Phillips who told me in early December over a bottle of whiskey that Chief Justice Hosmer had convened a Virginia City grand jury, which included none other than Captain James Williams. The chief justice first credited the Vigilance Committee for its important work, in the absence of law, of "purging society of all offenders against its peace, happiness, and safety." He even singled out Henry Plummer, calling the late sheriff "the greatest villain of them all—with hands reeking with the blood of numerous victims." Next, though, Hosmer spoke out against future summary hangings, saying: "Let us erect no more impromptu scaffolds. Let us inflict no more midnight executions." What's more, he told the grand jurors that in the future, vigilantes could be tried for murder like any ordinary citizen.

"James Williams just sat there and took it," W.A. said with a chuckle and a sip. "What else could he do? The chief justice had spoken sense, and the vigilantes could *not* defy the court."

"I thought the vigilantes were finished earlier," I muttered. "But they keep finding a reason to hang somebody, even the poor unfortunate R.C. Rawley."

"Or you, Woodrow Hart. You might have swung like your brother, if not for me."

That was arguable—not even the fired-up vigilantes would likely have hanged a man for merely transcribing someone else's nasty note. But I nodded anyway, just as I had done through November whenever W.A. declared himself my personal savior. I surely felt some guilt that revenge-minded R.C. had suffered the full wrath of the vigilantes while nothing bad had happened to me except I kept getting drunker and drunker—and that was my own doing.

"I'll believe the vigilantes are done when I see it—rather when I don't see it." I said, staring into my whiskey glass as if it were a cloudy crystal ball. "Thing is—I always see their nooses when I close my eyes. That will never end."

"It will if someone puts a stop to it. Have you thought anymore about taking revenge?"

I tried to nod and shake my head at the same time.

"That's you all over," he said. "But you're young yet."

"Young or old, drunk or sober, there's nothing I can do."

"Stop being such a curmudgeon, Red," W.A. said as he called for Mitty to bring over another bottle of rye. "I thought you'd be celebrating my news about how old Hosmer put the vigilantes in their place. I like old Hosmer. He's more than a lawyer; he's literary. Four years ago, before the first shots of the Civil War were fired, he wrote the great book *Adela, the Oc-*

toroon, an octoroon being one-eighth negro and Adela being one of those."

"You read it?"

"Sure, some of it." He laughed and raised his glass. "It's not *Moby Dick;* for one thing it's about an octoroon not a white whale." He thought he was being clever and laughed harder. I didn't even smile, which caused him to frown and lower his glass. "Old Hosmer makes his point, though," W.A. continued. "He doesn't like the slaveholders any more than he likes the vigilantes."

"Cruelty raises its ugly head in many guises. Justice can be a long time in coming."

"So true, so true. Nice to hear you make a pronouncement for a change. But those vigilantes will get their just deserts when I write my Great American . . ."

"I know, Great American Novel of the West, sea of grass and all."

"Right you are. And gulches of gold."

"And when do you think you'll get around to it, W.A.?"

"You mean the writing part? Soon. Soon. I'm still accumulating the important information to give it the necessary strong foundation. As I told Lucia the other night, 'Masterpieces can't be rushed, no more than matrimony.' "

"Matrimony? You were talking about that to her?"

He laughed again, showing no restraint. "Cruelty isn't the only thing that raises its ugly head. So does that green-eyed monster." He accidentally knocked over his glass, but it was empty, so he picked it up and kissed it.

"That's not funny," I said. "Matrimony is . . . eh . . . serious."

"You speak from experience, do you, Woodie?"

"My mother and father were married."

"Do tell. Serious matrimony was it?"

"Sad mostly."

W.A. Phillips fell silent; it lasted half a minute. "Look," he finally said, pointing a wobbly finger so close to my face that he nearly poked me in the eye. "It wasn't me who talked matrimony. It was Lucia."

I found that sad, if he was telling the truth. I poured myself more rye.

"I set her straight," he said, filling his own glass. "My writing comes first . . . and my information gathering, too. She's an educated schoolteacher from Ohio with an uncle totally opposed to human bondage, yet she had never heard of, let alone read, *Adela, the Octoroon,* and what's more never dove into *Moby Dick.* Can you believe that? One would think she would be more supportive of my literary ambitions."

"Will your literary ambitions pay for this?" Mitty Bessette asked as he set another bottle on the table, sighed, and sat down himself.

"No worries, Mr. Proprietor," W.A. said. "Red, here, earns a regular working man's salary peeling bark and is delighted to support your establishment as well as the art of writing. Right, Red?"

I grunted and fumbled about my person to find my small sack of gold dust.

"How come you never wear the red cape Moll Featherlegs gave me and I gave you?" W.A. asked as he used both hands to size my head. "You should take it out of the closet once in a while."

I didn't bother to answer. I had told him a dozen times it was "too girlish" and anyway wasn't my color (sort of a joke since it was almost as red as my hair). At the same time, I couldn't bring myself to throw or give the cape away since it was a present (albeit not directly to me) from a lady who had cared for me such a long time in her Virginia City establishment while I was out of my sore head.

"Just look at our young friend, Mr. Proprietor," said W.A., joggling Mitty Bessette's shoulder until the bar owner turned his head toward me. "He is constantly in deep thought, but he has no need to fill the air with words. Though still a greenhorn in many respects and a relative novice at wetting his whistle with whiskey, he is my hero. Even as I speak, he is thinking extra hard about taking serious revenge against cruel men. Hell, I'm just liable to write about heroic Red someday."

"Well, watch what you write in here," Mitty said. "It could be dangerous to your health."

"A point well taken, Mr. Proprietor. Right now, I'm simply gathering as much information as I possibly can."

"Right. The whole world is divided between hunters and gatherers."

"Aren't you the philosopher, Mr. Proprietor. The gathering, I'll have you know, isn't easy. Red is a reluctant hero."

"Smart boy. Most heroes are dead."

"I like you, Mr. Proprietor. How 'bout joining us in a toast to Mr. Anti-vigilante, Hezekiah Hosmer."

"Anti-vigilante?" whispered Mitty, turning his head from side to side to get a read on his other customers. "I shall raise a glass to that without reluctance."

Did the vigilantes stop operating once Justice Hosmer's court system was in place? It might have seemed that way to me because they left me alone and didn't hang anyone else in 1864 or well into the new year. But Lucy told me the Vigilance Committee had stayed intact and that in February 1865 its president, Paris Pfouts, got himself elected mayor of Virginia City. The voters clearly still backed those self-appointed judges and hangmen and supported their drastic, unlawful actions. That news made me want to vomit. It couldn't have been the whiskey; I was too used to it by then.

Meanwhile, back in Bannack, Governor Edgerton wasn't

making new friends, not even in the new legislature, because of his intolerance of all Democrats, even those who were antiwar and wanted the South back in the Union. Defenders of the vigilantes made their voice heard, and often these were the same men who were critical of what the territorial government did or didn't do. Governor Edgerton did sign into law on February 2 a bill introduced into the legislature by his friend and my boss Francis M. Thompson that created the Historical Society of Montana. The incorporators included, among others, Thompson, Hezekiah Hosmer, Wilbur Sanders, and one of my old bosses from Hell Gate, C.P. Higgins. I made a note to myself that it would be good to see Mr. Higgins again; he and Mr. Worden had been mighty good to me and Rufus. But I had no wish to return to Virginia City, so I went back to drinking and not thinking about it or most anything else that might do me some good.

In March the Historical Society's members elected Sanders president, merchant Granville Stuart secretary-treasurer, and Justice Hosmer historian. Its primary purpose, according to my sister, was "to collect and arrange facts in regard to the early history of the territory, including the discovery of its mines." W.A. Phillips expressed only contempt for the new society, telling me: "They aren't any kind of scholars. All they care about is recording history so it makes them look good. They are the worst of the vigilante apologists. Hell, 'Will Bury You' Sanders was one of the damned founders. You can bet he made a deal with old Hosmer, the so-called historian: *Yes, Honorable Hosmer, we can grant you that honorable position as long as you don't take my name or that of my uncle in vain and as long as you keep out of print the horrendous truths about the cold-blooded vigilantes.*"

I did not stand up for Hezekiah Hosmer, who I had never met, or Wilbur Sanders, who I had never particularly liked, or even Mr. Higgins. You could say it was the whiskey talking or *not* talking, and indeed there were times I could not stand up from the table at Mitty Bessette's saloon. W.A. Phillips regularly brought copies of Virginia City's four-page *Montana Post* to the table. In a loud, if not always clear, voice, he would read aloud articles written by Thomas Dimsdale, who had been a private schoolteacher like Lucia Darling before becoming editor of Montana Territory's first newspaper the previous September. In the weekly paper, Mr. Dimsdale advocated churches, public schools, a fire department, and improved streets with streetlights and no gun play, and editorialized against whiskey, gambling, and hurdy-gurdy girls. W.A. scoffed at everything the man wrote, except for Mr. Dimsdale's suggestion to form a literary club even though no book had ever been published in the territory.

"That son of a bitch wants to write the first one," W.A. Phillips said to Mitty and me during one of our March drinking sessions. "He fancies himself well educated with a load of literary talent. Lucy told me she heard from Wilbur Sanders that Dimsy is in the collecting information stage, just like me."

"For writing a book, you mean?" I said. "He is already writing for the *Post.*"

W.A. tossed aside the copy of the *Post* he'd been reading and looked ready to spit on it. "It won't be like mine, not at all," he said, drooling whiskey. "It won't be a novel, but he won't be telling the truth. I know him. It'll be a book to justify vigilante action. He'll be pandering to the mayor and Captain Williams and all the other powers that be in Virginia City. No doubt his effort will be fully supported by the goddamn Historical Society of Montana and he'll greatly enrich himself."

I detected a degree of jealousy in W.A.'s words but said nothing about the green-eyed monster that he claimed tormented me. I told myself if this newspaperman Dimsdale ever wrote a book like that, I wouldn't read it but might buy it just so I could have the pleasure of burning it on some cold winter night.

"How in the hell is the dim fellow gonna justify the hanging of R.C. Rawley?" said Mitty Bessette, taking up the newspaper W.A. had discarded. "Charles Dickens should write about R.C. Rawley. My friend was a regular Oliver Twist, 'cept grown up and a little more twisted by society's cruelty and indifference."

W.A. Phillips began to clap, mostly getting his palms to connect with each other. I didn't clap but I was equally impressed. The Bannack barman had read Dickens, too.

"Don't you worry, Mr. Proprietor," W.A. said. "I've collected the information on Mr. Rawley. I'll put him in my book. You can depend on me."

"And you'll tell the truth about him?"

"You bet. The truth and then some. My answer to Dimsdale will be a novel that is strictly—or at least for the most part—anti-vigilante."

"Isn't a novel made up?"

"It'll be based on pure fact. Thousands upon thousands of people in the territory and from coast to coast will read it. Half of them will identify with my hero and the other half with the hero's girl. The sons of bitches in Virginia City won't like it, but they'll buy it, too, to see what I say about them. Without doubt they're going to hate my hero, but that's all right. They aren't my *true* audience."

"I haven't seen a true hero around here yet."

"Don't be so shortsighted, Mr. Proprietor. Could be we got one sitting right across this table from us."

I squirmed in my chair. Mitty Bessette reached over and tapped me on the top of my head. "You don't really mean him, do you?" he said. "Woodie is so young . . . and he drinks too much."

"You saying a hero can't drink? Well, hell, he doesn't have to drink in my book or else can drink everyone under the table."

"What will your hero do?"

"Save folks who need saving. Punish the punishers who don't."

"Are you still talking about Woodie Hart?"

"Why the hell not! *Everyman* can be a hero, including Red. I'll call him Red Rider. No. People might think he's a bloody Indian riding bareback. The Red Revenger would be the perfect name because revenge is what he'll be all about, except Ned Buntline wrote a book about a pirate with that name. It was ages ago, but . . . I know, The Red Ranger. Wait. Ax the *the*—too pretentious. Red Ranger is enough. Yes, Red Ranger. Now doesn't that sound like a genuine hero?"

"But it won't be genuine," said Mitty, peering at me and shaking his head as if I were a glass of bad whiskey. "How can this boy be Red Ranger! He has the red hair, but he's too, I don't know, stationary, and too . . . eh . . ."

"Drunk," I said. "But not as stewed as our would-be writer."

"To hell with you, Red. You already got the cape of the correct color. I gave it to *you*! I can make you my hero if I damn well please. It's a writer's pre . . . prerog . . . prerog . . . right!"

I fell into a deep silence, wanting to drink, not argue. The three of us were now the only ones left in the saloon. I figured neither W.A. nor I could even make it back to our room in the Goodrich Hotel that night, but I didn't care. I had no wish to move. My head would pay for it tomorrow at the sawmill, but I didn't care about that either. W.A.'s talk about me being a hero was just prattle coming straight from the bottle. I didn't like it much since it was so damn far from the truth, but I could live with it. Better that W.A. was with me instead of with Lucia Darling. I imagined her lying in her bed at the Edgerton home smoothing out her pillow while trying to forget that information-gathering cad brought west by the nice Lucy Hart, sister of that nice Woodie Hart. I had scarcely talked to Lucia in months, but a young fellow like myself had to think about somebody. And my thoughts didn't always stay nice. Drinking could do that to a man.

"I appreciate your business, Woodie, but shouldn't you find yourself a nice female companion for a change?" Mitty suddenly asked, as if he had been reading my mind.

"Nice?" said W.A "In this town?"

"Or Virginia City."

"No nicer there but more plentiful and more willing. Isn't that right, Red Ranger?"

"I'm *not* Red Ranger. Never will be. I don't even want to be Red. I'm Woodie. That's all."

"Sure you are. Remember Little Gold Bit from Moll Featherlegs's bordello? Of course, you do. You made a heroic stand in her place but couldn't ultimately overcome the wiles of a worldly whore."

"C'est pas gentil," Mitty said. "Not nice at all." He put a heavy arm over my shoulders, and with his free hand he pulled my glass away, and not to refill it. "There must be a nice girl somewhere around these parts, Woodie. You could put a classified ad in the *Post.* Just listen to this one."

Mitty began reading aloud, his voice softer and more melodious than W.A.'s:

> *Wanted—A correspondence with some lady, with a view to matrimony. One who has been divorced in the Territory preferred. Red hair, or one who stutters need not apply. Must not be averse to my being out late at night, and on my return must ask no questions. Money is no object, still would not let a few thousand paltry dollars separate an otherwise eligible couple. Have travelled all over the world, more especially in the Sandwich Islands. Profession, a gentleman; can support a wife like a lady. All letters addressed to the president of the Nevada Clam and Oyster Company will receive prompt attention.*

"Look how red-faced you've made Red, Mr. Proprietor," W.A. Phillips said, the whiskey still dribbling from the corners of his mouth in his merriment. "But this is good information, Red. This big bug in the *Post* isn't any competition at all for you. He doesn't want a female with red hair, and I know you do. I can just see you trudging off to the sawmill each day with a weary red-haired wife and three hungry redheaded brats waiting anxiously at home for your return."

"I thought you saw Woodie as a hero?" said Mitty Bessette.

"I do. I do. You don't think him surviving such a domestic scene would be heroic? We're talking about serious matrimony here."

I lay my head on the table, rather let it fall . . . and it hurt a little.

Mitty gave my shoulder a squeeze and then let go. With a mighty groan, he stood up. "I got nothing against wives in theory. Some men need them. What about you, Mr. Fictionist? What ever happened to you and the governor's niece? Not anti-vigilante enough for you?"

"On the contrary, Mr. Proprietor. Lucia Darling is against the vigilantes all the way. She has some fine attributes. But, just between you and me, she doesn't think all that much about writers either, except the dead ones with names like Homer and Shakespeare."

"I'll drink to that," I said.

Chapter Twenty-Five

On February 7, 1865, the Legislature moved the territorial capital to Virginia City. Governor Sidney Edgerton couldn't do anything about that, but perhaps he thought it a blessing. He didn't get along with some of those fellows and in any case didn't like people—except for my sister, Lucy—looking over his shoulder. The winter lingered, with the snow piling up like bad memories. The mountain passes between Salt Lake and the Montana Territory gold camps remained closed well into April. With freighters unable to get through, bacon, beans, rice, and especially flour either ran out or cost too much for many residents to buy. Over in Alder Gulch, miners were more interested in flour than gold, and some so-called regulators seized what flour they could, paid for it at more reasonable rates, and then sold it at the same rates to hungry residents. What the regulators did might be seen as a thoughtful act of mercy, but it wasn't exactly legal and was opposed by a sheriff and other duly appointed guardians of official government. Most of these regulators turned out to be vigilantes, with Captain James Williams "regulating" more forcefully than anyone. It didn't make me hate the captain and associates any less, but I must say that distributing the wealth to the people—as measured in flour—struck me as almost noble. Certainly, it was a far cry from dishing out death.

In Bannack the Edgerton family hardly suffered as their cupboards were well stocked for another long winter. Lucy complained that she even put on a few pounds since New Year's. Lucia Darling took a break from baking pies. According to W.A. Phillips, she had somehow gotten hold of a copy of *Adela, the Octoroon* and was reading it cover to cover. I didn't suffer, either. The snow piles and sometimes frigid temperatures shut down the sawmill for great stretches, so I could sleep in every morning. Flour wasn't an ingredient in whiskey and Mitty Bessette's stock hadn't run out yet. Sometimes when I couldn't sleep, I read from Mitty's copy of *Oliver Twist; or, The Parish Boy's Progress.* I was making progress. I was now a nearly happy drunk.

All that changed in mid-April. No matter how much I drank, I could no longer force happiness down my throat. It felt as if my heart was pumping dry, oxygen-depleted blood to my brain. It all started when I heard—about a week after it happened due to lack of telegraph service—the news that an assassin's bullet had ended the life of President Abraham Lincoln. About the time John Wilkes Booth was actually pulling the trigger in my hometown, we regulars at Mitty Bessette's saloon were toasting peace. We had just learned that Confederate General Robert E. Lee had surrendered in his home state of Virginia, effectively ending the butchery of the Civil War, and that the Yankees had decided *not* to hang the enemy general by the neck until dead. More than 600,000 people, mostly common men like two of my brothers, had died in the States during the four years of war, yet Lincoln's sudden death struck me harder. Lincoln had been my neighbor and my friend—at least in my own mind. W.A. Phillips delivered the bad news along with the latest copy of the *Montana Post,* which mentioned Appomattox but not Ford's Theatre. There would be no reading of Thomas Dimsdale that day.

After I got over the initial numbness, I became mournful, then bitter, and then mournful and bitter at the same time. I ran so fast to the Edgerton home that W.A. could barely keep up. I wanted to commiserate with Lucy, since I knew my sister's fondness for Lincoln nearly matched my own. When I got there, everyone was hugging each other and crying. Mary Edgerton was clinging to one of her husband Sidney's shoulders while Lucy clasped the other. Meanwhile, Lucia's face was pressed against the back of Lucy's neck and various Edgerton children were at the skirts of the women's dresses looking for legs to clutch. Mattie Edgerton broke away from family to wrap her arms around me, essentially giving me a bear hug.

"I can hardly bear up to this," she admitted. "He's the one who appointed Papa territorial governor."

"He did a few other things, too," I said, rather coldly I must say considering I was shedding my own tears. "Like freeing the slaves, saving the Union, and taking Mary Lincoln to see a play despite his premonitions of death."

"I know all that. What's premonitions?

"Forget it. They're done with now."

"I'm scared. What if one of the Southern traitors tries to kill Papa for being on Lincoln's side?"

"Don't worry. The vigilantes would hang the traitor. They're mostly Republicans."

"But Papa would be dead."

"Maybe. Maybe not. They'd still hang the traitor if he tried but failed. Anyway, it's pure speculation on your part. Unless you've had premonitions about the governor's death, forget about it."

"I'll try." Mattie hugged me even tighter. "Have you noticed how much I've grown, Woodie? I'm fourteen now."

I didn't answer. My mind was elsewhere.

"I said I am fourteen. I'm filling out fast. My mother won't even let me attend any of the dances and parties in town on account of Bannack being full of the drinking, loafing set."

"Well, girl, I'm seventeen . . . or will be in July. What's more, I'm one of them drinkers and loafers."

"I don't believe it. And I won't let go of you no matter what falsehoods you tell me."

"Look, Lincoln is dead, and I don't feel like talking, certainly not about you."

"You think about it, then. I'm terribly mature for my age."

I started thinking too much, but *not* about Mattie Edgerton. While I naturally detested the multiple hangings that had gone on in the mining camps, I thought anyone in any way connected to Lincoln's assassination ought to swing. *After a legal trial,* I reminded myself. Truth was, at that moment, I wouldn't have objected to seeing the whole lot of them lynched from the columns of the White House.

"Ouch," cried Mattie. "Must you squeeze so terribly hard?"

I excused myself and separated from the little pest. Despite my bitter mournfulness, I was pleased to see that Lucia was still crying on Lucy's neck and W.A. Phillips was still standing alone looking for someone to hug.

A nudge to the shoulder startled me. "It is terrible to think of it," Mary Edgerton told me. "What can these traitors possibly gain by such murderous deeds? Sidney doesn't need this kind of excitement on top of what has already happened."

"You mean the hungry miners and flour riots in Alder Gulch?"

"I mean the fact that the Legislature had voted to move the capital from Bannack to Virginia City. What is Sidney to do? What are we to do? With President Lincoln dead and most of the Legislature against Sid . . . How could he ever win office with all those Democratic voters in Virginia City! Bannack isn't much better. He—we—might do best by returning to Ohio. Do you realize that the government still hasn't paid him his salary as Montana Territory's first governor or given him a secretary?"

"I'm sorry."

"Frankly, I don't know what he—we—would have done

without your efficient sister helping out with the territorial paperwork and correspondence. I'm sure she would come along to help out wherever we go if Sid asks her. But Sid would *never* ask her to go with us to Virginia City, because I—we—simply won't go there."

"I don't blame you. I'm not too fond of the place myself. They hanged my brother . . ."

"Not that Bannack is so very much better. I've never really fit in with the townspeople. But it is our home. We have this house here."

"I know. I'm standing in it. You gave me a room and . . ."

"But why am I telling you my—our—troubles? You no doubt have your own little worries. Tell me, Woodrow, why have you been making yourself so scare lately? Lucy says you have been working at Mr. Thompson's sawmill but still, we'd all like to see more of you."

"Lucia Darling, too?"

"What? Yes. Why not. Our niece has always thought you an upstanding if unpolished young fellow, one quite a bit more educated than he may think."

"I don't think so, but tell me, Mrs. Edgerton, has Lucia become . . . you know, disenchanted with W. A. . . . eh, Mr. Phillips?"

"To say the least, and I am not one to talk, so I will say the least. I know he's a friend of yours, Woodrow, and once did Sidney an enormous favor by accompanying him back home from Washington, but for one who claims to be a gentleman with a literary bent, he can be quite crude. He has shown Lucia—and myself—his true colors. There, I've said enough."

"Thank you, Mrs. Edgerton." I had said enough, too. I wasn't sure I had shown anyone my true colors yet. I certainly couldn't share my current color with such a fine wife and mother. I bowed to her like I was a gentleman and backed away, telling myself I *must* be something more than a sometime bark peeler who in his free time was a loafing drunk.

Finally, Lucy and Lucia came over to me and both gave me a hug—Lucy in genuine sisterly fashion, Lucia as if I were a former student too big for his boots. As they spoke words in praise of the late Mr. Lincoln, W.A. Phillips came over and hugged both of them—each in what I believed to be crude fashion.

"You got one for Lincoln," Lucia told him. "That's all you get."

"I don't catch your drift," W.A. said. "You all been missing me?"

"If you'll excuse me." She pried herself free of him and shook my hand. "I know this is a terribly sad occasion, but it was still nice to see you looking sober, Woodie. Yes, Lucy has told me about your problem. It's no doubt a challenge for you, but I'm confident you can overcome it in time. Good luck to you and goodbye." She barely smiled and then walked away to join Mattie, who was observing us with hands on hips, admittedly, somewhat widened hips, though of course no match for Lucia's hips.

"It was terribly good to see you, too, Lucia," I finally called out. "You, too, Mattie," I added, probably for Lucia's and Lucy's ears more than those of the little Edgerton pest. But Lucia had turned away from me and was lost in thought, while Lucy wasn't even listening. She was busy telling W.A. that he didn't have to make himself scarce just because he wasn't courting Lucia anymore, and he was busy telling his old friend from Washington that he had become engrossed in answering the call of his writing muse.

"Information-collecting muse," I said, interrupting their business.

"At lease I have a muse," W.A. said.

"I am not amused."

"Neither am I, bark peeler."

"Are you two bickering?" Lucy asked. "This isn't the time or place."

"Woodie obviously needs a drink."

"You buying, W.A.? Never mind. It's about as likely as Lincoln rising from the grave."

"You look like you already have. Why don't you go wash your face, Red. And dry your eyes at the same time, you sentimental son of a bitch."

"You really are a crude bastard, aren't you?"

Lucy gasped because it was me, her little innocent younger brother talking. But she quickly recovered. "You two roommates sound like an old married couple."

"Hell, I'd rather marry the sentimental bastard's enchanting sister," said W.A., putting his arms around Lucy and squeezing her tight, but apparently not unreasonably tight. She elected not to pry herself away.

I thought that called for me to put my arms around Lucia, but she had drifted clear out of the room. She never did accept such bad language in her students.

Lincoln's death brought on temporary lugubriousness but did *not* drive me to further drink. Listening that April day to Mary Edgerton, Lucia Darling, my sister, and even Mattie Edgerton had made me ashamed of my intoxications and indolence. It so happened that Mitty Bessette did nearly run out of his stock whiskey soon after, but in any case, I had been planning to cut back. At the sawmill, they were letting me operate the levers that moved the cutting blades. A drunk doing that line of work risked losing his own fingers or those of a fellow worker. I didn't swear off whiskey, but I didn't swear by it too often.

That May, Blackfeet killed ten white people near Fort Benton in the northern part of the territory, but Governor Edgerton failed to raise a fighting force to run down the guilty parties. I am not even sure he tried, although W.A. Phillips expressed an eagerness to go—not to kill or be killed but to learn more about the natives, good and bad, for his future book. The Bannock Indians who visited Bannack for handouts were hardly a threat, and the governor dismissed what the distant Blackfeet did as an aberration, one likely brought on by overly aggressive gold seekers. The governor hardly raised an eyebrow when Justice Hosmer's court in Virginia City failed to convict several accused murderers. That stirred up the passions of the vigilantes. In July after robbers held up a stage from Virginia City and killed four passengers in Idaho Territory's Portneuf Canyon, vigilantes rode out to execute their own brand of justice. They, as reported in the *Montana Post,* failed to capture a single robber/murderer. Not only that but the *Post* quoted one outlaw as saying that the deadly robbery was payback to the "damned vigilantes" for hanging their friends.

The vigilantes had been having better luck 125 miles north of Virginia City in Helena, a boomtown originally known as "Last Chance Gulch." The diggings there had begun to flourish the previous year, attracting desperadoes as well as prospectors. The good citizens got rid of the camp's crass old name but not its bad men. In June 1865, X Beidler, who had worked neck in hand with Captain James Williams in Alder Gulch, brought the vigilante act to Helena and orchestrated the hanging of an alleged murderer. Helena's same "Hanging Tree" came into play in late July when Beidler and the captain teamed up once again to capture and string up a man pressured into a confession. Sidney Edgerton took these far-off executions in stride. After all, Captain Williams resigned as executive officer of the Vigilance Committee soon after, and things were downright peaceful in Bannack. As for me, though I had never been to Helena, I had no trouble conjuring up visions of men dangling from the tall pine there.

"We could use a little more action here in Bannack," W.A. Phillips told me one hot August night in our Goodrich Hotel room after he and Lucy had returned from a fact-finding mission in Helena, ostensibly for the benefit of the territorial governor but of more use to the would-be novelist. "Virginia City left this town half dead and in time Helena will leave it full dead."

"Bannack has enough activity for me," I said, but right away I started thinking of my lack of activity with Lucia Darling. As far as I was concerned, there could be no substitute—not in Bannack, not in Alder Gulch, not in Last Chance Gulch.

"This town has lost its old grit. What we have here is old dirt and not much true grit." W.A. walked around the room as if inspecting for dirt.

"Like in the days of Sheriff Plummer?"

"Exactly. I'm damn sorry I missed them. Do you know that Helena formed its own vigilante group—the Committee of Safety?"

"Lucy told me. I had a nightmare or two about it. Safety indeed."

"The show goes on, even with Captain Williams finding a new pastime besides hanging desperadoes."

"Do you have to delight in it, W.A.? I feel safer in Bannack."

"Man can only be truly alive when surrounded by death."

I nodded without the slightest conviction. Ever since Lucia ended their romantic relationship, W.A. had been nurturing his morbid fascination for shootings, knifings, robberies, executions, vengeance, and even women who poisoned their husbands (though I hadn't heard of any such cases in the territory).

"And if *not* surrounded by hate," he continued, "how can one truly experience love?"

That worried me, him using the word *love.* He easily read my frown lines.

"No, Woodie, Lucia barely acknowledged me when I returned from Helena. We are birds of a different feather. She's a white dove. I'm a red-tailed hawk. She wanted to educate me into her kind of potential mate. I wanted to teach her how to complement a man."

"Like tell you what a great writer . . . eh, fact-gatherer . . . you are?"

"Not that kind of compliment. Only a woman can *complete* a man, but it has to be the right kind of woman. It's hard to explain to a naïf like yourself."

"I understand what kind of woman Lucia Darling is. She doesn't need you to tell her what kind of woman she should be."

"She doesn't need a man for anything. She has her family, her school, and her God. That's fine, her not being *totally* human. While in Helena I was reminded what a real woman is all about—one who gives to others because she's a natural giver not because she wants to be rewarded for giving in this life . . . or the ever after."

"Oh. So you met a lady in Helena who you think is *right*?"

"Not exactly. What I did was rediscover a fine lady. Funny how we traveled all the way west together but we never . . . you know, shared the same bedroll. Now there is something to be said for platonic relationships, for half a loaf is better than none. But when you realize a woman is the right one, as I did while vigorously absorbing the latest doings in Helena, you want to have all the bread you can get. You need to fill your belly and feel fully alive."

My mind had drifted to hopeless thoughts about Lucia, so what W.A. was saying didn't register at first. But then it hit me. It may as well have been an actual punch to the stomach.

"Good God!" I shouted. "You're talking about my sister . . .

a married lady."

"Don't fret, Red. The country is at peace, and we should all be at peace."

"What does peace have to do with it?"

"Lucy will get her divorce from Mr. Norton when we get back to Washington . . . which is bound to happen someday."

I automatically nodded, but the truth was I had given very little thought to any of us ever returning to the city where Abe Lincoln was assassinated.

"But what about your so-called great Western novel?" I asked.

"I'm nearly full loaded with information. I can do the actual writing anywhere Lucy and I land—Bannack, Virginia City, Washington, Paris. That's the beauty of it."

"What I mean is you told me that women—specifically Lucia Darling—was a detriment to a writer."

"Lucia isn't Lucy. Your sister is an asset, a beautiful asset. She encourages a man in his work. Look at all she's done for the governor. There's no holding me back now. I'm going to write a novel that shall captivate the nation . . . hell, Europe, too. Lucy believes in me. She complements me, completes me to perfection, with or without her divorce."

I contemplated complimenting him on his good taste, but at that moment in our room at the Goodrich Hotel his being with Lucy seemed just as objectionable as his courting Lucia. Regardless, I was too tongue-tied to say anything clearly, let alone anything that made sense. What's more, I was suddenly wishing we were at our table in Mitty Bessette's saloon toasting most anything, except violence or romance, of course.

Chapter Twenty-Six

When in late August I finally asked Lucy on an otherwise deserted street corner about her recent intimacy with W.A. Phillips, she told me quite frankly that a woman had needs just like a man. She added that she felt safe with somebody so familiar, knew exactly what she was getting from "love-starved W.A." and needed a substitute for the preferred but unavailable (because of his marriage, not hers) Sidney Edgerton. She no doubt would have continued in that vein, but I had heard enough sisterly honesty. I tried to excuse myself to attend to some important business, but we both knew I had no important business. Banker, dry goods store owner, and lumberman Francis Thompson, with pockets filled with gold, had left Bannack for a new life in the East, and I no longer had a job.

"No need to rush off," she told me, taking hold of my left elbow. "I'm not saying I can no longer work with the governor; I'm saying my position is changing."

"Because of you and . . . you know?"

"No. Nothing to do with W.A. But President Andrew Johnson has at last named an official territorial secretary, Thomas Francis Meagher, who fought hard for the Union and is a highly spirited politician. Whenever Mr. Meagher gets here, my services as unofficial but well-paid secretary to Sidney could very well be curtailed. It can't go on like this forever, in any case. I'll have to find new employment somewhere—almost certainly not in this failing town—and you'll have to pay your own way again, dear brother. Such is life."

It was only proper that I nod, but the fact was she was scaring me too much to react.

"W.A. says you might go home to Washington to get a divorce," I finally said, leaning against an unused hitching post for support.

"I do want a divorce but not so that I can marry W.A. I've gotten a taste of the political life here, and while it can be unpleasant, it is something I wish to pursue. It's in my blood."

Politics certainly wasn't in my blood. "Oh," is all I said.

"In Washington everything is political. Naturally, as a woman, it would be impossible to hold political office, but there are ways a woman can influence policy upfront or behind the scenes. It might mean marrying again, but it might not. I will be free to decide."

"W.A. would go back to Washington with you, though?"

"He's free to decide. That goes for you, too, Woodie. I worry about your future. You seem at loose ends. W.A. tells me you drink twice as much as him now and can't sleep at night."

"The bastard lies. And he snores."

"And, as I've mentioned before, you use the kind of language you once rejected."

"I don't give a fart about polite words. I . . . Sorry, Lucy. Sometimes whatever I do seems ass-backward and thinking about it doesn't help."

"I only hope you can pull yourself together."

"Drinking helps."

"No. It will tear you apart. I have one question for you, and I would like a serious answer."

"Shoot."

"The question is this, dear brother: Do you want to return to the nation's capital when I do or remain by your lonesome in the territory?"

I pondered her question with great difficulty as if she had asked me the meaning of life. *Washington D.C. had nothing to offer me anymore, if it ever did. But what did Montana Territory have to offer me? Certainly not gold. Hopefully not a hangman's noose.* But finally, with Lucy waiting patiently for my answer, I thought of something.

"Lucia Darling," I declared. "I have her here. I'll stay."

Of course, I didn't have her, and of course Lucia Darling, coming off her short-lived romance with W.A. Phillips, still had no interest in an even younger man. Lucy knew this, of course, but she didn't laugh at my foolishness or tell me to find a girl my own age, preferably after first finding a way to support a family of two or more.

"Nothing is for certain, brother," Lucy said. "But it's best you know something about Lucia."

"I do know something. I'd like to know more."

"Lucia could very well be looking for greener pastures herself before long."

I nodded and kept nodding until my entire body trembled. Needing a drink, I excused myself and ran off to my favorite saloon. After one drink, I needed another, and so on. At some point I worked up the nerve to go to the Edgerton house to tell Lucia, once and for all, about her and me and the way it *should* be between us. After all I was older now, seventeen years and nearly two months . . . and counting. My plan was to take her onto one of the hilltops—definitely not gallows hill or cemetery hill—stare with her at the galaxy-filled sky and offer her nothing short of my universal love till the end of time. Fortunately, since I was in no condition to court or even walk, Mitty Bessette put me to bed in his backroom among the crates of whiskey. After that, my cowardice resurfaced and I convinced myself Lucia wasn't going anywhere, so there was no need to rush things.

And then it was September 1865, a month I keep trying to

forget but never can. For one thing, vigilantes dealt out death again that month despite Hezekiah Hosmer and territorial courts. First, they hanged a man accused of stealing horses in Confederate Gulch east of Helena, and then they went back to Helena's Hanging Tree to string up a man accused of picking pockets. Perhaps these two examples of extralegal justice (to use the polite term) inspired the Vigilance Committee, which soon after announced it would be inflicting punishment "where the civil authorities are unable to enforce the proper penalty of the law." True to its word, the committee put the noose to two suspected horse thieves on September 27 in Virginia City. If Chief Justice Hosmer objected, I didn't hear about it, and, as usual, neither did Sidney Edgerton. The governor had less reason to care than ever. He had already pulled up stakes.

It was supposed to be a temporary arrangement. Sidney Edgerton would go to Washington, D.C., to secure funds for the territory and himself and leave Territorial Secretary Meagher in charge as acting governor. I was suspicious, though, because the governor was hardly wanting, having cashed in on some mining claims I hadn't previously known about. What's more, the governor was taking his family with him, but only as far as Ohio, where he would resettle them in their old hometown of Tallmadge. I didn't find out about the seemingly sudden departure until two days before it happened. It was Mattie who told me all about it late one afternoon when I was aimlessly walking the streets of Bannack trying to work up the courage to ask Lucia if I could help her teach school every day, which I saw as the first step in winning her over for life.

"You all are really leaving Bannack?" I said, and suddenly Mattie looked better than she ever had. I mean some people just look better when you know they are going away.

"Really and truly. Papa says there is no future here. Mother never became attached to the rough ways that stick out so far from civilized society. And I say, well, I'll miss certain things about Bannack and certain people, too, but . . ."

"But what?"

"My parents worry terribly about the way men look at me here even though I am fourteen. I don't mind so much their looking because I know they are just lonely, but . . ."

"None of you were even going to say goodbye?"

"I'll say goodbye." She slipped between my arms and I let her, even squeezing the small of her back just a little. "You could come with us, Woodie. It's not too late. Mother wouldn't object."

"I don't want to go back to Washington, and Ohio doesn't interest me."

"Not me, either?"

I knew I couldn't answer such a question even if my tongue cooperated. "All of this is hard to digest," I said instead.

Mattie, still clutching, looked up at me until I caught her eye. Then, she winked. "Lucia is coming back to Ohio, too, to teach at a better school. You'll have to say goodbye to her, too, you know."

I didn't know. I quickly broke loose from Mattie and began to turn in a small circle like a cat looking for a place to curl up for the night. I had trouble catching my breath.

"You look sick," she said. "Like me the time I had the croup."

"I . . . I had better come with you."

"Really! To Ohio?"

"To . . . to your house here. To say goodbye to . . . everyone."

"Your sister would like that. She was going to come to the hotel later anyway."

"What for?"

"To say goodbye, of course."

"Oh. Lucy is leaving in two days, too?"

"She wanted to tell you herself. But, yes. She'll be going on to Washington with Papa. He says he'll need all the help he can with the new president and Congress and the political climate."

All I could think about was how much help I would need existing in Bannack without Francis Thompson, the Edgertons, Lucia, and Lucy. But Washington, D.C.? When I left there with brother Rufus, I had *not* left my heart behind. As for Ohio, if Lucia begged me to come along as her teaching assistant, I might consider . . . Hell freezing over seemed more likely. And then I dwelled on the concept of Hell for several minutes as Mattie tugged on my shirtsleeve before my thoughts switched smoothly enough to my roommate at the Goodrich.

"It's funny," I finally said, but I had to pause to wipe my eyes with my other shirtsleeve. I wasn't sure if the tears were for Lucia, Lucy, or myself.

"You aren't laughing," Mattie said.

"All right, it's strange, not funny, but W.A. Phillips said nothing to me about leaving with Lucy and the Edgertons."

"Oh, you see, he doesn't know about us going."

"How could he *not* know?"

"He isn't going. Lucy wants to go to Washington without him. At the hotel tonight she was going to say goodbye to him as well as to you."

I was possibly in a state of shock when Mattie led me by the hand to the Edgerton house. The family was busy packing. Everyone said hello instead of goodbye and then went back to work. Even Mattie let go of me and joined them. All I could do was watch until Lucy broke away from the important papers in the gubernatorial files to explain herself. Her desire for a divorce and a political career in Washington, combined with her loyalty to the governor and her need for at least a temporary separation from her demanding friend W.A. Phillips, made her decision to leave with the Edgertons an easy one.

"What about me?" I asked, for my sister's unconditional support, my drinking, and my lack of access to my true love had turned me into a self-pitying dependent. "What am I to do?"

"You are the hard part in this," she said. "I came west mainly to see about you and get away from William Penn Norton, but it was never to be a permanent thing. I will miss you, Woodie, though at this point I believe that leaving you here to make it on your own on the frontier is the best thing I can possibly do for you. Do you understand?"

I nodded and gasped simultaneously.

"And you will make it on your own, Woodie."

"I heard you were leaving W.A. behind, too. Is that also for his own good?"

"I'm not sure. But it's for my own good. It would serve no purpose for me to move on from my marital ties to Mr. Norton to take up similar ties with Mr. Phillips. I don't mean to sound selfish or cruel. I rather adore W.A. I will continue to do so from afar. He has been a great friend, but he has become *too great* for me. It is difficult to explain. Lucia has called him impetuous and self-important. I believe she has hit the nail on the head."

"She can do that," I said, rubbing my own poor, aching head.

"We'll talk more later, dear brother. I think it is time for you to say goodbye to Lucia. She's waiting for you in the kitchen."

Without even a nod, I went to the kitchen with my head down. I knocked on the door before stepping in cautiously, like a boy entering a saloon—which is what I was myself not so long ago. I arrived in time to see her put a pie pan and then a cutting board into a wood crate. She paused to look me over closely. I suspected I never looked better to her now that she was leaving. I did not look back directly but focused on the empty pie pan.

"I was born in Michigan, not Ohio," she said. "When I was fourteen, I said goodbye to my mother Pauline, Sidney's sister, to live with my uncle and teach school in Akron, Ohio. I wanted to come to Bannack with the Edgertons, and I am glad I did. I was able to interest a few young people here in learning. But I am not at heart a pioneering woman. Bannack is hard, especially when the bitter cold and snow comes. I shall continue to teach the young in Ohio or wherever I happen to be, and I will continue my own studies in college."

"And you will marry?"

"I am in no rush to do that. Education comes first—for me, for others. I don't ever want to stop learning. No adult human being should. It's what separates us from the animals."

"But someday you will?"

"Marry? Give me twenty years maybe."

"Good. I'll be twenty years older . . . old enough, right?"

"I'll be far too old for you, then, Woodie. You'll find someone right for you, someone a lot younger."

"I like education a whole lot. I could be a teacher, too. Didn't you tell me that once?"

"Have a passel of children with the right lady, Woodie. Teach them all well."

"I don't understand why we can't . . . I mean me and you . . ."

"It wouldn't work, Woodie, not if you came East now or later. You have a good heart. Stay here and make the West a better, more forgiving place. It needs more young men like you, young men who don't want to rob, shoot, or hang anyone and who are willing to let women have their say and act on their own however they wish. Lucy was right about you. You are decent."

"I don't want you to speak anymore, Lucia. I just want to kiss you on the lips."

"I'll kiss you, Woodie, as long as you recognize it for what it is and shall always be—a goodbye kiss."

I recognized only our lips and pressed mine to hers without restraint. My body and hands and tongue kept their distance even when I sensed her lips pressing back, so there was no way she could conclude I was forcing my affection on her. I reckon I was trying to be decent. I saw her nostrils flare and then closed my eyes to block out all distractions. Our lips were sealed together by mutual consent, I thought, for at least a minute until Mattie Edgerton entered the kitchen and as usual said what was on her young mind.

"Why, cousin Lucia," she said. "I never once in my life saw such a thing. You never kissed Mr. Phillips with such everlasting passion."

The spell was broken. Lucia withdrew her face from mine as if she had drunk a glass of vinegar by mistake. She wiped her mouth with the back of her hand. I licked my lips; I could still taste her.

"You are seeing things, cousin," Lucia said as she readjusted the pie pan in the crate. "It wasn't everlasting in the least. I was simply saying goodbye to Woodie."

"I'd like to say goodbye again to Woodie."

Mattie moved in with lips puckered but fortunately her mother entered the kitchen.

"Is everything all right in here?" Mary Edgerton asked.

"Oh, yes," Mattie said. "We are just bidding farewell to one of those bad men of Bannack."

I left the Edgerton house that day with my head spinning. Lucy made me promise not to say a word to W.A. Phillips. She said she owed it to him to tell him the bad news directly—that she was leaving for the East with the Edgertons and he *must* remain behind to pursue his separate dreams. I paced outside the Goodrich Hotel while she and him had their long goodbye up in the room, but at one point a high-pitched scream from above caused me to halt. I looked up at the cracked window and wondered which one of them had screamed. When she said, "That's it, get it all out," I knew he was the screamer. I could make out the words that followed, too: "I'm not saying you must fend for yourself; you and Woodie would do well to help fend for each other." W.A. responded with a howl, and then someone shut the window tight.

After Lucy left, I went up to the room and found W.A. lying on the bed chewing on a pencil. For several hours he told me how miserable he was, barely giving me the chance to tell him that I was just as wretched as him. We both sobbed and cursed, but no drinking was involved. Neither of us wanted to dull or redirect the pain. The next day, we went to the Edgertons together. He tried to get Lucy to change her mind but was so forceful and rude about it that Sidney Edgerton threatened to have him arrested. I wanted another kiss from Lucia but was too sober and sensible and decent to press the issue. I dragged W.A. back to our hotel room where he damned the governor for being cruel, ungrateful, and a bad influence on not only Lucy but also Lucia, at least as far as other men were concerned. I knew W.A. was wrong about all that, but I nodded anyway and once even suggested that the governor wasn't helping his daughter Mattie either. I may have suggested that the two of us go for a drink at Mitty Bessette's saloon, but W.A. preferred to just lie there chewing on his pencil.

On the very September day Lucy, Lucia, and the Edgertons left for the East, W.A. took the stub of a pencil out of his mouth and began scribbling on a pad of paper that Lucy gave him as a parting gift. His information-gathering stage was over. He had begun his novel at last. Lucia left me with no goodbye present after that long kiss, but her taste was still lingering on my lips, so I restrained myself for a week before going to Mitty's place alone to wipe my mouth with whiskey.

Chapter Twenty-Seven

September also saw Thomas Francis Meagher arrive in Bannack. With Sidney Edgerton going to Washington, Meagher became acting governor. He had been sitting in stagecoaches for a good three weeks, and he needed to stretch his legs, meet the locals, and take in liquid refreshment, not necessarily in that order. A proud Irish Brigade commander during the Civil War, he had seen so many casualties in battle that a few hangings in the territory weren't likely to cause him to raise an eyebrow. The acting governor was a Republican like Sidney Edgerton, but he was more flexible in his political beliefs and had a far less rigid code of personal behavior. By that I mean he was a drinking man and was willing to down more than a few with Mr. Edgerton's Democratic enemies and even with the likes of me who, since the death of Abe Lincoln, had made a vow to avoid politics like the plague.

One time in a drunken stupor at Mitty Bessette's saloon, the acting governor stood atop the bar and told the hard-drinking miners what he planned to tell Andrew Johnson: "Restore the Southern states if you will, Mr. President, but whether you do or not, do *not* neglect the West. We need forts and U.S. soldiers out here in the Montana Territory to protect our good citizens from Indian depredations and curtail the plundering of road agents and cold-blooded murderers." No doubt if the orator ever told Andrew Johnson anything, it would have to be in a letter; nevertheless, the drinking crowd roared its approval. Making sure their gold remained safe was paramount to them. I merely moaned into my empty glass.

"That's all the territory needs," I told W.A. Phillips, who had no gold but was still cheering and pounding his fist on our table, "soldiers shooting the poor men that the vigilantes haven't managed to hang."

"That's the real West, Red," he shouted, as if addressing the acting governor instead of me.

"You don't understand. I'm saying that's a bad thing. We have enough killing here."

"What if the federal troops shoot the vigilantes? Wouldn't that be a good thing?"

"No," I said, although I admitted I did hesitate before answering. "And we don't need forts and soldiers to protect us from the Bannocks."

"Don't forget the deadly Blackfeet to the north and the bloodthirsty Sioux to the east. We don't need a meager, mild-mannered politician in Montana. Give the red savages hell, Meagher!"

There was no talking to W.A. He had become something of a rabble-rouser since Lucy left for the East. Another time at Mitty's place, W.A. joined Mr. Meagher in railing against Wilbur Sanders for being a "radical and extremist and teetotaler." The acting governor wanted to be governor should Sidney Edgerton resign the post, and he saw the governor's nephew as his major rival. W.A. suggested that Sanders, who had prosecuted George Ives and encouraged vigilante action, be hanged by his neck to get a taste of his own medicine. "That's going too far," Mr. Meagher cried. "Hanging Wilbur by his toes would be enough."

When the acting governor visited Virginia City for the first time, W.A. went with him as a bodyguard and drinking companion. They raised more glasses than they did goodwill and entertained flocks of soiled doves, including Little Gold Bit from Moll Featherlegs's bordello and Varina Willingham, who was calling herself Virginia Nevada all over again. I stayed behind because I was not only tired of Mr. Meagher and W.A. but also working again, this time as Mittty Bessette's saloon helper (in other words I swept the floor, washed the glasses, toted the whiskey crates, and did whatever else he told me to do).

"Little Gold Bit was asking about you and that large salmon birthmark you have in back of your neck," W.A. told me in our hotel room as soon as he returned in October to wrap up his affairs in Bannack.

"I don't have a birthmark on the back of my neck or anywhere else," I told him.

"You know that and I know that but Little Gold Bit must have gotten you mixed up with some other young customer that came along. There was no reason to correct her. She did remember that you lay in bed a long, long time in Moll's place like a sick preacher and that you never drank. I corrected her on that last point and told her that at age seventeen you were drinking like a fish."

"Thanks."

"Now Virginia Nevada at the Pay Dirt said she remembered you, too, but that she remembered your brother better."

"That's good. Rufus hanged for her."

"She wanted me to tell you that her estranged husband, Wallace something, has stopped looking for her in Virginia City because he fell under a plow, the blade cut a vital artery in his fat neck, and he is now resting under the Kansas sod."

"That must be a relief for her. Guess she doesn't have to worry about the Willinghams any longer. It was Wallace's brother she shot in Virginia City when I was there."

"As far as I could tell, she isn't worried about a bloody thing. She and Meagher were quite the pair for nearly three days. Apparently, she has a good dose of Irish blood in her. And that's not all they have in common. They both claim to have been subjected to outrageous accusations and cowardly slander by their jealous enemies. The Acting One took good care of Virginia Nevada until he acted on another drunken impulse and left her to call on the Little Gold Bit."

"I don't need to hear any more of this, W.A. Those two women are of no interest to me and neither is the acting governor."

"I understand. All you care about, Red, is tending to dirty floors and dirty glasses."

I hung my head, even though I was glad to have a job, any job again. I suppose I would have liked to have possessed a gold claim, but I didn't and had neither the funds nor the ambition to pursue the stuff that made Montana Territory possible. All I had was the gold spoon Lucy gave me as a sixteenth birthday present. I kept it close to my heart sixteen months later and took it out to clutch now and then, even when I had nothing to scoop with it except the heavy air of Bannack.

"It's only temporary," I said. "By the way, how's the novel coming along?"

"Had no time to write in Virginia City. But don't you fret, Red, I'll get her done when I find the time."

"But not here in Bannack? You are really leaving?"

"That's right. I've had enough of Mitty's saloon, the Goodrich Hotel, and all the rest of this decaying metropolis."

"I see. You are returning to Virginia City to work for the acting governor?"

"I'm off to Helena. I'm on the payroll. I'll be Meagher's eyes and ears over there. Remember when I went there with Lucy on behalf of Governor Edgerton? Well Meagher considers me, with my experience and enthusiasm, to be the right man to get the lay of the land. We both agree that Helena is an up-and-coming place where we figure most of the future action will be."

"And by action, you mean?"

"Yes, armed robberies, killings, hangings. I need to break out of my writing lull, and a little modern mayhem will inspire me."

"Violence is your friend, huh?" I shook my weary head until he got mad and threatened to knock the righteousness clear out of it. I apologized, which inspired him to ruffle my red hair.

"Lucy and Lucia have moved on," he said. "You got to move on, too."

"Where to? I hate Virginia City and I'm not moving with you to Helena."

"I didn't ask you to. I don't think you could stand the action."

"I have thought some about Hell Gate. But I'm not sure I could get my old job back at the store of Mr. Higgins and Mr. Worden."

"What the hell. Go for it instead of thinking about it. That's my advice to you, Red."

"I'll think about it."

"Look, you got to move on with your life, even if you continue to spend it in Bannack. I want to write the Great American Western Novel. What do you want to do?"

All I could think about was fondling a bottle of red-eye. "I don't know," I said.

"If you could accomplish anything—I mean in your wildest dreams—what would it be?"

"I don't know. Well, maybe it would be stopping the hangings—you know, putting an end to vigilante action everywhere in the territory, everywhere in the world."

"But you wouldn't stop the robbing and killing?"

"Well, that, too. All violence everywhere. I know that's ridiculous. But you asked."

"If there was no violence anywhere, how could you appreciate peace?"

"I don't know. That's your old argument. I'd find a way."

W.A. walked to the window and stared out at the peace and quiet. "You know, Red, you've inspired me again. Stopping the vigilantes. That's a job for my hero."

"Your hero?"

"In the novel, in the novel. Remember how I mentioned Red Ranger before. That's my hero. You've convinced me."

"Me?"

"Red Ranger is just the man—the *only* man—to do the job. Doesn't it sound simply stupendous?"

"I suppose. I meant to ask you before, what's a ranger?"

"A ranger is a ranger. There were rangers in Colonial America. There were rangers in the Civil War. Remember John S. Mosby in Virginia? He was a partisan ranger. There are rangers in Texas even as we speak. Texas Rangers. Why can't there be a ranger in Montana . . . a red one!"

"Why red?"

"Now that's about the dumbest question I've heard in all my born days. It's you, Red. You are the inspiration. Take a look in the mirror. You are my bloody hero. You, by God, *are* Red Ranger. Have you tried on your red cape yet?"

"No. It's place as always is in the closet." Nothing had changed—I didn't even like being called Red, let alone having "Ranger" tacked on to the end of it. Making me any kind of hero seemed even dumber to me than any question I'd ever asked. I figured W.A. would just forget about the silly notion in time. If he ever really finished his novel, which I strongly doubted that October day in our room at the Goodrich Hotel, it undoubtedly would center on a real hero, even if fictional, and that character would bear no more resemblance to me than I did to Achilles, Hercules, or Abraham Lincoln.

W.A. kept staring at me as if he expected me to do something, like go to the closet, or at least say something even remotely heroic.

"I suppose I could be," I finally said, "after a thousand drinks."

"Could be what?"

"Heroic like your Red Ranger. It would have to be in a quiet sort of way. Isn't that what we are talking about here?"

"Let's forget the talk. It's time to take action, Woodrow Russell Hart."

"Whatever you say, Wilberforce Anaconda Phillips. I'm too tired to go to Mitty's. I'm going to bed."

By November, W.A. Phillips was gone from Bannack. I suppose he found what he wanted in Helena, where the Committee of Safety hanged at least three men by month's end. Truth is, I lost count of the executions as I went about my life as what Mitty Bessette, my only friend and only employer, called a *rat de salon,* which at least sounds better in French than it does in English—saloon rat. In early December I read a public announcement of sorts in the *Montana Post:* " 'Hangman's Tree,' in Dry Gulch, is barren this week—no crop, not a sign of one." Somehow that didn't improve my spirits. On New Year's Eve, Mitty produced a tally sheet he had kept under lock and key. It listed thirty-seven hanging "victims" either by their initials or by "NUK," for name unknown. When I saw one of the March entries—an NUK crossed out and replaced with "RH"—I lost it in front of a full house at Mitty's place. I drank directly from a bottle as I moaned over what the Virginia City vigilantes had done to Rufus Hart—as if it had happened just the day before—and declared (I quote myself here, as remembered by Mitty): "Men who break the law still accept the law of gravity, but men who take the law into their own hands defy gravity and are guilty of human depravity."

In my drunken state, I was condemning the vigilantes for raising men in the air and *not* letting them come back down to earth naturally. Most of Mitty Bessette's patrons ignored my inebriated tantrum but not so this one burly miner who told me to shut up and listen. He then quoted Thomas Dimsdale of the *Post* as saying, "Peace and good order must be preserved even if the sun of every morning should rise upon the morbid picture of a malefactor dangling in the air." Those were fighting words, even for a non-fighter like me. When the burly miner came at me with ham-hock fists raised, I broke my bottle on the bar, creating a jagged weapon that I somehow proceeded to thrust through the bottom of my own chin into my mouth. I, needless to say, created a bloody mess and fainted. But most of that blood must not have been critical and I apparently didn't sever any major artery and was also extremely lucky, depending on your point of view. The bottom line is that a Bannack doctor stopped the bleeding and I lived, albeit with many scars on the lower half of my face that have regularly frightened delicate women.

"You are damn fortunate, Woodie," Mitty Bessette told me while I was still lying on his back-of-the-saloon bed with my face half covered in bandages. "It could have been your neck or an eye you took out with your self-bottling maneuver."

I nodded. "Does W.A. Phillips know?"

"How could he?"

I shrugged, and even that slight movement aggravated my ugly jaw. "I thought he might be interested in what happened, seeing as how violence was involved."

"Haven't seen hide nor hair of our *ancien ami.* He must be having one hell of a time in Helena . . . that is if he isn't dead."

"Could be he's been locked away in some hotel room writing his Great American Western Novel. It's his obsession, you know."

"I rather doubt it. More likely he's been on a two-month drunk."

I don't know if he was writing then or not, in Helena or not. I do know it took W.A. Phillips three decades to finish what he had started in Bannack. True to his word, he finally made me, disguised as Red Ranger, the hero of his first and only completed novel, 1895's *Man from Montana: How He Escaped the Noose*. During my early years in Bannack, Virginia City, and Hell Gate I never actually got close to being hanged, unless you count that time those four misguided men came into Mitty's place and tried to seize me for writing that vehement anti-vigilante note on behalf of R.C. Rawley. But the author's Red Ranger was constantly threatened with extermination once he had challenged the authority of the various vigilance committees and begun rescuing men who were condemned without a trial by jury. Sometimes he was required to rescue himself.

On one unbelievably melodramatic occasion (and almost every occasion in the novel fits that description), Montana vigilantes go all the way to Salt Lake City to string up Red Ranger for killing in self-defense a Mormon man who falsely accused the hero of stealing three of his four wives. For maybe twenty seconds Red Ranger hangs by his incredibly strong, injury-proof neck (developed through years of neck-strengthening exercises) before he manages to free his hands, pull a knife from under his red cape, sever the noose, run like the wind to safety, and find the *fourth* wife to apologize to her (only to find out she is as delighted to be a widow as the other three are). You might think the *How He Escaped the Noose* part of the book's title comes from that particular incident, but there are similar incidents later. It becomes Red Ranger's specialty.

In the dime novel so much is wrong—history is distorted as well as my own character (I only passively opposed the vigilantes, of course, while Red Ranger does so with courageous, muscular action)—that it probably serves no purpose to point it all out other than to provide me with a small degree of peace of mind in what could be, not to sound too melodramatic, my final months on Earth. I mean readers of *that kind of trash* are not looking for truth or the slightest bit of honesty between the stained pages. And for those of you who have never glanced at the W.A. Phillips abomination, I am no doubt at fault for bringing it to your attention in my own true manuscript. Regardless, I have already noted some of W.A. Phillips's errors, almost all put in his novel intentionally.

And here are a few more of the things Red Ranger does in the novel that I didn't do in real life: Saves fifty-one men, in addition to Sheriff Henry Plummer, from hanging (out of the one-hundred-forty-nine men various vigilante groups supposedly targeted for the rope); kills twenty-one men who deserve killing (the Mormon man, six vicious vigilantes after his or other necks, and fourteen hostile redskins—tribes never identified—after Red Ranger's scalp); twice lectures Thomas Dimsdale of the *Montana Post* for choosing to support the vigilantes; forces, with a headlock, vigilante enforcer Captain James Williams into retirement and later drives him to suicide (guzzling laudanum) as "a kind of rough justice"; convinces vigilante president Paris Pfouts to take his family back east to tamer St. Louis; determines through "a kind of mild but effective water torture" that vigilante meanness, not too much whiskey, has caused Thomas Meagher's drowning on July 1, 1867; reforms Madam Moll Featherlegs (one of the few female characters developed to any degree in the novel) by turning her into Virginia City's first successful female doctor; helps a Methodist minister chop down Helena's Hanging Tree in 1875 and then gives the firewood to one of the vigilante victims; and four times successfully fights bids by Wilbur Sanders (called "Banders" in the book) to become territorial delegate to Congress (Banders does become a U.S. Senator in 1889 but only because Red Ranger is out of state busy helping with the Johnstown Flood cleanup in western Pennsylvania).

I could go on in this vein, but I will spare you. Comparing my life to that of Red Ranger has left me utterly frustrated and exhausted. I have, in short, never been a brave deed–doer. At the moment I can think of only one important thing Red Ranger and I have in common—we both ended up alone, having never landed a suitable woman (me because my one and only true love Lucia Darling had rejected me, Red Ranger because he didn't want to subject Lucinda Darlington to a lifetime of worrying about him—a hero devoting his entire existence to justice and fair play and thus unable to spend enough quality time with one lady, Mormon or otherwise).

Chapter Twenty-Eight

My story, of course, didn't end at the end of 1865. Neither does Red Ranger's story in *Man from Montana: How He Escaped the Noose*. There were still more hangings for both of us. I am still hanging on (if you will pardon this tired pun) at age sixty-five in 1913, though several Missoula doctors wonder how I managed it and also indicate—because my health has steadily deteriorated since I became an institution at Red's Saloon—I will be lucky to make it into 1914. It took me a long time to recover from the accidental stabbing of self with a broken whiskey bottle, and arguably I've never recovered from my alcoholic funk. The years have flown past like a bald eagle in a thick winter fog. They are all far less memorable than my first two years in what became Montana. In fact, I have no memory of some years. I shall quickly wade through the haze. My timeline might be crooked but so be it. My body is crooked, too. And I have already alluded to my whiskey-addled brain. I ain't much—that's for sure. But I am proud to have been a mostly honest man, and never a crook. And I'm even more proud to have never been a goddamn vigilante.

I was in such a state by 1866 that I hardly noticed or cared about the political turmoil in the territory that caused the Republican U.S. Congress to declare a couple of Montana legislatures "null and void" and to deny "Democratic" Montana statehood. A new "green" governor (Green Clay Smith was his name) finally succeeded Sidney Edgerton in the fall, but he went to the nation's capital on business, making Thomas Francis Meagher the Acting One once more. Mitty Bessette and many others said Mr. Meagher, who I suspected was drinking as much as me, made a further shamble of things. The Sioux Indians caused a scare along the Bozeman Trail, and the acting governor, wanting to fight them in a full-frontal assault the way he had fought the Confederates, raised an army. Nothing much came of his bloodless campaign except it cost a lot of money and his own life. It could have been an accident when he fell off a steamboat in Fort Benton, but then again it could have been suicide or murder. I guess I always thought some vigilantes killed him, but I certainly never looked for any real proof, and later when W.A. Phillips put the *murder* in his book, I began to doubt the cause of death (since W.A. Phillips wasn't likely to put in something that was true). Governor Green returned from Washington and apparently acted more sensibly than Mr. Meagher, but the only thing he said that made sense to me was his calling attention to Montana Territory's need for education. I pointed out to Mitty my need for educator Lucia Darling, teaching somewhere back in civilized society. Somehow the two issues seemed closely connected.

I got four or five letters (including two on the same spring day in 1867) at the Goodrich Hotel from sister Lucy, but, feeling low as I did, I didn't answer any of them. She gave me some news—she finally got her divorce from the unaccommodating William Penn Norton; black men were now allowed to vote in the District of Columbia; she was trying to get off the ground a prohibition political party whose main purpose was to convince communities and counties to outlaw the production and sale of intoxicating beverages; she was offering her services as a "vice president" to Andrew Johnson (who hadn't had one since succeeding to the presidency upon Abraham Lincoln's assassination in 1865); and the lynching of black men in the South was on the upswing with the establishment of the Klu Klux Klan. As was her way, she asked questions about how I was doing and how W.A. Phillips was doing and why she hadn't heard from either of us. In her last letter she expressed great concern that I might be drinking too much, working too little, not eating well, quarreling with W.A., antagonizing vigilantes, and suffering from lack of female companionship.

Three or four times I started letters to her. I thought she might like to know that W.A. had gone to Helena to acquire fodder for his novel and had not returned even though *only* two additional hangings had occurred there in 1866. I also thought I might mention something I had read in the *Montana Post* early in 1867: Vigilantes in Nevada City had hanged a "notorious scoundrel" named George Rosenbaum and "the world is well rid of him." After that, though, I couldn't think of any other news worth telling. How could I tell Lucy about *my* continued existence in Bannack, where I spent my days without female companionship working for drinks at Mitty's and my nights at the same place sleeping off my daily daze (ever since being barred from my Goodrich Hotel room for lack of sufficient funds)? I remember putting down on borrowed paper "The world is well rid of me," then crossing out "is" and replacing it with "would be" and finally crumbling the paper into a tight ball and trying to swallow it.

On July 4, 1867, I thought nothing about my birthday until I heard a cannon go off, followed by a series of musket shots. At least a few people in Bannack, no doubt Republicans, wanted to celebrate the birth of the United States of America. It took me half the day to figure out that the country was ninety-one years old and that I was *really* nineteen. That very night, a long-in-the-tooth freighter entered Mitty's place and said he was headed north with a load of supplies for Higgins and Worden in Missoula Mills. Even in my dazed state and though I hadn't thought about them in a long time, the names of those two men registered in my brain. Christopher P. Higgins and Frank Worden had been good to me.

"I know them!" I explained as I staggered up to him at the bar.

"Congratulations," replied the freighter, who only looked up from his glass when it was empty. "You and most everyone else in the territory."

"You don't understand, mister. I worked for them long ago."

"Long ago? You ain't nothing but a boy now."

"I'm nineteen. That's a man."

"More or less."

"Hey, wait a second."

"Ain't headed out till morning."

"But to Hell Gate, right? You must mean you're taking your load to Hell Gate."

"I mean Missoula Mills. I know where the hell I'm going. Do you?"

I thought about that a good minute. "Mr. Higgins and Mr. Worden must have moved," I concluded.

"Everyone and everything moved. Higgins and Worden didn't have enough water in Hell Gate for the lumber and flour mills they aimed to build. The whole settlement packed up in '65 and moved four miles east. Where you been?"

"Here. Right here in Bannack."

"That right? I say they should move this *old settlement* somewhere else."

To make a long story short, I borrowed from Mitty Bessette a $20 liberty head gold coin that had the words "In God We Trust" on the back, cried on his shoulder, packed up my meager belongings, drank myself to sleep, and caught a wagon ride in the morning to Missoula Mills. Mitty said he liked me well enough but that I was drinking him dry and should bestir my young bones to seek my fortune in a town that wasn't half-dead and full of misfortune.

Mr. Higgins and Mr. Worden remembered me if not my name. They both called me "Red" until I corrected them. They were happy partners still, prospering in their new location. Hell Gate had seemed a much too unfriendly name for the transplanted community, and Missoula Mills flowed nicely off their tongues. Missoula County had been created by Washington Territory legislators some seven years earlier, the name coming from *Nemissoolatakoo* or other Indian words related to the flow and direction of rivers. They had been pleased with my earlier work at their Hell Gate store and were impressed that Francis Thompson had employed me at his sawmill in Bannack. I didn't tell them how I had since become something just short of Bannack's town drunk. Of course, they were sharp enough to have seen it in my eyes or nose or smelled it on my breath. Regardless, they put me in their employment again right on the spot.

The partners also found me a room to call my own in back of a long log structure overlooking Rattlesnake Creek, whose channeled waters powered the sawmill and also the Higgins-Worden grist mill. Other employees—all male of course—occupied other rooms in the building. We were free to eat all the apples we wanted from the orchard that was the backyard, and many of my meals consisted of whole, sliced, or mashed apples. For some months I avoided visits to the Missoula Mills drinking establishments, to please Mr. Higgins and Mr. Worden, but I assisted an Irishman named McQuirk in making a sweet apple wine that we drank at the end of the workday. Because of the way I went for the apples and the wine, McQuirk called me "Red Worm," which I objected to so strenuously that he finally made it just "Worm," which somehow didn't bother me at all. I called him McOwl as he resembled a great horned one of those from the neck up and was naturally nocturnal. Women found his flat face, tiny ears, large dark circles around his eyes, and foul breath unappealing so he counted on me to attract the fairer sex. The end result was neither of us enjoyed female companionship, at least not the kind that is free on the surface.

And thus the years went by, productively for Mr. Higgins and Mr. Worden, who ran a quality store on Mullan Road and were the leading lights in the community they founded, and unproductively for McOwl and Worm. At least I kept my job and didn't cut off any body part at the sawmill. McOwl, who preferred to sleep by day, took to selling *our* homemade apple wine (limiting my input, so to speak) and petty theft, often from his bosses' store. He was caught once and given a second chance and then caught again and given a third chance. After he showed no signs of changing his ways, Mr. Higgins and Mr. Worden had no choice but to let him go. Actually, I suppose they could have put him in jail or worse, but they didn't press charges and the Irishman slept on the floor of my room and continued pressing their apples.

During Hell Gate's five years of existence, ten people died, none from natural causes. But nobody threatened to hang McOwl or anyone else in Missoula's early years. A mean drunk named Matt Craft, who had killed a man in Hell Gate, was behaving badly in Missoula Mills until shot through a window by a put-upon employee named "Black Tom" Haggerty. The authorities arrested Black Tom for murder but then freed him, and the town residents hailed him as a public benefactor. Another resident was convicted one fall of murder and sentenced to ten years in the twelve-foot-square Missoula jail. That winter he enjoyed the warmth of the stove-heated jail and three free meals a day. Come spring he dug his way out and disappeared into the hills. Nobody spent much time trying to catch him, but if somebody had, it would have simply meant a trip back behind bars, not to the gallows. Now I have never killed anyone (and only on rare occasion, such as when McOwl denied me my share of the wine, have I even thought I could), but I still found those two instances of the justice system at work (even if poorly) mighty refreshing—a nice change of pace from vigilante action in Bannack, Virginia City, Helena, old Hell Gate, and elsewhere in the territory.

The only person of the opposite sex I care to mention is Emma Slack, who arrived from Baltimore, Maryland, to become Missoula's first schoolteacher in 1869. That's one date I can remember because, yes, I was attracted to her—mostly to her educated mind but also to everything else that went with it. I should point out that I decided to make her acquaintance when I turned twenty-one. She told me she was eleven years my senior, but I swear she didn't look close to thirty-two and anyway I had a history with older teachers. I made the mistake of mentioning Lucia Darling and how she had started a school in Bannack five years earlier. Not that Miss Slack actually acted jealous or anything, but I could tell she didn't want to hear about her rival for my affections. I know, I know. I was probably thinking over my head. For a while I passed as her top-of-the-class student because I still looked younger than my age despite all the whiskey and apple wine I had poured down my throat. Anyway, she did have pupils of all ages, including at least two older than me. But being plenty sharp, she soon caught on. I then became her teaching assistant, but only for two classes. My mistake was trying to kiss her while we were jointly setting up addition problems on her small painted blackboard. I have no excuse except to say that the smell of chalk and lavender does something to me.

Flathead Indian children used to peek through the windows of her classroom, causing Miss Slack to clutch her two petticoats and perspire profusely. While still in my "student" stage, I set her straight by explaining how Bannock Indian children did the same in Bannack and how Flatheads like Bannocks were curious and hungry people, not maleficent. She was impressed I knew that word *maleficent,* but it did me no good in the long run. Two years later, Miss Slack resigned her position and became part of another Missoula first—the first couple to marry in the new town. Teachers at the time were *not* allowed to be married or to even keep company with men. I came to realize I was about the last man in Montana Territory she would care to wed, yet I was still disappointed in her for giving up her classroom on East Front Street. She did seem exceedingly happy with her chosen man, postmaster William Henry Harrison Dickinson, and they began having their handful of children to teach in their immaculate little home behind the post office. Early in their marriage, she broke her hip in a fall (running to get the mail, I heard) and developed a permanent limp, but that didn't slow the couple down one bit. As for me, I began to drink whiskey again about that time, but only in moderation. After all Emma Slack Dickinson never for a minute made me forget Lucia Darling.

One man of interest whom I became reacquainted with during my first years in Missoula Mills was Jean-Pierre, the Catholic Kootenai who still lived on the Flathead Indian Reservation at St. Ignatius Mission and was still doing business with Mr. Worden and Mr. Higgins. His belly was rounder than ever, and he rubbed it joyfully after shaking my hand and making the sign of the cross on my forehead. When I had last seen Jean-Pierre, his son with the musical name, La La See, had been only five or six. When I saw the boy again, he was about twelve and so unmanageable that the store owners couldn't settle him down with canned peaches, rock candy, soup, or pats on the head. They had sent him, with Jean-Pierre's blessing, out back to chase the hogs and chickens with his prized if primitive coup-stick. When I came along, he danced around me in a wide circle and then reached out with the stick to touch me none too gently on the forehead—a sign of something far removed from the cross. He clearly fancied himself to be a free-roaming Sioux or Blackfeet warrior rather than a reservation Kootenai or Flathead.

"Ouch," I said. "I come in peace."

"That's what they all say," he said in English. At least his father or somebody had taught him well in the language department.

"I am a good white man, really I am."

"The only good white man is a dead white man."

"Such talk in one so young."

"In another year I am old enough to be a warrior . . . if my people still fought."

"I once had an Indian pony named Togu. A Bannock boy named Manahuu traded him to me . . . well, not to me but to a store owner named Thompson who . . ."

"Never mind. Bannocks are weak. This Thompson, being white, no doubt cheated him."

"Haven't Mr. Worden and Mr. Higgins been good to you?"

"They are greedy like all you palefaces."

"I remember your father once telling me that we are all God's children."

"My father is weak. He believes the white man's God is the only true . . . But how is it you know the man who now calls himself Jean-Pierre?"

"I know you, too. One day when you were a boy—a much younger boy—we went fishing together and played with sticks."

"I don't play with my coupstick. I . . . I remember a big boy with red hair."

"That was me. I'm twenty-one years now . . . a man. Of course, my hair is still red."

"It would make a fine scalp."

"I don't want to be your enemy, La La See. You can see I'm

no fighter. I go unarmed."

"You are weak like my father. Did the Jesuits teach you, too?"

"No. I'm not Roman Catholic. Religion is foreign to me. I'm not anything."

"I know that. You are white, as pale as death."

"Death doesn't have red hair. We do have something in common, La La."

"Red hair is not the same as red skin."

"I meant we both had fun fishing in Rattlesnake Creek that day. We each caught a cutthroat trout. Don't you remember?"

La La nodded his head, but at the same time he rolled his pupils so that only the whites of his eyes showed for a moment. "For that reason," he said, pausing to show me the slight hint of a smile. "I shan't kill you."

the white
Ie has lost

with me,

e the eyes
went limp
one came.
he spirits.
art of the
can see or
guidance
takes what
No migrat-
he mission

ns are sup-
put. They
necessary.

n happy to
en and Mr.
te dispens-
keep me on

vhide, sur-
u'd be bet-

ivileges (he
count of he

Twenty-Nine

me fast friends thanks to our fish-
Creek, along the Bitterroot and
t often up on the Flathead River
e never went with us because the
a falling out over not only fishing
nethods, the Creator, spirits, misty, meaning of friendship, money,
sex, and life on the reservation.
e of the Ksanka Band, or "People
d took pride in such qualities as
. La La couldn't have been more
his father was feeble in body and
nan's world, and dexterous only at
pray to a false God.

La See told me one time when we
n a five-day fishing trip. To me he
ho had also wanted to be a man
g. "My father is a potted house-

head for a long time, not wanting
a, who had a hair-trigger temper
us streak. "Jean-Pierre is a good
quietly after he had landed a cut-

as he watched the fish flop in his

hand. "You say he is good because he is good with man. Never causes harm. He adores the reservation. I his red skin and turned pale."

"I'm not *pale* but I am a white man. You are goo don't forget."

"No need to remind me." He jabbed the trout abo just once, triggering a death shudder before the fish in his hand. I waited for at least a gill twitch, but r "My father has ears for the missionaries instead of The spirits, since the beginning of time, have been animals, the plants, the rocks, and everything else we feel. We would not survive on earth without help an from the spirits. The old man has forgotten this. He the white men give him. He has stopped traveling. ing at all. His tail end has grown fat from sitting on pews all day."

"To each his own, I say."

"You don't talk too much. I like that."

"I work some, drink some, fish a lot."

"I like that, too. White men can migrate. We India posed to stay put. I like the Sioux. They don't sta are never afraid. They will fight the white man if They are migratory men, like me."

"Well, you have no reason to fight me, La La. I' migrate with you to assorted fishing holes. Mr. Word Higgins are most understanding about that. I am qu able in their operations, but they are generous and their payroll . . . giving me enough to get by."

"Living in a Shacktown shack with walls of co rounded by the river and the ugliest of palefaces. Yo ter off with me in a tepee."

After McOwl and I had a loud fight over wine p threw the only punch, which missed my jaw on ac couldn't see a hole through a ladder) and were forced to give up our room in the log structure on Rattlesnake Creek, he wandered off somewhere while I moved into a shanty in Shacktown. The community, to use that term loosely, sat on an island in the Clark Fork River at the time (later someone decided to fill in the channel and make it part of the mainland) and earned the nickname "Rotten Row" because of all the poor and disreputable residents, including serious drunks and equally serious sporting women.

"You're right," I finally said. "It isn't much. But I don't ask for much."

"I like that plenty about you, white man. I will share the trout."

As the Indian boy grew older (of course, I was growing older, too), he continued to accept—even like—me despite the color of my skin. In the summer of 1877, La La wanted to join up with the Nez Perce Indians who had fled the U.S. Army in Idaho Territory and crossed into Montana Territory without any bloodshed by avoiding the log-and-earth breastworks set up south of Missoula by troops and local citizens. I pointed out to my cantankerous Kootenai friend that the Nez Perces were too busy *fleeing* to have time to fish. "Why should I flee then?" he said. "I never fled from anything in my entire life. I ain't afraid to stand up and fight any damn pale-faced long knives that come along. Anyway, the fishing is too good around here to take off for parts unknown." So instead of following the Nez Perces up the Bitterroot Valley and over to the Big Hole, La La took me to his favorite fishing hole on the Blackfoot River.

His other friends were all Indians who chose to roam, boast of their deeds, and sometimes terrorize the residents in the southern half of the Flathead Reservation. The worst of them, Pierre Paul, was known for torturing animals before killing them (and not always for food) and treating outsiders as if they were animals. Several times he might have killed—or at least maimed—me for petty offenses such as stepping on his moccasin tracks or accidentally brushing against one of his animal skins. Each time, though, La La See stepped up and set him straight: I was an exception to the rule—a white man who didn't deserve to be treated like a striped skunk, striped soldier, or uninvited settler. Other palefaces were fair game. Before the first bridge across the Clark Fork washed out, I saw Pierre Paul push a white man (who was crossing in the opposite direction) over the railing and into the water. The man didn't drown, though, so the authorities did nothing more than ban Pierre Paul and his aggressive Kootenai friends from using the crossing. When Frank Woody was elected Missoula's first mayor in the early 1880s, Pierre Paul bet La La See a buffalo tongue meal that he would steal the mayor's horse during a town meeting. And he did, though the horse was recovered two days later trying to ford the Clark Fork with nobody in the saddle.

In mid-decade a letter from my sister Lucy found its way to me in Shacktown, which struck me as some kind of miracle. She said she had learned of my presence from W.A. Phillips, although she said nothing about where he was or how he knew where I was. I certainly had not seen him or heard from him since leaving Bannack for Missoula. The letter was nice to get and had the usual inquiries about my drinking, health, work, and female relationships. She said she was doing fine in the nation's capital and was glad that Chester Arthur was no longer president as he had reneged on a certain, unspecified promise to her. She was confident, however, she could land some kind of advisory but nonpolitical position within the Grover Cleveland administration. "I suppose I am turning Democratic to a degree," she wrote. "It's not so much the white man's party anymore, though Grover is inconsistent in his social views."

Nevertheless, Lucy had stayed in touch with the staunch

Republican Sidney Edgerton, who was living comfortably with his family in Tallmadge, Ohio, and was once more practicing law. The former governor of Montana Territory told her a bit of devastating news—at least it was to me. For nine years Lucia Darling had served as lady principal of Berea College in Kentucky, but she had recently married and was moving to her husband's hometown of Warren, Ohio. She had given up teaching, of course, but planned to be active in the Ladies Aid Society and doing Presbyterian missionary work. It hit me hard, as if the jagged edge of that broken bottle was penetrating my chin all over again. The husband's name, Lucy saw necessary to tell me, was Servetus W. Park, and I muttered *that* name so often that one would have thought he was a lifelong enemy. That should have closed the book on Lucia Darling, but the lonely mind does not always recognize the sanctity of marriage. I still saw her face and figure too clearly in both my intemperate melancholies and sober dreams.

In other news, Lucy reported taking our ancient aunt Clementina to witness the formal dedication of the Washington Monument one February afternoon. The old lady who had been more of a mother to me than my own mother had demanded to see the tallest thing in Washington and the world before she died. Lucy reminded me that on the day of my birth—the Fourth of July 1848—our late father, Lyman Hart, had watched the cornerstone laying of what was now a completed 555-foot-high marble obelisk. "Wouldn't father, with his alcoholic architectural aspirations, have marveled at the finished product," Lucy wrote. "Auntie was certainly dying to see the structure. She told me it reminded her of both her brother Lyman and of you, his youngest son. She called you *Stone Hart* at first but then remembered your name was Woodie. I'm so glad she was able to see it. Her heart gave out five days later in bed." Almost as an afterthought, though it did come before the "P.S.," Lucy confirmed that Olive Hart and her second husband had indeed died in Atlanta within two days of each other fifteen years ago. "Olive Hart was our mother," Lucy added for some reason, even though she must have known a son could never drink enough to forget such a fact. Lucy's P.S. read, "I won't be marrying W.A. Phillips or any man. You are all so terribly *needy.* Oh, and I heard your new capital finally moved from Virginia City to Helena. About time, huh?"

"To hell with Helena," I muttered into the wind. I needed to squeeze a loving person after reading Lucy's letter. None was available, so I took hold of a crotchety, grandmotherly neighbor who almost broke in half in my arms. In exchange for food and drink, she used to read minds by pressing her skull-like head to the forehead of customers, but now she used the same method to tell futures. That was safer because it took some time to prove a fortune-teller wrong.

"You received bad news," she said after I let her go.

"You asking or telling?" I asked.

"I tell your future, Mr. Red."

"For what?"

"What you got, Mr. Red?"

"Not much, but I do have a different name. It's Mr. Hart. But nobody calls me that. I'm Woodie."

"I'm Madame Hoy."

"I know. We've been neighbors for quite a spell."

"So you hug me like a bear."

"Didn't mean to hold you so tightly. I'm sorry."

"I tell your future, Mr. Red."

I consented to undergo this procedure, mainly because I wanted to hear that a red-cheeked schoolteacher (an acceptable substitute for Lucia Darling) lay ahead, along with three or four little ones and a white house with a matching picket fence. I promised Madame Hoy two cans of Worden and Company peaches for the "telling." But when we sat down facing each other and the crone went head-to-head with me, it felt as if she were trying to peel my forehead with a dull paring knife. Even worse, she held nothing back: I would neither find nor lose a lady; I would be out of work; I would fail to drown my sorrows in a bottle; I would turn my back on civilization; and, in the next five to ten years, I would be hanged by the neck until dead—and quite legally, to boot.

When I howled, she laughed like a mad woman and pressed her forehead harder against mine. "I almost forgot," she said, curling her withered upper lip. "Your red hair will turn white."

"Before or after they hang me?" I asked as I pulled away from her.

"You wanted me to lie to you? Madame Hoy *never* lies."

"Why would anyone hang me?" I felt something oozing from my forehead that I thought might be blood. But I reached up to touch it with my fingers and then taste it. Pure sweat—that was all, but that was enough. "I have never done anything . . . I mean anything wrong. Why would I ever start to . . ." The lump in my throat cut off my next question.

"I cannot lie," she said, wiping her own brow with a black scar. "I don't know. I only see what . . ."

The lump dissolved and I shouted questions: "Who will hang me? Legally, you said. Not vigilantes, then?"

She leaned forward, trying to connect with my forehead again.

"Never mind!" I stood up and covered my throat with both hands.

"I have said too much truth, perhaps?"

"You haven't earned your peaches!" I complained, wanting to squeeze her again, this time in anger. "What you said, can't be . . . I mean the last part about . . . you know. How can you tell a man that, a neighbor no less?"

"I have told you what I've seen. Madame Hoy does not . . ."

"Lie. So you've said. But you don't understand. I wouldn't willfully hurt a fly. I've never killed or robbed anyone. Damn it! I am no hard case!"

"Never said you were. And I never said it was just. I only said you would . . ."

"I know what you said." I walked away but soon returned. To show her I was no hard case, I brought her the two cans of peaches. She didn't thank me, and I wasn't about to thank her. I hurried back to my shanty, closed and locked the door behind me, and missed the next three days of work. I only emerged to find something strong to drink. I had nothing on me to pay for it, though, so I decided to go look up La La See and friends who always managed to get their hands on whiskey. That meant leaving town and heading up to the reservation. I would be gone from Missoula for many a month.

While away from my home, such as it was, I mostly stayed with La La See in his lodge at a small Indian village about twenty miles from St. Ignatius Mission, where his pious parents lived. During this time La La, Pierre Paul, and several other full-blood Indians committed petty thefts and robberies on the reservation, occasionally assaulting those who got in their way. I never got in their way. I stayed back in and around the tepee (more comfortable than the shanty I left behind in Shacktown) to drink (cheap trade whiskey), gather (firewood, nuts, berries, roots, inner bark and sap of cottonwoods), fish (mostly for bull trout and whitefish), and cook (learning by trial and error). I didn't do anything warrior-like such as hunt buffalo, deer, or anything else. Pierre Paul started to call me "squaw," but I didn't care as long as he and the others kept supplying the firewater and meat. Occasionally, I headed over to St. Ignatius with La La (Pierre Paul wasn't welcome at the mission and in any case never wanted to go there) to pay my respects to Jean-Pierre, who mostly turned a blind eye to his son's criminal activities. "La La has always been wild, but he is good at heart," the old man insisted. "Pierre Paul is the evil one. He is the devil on earth. That he is a *Pierre,* too, makes my belly churn like the hooves of a horse stuck in quicksand. You, Woodie, as my son's good friend, must guide him away from that fiend." It was an impossible task, not that I tried very hard. I wasn't playing Indian; I was living as one. I didn't want to do anything to jeopardize that, which was only possible because La La liked me.

When I finally got back to Missoula sometime in early 1887, I was just passing through with La La See on a fishing trip to Rock Creek, twenty-some miles to the east. La La went off to obtain tobacco for himself and white grubworms for bait, while I visited Shacktown. My shanty had been usurped by none other than the old winemaker McQuirk/McOwl, who didn't recognize me at first because I wore buckskins and moccasins and my face was leathery and russet. Of course, my red hair, which even he could see through his glassy eyes, eventually gave me away. Neither of us made mention of our earlier fight. He did comment that I looked like a red savage and that he was making himself very much at home in my home, but I took no offense at either.

"I could pay you rent," he said.

I couldn't have been more startled had he told me he was elected mayor of Missoula.

"You can? Selling that much wine, are you?"

"No time to make wine no more, but I can pay."

"You rob a bank?"

"I got a store job, kind of."

"With Mr. Worden and Mr. Higgins?"

"Nope. There's a new top store in town, or city rather. Missoula become one of those in March 1885, you know."

"I forgot. But what's the store?"

"Missoula Mercantile Company."

"And you work there?" I never wanted to be so employed again, but I did pride myself in having served well in several dry goods stores. I couldn't imagine McOwl doing *my* job.

"They got a big barn, too," he said. "That's where I work, looking after their freight teams. It ain't full time. It's near half time. Good, honest work, though. Anyway, I can pay you a pittance."

"Forget about it, McOwl. I abandoned this place and left my job. I live in a tepee now. I don't aim to come back here permanent."

"Thanks, Worm. C. P. Higgins ain't hiring at the store or anyplace else right now. And Frank Worden is gone."

"Gone where? You don't mean he broke up his partnership with Mr. Higgins?"

"No, I don't mean that. I mean Worden is dead. He caught a cold in early February while working on the city water system and . . . well, obviously the cold got worse. He left a youngish wife and seven children behind, you know."

I couldn't talk right away, so I turned in a circle kicking at the side of my former shanty, thinking how Mr. Worden had treated me right, and letting the tears build up.

"You're all choked up, Worm. Come with me and let your old friend buy you a drink . . . I mean whiskey, not apple wine."

"Thanks, but I don't have time. I have to meet up with my best friend, La La See, at the bridge."

"I don't see. Your best friend is a no-account red savage?"

"I could do worse. Say, is Madame Hoy still living next door?"

"You mean that vile old witch who claimed to tell fortunes?"

"Yes. She predicted I'd be out of work, which is true—that is I don't do white man's work anymore—but that's a good thing. She also predicted I would drown my sorrows in a bottle, but living in the tepee on the reservation suits me fine. I don't seem to have so many sorrows anymore. They sort of faded away naturally out there, which is, like she said, away from civilization as I knew it. Thing is, and this continues to trouble me some, she also predicted I would get my neck stretched one day. Imagine that! I'd sure hate for that to come true."

"Don't worry. Madame Hoy is dead. She went wading in the river one stormy morning, toppled over, and was swept away—she never saw it coming."

"Too bad. You figure her dire prediction about me died with her?"

"You can only hope. I figure you'd better have a drink with your old friend, in any case."

"Sorry, but I . . ."

"I know. You'd rather drink with the La La Injun!"

"We aren't drinking. We're going fishing."

"Well, good luck, Worm. You'll need it associating with the likes of him."

Chapter Thirty

McOwl was right, I am sorry to say. By the summer of 1887, La La See had folded up his tepee and moved into a cabin on the banks of the Jocko River on the Flathead Reservation. I went along because I had nowhere else to go. I had no wish to return to the society of white men and white women in Missoula or anywhere else. The simple life suited me, and though I preferred when I was surrounded by buffalo hides instead of log walls, I continued to clean and cook for my friend and to console him first when a white man killed his brother and then when a white doctor and the prayers of everyone at St. Ignatius Mission could not save his father, Catholic convert Jean-Pierre, from the ravages of typhus fever.

My remoteness from people of my race left me so at peace with myself that I all but forgot about my lost love (Lucia Darling) and other women I had almost known, lynched brother (Rufus Hart) and the rest of my departed family, and the hated vigilantes of Montana Territory. I did learn during Jean-Pierre's burial ceremony at the mission cemetery the fate of Captain James Williams, whose cry of "Men, do your duty" had haunted me for years. The one-time zealous vigilante had turned to cattle ranching, but when the merciless winter of 1886–87 devastated his herd, he drank a fatal dose of laudanum. Did his guilty conscience about all those illegal hangings have something to do with his suicide? I like to think so now, but at the time I barely gave him or his motive a second thought. Why, I was so almighty content that I all but gave up alcohol consumption, leaving the periodic bouts of whiskey drinking to La La and his "non-missionary" Indian friends.

Toward the end of that summer, La La went with Pierre Paul and others on a hunting trip, and I was alone in the cabin when two white men came along who said they were prospecting on the reservation for gold and silver. I told them I didn't know about any valuable ore around and that such things had never interested me even when I resided in the gold camps of Bannack and Virginia City. They were skeptical, in part because they caught a glimpse of the gold spoon Lucy had given me and thought it strange I should be living alone in the middle of nowhere unless I had found a private gold mine or something. I told them I had found peace, which made them both laugh. I told them that I had no meat to give them because the hunters weren't back. They wanted to know who the hunters were, and when I said Kootenai friends, they stopped laughing and looked at me as if I were the Sioux warrior who killed Lt. Col. George Armstrong Custer at the Battle of the Little Bighorn. But still they accepted my offered meal of roasted camas, fresh huckleberries, and larch bark tea before they retired to their nearby camp.

La La See returned to the cabin with Pierre Paul that evening. The hunt had not gone well, and they only brought back the meat of one deer and two rabbits. They were in foul moods and were also hungry; I immediately prepared a rabbit stew. As they ate, I had cause to mention the two visiting prospectors and that did not help their mood. In the morning, I showed them to the prospectors' camp, where the two white men were cooking breakfast over a small fire. We watched them unseen from the bushes.

"Let's kill them," Pierre Paul said, raising his hunting rifle.

"Why?" La La See asked, studying his own rifle, which had

failed him during the hunt.

"Why not! We'll kill them and eat their breakfast."

"Hey, no joking," I said, but I knew Pierre Paul wasn't joking.

"Shut your trap, squaw," Pierre Paul snapped. "Squaws never give orders."

"You can't shoot them in cold blood."

"Their bones have warmed from the fire. Palefaces killed La La's brother. What right have they to make themselves at home on *our* land! And what right have you to say anything! Only your head is red, pale-faced squaw. What say you, La La? You take the fat one on the right. I'll take the bony one on the left."

La La nodded his head as I shook mine. Two shots pierced the rising smoke and the chests of the two seated men. They both went down like sacks of flour, but when they squirmed on the ground like landed fish, the two Kootenais let loose with two more rounds each. What did I do while the shooting was going on? I don't like to recall. I just stood there with bulging eyes, trembling knees, sweaty palms pressed hard against my thighs, and a pounding head that sounded to me like Sioux war drums, though I had never actually heard them. It was like watching a hanging—but this was worse. It was cold-blooded murder in its rawest form. Pierre Paul expected me to participate.

"You shoot, too," he ordered as he forced his Winchester into my hands. "Plenty more bullets."

I dropped to my knees but held onto the rifle, terrified to drop it. Neither hand was near the trigger. The lump in my throat felt as large as an infant's head.

"You with us or against us?" Pierre Paul asked, but he didn't wait for an answer. "You best have a hand in this or we'll kill you, too."

"I can't," I pleaded, trying to hand him back his rifle. "I

never shot anything, let alone anyone." I found a touch of courage from deep inside and rose up, at least off one knee anyway, and added, "So shoot me if you *must.*"

La La See nudged my back with the butt of his rifle. "You can do it; they're already dead dogs."

As I shook my head, Pierre Paul took control of his rifle and pointed it at my temple.

"Wait!" shouted La La. "He didn't kill my brother."

"Neither did those two lying in the dirt," Pierre Paul said. "But they're all white."

"Not all the same, though. Woodrow Hart is a different kind. No need to kill him. Lower your rifle. We'll make him swear to keep this a secret."

Pierre Paul poked me in the ear with the barrel before lowering the rifle. He made me swear a half dozen times. Two Indian acquaintances came along, having heard the shots, and Pierre Paul also threatened them with death should they breathe a word about the two dead white men. The four Indians then weighted down the two bodies with stones and threw them into the Jocko River while I shuffled my feet on the riverbank. An Indian woman on the river to wash clothes much later discovered the partly decomposed bodies and told her husband who told someone else who told a subchief. None of them told Indian agent Peter Ronan or any other white authorities out of fear of what La La See and Pierre Paul, primarily the latter, might do to them. I suppose I was afraid, too, but mostly I just wanted to go back to the home cabin and forget about the murders just as I had all the vigilante hangings. I succeeded, too . . . for a while.

About a year later, one of the Indians, jailed for some other crime, divulged all he knew about the Jocko River double murder and warrants went out for the arrest of Pierre Paul and La La See. A sheriff's posse out of Missoula came north to Ravalli and almost ran into an ambush in a thicket, except an

Indian supporter of the two murderers rose up too soon and was shot dead. Plenty of other Indians were in the thicket, but not Pierre Paul or La La See, so the lawmen withdrew. Within two hours, the two wanted men appeared on the scene, each with two six-shooters in their belts, rifles slung across their shoulders, and short-barreled shotguns in their hands to parade about, yelling and laughing and no doubt feeling invulnerable. The governor, Benjamin White, traveled from Helena to Ravalli and offered a $1,000 reward for the two outlaws, dead or alive, but nothing came of it for another year. The two accused Kootenais knew the land, of course, and knew when to lay low, but they couldn't have avoided capture had not the reservation been full of relatives, sympathizers, and fearful folk unwilling to assist the authorities.

In June 1889, a sheriff's posse showed up for an Indian feast at St. Ignatius hoping to seize the wanted men, but they came up empty and later shot an armed but innocent Indian who looked like he might resist. Fearing that the killing of an unwanted Kootenai might cause an uprising on the reservation or at least an attack on his posse, the sheriff called for soldiers. He got them in the form of three companies of the 25th U.S. Infantry troops out of Fort Missoula and figured as long as they were on the reservation, they might as well track down the wanted men. Easier said than done. La La See got wind of this "white invasion" (even though it was technically a "black invasion," seeing as how the soldiers of the 25th were all colored) and fled *our* cabin for the hills where Pierre Paul was already hiding out.

What the sheriff and the soldiers couldn't do, a half-blood Indian policeman did, at least in part. He rode his fast horse ahead of another posse, disarmed and arrested Pierre Paul, and then turned him over to the exhausted white men. Agent Ronan called the policeman "fearless and true" for capturing the desperado, who was less than fearless and not true to anybody. I don't know for certain that Pierre Paul said anything or not, but a week after he was taken into custody, a fifty-man posse showed up at the cabin door and arrested me—without a fight, of course. I wouldn't tell them where La La See was. For one thing I didn't know, and for another I resented my "native" way of life being disrupted and refused to cooperate with the authorities. The hunt for La La See had become too tiring and too expensive for the county, so Sheriff Bill Houston disbanded his posse. But the Indian police kept the pressure on the so-called "Most Desperate Character of the Whole Lot" and now had the cooperation of some of the chiefs on the Flathead Reservation. Seeing that escape was impossible or perhaps finding it impossible to carry on without me keeping house in the cabin (a stretch, I must admit now), La La See surrendered in August 1890 and joined Pierre Paul, two other Kootenais accused of murdering white men, and me, the only paleface in the bunch, behind bars in Missoula.

The cases moved swiftly through the court system. It seemed clear to me, with Madame Hoy's dire prediction still revolving inside my head, that I was as doomed as the four red men who had committed the various murders. Pierre Paul, out of nothing but sheer spite, stood up in the courtroom, practically jumping clear out of his moccasins, to assert that I not only had set up the ambush in the Jocko River killings but had fired the fatal bullet in at least one of the two victims, had helped beat their brains out afterward, and had suggested the dead men be weighted with stones before tossing them in the river. It didn't help that McQuirk/McOwl, supposedly my old friend, testified that I had lost all reason and gone Indian to such an extreme that it should be no surprise to anyone that I had become a traitor to my race. I guess I was afraid and wanted to live, so I told the court that I had been a city or town dweller most of my from the reservation, reject the red heathens and their murderous conduct, and become a fully functioning civilized white man again! I don't doubt that either, my friends, but it can only come true if he is found innocent of the dastardly and decidedly untrue charges against him. Even while living in Indian country as a lost soul, Woodrow Hart could no more participate in the killing of a white man, let alone two, than his dear sister could. Both Harts, no matter how you spell it, are outstanding. Do your duty, men: Set Woodrow Russell Hart free!"

That the judge and prosecuting attorney allowed W.A. Phillips to carry on that way amazed me. He played with the truth but so well that he dazzled the members of the jury and made me believe—almost as much as they did—that I did *not* deserve to die. When the not guilty verdict came in for yours truly, I didn't exactly jump for joy, though I was pleased enough to want to give someone a hug. The defense lawyer who took my case even though he expected us to lose was gaunt, deadly serious, and at times reluctant to shake the hands of his own clients. I bypassed him for La La See, but they took my old cabin mate away before I could get to him—just as well, because though he had stuck up for me in noble fashion, he would never be caught dead hugging a white man in public.

I then turned to W.A. Phillips, who came at me with open arms. I have to admit he was a great speechmaker (though, I'll never admit he was a great writer). His silver tongue could effortlessly cast aside honesty and accuracy when necessary, just as his pen tip would do. In the courtroom his words helped save my life; on paper his words made my life not my own. I was no murderer, of course, but just as certainly, I was no hero. I will admit that after he saved my neck and I was a free man, I did dig up the red cape that once belonged to Madam Moll Featherlegs and that I had been saving all those years. I put it on for only a minute for W.A.'s benefit and then gave it back to him as a parting gift. He wanted to return to Washington, D.C., and get back to his writing. "I don't want the damn thing anymore," I told him.

In his *Man from Montana: How He Escaped the Noose,* I—that is Red Ranger—never turns "Indian," but he is falsely accused of murdering two old but vicious vigilantes and, in one of a dozen climactic scenes, only avoids the hangman's noose by overpowering a guard in the Missoula lockup and fleeing on the back of a plow horse and then, after the horse throws a shoe, on the hump of a young bison. Simply running away would not do for a full-fledged hero, so Red Ranger (me) goes to the reservation and apprehends, at great personal risk of course, the four red savages (called "crazed Blackfeet" in the book instead of Kootenais) that actually did the killing. When other vigilantes (not the legal court system) in Missoula condemn the foursome to death, Red Ranger rescues them from the noose by single-handedly overpowering a half-dozen more guards. He then transports the condemned Blackfeet to Dakota Territory for rehabilitation among the reservation Sioux, but their lives end shortly thereafter anyway in a blaze of Hotchkiss gunfire during the Massacre at Wounded Knee. The "Man from Montana," after saving several children and mothers from the massacre, goes on to have several unbelievable and pointless post-vigilante, post–Indian wars adventures in the West but can never quite escape his recurrent nightmares about the noose (rather the nooses) that nearly took hold of his "sensitive but leathery and reddish" neck.

But enough about the made-up Red Ranger! Yes, in W.A. Phillips's *Man from Montana: How He Escaped the Noose,* this superman in a red cape makes many miraculous escapes from the hangman's knot. But, as you now know, I made at least one such escape in *real life.* I could very well have used that same title for my manuscript, but I like my title better—*Man from*

Montana: The Man Who Wasn't. And, don't you know, *my* title also can apply to either Red Ranger or me.

Back to real life for a closing moment. On December 19, 1890, the sheriff and associates hanged four Kootenais—La La See, Pierre Paul, and two other convicted murderers—behind the Missoula County Jail. I was not there to witness the horrific spectacle, which was by invitation only. I wasn't invited. W.A. Phillips had told the authorities that it was better for me *not* to see another multiple hanging, so that I could more swiftly forget my "redskin interlude" and move on with my life in civilized society. How people did listen to that man! And how they read him five years later when he came out with his damned dime novel! Would I have gone had I received a formal invitation to the execution? The sad answer twenty-three years later is this: *Almost certainly—how could I have turned it down?* The world has its share of doers but far more watchers and gawkers. For better (at least as far as longevity is concerned) or for worse (as far as most everything else is concerned), I am one of the latter. Instead of attending the quadruple hanging that day, I discovered a newly opened drinking establishment in downtown Missoula—Red's Saloon. It seems like I've been there ever since.

ABOUT THE AUTHOR

Gregory J. Lalire, who majored in history at the University of New Mexico and worked for newspapers in New Mexico, Montana, New York and Virginia, has been editor of *Wild West* magazine in Virginia since 1995. He is the author of the children's book *The Red Sweater* (1982) and the novels *Captured: From the Frontier Diary of Infant Danny Duly* and *Our Frontier Pastime: 1804-1815* (2019). He was a Western Writers of America (WWA) Spur Finalist for his article "Custer's Art Stand" in the April 1994 *Wild West*, and a WWA Stirrup Award winner in 2015 for his nonfiction article about baseball in the West. He is *not* from Montana, but his heart resides there.

The employees of Five Star Publishing hope you have enjoyed this book.

Our Five Star novels explore little-known chapters from America's history, stories told from unique perspectives that will entertain a broad range of readers.

Other Five Star books are available at your local library, bookstore, all major book distributors, and directly from Five Star/Gale.

Connect with Five Star Publishing

Visit us on Facebook:
https://www.facebook.com/FiveStarCengage

Email:
FiveStar@cengage.com

For information about titles and placing orders:
(800) 223-1244
gale.orders@cengage.com

To share your comments, write to us:
Five Star Publishing
Attn: Publisher
10 Water St., Suite 310
Waterville, ME 04901